LUKE JENSEN
BOUNTY HUNTER
HIRED GUNS

LUKE JENSEN BOUNTY HUNTER
HIRED GUNS

WILLIAM W. JOHNSTONE
AND J. A. JOHNSTONE

PINNACLE BOOKS
Kensington Publishing Corp.
www.kensingtonbooks.com

PINNACLE BOOKS are published by
Kensington Publishing Corp.
119 West 40th Street
New York, NY 10018

PUBLISHER'S NOTE
Following the death of William W. Johnstone, the Johnstone family is working with a carefully selected writer to organize and complete Mr. Johnstone's outlines and many unfinished manuscripts to create additional novels in all of his series like The Last Gunfighter, Mountain Man, and Eagles, among others. This novel was inspired by Mr. Johnstone's superb storytelling.

All Kensington titles, imprints, and distributed lines are available at special quantity discounts for bulk purchases for sales promotions, premiums, fund-raising, educational, or institutional use. Special book excerpts or customized printings can also be created to fit specific needs. For details, write or phone the office of the Kensington sales manager: Kensington Publishing Corp., 119 West 40th Street, New York, NY 10018, attn: Sales Department; phone 1-800-221-2647.

PINNACLE BOOKS, the Pinnacle logo, and the WWJ steer head logo are Reg. U.S. Pat. & TM Off.

ISBN-13: 978-0-7860-4424-5
ISBN-10: 0-7860-4424-1

First printing: January 2020

10 9 8 7 6 5 4 3 2 1

Printed in the United States of America

Electronic edition:

ISBN-13: 978-0-7860-4425-2 (e-book)
ISBN-10: 0-7860-4425-X (e-book)

THE JENSEN FAMILY
FIRST FAMILY OF THE AMERICAN FRONTIER

Smoke Jensen—*The Mountain Man*
The youngest of three children and orphaned as a young boy, Smoke Jensen is considered one of the fastest draws in the West. His quest to tame the lawless West has become the stuff of legend. Smoke owns the Sugarloaf Ranch in Colorado. Married to Sally Jensen, father to Denise ("Denny") and Louis.

Preacher—*The First Mountain Man*
Though not a blood relative, grizzled frontiersman Preacher became a father figure to the young Smoke Jensen, teaching him how to survive in the brutal, often deadly Rocky Mountains. Fought the battles that forged his destiny. Armed with a long gun, Preacher is as fierce as the land itself.

Matt Jensen—*The Last Mountain Man*
Orphaned but taken in by Smoke Jensen, Matt Jensen has become like a younger brother to Smoke and even took the Jensen name. And like Smoke, Matt has carved out his destiny on the American frontier. He lives by the gun and surrenders to no man.

Luke Jensen—*Bounty Hunter*
Mountain Man Smoke Jensen's long-lost brother Luke Jensen is scarred by war and a dead shot—the right qualities to be a bounty hunter. And he's cunning, and fierce enough, to bring down the deadliest outlaws of his day.

Ace Jensen and Chance Jensen—*Those Jensen Boys!*
Smoke Jensen's long-lost nephews, Ace and Chance, are a pair of young-gun twins as reckless and wild as the frontier itself . . . Their father is Luke Jensen, thought killed in the Civil War. Their uncle Smoke Jensen is one of the fiercest gunfighters the West has ever known. It's no surprise that the inseparable Ace and Chance Jensen have a knack for taking risks—even if they have to blast their way out of them.

Chapter 1

Luke Jensen was in a fix. A bad one.

What made it worse was knowing that he had been put there by the likes of the Turpin twins. How galling would it be if, after all the hardcases he had gone up against and survived, he would end up having his sun finally set by a pair of no-account knotheads like Oscar and Augie?

Not that Luke was ready to give up. Giving up wasn't something that ran in the Jensen bloodline. But at the same time, neither did foolishly refusing to face the facts—and the facts when it came to his current situation were pretty grim.

He'd followed the two fugitives into this cramped, twisty canyon with its high, ragged rock walls knowing full well the risk that he might be riding into an attempted ambush. But having narrowed the gap between him and the brothers to such a slim margin after being on their trail for more than a week, he was anxious to close in the rest of the way and complete his mission of taking them into custody for the prices on their heads.

That was Luke's trade. He was one of the most

renowned bounty hunters in the West. Good enough, he reckoned, to pit his skills against the risk of anything the Turpins might try to spring against him.

As it turned out, he'd underestimated the craftiness of his prey. The only thing that saved him was that whichever of the brothers had skinned out of his saddle and clambered to a hidden crevice high up on the canyon's north wall miscalculated when it came to firing at a downward angle in his attempt to backshoot the bounty hunter as he passed below. The bullet sliced through the front brim of Luke's hat, harmlessly knocking it from his head and sending it tumbling end over end rather than splitting the skull it had been resting upon.

The fraction of a second Luke had before a second bullet came sizzling in his direction was enough—though just barely—for his lightning reflexes to kick in and once again save him from the bite of hot lead. He pitched to his left out of the saddle and hit the ground rolling, scrambling immediately in amongst some various-sized boulders that littered the base of the canyon's south wall. Luckily, some of these broken, ragged chunks remained large enough that they provided him cover against the continuing rifle fire angling down from the opposite wall.

But while Luke was safe for the moment, the same did not prove true for his horse. Without its rider, panicked by the repeated roar of the rifle and the *craack-whine!* of slugs ricocheting wildly off the surrounding rocks, the animal wheeled and tried to bolt away. It went barely a step, however, before the rifleman planted a bullet in its brain. As the unfortunate horse's legs buckled and its heavy body began sinking to the ground, the shooter drilled home a follow-up round for good measure.

At least the loyal critter that had served him well over many a hard mile hadn't suffered, Luke told himself . . . but that didn't necessarily mean he could guarantee the same for the piece of vermin who'd gunned it down.

The loss of the horse itself was only part of Luke's concerns. His Winchester was still in the saddle boot, still attached to the fallen animal where it now lay twenty feet away. And all the while there was the on-going rifle fire that continued to slap and chip at the boulders behind which Luke remained pinned down.

As he hunkered tight to the ground, eyes narrowed and teeth clenched against the gritty dust being kicked up all around, Luke's mind raced. He saw then how it had played out, how one of the brothers had quit his saddle, taking care not to touch the ground and leave a footprint that might have provided Luke some warning, and climbed quickly to a concealed spot up on the sharply sloping, deeply seamed canyon wall. He'd then waited patiently for the pursuing bounty hunter—still following the double set of hoofprints that continued along the canyon floor—to show himself and move into a spot where the ambusher had a clear shot.

Luke silently cursed himself for failing to notice that one of the sets of hoofprints must have started appearing more shallowly sunk into the sandy canyon floor after the horse's rider left the saddle. It was oversights like that that got men killed, and the kind of mistake Luke prided himself on never making. Yet he had. And the only reason he didn't end up dead as a result was due to the ambusher not being accurate enough to score the head shot he foolishly tried to pull off instead of aiming for the larger target of his intended victim's torso.

So things could have been better, but they could have been a lot worse. As long as he was alive, he still had a fighting chance. And the brace of Remington .44s strapped around his waist, butts forward for the cross-draw, gave him the means to put up a fight. His ammunition was limited to only the full wheels in each gun and the extra cartridges snugged in the loops of his shell belt, but if he made each round count, they represented a heavy toll for anyone bent on coming at him.

The only thing lacking was some kind of opening so he could bring the Remingtons into play. The way he was pinned down, not only was he being given no chance to shoot back, but he hadn't even been able to determine exactly where the rifle fire was coming from.

As long as he stayed hugged tight to the boulders currently protecting him, Luke was safe. But he figured it was just a matter of time before the rifleman pouring lead his way would try to shift to a position where he had a better angle and could plant a slug where it would do more damage.

It also seemed likely that before too long, the *other* Turpin brother—the one who had continued riding and left the misleading hoofprints for Luke to follow—would double back and join in the ambush. If this second brother took to the high rocks of the canyon wall on the same side where Luke was hunkered, he would have a better vantage point to shoot from and Luke would find himself in even worse shape.

Luke had to make something happen before it came to that.

Despite the craftiness they'd displayed so far, Luke reminded himself that the Turpins remained a couple of dim candles in even the densest gloom. He had to try to use that as part of his defense against them.

When there was a lull in the shooting, probably while the rifleman was reloading, the bounty hunter called, "Hey, Turpin! You're a holy terror when it comes to blasting horses and rocks! I'm surprised I've never seen that mentioned on any of the wanted posters issued against you."

"You just shut up and don't worry about it," came the response. "One more inch and I'd've took your whole head off, instead of just that stupid hat!"

"Aw now, don't go running down my hat. It was a perfectly good one until you went and ventilated it with a bullet hole."

"Yeah, and I'm gonna ventilate your worthless hide, too, before I'm done!"

Luke went quiet again, his mouth curved in a thin smile. The exchange of words had been enough for him to tell that Augie was the twin he was talking to. Augie had a speech peculiarity he was left with after a knife blade split his lower lip back when he was a youth.

It also made sense that Augie would be the brother chosen to do some climbing and hiding up on the canyon wall. Though both he and Oscar had nearly identical facial features—both ugly—the years had packed a number of added pounds onto Oscar, leaving him bloated and ponderous while Augie remained relatively lean and spry.

This made for another slight break in his favor, Luke told himself, as far as the notion of Oscar doubling back and trying to close in on him from a second elevated position. Oscar's bulk would make any such attempt mighty difficult, and if he *did* attempt it, it was bound to be slow, awkward going for him.

That gave Luke even more incentive for trying to turn the tables on Augie, while he was without the usual backup of his brother.

Considering the reports he'd heard about Oscar being the brains of the pair, according to most who'd spent any time around them, Luke calculated there might be something there he could use to needle Augie, maybe fluster him some.

"Boy, I bet your brother is gonna be mighty impressed when he sees that dead horse and all those rocks you've killed. That'll sure make him proud he left you to take care of ambushing me, won't it?"

"Shut up!" Augie hollered, his voice quavering with rage. "I've got you pinned down like a bug under a cup, don't I? You ain't got a chance of crawlin' out of there alive!"

With that, he loosed another relentless volley, the rounds hammering and slamming the boulders shielding Luke until the canyon for dozens of yards in either direction reverberated with the roar of the gun punctuated by the scream of wildly ricocheting slugs.

This time when Augie momentarily halted, Luke was ready. Although he hadn't dared poke his head up to gain an actual sighting, getting Augie to talk had allowed Luke to make a good estimate of where he was positioned—close enough, at any rate, to throw some return lead and demonstrate he was hardly a hopelessly trapped bug like Augie said.

Gripping one of the Remingtons in his right hand, he shoved up on his left elbow, thrust the Remy out over the crest of his protective boulder, and triggered four quick rounds at the spot where he judged Augie to be. He made a short sweep with the gun muzzle as he fired, planting slugs at two-foot intervals just above the bottom lip of a horizontal slash on the face of the canyon wall little more than a dozen feet above its base. The hollowed-out area filled with the spang of bullets and the rattle of flying rock chips. An alarmed curse spat out from the midst of all that and Luke very briefly saw a flash of orange—the same color as the shirt Augie had been wearing when Luke caught a glimpse of him through field glasses a couple of days earlier.

Luke dropped flat behind the boulder again, pressing the smoking Remington tight to his chest. One corner of his mouth quirked slightly upward. He didn't believe he'd been lucky enough to score a serious hit on Augie, but he had the satisfaction of knowing he'd been accurate in placing the bushwhacker's position and had sure made it hot for him. The thing now was to go for a quick follow-up before the dim-witted Augie saw the urgency in shifting to a different spot.

As he rapidly thumbed fresh cartridges into the Remington to replace the spent ones, Luke called out, "Hey, Augie! In case you didn't notice, I guess the bug under the cup is a little more lively than you figured, ain't he?"

"Even a dyin' bug sometimes manages a death

twitch—but that still don't mean it's got long to live!" Augie hollered back, a sneer in his voice.

Then he cut loose with the rifle again, raining more lead down on Luke's boulder. As far as Luke could tell, the angle of fire remained the same, meaning Augie figured to use this latest bit of blasting as cover fire in an attempt to move to a new position—or he was even dumber than Luke thought and was sending a signal that he intended to hold right where he was and wait for Oscar to show up in order to help seal the lid on the man who'd been dogging their trail for so long.

Luke drew his second Remington and once more readied himself for a lull in the shooting. If Augie lingered just a little bit longer in the ragged cavity where Luke had caught sight of him, the bounty hunter had an idea for possibly eliminating him in a way that didn't necessarily involve trying to plant a bullet in him or even needing to gain sight of him again. It was a long shot, but no worse than trading fire blindly until he ran out of bullets.

In his mind's eye, Luke re-played a vision of the spot where Augie had chosen to conceal himself—the horizontal slash in the rock face of the canyon's north wall. It was apparent this cavity had been created many years ago by a large rock slab, loosened over time by rain and wind, breaking away and toppling down to leave the hollowed-out gap behind.

But what was also left behind, Luke had noted, was a ragged ledge jutting out all along the top rim of the cavity. Like the larger slab that had torn away years earlier, it appeared inevitable that this ledge would also one day break free . . .

And maybe, with a little help, that could happen sooner rather than later.

The instant the lull in the shooting came, Luke sprang into action. He jackknifed to a sitting position, extended both arms over the top of the boulder, and began triggering the brace of Remingtons, one in each fist. This time he didn't fire *into* the cavity at all, making no attempt directly on Augie, but rather he concentrated strictly on the ledge running across the top of the hollowed-out area. His slugs slammed in, chewing just above the jagged outcrop, chipping away at a weathered seam where the ledge appeared to be clinging to the rest of the canyon face.

Chips of rock flew and puffs of dust geysered upward. Bullets whined. And another kind of whine—coming from a confused and panicked Augie—could also be heard from deep within the cavity.

Then, just as Luke was triggering his last rounds, it happened. A loud cracking, ripping sound seemed to issue from the rock wall. It was like part of the canyon was groaning in pain. Until, suddenly, section after section of the ledge began crumbling away and tumbling down into a roiling, climbing cloud of yellow dust. From this a new sound grew, a low rumbling that rolled the length of the canyon. And with this was mixed Augie's agonized screams as he was jarred out of the previously hollowed-out pocket and caught in the crushing spill of freshly loosened rock.

Chapter 2

Luke's gamble had paid off better than he'd expected or even hoped.

Once the final piece of dislodged rock had settled, an eerie silence fell over the scene. It was made even more intense by the thick, choking cloud of dust that hung in the air and cut visibility to mere inches.

Luke remained kneeling behind his boulder. As if by their own volition, his hands quickly but silently went through the motions of reloading his guns. He was mindful of the fact that Oscar was still lurking somewhere and it was just a matter of time before he was bound to show up. For this reason, Luke kept his ears pricked sharp, listening hard for any sound coming from farther down the canyon, off to the west, the way Oscar had continued on with his and Augie's horses.

Everything stayed still and quiet. Slowly, the dust haze dissipated. When he was able to see that far, Luke's gaze sought out the pile of rubble directly below the hollowed-out area where Augie had lain in ambush.

The cavity was dramatically changed now, scoured

away to a barely discernible indentation on the canyon wall. The ragged ledge that had jutted out above it was gone entirely, leaving its own fresh scar. The resulting heap of fallen, broken rock now lay on the canyon floor, sprawled halfway across the passage.

Within this heap, Luke could make out the twisted, half-buried form of Augie Turpin. One leg thrust out at an impossible angle; one arm, still clad in tattered remnants of the orange shirt, was bent at the elbow in a way no arm was ever meant to bend.

Luke was still gazing at these remains, feeling no remorse for the man who'd tried to back-shoot him, when a new voice boomed down the canyon from off to the west. "Augie! What happened? Are you all right?"

Oscar had arrived.

Luke immediately shifted away from his boulder and slipped into a shallow crevice worn into a sloping section of the south canyon wall. This gave him cover against Oscar's approach and also provided the option of being able to lean out and return fire or, if need be, fall back to another position. He meant to avoid getting pinned down again.

The biggest problem, he reminded himself bitterly as he glanced back over his shoulder at the carcass of his fallen horse, was that the time it took for the dust cloud to clear hadn't given him the chance to retrieve his Winchester or any additional ammunition. Once again he'd have to deal with a Turpin brother, likely armed with a rifle of his own, and only have the Remingtons and the diminished supply of cartridges left in his gunbelt to do so.

"Augie!" Oscar's voice boomed again. "Talk to me!"

"I'm afraid Augie's talking days are all over with," Luke called back.

There was a moment of silence. Then: "Is that you, Jensen, you blasted bloodhound?"

"The name's Jensen, right enough," Luke said. "But the insult to my parentage—the kind of thing I understand you and your late brother knew about firsthand—is as far off the mark as Augie's attempt to back-shoot me."

"Are you sayin' you did for Augie?"

"I'm saying he tried to kill me and I defended myself. I don't know how to make it any plainer."

Nothing more was said for several minutes. What had been an eerie silence now took on an ominous overtone.

Oscar was far enough back that the canyon walls had echoed his words somewhat, making it difficult for Luke to judge how far. Nor, no matter how hard he peered around the slope of rock he'd moved behind, could he pick up any sign of movement from the big man. The canyon in that direction bent slightly to the south after about forty yards. Luke guessed that was where Oscar was hanging back, just around that bend. That meant he didn't have a very clear line of sight on Luke, either.

Luke licked his lips and glanced again at his fallen horse. If Oscar was indeed around that bend some forty yards to the west, and the horse was about twenty feet diagonally toward the east, maybe he had a chance to retrieve his Winchester after all. He could make a desperate dash and dive in behind the horse, using its carcass for cover. From there he'd have access to his rifle and plenty of ammunition and even a canteen of water in case of a prolonged gun battle with Oscar.

The only trouble with that notion—apart from the risk of making the dash in the first place—would be that falling behind the horse carcass would leave him pinned down once again. Sure, he'd have plenty of cartridges to throw lead with, but if Oscar was cautious about keeping to cover himself, they could play a game of duck and shoot that might drag on for hours without either of them gaining an advantage.

Luke didn't like the thought of that.

His gaze once more touched on the crumpled, half-buried body of Augie and another idea started to form in his head. Oscar wasn't all that much brighter than Augie had been. Maybe Luke's previous plan to try and needle a Turpin brother into doing something stupid was worth another try.

"You know, Oscar," he called after some quick consideration, "could be I'm mistaken about how bad a shape your brother is in. Could even be that he's still got some life left in him."

"What kind of crawfishin' talk is that?" Oscar demanded. "Either you shot him and kilt him, or you didn't. I reckon you've plugged enough men in your time to know the difference."

Luke smiled. He sensed he'd succeeded in hooking the barb in Oscar.

"You see, that's the thing. I didn't actually shoot Augie. I was shooting *at* him when part of that canyon wall came loose and he got caught in a rockslide. He's lying over there in the rubble. No doubt he's hurt pretty bad and I haven't seen him move or anything . . . but it could be he's still alive and breathing in there."

Oscar cursed again. "That's mighty lowdown, tauntin' me that way about my brother's life."

"And him trying to kill me—from the back—*wasn't* lowdown?"

"You been doggin' us for days. You been askin' for it!"

"Okay," Luke grated. "So now I'm asking something else—you man enough to finish the job face-on? You sent Augie to do the dirty work, to sneak around and try to take me out like a yellow cur. Now he's left crushed and maybe dying a slow death. You going to keep hanging back, just blowing hot air and talking mean, or are you ready to take a turn at coming for me and maybe having the chance to still save your brother's life?"

Things went quiet again for a tense few seconds. This time, however, Luke could hear the sounds of movement from Oscar. Faint grunts of effort, the scrape of a boot against rock. And then came a sharp intake of breath and Luke recognized it meant that Oscar had moved to where he was able to finally see what was left of his brother.

"Augie . . . !" The name came out in a mournful groan.

"I don't think he can help you now," Luke said, poking the barb deeper.

"Shut up!" Oscar roared. And then, almost immediately, his voice broke and softened into a barely audible whimper. "Oh, Augie . . . I'm so sorry . . ."

"Look there!" Luke said suddenly and with exaggerated urgency. "Did you see that, Oscar? Did his arm just move a little bit, or was it only a piece of his shirt stirring in the breeze? Maybe he heard your voice and he's trying to signal you, begging you to come help him before—"

"Shut up, I told you!" Oscar roared again. "Haven't you done enough?"

"I think that's a question it's time to ask yourself," Luke responded, really laying on the taunting tone in his voice. "You're partly responsible for Augie being in that condition. Is *that* enough? Is that all you're going to do, besides whimpering and saying you're sorry? Or are you going to make me pay and maybe—just maybe—try to get to Augie in time to—"

"You're damn right you're gonna pay!" Oscar bellowed, his rage making his voice ring out louder than ever. He burst around the bend of the canyon and came rushing forward in long, lumbering strides. He held a Henry repeating rifle at waist level and began shooting from the hip, levering and firing round after round as he ran. With a maniacal fire dancing in his eyes, he screamed, "I'm comin' for you, Augie! Comin' for revenge and to save you!"

Even though he'd been trying to provoke some kind of response along these lines, the suddenness and recklessness of it still caught Luke a bit off guard. What was more, the accuracy of the volley Oscar threw ahead of himself as he launched his frantic charge came too close for comfort. Luke was forced to jerk back momentarily as bullets came whistling in and blasted away slices of the rock slope he stood behind, mere inches from where his face had been peering around it just a fraction of a second earlier.

After those first few moments, though, it really was no contest. It became just a matter of bringing the trackdown of the Turpin twins to a grim, bloody conclusion. Though the terms of the wanted posters issued on them were "Dead or Alive," Luke had been hoping, as he always did, to take them in upright in their saddles. But for the sake of his own survival, that option was closed to him, first by Augie and now Oscar.

Dropping low, where he wouldn't be expected to re-appear, Luke leaned suddenly out around the base of the sloping rock and returned Oscar's fire. Although his breath was now coming in hard puffs and he was starting to slow, the big man had covered a surprising amount of ground from where he'd started, and the Henry was still spitting flame and lead.

Meaning to give his target one more chance to come out of this alive, Luke extended his right-hand Remington and fired three rounds, aiming to cut Oscar's legs out from under him. He succeeded, planting lead in each of the man's heavy thighs and sending him crashing to the ground. The Henry went flying from his grasp.

Wanting to believe he'd brought this to an end, Luke straightened up and eased cautiously out from behind his cover. He kept the gun in his right fist leveled on the fallen man while his left hand rested on the butt of the still-holstered Remington.

"Just lay real still, Oscar," he said in a steady voice. "Hold your hands out away from your body and don't try anything foolish."

"You've crippled me," Oscar groaned, dust puffing up from where his mouth was pressed against the ground.

"You're wounded but still alive," Luke told him.

"You don't know but what a good doctor can fix those legs so you'll be able to walk fine."

"For what? So I can walk up the gallows steps?" After those words, Oscar issued a different noise, a mixture of another groan and an agonized animal sound. "No! I ain't goin' thataway!"

He jabbed his hand in where his bulging stomach was mashed to the ground and clawed at the waistband of his trousers.

"Don't try it, Oscar!" Luke warned.

But it was no use. A second later, Oscar's hand pulled free and this time it was gripping a short-barreled Colt revolver that he tried to swing in Luke's direction.

The Remington spoke one more time. A red-rimmed hole appeared above Oscar's left eyebrow and a chunky mist of scarlet sprayed out the back of his head. His face and the revolver dropped simultaneously to the ground.

Luke stood very still for a long count. Then, holstering the Remy, he said in a husky voice, "You had your chance. Now you can walk into hell on those crippled legs."

Chapter 3

The first thing Luke did was walk up the canyon and collect the Turpin horses before they wandered off. Luckily, Oscar had shown the sense to hobble the animals so they wouldn't be spooked by the sound of gunfire. Luke followed suit, hobbling the pair once again after he got them back to the ambush site, ensuring that neither the scent of fresh blood nor the touch of a stranger would make them want to scatter.

Then came the task of loading the two dead bodies onto the back of the sturdiest-looking of the two horses, a deep-chested paint. It was only early May, but the sun was climbing steadily higher and hotter in the cloudless Montana sky and there was precious little in the way of shade in the canyon. Luke knew that by noon the rocks all around him would be blistering to the touch and he wanted to be out of here before then.

The task of loading a limp, lifeless body up onto a horse was never easy, even though Luke had had plenty of practice at it. And Oscar's bulk certainly added to the difficulty. But the tall, craggy-faced, black-clad bounty hunter's own powerful physique and the techniques he'd developed during all the times he'd done it before prevailed, though he was dripping sweat by the time he was done.

Next came the job of not only loading up Augie but having to first dig him out from under the rock-slide rubble. Before tackling that, Luke took a few minutes to sit down on a slab of broken boulder and catch his breath between long swallows from his canteen.

It was during that still, quiet moment of rest that the faint sounds began to reach him . . . the periodic click of horseshoes against rock.

Someone was approaching from the east. Not hurriedly and apparently not making any attempt to hide the fact they were out there. That was potentially a good sign. But Luke had survived too long on the edge of danger to accept anything for granted and not take precautions when he had the chance. He once again slipped behind some cover and became motionless. Waiting.

It took a few minutes for the approaching horse-man to appear. When he did, he showed himself to be a man of about forty, average height, solid look-ing, sitting easy in the saddle of a gleaming black gelding. The rider wore a high-crowned black Stetson and a black leather vest over a maroon shirt. A walnut-handled Colt was holstered on his right hip. His facial features were evenly chiseled, conveying a measure of hardness especially around the dark eyes that swept alertly under thick black brows. He gave an overall impression of competence but not someone who went looking for trouble.

As he drew nearer and his gaze touched on Luke's

dead horse, Augie still in the rubble pile, and then Oscar over the back of the paint, his expression seemed almost as if he'd been expecting what he saw.

Luke spoke without exposing himself. "Rein up easy, mister. Keep both hands where I can see them plain."

The stranger did as he was told. His gaze searched calmly in the direction of Luke's voice. After a moment, he said, "Looks like you've already had a fair share of trouble here. I'm not looking to bring any more."

"That's good to hear," Luke said. He stepped out slowly, revealing himself. "It still leaves me wondering, though, just what *does* bring you here. This canyon is hardly a commonly traveled route for most folks."

"True enough," the stranger said with a faint tip of his chin. "The short answer to your question is that— providing you're Luke Jensen, which I believe is the case based on the description I was given—I'm here looking for you. I've been following you, trying to catch up, for a couple of days now."

Luke's eyebrows lifted. "I'll confess to being Jensen. Now let's hear the rest of it—who are you, and why have you been trying to catch up with me?"

"My name's Patton. Asa Patton. I work for a man named Parker Dixon." The stranger paused, wagged his head. "I can see by your expression that neither of those names mean anything to you. Nor should they, especially mine. But Mr. Dixon is a prominent businessman with holdings throughout much of western Montana. He wants to meet with you and discuss a business proposition. When he learned you were in the area and had passed near Helena as recently as a few days ago, he sent me after you. He asks that you return with me at your earliest convenience and gives assurance that he will compensate you for your time and the trip."

Luke cocked his head to one side. "That sounds mighty intriguing, not to mention mighty generous. No offense, but almost *too* generous. Enough so to make it smell a little fishy. Just what is this 'business proposition' of Dixon's about?"

"I can't say," Patton replied. "Mainly, because I don't know the details. But to be honest, even if I did, I'm pretty sure Mr. Dixon would want me to leave them for him to reveal. What I can tell you—make that *assure* you—is that Mr. Dixon isn't in the habit of making overly intriguing or overly generous offers without good reason. And those who have entered into business dealings with him in the past have tended to benefit very well."

Luke continued to regard the dark-eyed messenger. He asked, "How much do you know about me, Patton?"

Patton met his gaze with a level one of his own. "Not much. Basically, that you're a bounty hunter with quite a reputation." He glanced at Augie and Oscar. "I gather these two gentlemen represent your latest accomplishment in that line of work. The Turpin brothers, I assume, since I heard that was the name of the most recent fugitives you were on the trail of?"

Luke smiled wryly. "That's right. These are the Turpins. I don't make a habit of shooting up men I'm *not* on the trail of. Wouldn't have had to shoot up these two if they hadn't sort of insisted on it. Augie, over there in the rocks, tried to ambush me. His brother Oscar, the one on the horse, failed to learn anything from his brother's misfortune and decided to make his own run at me."

"I heard the shooting from back down the canyon," Patton explained. "I was too far away to make it in time to intervene. And, to be honest, without knowing what the situation was, it didn't seem particularly wise to get in too big a hurry to try."

Luke nodded. "Smart thinking."

"So," Patton said, "since this matter is concluded, it seems reasonable to assume you are now, ah, between engagements. Is that an accurate statement?"

"Close," Luke conceded. "But this matter isn't all the way concluded until these bodies are turned in to a proper legal authority who can match them to their wanted posters and my payment for delivery has been arranged. There's a sheriff in Marysville who's worked with me on that sort of thing in the past. I figured that's where I would head next."

"Not all that far from Marysville to Helena, where Mr. Dixon is waiting to meet with you," Patton pointed out.

"You're persistent, I'll give you that."

"So is Parker Dixon."

Luke considered. Then he said, "Tell you what. If you're willing to help me dig Augie out from that rock pile, load him up with his brother, ride with me to Marysville and give me a chance to take care of my business there . . . then I'll go on with you to Helena to meet your Mr. Dixon."

Chapter 4

Parker Dixon was a tall, lean, square-shouldered individual who looked to be a couple years one side or the other of fifty. His bearing was ramrod-straight, suggesting former military, though the impression was softened somewhat by the fine tailoring of his suit as well as the silk shirt and crimson string tie complimenting it. A single streak of silver running slightly off-center from the top of his forehead and then up through a sweep of pomaded, precisely barbered hair provided an added touch of distinction to the carefully cultured image of a successful, wealthy man.

But for all that, Luke sensed a certain hardness around the eyes and mouth that suggested here was someone who hadn't always led such a pampered life.

Rising from behind a massive desk that dominated his handsomely appointed private office—the headquarters for Dixon Enterprises, a name prominently displayed on the front of the building as well as several others to be found throughout Helena—the man himself managed a brief smile that appeared as if it might be a rare departure from his otherwise stern expression.

"Mr. Jensen," he said by way of greeting. "I'm glad you agreed to this meeting."

Dixon made no attempt to come around the end of the desk and shake hands. That suited Luke just fine. Although he could draw with either hand, he never liked to willingly place himself in the grip of another and diminish his chances to react in case of trouble.

Plus, in this instance, he'd opted against wearing his rather showy brace of Remingtons for the meeting with Dixon and was instead heeled more discreetly with a short-barreled .38 holstered in a shoulder rig under his left arm, covered by the suit jacket he had also donned for the occasion. Luke had made too many enemies over the years—a few of them still on the loose—for him to go completely unarmed in even the most refined setting.

"Have a seat, make yourselves comfortable," Dixon said, gesturing toward a pair of deeply cushioned leather chairs arranged in front of his desk.

Luke, along with Asa Patton, who had escorted him into the office, did as instructed. Dixon lowered himself back into his own chair on the other side of the desk.

Leaning forward, interlacing his long, blunt-tipped fingers on the desktop before him, Dixon announced, "When it comes to matters of business, as well as most other things, I believe in getting right to the point, Mr. Jensen."

"Same here," Luke replied.

"Good. Then, in order to prevent wasting time,"

Dixon suggested, "why don't you tell me what Mr. Patton has already revealed about the nature of why I sent for you."

A corner of his mouth quirking upward, Luke glanced over at Patton. In the five days the two of them had spent together on the trail—part of it to reach Marysville, the rest to proceed on here to Helena— the dark-eyed messenger hadn't spilled a peep more about Dixon's "business proposition" than he had in that first handful of minutes in that nameless canyon where he showed up after Luke had bested the Turpins.

Cutting his gaze back to Dixon, Luke said, "That's easy—nothing. Your Mr. Patton was firm in his belief that you should give me the details yourself. He said only that it was a matter important to you and one that could prove lucrative to me in the event we ended up doing business together."

Dixon gave a satisfied bob of his head. "Very well. The long and the short of it, then, is this: You, sir, have the reputation of being a highly skilled bounty collector, a manhunter, widely considered one of the best in the business. I am plagued by a black-hearted scoundrel—a robber and a killer—who needs to be run to ground. When I require a job done that falls outside my own capabilities, I have a habit of hiring the best I can find to take care of it for me. You fit that description for a matter of this nature and so, when I heard you had been spotted in the vicinity, I naturally thought to contact you."

When Dixon paused, clearly expecting a response, Luke said, "This *scoundrel.* He have a name?"

"Tom Eagle. He's a half-breed Shoshone."

"Are there papers on him? Reward dodgers?"

"Not that I am aware of, no. One of the problems, you see, is that the area where Tom Eagle is raiding and killing is basically lawless and lacking in men willing to stand up and try to enforce what meager laws do exist." Dixon's mouth curled into a sneer. "Ironically, at one point Tom Eagle was the sheriff, one of the few anywhere for miles, of a small town called Hard Rock. But that was before greed turned him bad and he became worse than anything he ever faced when he was on the right side of the badge."

"This lawless place, this town of Hard Rock . . . where is it exactly?"

"To the north and a bit east," Dixon answered. "Hard Rock lies in the valley of a small mountain spur called the Spearpoints, an offshoot of the larger Flathead Range that runs not too far to the west."

"About three days' ride from here," Patton added.

"And your interests there?" Luke said to Dixon.

The businessman unlaced his fingers and spread his hands. "A mining operation in the Spearpoints. Gold. It's producing now, has been for going on two years. Not panning out as good as projected, but it still manages to show in the black and my engineers assure me there remains promise for a richer vein to be struck if we just stay with it. In the meantime, I can ill afford for repeated shipments of what we *do* yield to be stolen by this blasted half-breed."

"Are your shipments all that he hits?"

"Not strictly. There are reports of him robbing at least one stagecoach, maybe a bank or two. But there isn't a lot else up that way *to* hit." Dixon scowled fiercely.

"My gold shipments are his main meat, no two ways about it."

Luke leaned back deeper in his chair. His brow furrowed. "I'm sorry to hear about your trouble up around Hard Rock. And I appreciate you thinking of me as a possible solution, Mr. Dixon," he said. "But I'm afraid it sounds like a job I can't accept."

Dixon's scowl intensified, displaying the reaction of someone who wasn't used to being turned down.

"Why in blazes not?" he demanded. "I can't believe you're afraid of Tom Eagle as I've described him. Surely you've gone up against men more dangerous than him."

"Maybe, maybe not. But that isn't the point. The thing is," Luke explained, "when I go after a man it's because there are papers on him issued by proper legal authorities. A lot of folks view bounty hunters as being not much different than the fugitives they track down. But I see it different—I see what I do as an extension of the legal system, one that's been recognized for a lot of years, and that's how I treat it. What you're asking . . . well, it sounds more like a job for a hired gun."

"Nonsense," protested Dixon. "It's not like I'm some greedy cattle baron looking to hide behind your gun in order to gobble up more land. What I'm looking for is to see justice done, to have this blatant outlaw apprehended and brought before legal authorities, exactly as you're suggesting. I'm not asking you to go out and gun him down, for Christ's sake—though I'll admit that seeing him dead would not displease me. At the end of a rope, however, if that's the verdict of a proper trial . . . You see, if you reconsider and *are* willing and able to take Tom Eagle into custody and place him in the hands of appropriate authorities, then there are witnesses ready to testify against him and his crimes. But until he's captured, they're afraid to come forward."

Luke frowned in thought, chewing on this new slant to what Dixon had at first seemed to be proposing.

In the chair next to Luke, Patton addressed Dixon, saying in a quiet voice, "Tell him the rest of it."

Dixon winced faintly at this. For a moment, he glared disapprovingly at Patton. Then, after brief consideration, he shifted his gaze once more to Luke. His expression and his tone turning quite grave, he said, "There is, it is only fair for you to know, another aspect to this. A very personal one, though it in no way changes anything I have previously stated. It involves my son Roland . . ."

Dixon paused, took a breath, and went on, "He was somewhat pampered by my late wife. After she passed away, I was afraid that her pampering had had an undesirable effect on the boy. Made him too soft. As he grew up, I took it upon myself to make sure that influence was countered. Toward that end, about a year ago I sent him to run our mining operation up near Hard Rock. He had the brains, he knew the business. It was his chance to prove he could control the men, make the tough calls, keep the operation running smoothly."

Luke remained silent as Dixon paused again. The businessman seemed to have to force himself to continue, but continue he did.

"He did well. He pushed himself hard to show me he could measure up. He even took it upon himself to ride shotgun on some of the shipments that left the mine. Until, on one of those trips, the shipment Roland was riding with got waylaid by Tom Eagle's gang. Roland resisted. They blew him off the wagon seat. He was dead before he hit the ground."

Dixon's voice thickened on those closing words. He went silent for several moments after that. Luke stayed quiet, too, not knowing what to say.

His businesslike tone, though still decidedly grave, returning, Dixon spoke again. "I'm asking you to reconsider my proposal, Mr. Jensen. For all the right reasons, apart from my personal hatred for the man, and following all the proper procedures you feel bound to . . . apprehend Tom Eagle. Please. Bring him to justice." And then, after a measured pause, he added, "I will pay you five thousand dollars for the job. Twenty-five hundred now; the balance when you return with that murderous half-breed."

Luke met his eyes, noting the sadness in them. "All right," he said. "I'll go after Tom Eagle."

Dixon expelled a sigh of relief. "Excellent. When can you start?"

Luke shifted a little in his chair. "Well, I'd like to hang around long enough for a visit to a barber and a long, hot soak in a bathtub. A couple sit-down meals that I don't have to cook for myself over a campfire. Maybe a taste of Helena's nightlife after the sun goes down this evening. And then, by this time tomorrow, I figure I ought to be re-supplied and ready to head out."

"Excellent," Dixon said again. "Stop back right after lunch and see my secretary out front. She'll have the first part of your payment ready. Anything else you need before leaving town—directions to Hard Rock, the names of some of the personnel at our operation there, whatever else you might think of—you can get from Asa."

Sensing this amounted to a dismissal and taking his signal from Patton, who rose up out of his chair, Luke did likewise.

"One more thing," Dixon added, remaining seated. "There's a telegraph office in Hard Rock. It's of some use when the line isn't down. If you find it up and running, try to keep us posted on your arrival and progress. Address all of your transmissions to Asa. He'll see to it I'm kept informed."

With that, Dixon began rummaging through some papers on his desk and it was for certain their dismissal was now complete. Patton turned to depart the office, and Luke followed.

Chapter 5

Luke's overnight stay in Helena proved most pleasant. He had his long bathtub soak, preceded by a barber shave and hair trim, then followed by some fine food and drink, a modestly profitable session at the gaming tables, and all capped off by a very enjoyable dalliance in the company of a frisky redhead named Lucille, who worked as a waitress at the restaurant where he had supper.

When he was ready to ride out late the following morning, decked out once again in his customary trail attire of all black—boots, trousers, shirt, and hat—Asa Patton was on hand to see him off. In the previous days they'd spent together, Luke had grown fairly at ease with the dark-eyed, tight-lipped messenger. More so than he normally did with someone he'd been around for such a short time. Life had taught Luke to be on guard against people in general and he tended to stay distant from most he came in contact with. Yet something about Patton had given him cause to relax a bit more than usual.

Something else, though, a curiosity, had been

building in him to the point where he wasn't ready to ride off without addressing it.

"You effectively stonewalled my questions about Dixon for five days," Luke said now, as they stood out front of the livery stable he was preparing to depart from, "but I'm stubborn enough to give it one more shot—this time a question related to yourself as well as Dixon."

Patton smiled tolerantly. "You're welcome to try your luck. Ask away."

"I can't help wondering," Luke said, "why Dixon didn't assign this job to you. I mean, you've proven yourself capable on the trail, even to the point of tracking me to that remote canyon where the Turpins attempted their ambush. You pack a gun, and my sense—even though I've never seen you in action— is that you're likely quite capable with it. And you already work for Dixon. Why bring in an outsider like me?"

Patton's smile stayed in place. "I guess he thinks you're better suited. You heard what he said about always hiring the best. You're the one with the reputation as a manhunter."

"But a reputation is just the perception of other people. To Dixon, you're a known quantity. One he already clearly thinks highly of."

"Maybe that's it. Maybe he likes keeping me around close," Patton suggested. "Or maybe he asked me to take the job up in Hard Rock and I turned it down."

Luke cocked an eyebrow. "I get the impression that men who turn down an offer from Dixon don't stick around too long . . . at least, not still in his employ."

"Maybe he's willing to cut some slack when it comes to Hard Rock."

"Why would that be?"

Patton's smile widened, became a lopsided grin. "You ever heard the old expression about a place not necessarily being the back end of nowhere . . . but close enough to see it from there?"

"I've been to a few of those places."

"Uh-huh. Well, when you get to Hard Rock, you'll be in another one."

"That not only isn't any kind of straight answer to my question," Luke pointed out, "but neither is it much in the way of incentive for me being in a hurry to get there."

"You don't need incentive from me," Patton told him. "You've already got five thousand other reasons for making the trip."

Luke didn't have a response for that. And Patton, he could see, was once again going to avoid responding to his latest question.

It was time to hit the trail.

After his previous horse was killed, Luke had decided to stick with the pair he'd inherited from the Turpin twins. The deep-chested paint had proven itself to be sturdy and obedient—first when it came to hauling the brothers' dead bodies as far as Marysville, then as Luke's mount for the remainder of the way to Helena. Based on this, he put his saddle on it again for the trip to Hard Rock. The second animal, a big dun, was somewhat less impressive but would do all right for a packhorse.

With the sun nearly at its peak in a partly cloudy sky, Luke pointed the noses of the two horses north and put Helena behind him. He rode quite a ways before the last of the outlying buildings and pockets of activity, most of it related to mining, fell away and he found himself alone and passing through empty land. The terrain was hilly, covered by numerous stands of trees and frequent outcroppings of shale or sandstone. Now and then there were relatively flat stretches of prairie grass.

A few times Luke spotted wisps of distant chimney smoke and occasional clumps of livestock. Homesteaders trying to make a go of a farm or ranch, he guessed. But he steered clear, having neither the need to know nor enough curiosity to particularly care. And when at one point, from the top of a rise, he spotted a sprinkling of far-off buildings that marked a settlement of some sort, he steered wide of that also.

Luke had no intention of stopping anywhere until he got to Hard Rock. His focus was to reach there, conduct his business with Tom Eagle, and make it back to collect the balance of his pay.

As significant as the latter was, something about the job still didn't sit quite right with him. He still felt a little too much like a hired gun, despite Dixon's assurances that Tom Eagle would stand trial in a court of law and face sworn witnesses to his crimes before any punishment was meted out. If Tom Eagle was guilty of the charges against him—including murder—then he deserved to pay the ultimate price. But only if that was a properly arrived at verdict. And Luke meant to make sure it went down that way.

As darkness descended, Luke found a good spot for night camp in a clearing atop a grassy knob overlooking a winding creek that provided cold, clear water to slake his horses' thirst. He would top off his canteens and water skins before starting out again tomorrow. A fringe of thick pine growth made both a good windbreak should the night air turn chill and also obscured the small fire where Luke cooked some coffee and biscuits.

The fine meals he'd enjoyed in Helena yesterday and the hearty breakfast he'd stuffed himself with early this morning already seemed like a long time ago. But such were the fortunes of this life he'd chosen, Luke reminded himself. And, besides, he made a mighty fine pot of coffee and his trail biscuits were pretty fair, too, so it could have been worse.

After he'd eaten, Luke extinguished the flames. The night wasn't going to get that cold and the sky was clear except for a few stringy clouds trailing across the face of a waning moon. No sense keeping the fire going and taking even the slim chance of it attracting drifters who might be out and about and inclined toward no good.

Being careful kept a man alive.

Chapter 6

Luke rode hard for the next two days, holding to a steady, miles-eating pace aimed at getting him to Hard Rock as soon as possible. He checked his back trail regularly, especially on the first day, but saw no sign of anybody following him.

The weather stayed fair, neither too hot by day nor too chilly at night. A scattering of clouds hung stubbornly in the sky, but never formed into anything threatening rain.

As for the land, it gradually grew more rugged. Sharper ridges, steeper slopes, numerous stands of trees yielding to fewer open, grassy stretches. Mountains were perpetually on the horizon, looming higher and denser to the west, with frequent buttes and other rock outcroppings dotting the landscape in all directions.

Through it all, Luke got a fine performance out of his horses, especially the big paint. Cool streams were frequent and Luke made sure to give them plenty of chances to slake their thirst. Good graze was easy to find whenever he was ready to make camp, and after unsaddling and hobbling the animals where they had access to plenty of it for the night, he additionally gave each a generous scoop of grain from the supplies he had packed.

In those quiet moments after he'd finished his evening meal, Luke usually stretched out with a final cup of coffee, laced with a splash of bourbon from his saddle flask, and by the campfire light read from one of the books he also made it a point to include in his supplies. Self-educated, always hungry to increase his knowledge and improve his demeanor for settings a bit more refined than the barely tamed frontier where he plied his trade—settings to be found in places like Denver or San Francisco, for example, where he enjoyed spending time when he could—Luke pored through everything from the Bible to Shakespeare to historical accounts to even a few lurid dime novels now and then. It all served to enlighten or entertain, sometimes both, and it transformed those late moments from what might have felt like loneliness to more a welcome solitude.

On the third night out from Helena, expecting to arrive in Hard Rock the next day, Luke followed his usual routine after he was done eating but the book he'd selected to read from for a while, a collection of stories by Washington Irving, was failing to hold his interest. Thoughts about the job at hand, now close to actually beginning, kept rolling through his mind instead.

He was anxious to find out more about Tom Eagle—the former sheriff who had "gone bad from greed," as Parker Dixon described him. It still troubled Luke a bit that he didn't have a properly issued reward dodger on the man, or hardly anything at all in the way of particulars except for that provided by Dixon. Going after somebody under such circumstances continued to feel uncomfortably close to acting like a hired gun, especially considering the unusually large payment being offered.

What was more, Luke realized he'd be lying to himself if he didn't admit that the five grand was largely responsible for him accepting the job in the first place.

As a result, he had long since decided that how far he'd proceed would hinge on what he found out once he got to Hard Rock. If the people of the town backed up Dixon's account of things and some of them indicated they would in fact be willing to testify at a trial of Tom Eagle, then that would seal the deal. Luke would go ahead and try to apprehend the outlaw.

However, if he got conflicting reports on the situation, then he'd be riding back to Helena and returning Dixon's advance money, minus expenses.

For some reason, though, the closer he got to Hard Rock, the stronger an odd sort of hunch grew in Luke that—no matter what he found once he got there— simply turning and riding away might not be so easy.

Luke got his first look at the town from the rocky crest of a ridge on the south side of the valley. The cluster of buildings lay toward the east, near the narrow end of the rolling, grassy, teardrop-shaped expanse.

To the west—the fat, rounded end of the valley— lay some lumpy gray foothills and then the tall thrust of the Flathead Mountains beyond. To the north, slanting across the top of the valley and then curling down like a tail to partly force the eastern narrowing of the teardrop, ran a line of spiky peaks Luke reckoned were the Spearpoint Mountains. Farther east, past the point of the teardrop, from what he could see the land appeared to turn considerably more rocky and barren.

Cloud cover had thickened during the night, dimming daybreak and casting a dreary chill over the unfolding day. A couple hours before noon, a drizzling rain began to leak down. It was due to this added murkiness that, even with the use of the field glasses he dug out of his saddlebags along with the long, loose slicker now draped over him, Luke was unable to make out the features of Hard Rock very clearly.

"Still," he said aloud, speaking to the paint, "it doesn't appear *quite* as close to the back end of nowhere as Patton gave me to believe. Of course, this cold rain dripping down the back of my neck might have something to do with that. Right at the moment, any place offering a roof to get under looks mighty appealing to me, and that's a fact." Luke tucked the glasses back in under the slicker, leaving them to hang by the lanyard around his neck. Taking up his reins again, he said, "So what do you say we kick up some mud, critters, and hightail it on down there to where we can find ourselves a dry spot?"

From there, it took the better part of an hour to cover the distance to the town. The rain continued, but at least it never came down any harder. Still, man and horses were feeling plenty cold and drenched by the time they reached the first of the outlying buildings.

Luke scanned the layout as he steered the paint

down the main street. General store, pair of saloons, barbershop, café, boot repair shop, hardware store specializing in mining tools, telegraph office . . . all the standard businesses you might expect for a small town serving ranchers, farmers, and miners. Down the line, Luke spotted a small brick building with a sign nailed above its door: SHERIFF. Beyond that he saw a barn and some corrals that marked the town livery stable.

What Luke *didn't* see, however, was any sign of life.

In this weather, it wasn't surprising that no one was moving on the street. But equally absent was any sense of movement or activity inside the buildings, on the other side of the blank windows that stared back at him like empty eye sockets. Given the dreariness, there should have been the glow of lanterns in at least some of those windows. And since it was still the noon hour, surely the café ought to be doing some business.

Yet, as Luke rode by, it stood as silent and vacant-looking as everything else. The same for both of the saloons.

On both sides of the street, emptiness. No signs of life. Silence, except for the steady hiss of the rain, the splatter of the drops hitting the muddy street.

Luke plodded on toward the livery barn, figuring to get himself and his horses in where it was dry even if there was nobody there to welcome them. As he moved along, he continued to sweep his gaze from side to side. Adding to the eeriness was the fact that he had no feeling anyone was looking back out at him. Nor did he get any hint of menace.

He'd been in ghost towns before—old, withered, leftover shells of places, some of them thriving communities at one time, but now gutted and abandoned and left to the elements. Hard Rock had that same abandoned feeling. But it was more like a fresh, very recent development. Like everybody had just simultaneously packed up and lit a shuck, all at once. Only what sense did that make? What could cause such flight?

Reining up in front of the livery barn, Luke gave a loud shout. "Hellooo! Hello, is anybody around?"

Nothing. No kind of response.

After a minute, the paint chuffed somewhat impatiently, as if to say, *What's the point of standing here waiting in the rain when it's clear nobody is in there to answer?*

"Reckon you make a good point," Luke muttered under his breath.

He swung down from his saddle, walked up to the wide double doors, and shot back the two-by-four that had been slipped through metal brackets on each side to hold them shut. Pulling one of the doors open wide, Luke immediately felt the release of warm, dry air washing out over him. And mixed liberally in this was the familiar smell of horse—not just one or two horses, but several of them. Not a stale, lingering scent, either, but rather a fresh, current one. While his nostrils were assessing this, his ears picked up the scuff of hooves and a few curious snorts from deeper inside.

For the first time since arriving in town, despite all its oddities, a bolt of alarm stabbed into Luke. Heightening this came the awareness that he was standing silhouetted in an open doorway—something he instantly changed by hurling himself to one side and hitting the ground in a diving roll!

Chapter 7

Luke rolled to a stop, bumping against some bundles of straw in a pool of thick shadows off to one side of the door that was still closed. He quickly pushed into a crouch, coming to rest on one knee with both Remingtons gripped in his fists. He froze in that position for several seconds, keeping his breathing shallow, his slitted eyes darting from side to side, exploring as far as he could into the shadowy cavern that was the long, high-ceilinged barn.

The sound of more hooves scuffing the floor and a restless chuff here and there reached his ears. The rain continued to patter down outside. No hint of any human presence, inside or out.

Luke tried again. "Hey! Hello! Anybody in here—anybody at all?"

More of the same. Nothing.

He rose slowly up out of his crouch, took a couple steps forward. He pouched the iron he'd been holding in his right hand, kept his left filled. By now his eyes had adjusted to the gloom inside the barn. He could make out his surroundings pretty well.

A long aisle extended straight back, with horse stalls on either side. At the rear was a wide, fenced off area with a loft overhead. Each of the stalls—twelve in total, six on each side—appeared to have a horse in it. And more were milling around in the fenced area at the rear.

The fact that none of these animals seemed unduly agitated, like they would be if they'd been without food or water for a long period of time, indicated to Luke they must have recently received proper attention.

But from who? And where was that caregiver now?

Movement from the doorway snapped his head around and he saw the paint entering with a tentative step, its nostrils flared at the scent of the other horses already present.

Luke grinned. "Sure, why not. Why should they be in here where it's dry and warm and you two are still stuck out there in the rain, right?"

He walked over, took the paint's reins, and led it on in, the dun following on its tether. Near the bundles of straw, there stood a hand pump and a wide-mouthed wooden bucket. Luke led his horses over, pumped some fresh water into the bucket, then stood by while they dipped their heads and noisily drank. When they'd had enough, he led them a little farther into the barn and tied them to an upright post near where the rows of stalls began. They'd grazed recently enough not to have to worry about that for the time being. Nor did Luke deem it necessary to strip them of their saddles and gear right away—not until he'd poked around some more to try and find an answer to what was going on in this mysterious place.

He pulled his Winchester from its saddle scabbard

and then walked back to the doorway. Standing at its edge, exposing only a slice of himself, he gazed out once more through the rain and surveyed the town. Nothing had changed. Still no sign of activity, no hint of anyone being behind the flat, lifeless facades of the buildings that lined the street. From this new perspective, he could see that, behind the structures along the right side of the main drag, lay a cluster of houses that constituted the residential district. Same story there. Dull, dark windows, no "lived in" look whatsoever.

To the left, near the top of a slight slope, catty-cornered across from the jail building, stood a building Luke hadn't noticed when he first approached the livery barn. It was a church. Recently whitewashed, sturdy-looking, with straight, clean lines and sharp angles. From the roof peak over the front entrance, a bell tower rose tall and proud.

Luke's interest sharpened. Other than its obvious purpose, there wasn't really anything that different about this building . . . and yet there was. Somehow, it didn't appear quite so un-inviting. Plus, Luke asked himself, what was a church? A place of worship, yes, obviously. But often, also simply a gathering place. A place where a large section of townsfolk could meet, could come together in order to discuss and make plans for the community as a whole . . . Could it be that's what was going on now? Was that where everybody was—all gathered in the church for some kind of town meeting?

It seemed a little far-fetched, probably just some wishful thinking, Luke told himself—yet it was *something* that might explain all the emptiness everywhere else. Drawn by that thought, nudged along by the frustration of having no better idea, Luke pushed out of the doorway and started walking toward the church.

At the front door he paused, feeling suddenly uncomfortable carrying a rifle and having the Remingtons strapped around his waist. But, considering the strangeness of the overall situation, he decided it was of minor consequence. Finding the door unlocked, he worked the latch, pulled it open, and stepped inside.

He found himself in a rather cramped foyer directly under the bell tower. A set of wide double doors leading into the church proper were standing open and through them Luke could see rows of pews on either side of a center aisle leading up to the pulpit. Unfortunately, what he also could see was that the pews and the rest were as empty as every place else he had encountered in Hard Rock so far, save for the horses in the livery barn. A herd there, but no flock here.

Luke felt like swearing, but in deference to where he was, he held any epithet in check. Instead, useless though it seemed, he once again raised his voice in a shout. "Hellooo! . . . Reverend? Anybody?"

The same lack of response he was getting used to but found no less frustrating. Before turning to leave, Luke walked a few steps farther into the church and ran a hand across the back of one of the pews. His fingers disturbed a faint layer of dust. So the church may not have been abandoned for very long, but it *had* sat empty for days, maybe close to a month.

Back out in the foyer, Luke glanced over and noticed a closet-like room to one side. Stepping over and pulling open the door to the little room, he saw a rope extending down through a hole in the ceiling and tied to a metal hook on the room's back wall— the rope that led up to the bell in the tower.

On a whim, Luke leaned his Winchester against the door frame and went into the room. He untied the rope and gave it a light tug, until he felt the resistance of the heavy bell up above. A roguish smile touched his lips. Instead of going around wasting his breath shouting in all the doorways he came to, why not raise a kind of shout that the whole town could hear? Luke had no explanation for most of what he'd encountered so far, but the presence of the horses in the livery barn and the evidence of their recent care meant that *somebody* had to be close by.

He went to work pulling the rope and setting the church bell to clanging and clamoring for a full minute or more, drowning out the sound of the rain and making the little room and the whole foyer tremble from the reverberations. When he figured he'd made enough noise, Luke re-tied the rope to its hook, retrieved his rifle, and left the little room. Then, flipping up the collar of his slicker and pulling his hat down a little lower over his eyes, he passed through the foyer and stepped back out into the rain.

Whether as a result of the bell or merely because they'd decided it was time to make their presence known anyway, several men were gathering down along the base of the slope when Luke emerged from the church. Three were directly in front of him, fanned out slightly apart from one another. Two more were off toward the livery barn, as if they had just emerged from there. In the other direction, off toward the main

street area, a full half dozen more were in evidence—
four advancing from the nearer buildings, two others
hanging back, planted in the middle of the street. All
wore grim expressions well suited to otherwise hard,
rugged features and all were heavily armed, brandishing their weapons openly.

It didn't take a lot of study for Luke to determine
that here, very clearly, was *not* the local merchants'
welcome committee.

Chapter 8

"Just hold it right where you are, mister. Shuck your hardware and stand easy, there won't be no trouble."

These words came from the centermost of the three men directly in front of Luke. He was a thick-bodied individual with close-set, piggish eyes, and a wide, sneering mouth set in a bloated face. He held a long-barreled shotgun, butt resting on one hip, and behind the open folds of his slicker could be seen a set of bandoleers crisscrossing his swollen gut.

Luke held the shotgunner's eyes for a long count before sweeping his gaze once more over the others, who seemed to be poised awaiting his response. Then, cutting back again to the shotgunner, he said in a calm, flat voice, "I believe I'll decline that offer. It's no trouble at all, thanks, for me to hang on to my hardware."

A pair of bristly brows pinched together above the piggish eyes. "You some kind of smart mouth or something? Or are you maybe a little short in the brains department? That was no stinkin' *offer*—it was an order. And you'd best hop to it quick or there damn well is gonna be trouble, and plenty of it!"

"Well, since you put it that way . . . If you're so hell-bent on trouble, let's quit wasting time and get to it!"

With that, he wheeled and sprang back inside the church, slamming the door behind him. After a moment of startled inaction, several of the guns outside were put to use and a volley of shots roared nearly in unison, sending a leadstorm of bullets hammering against the door and pounding the frame all around it.

A harsh voice knifed instantly through the gunfire, shouting angrily, "Hold your fire! Hold it, you fools—we're supposed to take him alive!" As the shots began to falter, the voice hurled more commands. "Surround that church! If that's where he wants to be, we'll make sure he stays there!"

But Luke was already in motion, having hesitated barely a second once he'd plunged inside. His first impulse had been to leap to one of the foyer windows and try to cover the men outside with his rifle, return the fire they'd been so quick to throw his way. But Luke quickly changed his mind, realizing the risk of getting trapped and knowing the longer he stayed in the church the greater the chance of that happening.

So instead of trying to make even a momentary stand in the foyer, he had broken into a full-out run and raced toward the rear of the building, aiming to flee out the back. He didn't know what awaited behind the place of worship, his vague recollection of what he'd seen from the livery barn doorway being that it was open ground, no other structures close around where he might find cover. But even if that was the case, it would at least still give him the chance to put up a running fight.

Past the pulpit area, Luke reached a small, office-like room where he assumed the minister prepared his sermons and such. Whatever the case, it had an exit door and that was enough for Luke to give a little thanks of his own. He shouldered open the door and plunged outside. He could immediately hear shouts and curses as men came swarming closer to the front of the church, demonstrating understandable caution that he was in there ready to open fire on them. Good, let them take their time. The slower and more cautious the better. The main thing that mattered right now was that there was no one in sight to witness his exit out the back.

Unfortunately, the other thing that wasn't in sight was any sign of something Luke could use for cover. And he knew it wouldn't be long before some of those men would be moving up on one side or the other of the church, until somebody reached a point where they were certain to spot him if he stayed exposed the way he was.

Luke weighed the choices he had for his next move. Straight out from the back of the church, stretching for a dozen or so yards, was a patch of high grass and weeds that dropped off into a steep-walled ravine. Beyond was open country made up of choppy hills studded with rock outcroppings. Eighty yards off to the left and down a shallow incline was an empty corral area out behind the livery barn. To the right, just back from the rim of the ravine, was a cemetery. A combination of stone and wood markers stood within the border of a fence made of weathered, widely spaced wooden slats. Beyond the end of the cemetery and down another long, shallow incline, maybe a hundred yards away, were the backs of the buildings lining the near side of the town's main street.

Luke made his choice. If he could make it in among those buildings, he'd have a chance to play cat-and-mouse for a while with the men trying to close in on him. Long enough to, hopefully, find a way to eventually make it all the way clear.

At the same time he'd have the chance to take a toll on them. Any other way would leave him too exposed, allow them to continue swarming until they were certain to run him down.

Shoving away from the church, Luke broke for the cemetery as hard as he could run. He carried the Winchester in his left hand, gripped one of the Remingtons in his right. He dug his boot heels into the wet grass to keep from slipping as long tendrils of weeds slapped and clung to his churning legs.

He made it amongst the tombstones before somebody started hollering, signaling he'd been spotted. Quickly following that came the crack and roar of more gunfire. Bullets whacked against the slats of the cemetery fence and whined off some of the stone markers. One of them chipped away a marble corner and broken bits of lead and stone sprayed like shrapnel, slicing and stinging the side of Luke's face as he ran.

And then the hoarse bellow of the bloated-faced man with the shotgun rolled up the slope again. "Watch where you're shootin', dammit! Aim low—cut away his legs, but keep him alive!"

There it was again. The order to keep him alive. The

first time Luke had heard it, in the din of the initial volley as he was scrambling to get back inside the church, he thought his ears must be playing tricks on him. What sense did it make for a pack of gun wolves to show up and come after him if they weren't out to kill him? For that matter, who were they and why were they after him at all?

All Luke knew for sure was that calling a halt to discuss the finer details of what this was all about wasn't something he was ready to do right at the moment. Not as long as he had a chance to elude these hombres. Just because they weren't fixing to kill him right away didn't mean they weren't prepared to get around to it later on. And what they might have in mind to do in between wasn't exactly pleasant to speculate on. Bad as Luke wanted answers to whatever this was all about, he meant to try and find them in his own way and time—not have them dished out to him by Bloated Face and his bunch if they managed to get their paws on him.

Luke kept running. He cleared the far end of the cemetery and began his angle down the slope toward the buildings on Main Street. Bullets continued to sail his way but they were more intermittent now, more carefully aimed. They gouged the ground around his feet and sliced the air just ahead and behind his pumping knees.

The bunch from the front of the church were swinging his way in a frantic, jumbled mass, hoping to try and intercept him. More than once when somebody slowed to take a shot, one of the others running up from behind would inadvertently bump against the shooter and spoil his aim. A lot of cursing got hurled along with the lead.

Luke could see that the only ones who stood any real chance of getting in his way to prevent him from making it to the buildings were the two skunks he'd spotted out in the middle of the street when he'd first stepped from the church doorway. One was heavyset, moving ponderously, the other was a stringbean with loose-limbed, awkward movements of his own. They were cutting over, trying to get in front of him, but both seemed somewhat tentative about a confrontation since they were out in the open and the rest of the gang was still a ways off.

Without breaking stride, Luke decided to add to their tentativeness. Extending his right arm, he rapid-fired the Remington as he ran, emptying the whole wheel on the hapless pair. His arm was jarring too much for any real accuracy, he was aiming mainly to make them duck and scatter and allow him to reach his destination.

The result was one of his shots blew off the hat of the stringbean, another nicked the heavyset one in the thigh. The rest of his slugs came close enough to rattle nerves but struck no flesh or bone. But he succeeded in eliminating the pair from blocking his way. The heavyset one dropped to the muddy ground, clutching his wounded leg, the stringbean tripped and fell over him. By the time they got untangled and tried to make it back up to their feet, Luke had reached the nearest of the buildings and disappeared around the corner.

Chapter 9

Luke pressed against the outside of the building, taking a moment to try and catch his breath and to also reload the spent Remington. He backhanded away a smear of blood and rainwater from the cut on his cheek. He knew he'd managed to buy himself a few precious minutes. Nobody was going to be in a hurry to come around that corner after him, not any time soon.

But that didn't mean that some of them wouldn't go rushing up the street in an attempt to get ahead of him. And sooner or later, *somebody* would have to follow the way he'd gone for the sake of catching him in a crossfire.

The trick for Luke then, if he was going to succeed with his cat-and-mouse plan, would be to slip into one of the buildings in between without anybody seeing exactly which one. From there he could do some maneuvering of his own, popping in and out when and where they least expected, picking off a few of them—one by one—in the process.

If he could keep that up long enough, work on their nerves, get them chasing their own tails, then he might be able to create an opening to make it to his horses in the livery barn for a chance to ride clear of this crazy town.

Luke began working his way down the back ends of the businesses lining this side of Hard Rock's main street. His mind raced, trying to picture the layout of the buildings as best he could remember from his single trip down the street. What he needed to best suit his plan was a large structure, preferably two stories high, with several rooms or sections inside. A hotel would have been ideal, but he couldn't remember seeing anything so identified.

The rain seemed louder back here, spattering off the roofs and back porch overhangs. But Luke could still hear the somewhat muted voices of the men moving out in the street now, angry curses and threats being spat as they surged along just as he'd expected, trying to get ahead of him in anticipation of whatever he might do next. He darted cautiously through the gaps between buildings, making sure he wasn't seen from the street or that none of his pursuers were trying to work their way back through one of those gaps.

Some empty beer kegs and wooden cases marked as having contained bottles of whiskey, stacked out back of one of the buildings Luke came to, were welcome indicators of what he'd been hoping for. A saloon. A big, gaudy, two-story saloon that should give him plenty of room to operate.

The back door to the place was locked and opened inward, making it difficult for Luke to force the door with a shoulder block even if he'd wanted to risk the noise. Instead he pulled the Bowie knife from its sheath behind his right-hand Remington and used the stout, razor-sharp blade to start digging at the door's latch. Trying to do so without making a lot of noise or leaving behind visible damage was nerve-wrackingly tedious. Luke kept glancing over his shoulder to make sure no one had started around the back way while the voices of the men out in the street were growing in anger and intensity.

Finally, the latch popped and the door opened. He slipped into a cramped storage room with a single small window almost completely obscured by a stack of wooden boxes. The gloom forced Luke to pause for several seconds until his vision adjusted. When he could see well enough, he pressed the door shut and moved one of the wooden boxes over to hold it that way. Then he turned and carefully picked his way out through other stacks of barrels and boxes.

Exiting the storage room, Luke found himself in a short, wide hallway lined by ornate wallpaper and brass candle holders. The latter were unlit, but thankfully, a door at the opposite end of the hall was standing open and this allowed illumination from a large room beyond to spill in.

There were closed doors on either side of the hallway, but Luke ignored them. At the end of the hall he found himself gazing out at the main room of the saloon. It was spacious and fancily decked out. A long, brass-railed bar ran along one side, several gaming tables filled the center area, and a stage presumably for dancing girls extended out from a curtained doorway off to the right of the doorway where Luke now stood. Hanging from the center of the ceiling directly over the middle of the whole works was a glittering chandelier at least a dozen feet in diameter. On the other side of the stage, an open stairway led up to a second floor balcony that extended out above Luke's head. At the front of the room, a set of high, wide windows bracketed the main entrance and looked out on the street, at the same time providing passersby a beckoning peek at the opulence within.

Once again Luke had to wonder about Asa Patton's assessment of Hard Rock being so close to the back end of nowhere. Although there were different ways to measure a place, a well-appointed business establishment such as this, even though it was a saloon, seemed to indicate a level quite above hardscrabble.

At least it *had* indicated that, until some fairly recent point. As it stood now, some ransacking—apparently as part of the whole town's emptying-out—had left the place decidedly worse for wear. Although things weren't completely wrecked, the mirror behind the bar had been smashed, all the gaming tables and most of their accompanying chairs had been overturned and scattered, the curtains that opened onto the stage were mostly in tatters, and most of the glass in the front windows had been broken out.

As a curious aside to all that, Luke couldn't help noticing that several bottles of liquor that had lined shelves behind the bar still stood intact. There were gaps, many were missing altogether and the mirror that had been in back of them was in shards, but the remaining bottles stood tall and proud like soldiers ready for another battle.

Luke shook himself from this bit of musing. He couldn't afford it. What he had to concentrate on now was positioning himself to strike back at the gunmen. His gaze swept over to the stairway and then followed it upward to the second floor. He moved forward to get a better look at the layout up there, edging in behind an overturned table to stay hidden from anyone who might happen to glance in through the front windows.

A balcony extended a third of the way out over the main floor and the near end of the bar. Narrower sections of it also ran along the two side walls. There were doorways visible behind the railing all the way around—opening, Luke guessed, into some sleeping rooms and also probably rooms for bar girls to entertain customers. This made the upstairs appealing to him for his present circumstance. He'd have a good vantage point, both inside and out, from up there. He could move from room to room, assuming at least some were adjoining, and still have reasonable escape routes out the front and rear or even from one of the side windows if necessary, since he wouldn't be *that* high off the ground. Luke never lacked for confidence that, as long as he had his guns and plenty of ammunition, he always stood a chance of blasting his way out of a tight spot.

His mind made up, Luke was ready to head upstairs. But before he did, there was one piece of business he meant to take care of first. Slipping away from the overturned table, he glided around the end of the bar. From a shelf behind it, he reached up and snagged one of the undisturbed bottles of liquor.

Earlier, he had taken note of its distinctive label—it was a brand of brandy that he'd taken a liking to during one of his stays in Denver. Since it would likely be a while before Bloated Face or any of his bunch showed their ugly faces here, he might as well spend the time waiting in good company . . .

Chapter 10

It took a little over half an hour for them to start closing in on him again. The first indicator was a quick series of movement flickering across the busted-out saloon windows. Next came the clump of boot heels on the boardwalk out front. Luke thought he also might have heard some sounds from downstairs, toward the back, but couldn't be certain.

The outer front door was suddenly yanked open and flung wide. Luke tensed, ready with his raised Winchester, but the doorway stayed empty. The now exposed batwings hung undisturbed, no one yet ready to push on through.

Then the familiar voice of Bloated Face called out once again. "We know you're in there, Jensen. We found the jimmied door in back and we've searched all the other buildings on both sides of here. You got lucky and bought yourself a little time, but it's over now. Make it easy on yourself and give up before somebody else gets hurt."

Luke made no response. He was crouched behind an overturned padded chair at the balcony railing

just off center above the main room down below. A
hallway running back deeper into the upstairs level
was just off to his right. Half a dozen rooms branched
off from it, in addition to some smaller rooms opening off the narrow walkway that wrapped around the
sides.

At the far end of the hall behind him, a steep,
narrow stairwell led down to the first level. The door
at the bottom was locked and Luke had jammed a
straight-backed wooden chair under the knob to help
secure it. No one would be coming through that way
without some force and without making some racket
that would give him warning.

The chair he was hiding behind was in keeping
with the furnishings of the rest of the upstairs that
had been ransacked and tossed about much like the
lower barroom. So anyone looking up from down
there would not only be unable to see him but neither
would the overturned chair appear as anything unusual to draw their attention.

Luke stayed silent and waited. Peering around the
edge of the chair seat and down through the balcony
railings he had a clear view of the saloon entrance
and three quarters of the barroom.

"Blast it, Jensen, this is gettin' tiresome!" hollered
Bloated Face, showing his irritation and impatience.
"You must have heard me say our orders are to take
you alive, so maybe you think you can afford to be
cocky. But nobody said nothing about not roughin'
you up plenty! So I'll warn you right now that the
more you drag this out and the more you piss me off,
the rougher the treatment you're gonna get when we

do get our hands on you! You'd best do some thinkin' about that!"

Bloated Face went quiet again, waiting. And Luke continued to stay still and silent.

Some mutterings from down below—through the broken windows and past the batwings—began to drift up to him. He could make out snippets of agitated conversation.

"He's *got* to be in there."

"He's pretty slippery, maybe we missed him somehow in one of the other buildings."

"Well just standin' here jawin' about it ain't gonna flush him, that's for stinkin' sure . . ."

Luke smiled wolfishly. *Confusion to the enemy.* Where had he heard that saying before? No matter, it was a good one all the same. The more confusion and agitation he could stir up in that pack of varmints out there, the better it was for him.

Luke heard the vague creaks and bumps of movement as some of the gang members entered down below at the rear, moving in through the same storeroom. But they were of minor concern to him at this point. They couldn't get at him without using one of the two sets of stairs. He'd easily spot anyone attempting to climb the stairway down in the barroom, and trying to access the inside stairwell would create enough racket to warn him in time to deal with it. His main focus needed to remain on the front entrance— and, half a minute later, activity there proved he was correct.

To give the devil his due, Bloated Face showed himself to be neither a coward nor a shirker. He pushed

through the batwings and led the way in. The shotgun
was still gripped in his meaty fists as his piggish eyes
whipped anxiously in every direction. Three other
grim-faced gents edged in behind him, fanning out
slightly once they were through the doorway. Two of
them brandished rifles, one held a drawn pistol. A
fifth man, also prominently displaying a handgun,
stepped over the sill of the busted-out window to
Luke's left and veered off to start making his way
behind the bar.

Hard as it was, Luke remained stone still, letting
the men in the center advance cautiously. He was
waiting, hoping intently for them to continue on just
like they were . . . until they reached a certain spot in
accordance with some of the other preparations he'd
had time to make while he was alone in the empty
saloon.

And then they were there. Positioned almost too
good to be true.

Luke sighted on his target, held his breath, stroked
the Winchester's trigger. The rifle belched flame
and lead and a silence-shattering roar. The heavy slug
it hurled sizzled across the room and cleanly snapped
the length of chain from which dangled the ornate
chandelier in the middle of the ceiling. Down slammed
the massive assembly of glass icicles and the outer
ring of individual globe lamps, the twelve-foot span
across its diameter wide enough to cover Bloated Face
and all three of the men bunched around him. All
were instantly driven to the floor as if swatted flat by a
giant palm.

As the chandelier came crashing down, the pistoleer

who was moving up behind the bar remained in the clear. His reaction at seeing his cohorts get so brutally pounded down was cool and professional. He didn't waste any time looking shocked. Instead he immediately swung his attention to find the source of the shot that dropped the chandelier. His eyes locked right away on the powder haze hanging in the air from Luke's Winchester and his gun arm was rising just as fast.

But Luke was far from inexperienced at the game himself. Even before he saw that his shot struck true and the chandelier was falling, he'd been aware that the man behind the bar would still be in the clear and therefore a potential threat. So while the chandelier was still in the air, he adjusted his aim and swung his sights to the bar area.

The pistoleer was almost as fast as he was cool-headed. But his accuracy failed to match his speed. He got off a shot, but the bullet sailed half a foot over Luke's head. In the same instant, Luke's rifle roared once more—and once more his shot was true. The slug hit the pistoleer high in the center of his chest and slammed him back against the shelves behind the bar, leaving him to hang there a moment and then begin a slow slide into a limp, lifeless heap.

Drawn by the shooting, another man clomped up on the boardwalk out front and recklessly shoved the batwings open. He never even got his eyes raised to where Luke was—let alone the muzzle of the Henry repeater he was carrying—before another slug from Luke's rifle knocked him staggering back out into the street.

Directly below him, through the floor, Luke could make out slightly muffled voices start to chatter excitedly.

"He's upstairs!"

"He's mowin' down everybody out in the barroom!"

And then one of the idiots foolishly began shooting up at the ceiling, as if he expected a bullet to penetrate and have any chance to hit Luke. He triggered three rounds before somebody's hollering got him to stop. Crazy as the attempt was, the loud *whaps!* and vibrations pulsing through the floorboards right under where Luke was crouching were enough to make him do a little nervous shifting.

"There's a door back here that I think leads up a stairwell," said one of the muffled voices. "We can go up after him that way!"

This drew another wolfish grin from Luke. Having some of his pursuers try the stairwell was one more thing he'd had time to make some preparations for. Before that, though, he needed to take one more quick scan of the barroom below. One of the four men who'd been caught under the chandelier wasn't moving at all, obviously knocked cold. The other three were doing some struggling to pull free, but were so stunned and battered that it amounted to pretty weak attempts. It was plain that none of them were getting out from under any time soon.

Satisfied with that, Luke turned and hurried back down the hall. As he moved in long strides, he pulled from a slicker pocket the bottle of brandy he'd brought upstairs with him. It was now half empty and into the neck of the bottle was stuffed a wad of bed sheeting, two or three inches of it trailing loose, that he'd gotten from one of the rooms off the hall. Another piece of the sheet material, wetted with brandy, had served to clean and finally help stop the bleeding from the cut on his cheek.

From the top of the stairwell, Luke looked down on the jammed door at the bottom. It was shivering violently and already starting to split apart under heavy blows from the other side. Luke had no time to waste. He leaned his Winchester against the wall and pulled a sulfur match from his shirt pocket. He snapped the lucifer to life with a thumbnail and held the flame to the tail of sheeting poking out the top of the bottle.

As soon as the cloth was burning good, he hurled the bottle as hard as he could at the door. The glass vessel shattered on impact, its contents splashing out. The fiery cloth ignited the liquor. Blue alcohol flames instantly burst out all over the face of the door and in only seconds the paint and wood began to crackle from the heat as the fire took hold and spread wider.

The pounding on the door abruptly ceased and then only curses sounded from the other side. With a wall of flame now in place to prevent his attackers from getting at him via the stairwell, Luke had no time to stay and savor the accomplishment.

Once more wheeling around, he again raced the length of the hall and returned to his previous vantage overlooking the main barroom. As he covered this distance, he pulled from a slicker pocket a second liquor bottle—one he'd found empty in one of the second floor rooms and had partly filled with brandy from the first bottle then also rigged with a cloth wick.

A glance at the barroom below showed that not too

much had changed. One of the men under the fallen chandelier was still motionless. Two of the others, however—one of them being the durable Bloated Face, complete with a streak of bright blood flowing from a gash on the back of his head—had managed to pull almost all the way free.

That was all Luke needed to see. He wasted no time snapping another match to life and igniting the wick on the second bottle. As soon as the cloth was wrapped in flames, he demonstrated he was nearly as accurate with an overhand toss as with a rifle shot. Down the flaming bottle arced, landing in the center of the chandelier and immediately shattering into outward blossoming fingers of blue fire that instantly touched off the spilled oil from the ring of broken globe lanterns. In a matter of seconds, the entire framework of the chandelier wreckage was afire, licking higher and wider. The men caught under part of it screamed and began flailing and kicking even more frantically to get clear.

Luke had to keep on the move. Voices downstairs from those who'd been turned back at the stairwell were being raised in increased anger and alarm. And more shouts were coming from out in the street. Based on the number of varmints he'd seen when he first stepped out of the church, Luke figured he had at least a half dozen more to deal with.

But the sprawling saloon had served its purpose. It was time to take the game of cat-and-mouse to a new location. Luke didn't know exactly where yet, he just knew it was necessary to move on.

With this in mind, he turned again to the hallway behind him. Heavy smoke was rolling up out of the stairwell at the opposite end. Luke proceeded only partway this time before ducking into a doorway on his right. This placed him in a room where he judged one of the saloon's soiled doves had entertained customers. Continuing to move quickly, he crossed to a doorway on the far side and barged through it into an adjoining room. The far side of this room was the outside of the saloon building and there was a tall, narrow, shuttered window there. Luke went to the window and pushed the shutters open a crack. He had tested them earlier to confirm they swung back freely on their hinges.

Peering through the crack, he checked below to make sure that the space between this building and the next, an alley only about six feet in width, was clear of any activity. Same when he swept his gaze to either end. The building across the alley was a flat-roofed, single story structure, its top about the same distance lower from Luke's window as the gap between the two buildings. In other words, an easy jump to make.

Luke had determined all of this earlier during his exploration of the upstairs. It would have suited him better if he'd found a way to transfer to the building on the saloon's opposite side, the one back in the direction of the livery. Unfortunately, the distance to that structure was too great and its design offered no reasonable purchase for Luke to grab hold of if he'd tried to make that jump.

So that left the flat-topped building on this side. It wasn't ideal, but it would have to do. It gave him a way out of the saloon and a way to move on in order to keep eluding his pursuers. For now that was good enough. It just meant he'd have to do some more dodging and maneuvering before he got his chance to make it back to the livery and his horses.

Luke pushed the shutters open wide, braced one foot on the windowsill, then shoved out and away. As soon as he touched down on the opposite roof, he went into a smooth tuck and roll, Winchester hugged tight to his chest. He came up on one knee and froze there, head ducked low, eyes scanning alertly in all directions. First, he made sure no one happened to be looking out any of the saloon windows to see what he'd just done. Smoke was beginning to roll out both ends of the structure and the excited voices on the street were more frantic than ever. Luke didn't dare move to the front of the roof to try and spot how many men were down there because it would have meant too much of a risk of being seen.

He crossed to the opposite side of the roof to get a look from that vantage point, seeing if he had the chance to make another jump to the next building or if he'd have to drop to the ground before moving on. The next building being taller and again having no good purchase, it was evident the only way to proceed from this roof was to climb down from it. To do that, he moved to the back edge where he hoped he'd find a shed or perhaps a back porch overhang to aid in his descent.

Unfortunately, nothing like that presented itself. The back of the building dropped off as flat and bare as the roof itself. Weeds and open prairie stretched beyond for dozens of yards before dipping abruptly into a gully of indeterminate depth. But the gully promptly seized Luke's interest. If he could make it there, maybe it would be deep enough to use for cover and follow it back toward the livery barn and a chance to reach his horses without any more cat-and-mouse games among other empty buildings.

He was gazing at the ragged rim of the depression, still considering its possible use when suddenly, at almost the exact spot he was studying, the heads of a horse and rider lunged up into view. And following behind, being led on a rope gripped by the rider, came two more horses—the paint and the dun Luke had arrived in town with!

Once all the way up out of the gully, the rider nosed his little caravan straight toward Luke, advancing at a full gallop. When he'd reached the flat-topped building directly below where Luke stood looking down with his Winchester held at the ready, the stranger reined up sharply. All the horses skidded to a halt on the wet grass.

Looking up from under the wide brim of a slouch hat with an Indian design decorating the band around the base of its crown, the rider said calmly, "Not that you ain't doin' a pretty good job so far on your own—but it appears to me you're a fella who might could use a little help."

Chapter 11

Due north they rode, pushing the horses hard. They passed quickly in and out of the gully Luke had had his eye on and he saw that part of it was indeed deep enough to have given him cover, but its length only ran a short distance in either direction before it narrowed and choked off into little more than a crack in the ground. It wouldn't have taken him anywhere close to the livery barn.

But that problem had been unexpectedly solved and now it felt mighty good to be back in the saddle again—his own saddle, no less—and pounding clear of the craziness he'd encountered in the town of Hard Rock. He still had a score of questions rolling around in his mind about what was behind all of that, but for now he was just glad to have some distance between him and the hot lead welcome that had been waiting for him there.

Of course, he also had plenty of questions concerning this hombre who'd shown up out of nowhere to help him make a getaway. But if ever the old saying about not looking a gift horse in the mouth—literally, in this case—was worth following, then this was it.

The stranger seemed to know the area and have a specific destination in mind, and that was good enough. Concentrating on putting the gun wolves farther behind them suited Luke just fine.

As they rode, the drizzling rain turned gradually into a heavier downpour. What was more, the bank of thick, dark clouds rolling in over the mountain peaks directly ahead seemed to indicate no letup anytime soon. But Luke didn't mind all that much. The moisture on his face felt cool and bracing, almost refreshing after scrambling around inside that closed, eerily empty saloon . . . empty, that is, until his attackers started showing up. The only bad thing about this heavier downpour, he thought as he cast frequent glances over his shoulder, was if it reached the town, too, it would help the gunmen back there put out the saloon fire and be able to give pursuit that much sooner. *If* they'd ever intended to fight the fire to begin with, that was. For all Luke knew they'd be inclined to let it burn and spread to the whole town. They hardly struck him as civic-minded types who cared about nurturing the community.

Somehow, though, the thought of a whole section of the town burning bothered Luke. It shouldn't be any skin off his nose, one way or the other. But it would be a shame, more of those deserted yet still sturdy buildings ending up in ashes. And it would leave him as the one who'd triggered it. But more reflection on the matter, since he was hardly in a position to go back and help beat down the flames, was a waste. He had plenty else to worry about.

Before they'd gone much farther, the stranger in the Indian-band hat veered suddenly to the right and headed toward an outcropping of tall, ragged rock. Cutting in behind it, he led the way to a dry, sandy-bottomed pocket under the twelve-foot-high arc of a natural bridge that connected two halves of the over-all formation. Here he reined up and promptly slid from his saddle.

"There's some room for the horses over toward the back, where they'll have decent shelter, too," he announced, crowding his mount toward where he'd indicated. "We can slap feed bags on 'em after they've cooled some and they'll be fine."

As Luke dismounted and positioned his own animals, he got his first chance to study the man at any length. He saw that he was of average height, solidly built through the chest and shoulders, roughly forty years old. He had a lean face, evenly featured, with long, coal black hair showing under the Indian-band hat and dark eyes that appeared intelligent and alert. A Colt Peacemaker was holstered on his right hip and a long-bladed Bowie knife in an Indian-beaded sheath hung on his left.

"You figure on holing up here for a spell?" Luke asked as he swung down out of his own saddle.

"A bit. Any objections?"

Luke shrugged. "Not particularly. After the way you helped pull me out of that tight spot back there, I reckon I owe you not only my gratitude but the courtesy of letting you make the call."

The stranger grinned. "And I reckon you ain't one to give up calling his own shots very easy. Am I right?"

"Not exactly a habit I have, no," Luke agreed.

"The thing I got in mind, now that we're in the clear," explained the stranger, "is takin' ourselves a breather and usin' the opportunity to clear the air on some things. I expect we're both bustin' with questions and that means we'll each have some answers owed in turn. Ain't that about it?"

Luke nodded. "Sums it up pretty good, I'd say. But are you sure we're in the clear?"

The stranger pulled a spyglass from his saddlebag. "Reasonably so. I'm aimin' to shinny up higher on one of these rocks, though, and have a good look to make certain. But I didn't see no sign of anybody lightin' out after us, and I got half a hunch they might not even know yet that you squirted out the back of that saloon. Even if they did figure that much out and then that you'd made it to horseback, it'd take 'em time to run to the livery in order to saddle up their own mounts and give chase."

"Comes to that, this rain works in our favor," Luke pointed out. "The way it's coming down now, they'd never be able to track us."

The stranger twisted his mouth wryly. "Especially not this bunch. Trust me, you could carry a leaky paint bucket across a clean floor and they'd have trouble pickin' up the trail. I been dodgin' 'em for near to three months now, and they've never come within a quarter mile of me."

Luke wondered about that statement but figured it was something to be explained when he and the stranger had their palaver. Now wasn't the time to delve any deeper.

As if sensing the same thing, the stranger said, "I'm gonna go ahead and climb up for my look-see now. Since I've seen you're pretty handy at startin' fires, maybe you could scratch together the makin's for one while I'm gone. Then, after I'm back and we've tended the horses, we might could have our talk over a pot of coffee."

"I'll see what I can do," Luke told him.

A handful of minutes later, when the stranger came slipping back down from the high rocks, Luke indeed had a crackling fire waiting. He'd found sufficient dry fuel in the form of some thick brush stalks and a few stubborn, twisted scrub trees poking up through cracks in the rocks. And he already had a pot of coffee starting to brew on the edge of the coals. By the time he and the stranger had snugged their horses a bit more securely into the natural shelter and fitted them with feed bags, the coffee was ready.

With a steaming cup in hand, the stranger settled back on a hump of wind-smoothed rock and said, "Like I figured, no sign of pursuit. And like you was thinkin', this harder rain also made it to town and is drownin' that saloon fire to nothing but a smokin', smolderin' husk."

"So if those gunmen aren't chasing us or fighting the fire, what are they doing?"

"Can't say for sure. Couldn't see much of 'em. They usually hole up in a building across the street from the one you picked to set afire. I expect that's where they've regrouped, after you had 'em chasin' their tails and shot 'em up some." The stranger squinted at Luke. "You *did* thin their ranks a mite, didn't you?"

"I took out a few," Luke allowed. "A couple permanently, two or three more I nicked up pretty good."

The stranger gave a faint nod of approval before saying, "I'm guessin' they've probably discovered by now you made it out of the saloon somehow. The fact there ain't no activity around the livery barn tells me they got no idea yet that you made it clean out of town, though. What that leaves, as far as what they're up to, is goin' back to a search of the other empty buildings to try and pin you down again."

Luke frowned. "All those buildings . . . the whole town . . . empty and deserted the way it is. But it doesn't appear to have been that way for very long. What's the story there, anyway?"

"The short answer?" A distinct tone of bitterness crept into the stranger's voice. "Everybody got driven out. Driven out or, in the case of a few who resisted too hard—killed. And not just in the town, but all through the whole valley."

"All this by the same men who came after me?"

"Them, and others cut from the same cloth."

Luke eyed him more closely. "You don't mind my saying, you hardly strike me as the un-resisting type yourself. The fact you're still hanging around and the way you threw in to help me pretty much backs that up. What's your story?"

The bitterness was still there in the short laugh the stranger grunted out. "Pretty simple, really. I used to be the sheriff hereabouts."

The craziness Luke had already encountered in Hard Rock suddenly turned even more loco.

"You're Tom Eagle?" he said.

A stab of suspicion cut across Eagle's expression. "How is it you know my name?" he demanded.

"The answer to that is pretty simple, too," Luke replied, holding his voice calm and steady, hoping to keep any further reaction from Eagle the same. "You're the reason I'm here. You're the man I was sent to find."

Eagle's reaction was anything but calm. All of a sudden his Colt was drawn and Luke found himself staring into its muzzle.

Chapter 12

"Before I fetched your horses out of the livery barn," Eagle grated, "I took a couple minutes to check through what they were carryin'. The weapons and handcuffs, the rest of your gear—and the clump of wanted posters you keep real close at hand in one of your saddlebags. It was plain enough you're a bounty hunter!"

"That's right. I don't deny it. My name's Jensen, Luke Jensen. And it's true that bounty hunting is my trade."

"Then how is it you're here lookin' for me?" Eagle's eyes blazed. "There's no bounty on my head! I figured you must have been after somebody in that pack of coyotes who took over the town."

"I suspect there's a good chance some of them do have papers on them," Luke said. "Can't say as I recognized anybody, though. And once the bullets started flying, it wasn't like I had a whole lot of time to match any faces to those dodgers I carry with me."

"That still leaves the part about you comin' after me. You sayin' you got a dodger that *my* face matches?"

Luke shook his head. "Nope. As far as I know, none

exist. Not yet. That's why I was sent to bring you in. Since you represented the only law anywhere around here until you—the way it was told to me—went bad and turned outlaw, I was hired to bring you within the jurisdiction of proper authorities to the south where charges and papers *could* be issued against you."

"*I* turned outlaw?" Eagle's face flushed almost purple with rage. "What kind of hogwash is that? It's a filthy lie!"

"It's beginning to register with me," Luke said measuredly, "that I've been fed a sizable helping of lies."

"By who? Who hired you and filled you so full of this garbage about me?" Eagle wanted to know.

Luke watched his face closely as he said, "Man by the name of Parker Dixon."

The purple flush had never faded even the slightest from Eagle's face and it certainly showed no signs of doing so now. When he spoke, it was like the color was infused so deep it was squeezing his voice box, causing his words to come out in a half-strangled growl.

"That lowdown varmint! I should have known it'd be him. Who else? He can't hurt me bad enough by ruinin' everything and everybody around me, he's got to make sure he ruins me the rest of the way."

Luke didn't say anything right away. He drank some of his coffee, gave it a few moments. Eagle's Colt remained trained on him, but the former lawman seemed barely aware he was even holding it. Then Luke said, "From what I saw, Dixon is a wealthy, successful, highly respected man in and around Helena. What makes a man like that interested in reaching all the way up here to, as you put it, ruin everything and everybody—including you?"

Eagle's eyes bored into him. "What makes most men go bad? Sometimes a woman, sometimes spite. More often than anything else, though, it comes down to greed. The lust for more power and more money."

"I wouldn't argue against that, generally speaking," Luke said. "Only, meaning no disrespect to your former town or this surrounding valley, I'm having a little trouble seeing what's here that represents the kind of power and wealth that would turn somebody like Dixon so ruthless in order to gain control over it."

"If you were to dig a little deeper into his background," Eagle responded, "I'm bettin' you'd find that your prominent and respected Mr. Dixon didn't all of a sudden discover a ruthless streak in himself after he laid eyes on Hard Rock. Havin' a ruthless side is likely how he gained a chunk of his so-called prominence to begin with."

Luke thought about Dixon's man Asa Patton. Even though he'd grown to feel comfortable around him, it was plain that his services for Dixon included being available for gun work from time to time. Which made it equally plain that Dixon's business dealings weren't always conducted without some degree of force—or at least the implied threat of force—being involved.

"Going back to these new truths that are starting to register with me," said Luke, "let's include me having my eyes opened to the fact Parker Dixon may conduct part or all of his business in a manner that isn't exactly polite or gentlemanly. With that established then, tell me what makes him want to employ such an extreme level of those tactics here in your valley."

"Another simple answer. Gold."

"Dixon's already got gold. In addition to his other business interests," Luke said, "he has several mines around Helena. Plus one up around here somewhere . . . unless that was another lie."

"No, there's a Dixon mine up in the Spearpoints. That much is true," Eagle conceded. "The Gold Button—best producin' one around, as a matter of fact."

"I was led to believe it was barely holding its own. Not yielding all that much."

A trace of a wry smile touched one corner of Eagle's mouth. "Not much by some standards don't mean it ain't still a lot compared to others. And right there is the hinge of this whole thing. Not the amount of gold that's showed up so far . . . but the gold still waitin' in the belly of those mountains to be brung out!"

"You're going to have to chew that a little finer," Luke growled irritably. "This whole thing is getting fuzzier instead of clearer. Where I fit, where you fit, what it is that Dixon's after . . . What the blazes is it all about? And it might help me think a little straighter if you'd quit pointing that gun at me!"

Eagle looked somewhat taken aback. A bit of the high color faded from his face. He glanced down at the gun in his fist, as if he'd forgotten it was there, then looked up at Luke and back to the gun again. After a moment's hesitation, he pouched the iron.

"I ain't sure why, but my gut tells me you're to be

trusted," he said in a subdued voice. "No matter the reasons that brung you here."

"What brought me here had to do with a crooked sheriff who'd turned to robbing and killing," Luke told him. "Is that you?"

"I already gave you the straight on that."

"Then you've got no call to worry about me. The one thing that *does* seem clear is that what each of us has to worry about is back there in that town—the pack of gunnies who've taken over, and whoever's behind them and whatever the ultimate goal is."

"The answer to that is wrapped up in two words. Parker Dixon."

"Him and gold."

"Okay, three words."

Luke's jaw muscles clenched. "Since I got no argument in favor of Dixon and a growing list of reasons to doubt him, let's consider that part of it settled, at least for now. So tell me about the other—the gold you say is still in the belly of the mountain."

Chapter 13

After replacing the pot on the coals, Tom Eagle settled back again and went on, "Right from the first, practically as soon as the Gold Button started operation, Dixon kept sendin' more engineers to dig and sniff all around the area. Pokin' holes, takin' samples, buzzin' amongst themselves but not sayin' much to anybody on the outside. Finally, right about the time of this past winter's first thaw, they found something. Something big, you could tell by how excited they got."

Eagle sipped his coffee. Luke restrained his impatience.

"'The mother of all mother lodes' was the rumor that one of the engineers was supposed to've been overheard to say. Whatever it was, it was enough to bring Dixon himself up here for the first time since the start-up of his existin' mine. He went out of his way to talk to me personally and say a lot of vague stuff about how this whole valley was sittin' on some great changes that could benefit everybody if they were smart enough to go along and not try to stand in the way of progress."

"Sounds like a thinly veiled threat as much as anything," Luke observed.

"That's sorta what I thought. Trouble was, I didn't take it serious enough and didn't realize how fast Dixon was gonna start makin' good on it. Not that he came back around himself to do it," Eagle said with a scowl. "No, he sent others. 'Advocates' they called themselves. Guess that's a fancy term for lawyers. That's the way they talked, like lawyers. Goin' around tellin' folks how they represented a major corporation—never sayin' Dixon by name, mind you—that wanted to move into the valley and needed land for growth and development. They offered money at first. Decent enough amounts, I guess, but nothing overly generous. A few, mostly those who were strugglin' hard anyway, took 'em up on it. But not everybody, certainly not enough to suit their big plans. And that's when the advocates stepped out of the picture and Dixon's next wave of hired help showed up."

Luke gave a disdainful grunt. "Not too hard to guess that now you're talking about the same friendly gentlemen I had the pleasure of meeting."

"Them, and more just like 'em. That's when the rough stuff started happenin'. Folks flat-out threatened if they didn't pack up and move out. Property damaged and destroyed to help 'em make up their minds. Mysterious fires and explosions at some of the other mines. Cattle run off, some of 'em even slaughtered and left to rot where they fell." Eagle looked forlorn. "It got real bad real fast. It was just a matter of time before some shootin' started to take place. A handful of good people got hurt, a few even killed. Unfortunately, none of 'em were Dixon men."

"And you weren't able to stop any of it?"

Eagle shook his head in exasperation. "Never any proof. I knew exactly who it was, or at least who was behind it. And so did everybody else. But those who'd received direct threats were too afraid to identify who made 'em. And the rest of the stuff that happened—the fires and explosions and other kinds of damage—mostly took place at night so the ones who caused it couldn't be identified, even if somebody had been willing. Besides . . ."

Eagle stopped abruptly, letting his voice trail off.

"Besides what?" Luke wanted to know.

Another headshake from Eagle, this time firm, dismissive. "Never mind. It'd just sound like sour milk, like I was feelin' sorry for myself."

Luke took a drink of his coffee, then said, "You didn't have much in the way of backup, did you? No deputies, not enough men to ride behind you in a posse. That it?"

"It was what it was and it is what it is," Eagle replied sternly. "None of that likely would have made any difference, anyway, except maybe gotten some more innocents killed. The businessmen around town are—were—quiet sorts. Gentle. Clerks, family men, a lot of them gettin' on in years. Hardly the kind you could rally and throw against Dixon's gun wolves."

"What about the outlying ranchers and farmers? Or some of the independent miners? Those tend to be pretty hardy types."

"True enough. But when the trouble broke out, they were all bein' kept busy tryin' to protect their own interests. Expectin' 'em to abandon their individual fights to form a posse or help protect the town or their neighbors . . . No surprise, that wasn't very appealing. Can't say as I blame 'em. And then they got broken, one by one, and the fight got wore out of 'em."

"So any fighting back ended up all on your shoulders," Luke said, a touch of admiration in his tone. "I'm surprised Dixon allowed you to stay alive."

"*Allowed*, hell!" Eagle snapped back. "Next to tappin' that big vein of mountain gold, I don't think there's anything in the world Dixon would like better than seein' me dead. Trouble is, his hired guns haven't been up to the job, no matter how hard they've tried. I've spent my whole life in this valley and these mountains. I don't get cornered, and I don't kill easy!"

A corner of Luke's mouth quirked upward. "You've got me convinced. I'm glad things have turned out so I don't have to follow through on my original job of coming here to hunt you down."

"Comin' here to *try* and hunt me down," Eagle corrected him, a wry smile touching his own mouth.

Luke let that ride and simply took another drink of his coffee.

Eagle's teasing smile quickly faded and his mouth pulled instead into a grimace. "That blasted Dixon. Just 'cause he couldn't kill me one way, that didn't mean he was willin' to let up on me. Not by a long shot. What he did instead—no, make that at the same time, on account of he started right off, just as soon as his thugs showed up in place of those fancy-talkin' 'advocates'—was to kill my reputation."

Luke frowned. "Not sure I'm following what you mean."

"What line did he feed *you* about me? How I'd

turned from sheriff to outlaw, robbin' gold shipments, bein' a murderer. Right?" Eagle made an imploring gesture with his free hand. "Don't you get it? You weren't the first he dished that out to. Once he set out to take this whole valley and all the gold for himself, he started spreadin' the false talk about me. Went so far as to stage a couple phony robberies of his own gold shipments and rigged it so witnesses were willin' to say that one of the robbers, even in a mask, sounded and acted like me. Then, when folks started gettin' threatened and roughed up and the rest, and I wasn't able to do nothing to stop it, there were some who even wondered out loud if I wasn't in on that, too. It was like a poison bein' spread and what was gettin' poisoned was my good name."

"Occurs to me," Luke said, "that among the things Dixon told me was a claim that he'd put his own son in charge of the mining operation up here—until he got killed in one of those robberies you supposedly pulled."

Eagle's jaw dropped. "He must have wanted to convince you real bad that I was an evil dog who deserved to be taken down. The accusation that I killed his son is one I never heard before. It's a surprise to me and would be to Roland, too, I bet."

"His son, you mean?"

"None other."

"So he really does have a son. I'm surprised even that much of what he told me is true."

"Oh, it's true, all right," Eagle said. "Sounds like the only lie he told you about Roland was that he was dead and I killed him. Other than the robbery part, I wouldn't even mind takin' credit for it. You see,

Roland *does* run the Gold Button mining operation up here and not only is he still alive but he's almost as rotten as his father."

"Must make the old man real proud," Luke muttered. "But never mind the kid for now. My purpose in bringing him up wasn't meant to divert you from the rest of what you were saying."

Eagle made a sour face. "Not much left to tell. What it came down to was that, before I could do enough to stop it, Dixon had effectively painted me as crooked. A whole lot of people were quick to believe the lies he planted. Me bein' a half-breed made it plenty easy for those who never completely trusted me on account of that to begin with. Our town and our little valley bein' up here in the middle of nowhere didn't help, either. Nobody down to the south gave a damn about us when things were goin' okay, they sure didn't want to hear about our troubles. Not even other lawmen I tried to contact. By the time I was willin' to put aside my stupid pride and ask for help, Dixon's lies—and, again, my mixed blood, I suspect, in some cases—resulted in all of 'em turnin' a deaf ear. And with Dixon's status and shiny clean reputation all around Helena, I shouldn't have to tell you how far I got tryin' to get anybody down that way to listen to the truth about him."

Luke regarded him. "So you ended up one man left holding a mighty big bull by the tail. Not often I'd encourage a man to run from a fight, but what was left for you to keep hanging on for? Why didn't you say to hell with it and just ride off while you were still able?"

Eagle paused with his coffee cup raised partway to

his mouth. He held it like that for a long moment, staring into the cup as if he saw something more than the black liquid inside. Then, lifting his gaze to Luke, he said, "It ain't that simple. I might be the one carryin' most of the fight to Dixon's thugs, but I'm not all alone in this."

"So who else is there?" Luke asked.

"We'll get to that. But first, I think it's time for you to take a turn at fillin' in a bit more from your end."

"Such as?"

"The big thing I'm wonderin'," Eagle said, "is why—if Dixon hired you to come here after me—were his men waitin' to basically ambush you as soon as you hit town?"

"That's a question I've been asking myself ever since the bullets started flying," replied Luke. "I not only don't have the answer, I can't even make a decent guess. It just flat doesn't make any sense."

"Could it be those halfwits in town mistook you for somebody else?"

Luke shook his head. "Wasn't that. One of them—the heavyset fella with the bloated-looking face—"

"That was Ferris. Hacksaw Ferris."

"Okay. Ferris, then. The thing is, he called me by name. What was more, he kept ordering his men to take me alive, not shoot to kill."

Eagle gave a low whistle. "For not meanin' to kill you, they sure were throwin' a lot of lead your way."

"That's why Ferris had to keep reminding them to take it easy. And that only adds to the strangeness of the whole business. Why ambush somebody with orders not to kill? And since they're Dixon's men and seemed to be expecting me as well as knowing who I was, they must have gotten the word from him. Yet if he wanted me captured for some reason, why wait until I was clear up here to do it? He had me totally off guard and right there at his fingertips down in Helena. Surely he could have hired thugs to try for me there."

"It almost sounds like he has a notion to do some kind of toyin' with you, and up here is where he wants it to take place," Eagle suggested.

Luke's eyes narrowed. "If that's the case, I hope he also has a notion to show up and participate in the fun and games. I'm eager for the chance to have him in front of me again."

Eagle's tone hardened. "There's a sentiment we share."

After draining the last of his coffee, Luke said, "The only thing that seems clear is that Dixon's reasons for getting me up here, whatever they are, actually have little or nothing to do with you. If there was any chance he was hoping for me to get rid of you before he revealed the rest of what he has in mind for me, that went out the window when his men were laying for me outside the church. But that don't mean those same men aren't still gunning for you."

"And neither does it mean they're done gunnin' for you."

"Yeah, I get that now. I had no clue, though, when I first rode in." Luke's brows pinched a little tighter together. "But what about you? What brought you so close to town, knowing those varmints had to be hanging around there and are on the constant lookout for your hide?"

"Supplies," Eagle answered. "I was using the rain for cover to sneak in and gather up some supplies. When folks cleared out, see, a lot of 'em left behind useful things in root cellars and pantries and so forth. Things that Dixon's pack of rats give no thought to or care anything about. Booze, money, any baubles that looked like they might have some value—those kind of things they scooped up right away.

"But canned goods, medicine, blankets, and the like got paid no attention to. I even know where there's a couple barrels of cured meat they never discovered that I draw from a little at a time." Eagle's expression grew more intense as he locked eyes with Luke. "Dixon sees to the needs of his hired thugs real good," he went on, "but the folks he ran out from their homes with nothing but what little they had on their backs, he don't give a damn about. Yet some of them are . . . still around. It is for them that I scrounge and hunt supplies. And continue to remain here myself. They're who I was talkin' about before when I said I wasn't in this alone."

Luke was at a temporary loss for words. Springing from the discussion of so much betrayal and deceit having already taken place, a delayed suspicion had suddenly gripped him about the hunted man's motives for being so conveniently present back in town when it seemed like a place he should have avoided at all costs. Now that Luke had been given the answer, he was left with a pang of guilt for his suspicion.

Before he could say anything, Eagle had more to add. "You'll note that your packhorse has a few extra bundles on its back. Those are the result of my foraging. I left my own horse stashed out back and had snuck into the barn to grab one of the gunnies' nags for a packhorse when you showed up and conveniently left off your animals. At that point, I figured you for just a new recruit to the gang and I decided your horses would suit me just fine. By the time I got 'em out back, though, and was up in my own saddle once more, you'd made it to the church and commenced that commotion with the bell. I found that powerful curious. Then I saw Hacksaw and his boys closin' in, gettin' ready for you to step outside again, and it was startin' to look like you wasn't such a welcome guest after all.

"Next, when the bullets started flyin', that got more clear than ever. But to be honest with you—and I ain't especially proud to admit this—my first inclination was that none of it was any of my business, and in fact, the gunplay would make good cover for me hightailin' away."

"I'm glad you changed your mind," Luke said.

Eagle shrugged. "Somehow, it didn't seem like I had a choice. When I saw you skin out the back of the church and make your break across the cemetery, I started pullin' for you. I had no idea what all the ruckus was about, but you was fightin' the same lowdown scum I'm up against, so that's really all I needed to know. When I saw you duck into the back of the old saloon and watched Hacksaw and his bunch scatter all down the street tryin' to corner you so they could root you out, I had a pretty good idea what you was up to. That's when I took the horses down into that gully and waited, figurin' that when you popped back out again you'd likely be in the mood for some help when it came to a getaway."

"Well, your figuring certainly turned out handy for me," Luke stated. "And, in case I haven't expressed my gratitude sufficiently before this, allow me to say it again now."

Eagle cocked an eyebrow. "You might want to stop and remember what you're in the middle of before you go gettin' too grateful. The thing about it, though, is that you still got yourself an option left. Me, I'm pretty well locked in for all the reasons I've already explained. But you—and I heard something along these lines from a fella not too long ago—what have you got left to keep hangin' on for? Why don't you just ride away while you're still able?"

Luke gave a quick, firm shake of his head. "No, that's not the way it's going to go. Dixon sent me here to toy with me, play some games. Call it curiosity or plain stubbornness, but I'm not leaving until I find out why . . . And then, when I do, I mean to have a say in how the game ends."

"Well don't look for me to put no more effort in tryin' to talk you out of it," Eagle declared. "After watchin' the way you had Hacksaw and his boys dancin' to your tune back there in town, I'm interested in seein' what other moves you got. But before that, I've got some supplies to deliver and you're invited to come along, especially since they're loaded on your horse. There's some rugged miles between here and there, though, so we'd best get a move on if we want to make it ahead of dark."

Luke made a sweeping gesture with one hand. "Lead on, Sheriff. I'll be right behind you."

Chapter 14

Roland Dixon wrinkled his nose in disgust. "You stink of burnt hair, burnt flesh—and failure," he snarled. "On top of that, the gash on your head is threatening to drip blood on my carpet. Didn't it occur to you to at least take time to clean yourself up before you came barging in here?"

Standing just inside the doorway of Roland's private living quarters at the Gold Button mine, Hector "Hacksaw" Ferris looked down at the ornate carpet under his feet and stepped back as far as he could toward the edge. When he lifted his round, beefy face again—a face streaked with soot and dust along with tracks of dried blood from the wound Roland had mentioned—his expression resembled that of a scolded child.

"Jeez, Boss," he mumbled, pressing an already blood-soaked handkerchief to the back of his head, "I guess I wasn't thinkin'. I figured the most important thing was to not waste no time lettin' you know what happened with that Jensen fella."

"And why would I be in a hurry to hear the bad

news about how you and the others bumbled your apprehension of Jensen and instead allowed him to get away?" Roland said acidly. "The thing you *shouldn't* be wasting time about is going after him and running him to ground before he causes more trouble here or, worse yet, starts back to Helena."

"I did that. I sent boys out after him right away," Ferris was quick to say. Then, glumly, he added, "But with this doggone rain and night startin' to settle in . . . I don't know how much luck they're apt to have."

"Well, if it's anything like the luck you've had so far," Roland sneered, "then we can expect the worst, can't we?"

He remained in the plush easy chair where he was seated long enough to pound a fist on one of the thickly cushioned arm rests before shoving to his feet. He stood uncertainly for a moment and then started to pace in long strides back and forth across the width of the well-appointed room.

He was a tall, lean man not yet thirty years of age, the angular features of his face bearing a definite resemblance to his father. Unlike the older Dixon, however, his son conveyed no sense of being former military, not in the faint slouch to his shoulders or the longish cut of his dark hair or the petulant twist his mouth seemed always on the verge of displaying. And in lieu of any genuine hardness around his eyes there was only a glint of bullying meanness.

The latter had been on full display when addressing Ferris. But now, as he abruptly stopped pacing, he returned his gaze to the bloated-faced man and his expression became more tolerant.

"Blast it, Hack, I had no business coming down on you so hard," he said, pointedly stopping short of an actual apology. "Look at you, you're battered and burned as a result of trying to carry out a senseless task and all the thanks you get is a berating from me."

Roland turned to the third person in the room, a tall Oriental woman who had been standing silently and motionlessly behind the easy chair he'd been sitting in. She was of indeterminate age—maybe twenty, maybe forty. Her facial features were flawless: skin as pale and smooth as porcelain, lush mouth glistening with a touch of scarlet, striking almond eyes. Glossy black hair poured down around her face and over her shoulders, blending almost perfectly with the wrap of black silk that encased her Amazonian-proportioned body like a second skin.

"Ying-Su," Roland addressed her. "Go and fetch Mr. Ferris a glass and a bottle of good bourbon." As Ying-Su glided wordlessly away, Roland turned back to Ferris and said, "Come in and sit down, Hack. You look badly in need of taking a load off your feet."

Ferris had trouble tearing his eyes away from the departing Ying-Su. When he finally did, he spread his arms out and glanced down at himself before replying, "I better not, Boss. I'm a mess, like you said before—I don't want to ruin any of this nice furniture you got here. I'll sure take a touch of that bourbon, though."

"I appreciate your respect for the furnishings," Roland said. "We'll keep the rest of this brief so you can go get cleaned up and dried off. But before that, you need to stop by the infirmary and have Carstairs look at that head wound."

"I intend to," Ferris said. "I told the sawbones I'd be back when we dropped off the other injured men."

Roland scowled. "Who was that again, the men who were hurt?"

"Stuckey, Rogers, and Hollister. Stuckey took a bullet to the thigh, Rogers burned his hands pretty bad in that stairwell fire." Ferris's forehead puckered with concern. "It's Hollister I'm worried about the most, though. He got knocked loco when that chandelier fell on us and nobody's had any luck bringin' him back around, not even a little bit. He's still laid out cold on one of those cots in the infirmary."

Ying-Su returned carrying a serving tray upon which rested a glass and a bottle of bourbon. She carried this over and rested it on the ledge of a bookcase built into the wall next to where Ferris stood. Silently, with deft movements but without making eye contact, she uncorked the bottle, poured the glass three-quarters full, and handed it to Ferris. As soon as he took the glass, she backed away and then turned and retreated to a corner of the room where she sank onto a short divan strewn with multi-colored pillows. As she sat, she crossed her legs and a slit up the side of her gown parted to reveal a daring expanse of thigh as pale and smooth as her face.

This time Ferris had so much trouble tearing his eyes away that he nearly tipped up the glass of whiskey and poured it down the front of his chin. He caught himself at the last second, though, and managed to lift the fiery liquid to his lips instead. After he'd knocked back a healthy swallow, he cut his gaze to Roland and said, "Ain't you havin' a touch with me, Boss?"

Roland had watched Ferris's uncontrollable gawking with amusement. He was used to it when any of his employees came within sight of Ying-Su. There'd been a time when such drooling behavior had angered him. But he came to realize that they couldn't help it, and as far as the remote chance any of them would draw even the tiniest speck of return interest from Ying-Su, it was impossible to fathom. So let the fools make do with the whores working the tent cribs that the company allowed to occupy a corner of the mining property while they fantasized fleetingly about the unattainable that belonged to Roland alone.

In response to Ferris's question, Roland let his smile fade and gestured to a crystal glass of amber liquid perched on the table next to where he'd been seated. "I'm a brandy man, Hack. Was already working on one when you showed up." He reached over and picked up the glass. "So I'll save us both from drinking alone."

Once he'd tipped up the brandy and then lowered it, Roland's expression again grew somber. "You said we also lost two other men who were shot to death."

Ferris's nod was barely perceptible. "Cleve Rolly and Jim Dreyford. Good men, both."

"Yes. Dreyford, especially, was a top gun." Roland's free hand balled into a fist that he raised to chest level. "What a waste! Five men—two hurt, two dead, one perhaps hovering near death—all lost for the sake of my father's overly complicated vendetta against an elusive ghost from the past."

Ferris took another drink of his whiskey and then

set his jaw firmly as he lowered the glass. "Not to argue, Boss, but that Jensen ain't no ghost. I seen him bleed. But if we'd've been allowed to, we damn sure could have *made* him a ghost. I ain't makin' excuses, mind you, but tryin' to take a gun hand like Jensen alive—especially when he's shootin' back, and shootin' to kill—makes for a mighty awkward set of rules to operate by."

"You think I don't know that?" Roland snapped. He raised his brandy glass again but paused, merely glowering into it. Then he said, "But what I also know is that when my old man issues a set of orders, there are those of us who hop to whatever he says, few questions asked." He took his drink, then lowering the glass again, he said to Ferris, "I have little choice in the matter. But you and the others always have the option to draw your pay and ride off. Is that what you want, Hack?"

Ferris thrust out his chin defiantly. "Hell no. Especially not now, not where this Jensen is concerned. Me and that varmint have a score to settle—for what he did to my boys, and what he damn near did to me. I don't know what this 'vendetta' thing is that your old man has in mind, but I'm countin' on it not bein' very pleasant for Jensen when all is said and done. And I aim to be around to see how it ends."

"If my father has his way," Roland said, "I'm sure you won't be disappointed in the final outcome. But first, Jensen's apprehension needs to be accomplished."

"Me and the boys will see to that," Ferris said confidently.

Roland arched an eyebrow. "You said you saw him bleed. What did you mean by that?"

"Just what I said. There was a cut on his face—maybe a bullet graze, a ricochet or some such," Ferris explained. "Whatever it was, I saw blood on his cheek when he went runnin' out of that cemetery."

"Maybe it will be enough to slow him down, aid in your eventual capture of him."

"All I know is that slippery skunk may have dodged us once, but he won't again. He may last through the night, but come daylight we'll run him down sure." Ferris bared his teeth menacingly. "I'll sic Dog DeMarist on him. Dog's the best tracker we got."

"He hasn't managed to impress me much in the past, not with his inability to ferret out that troublesome half-breed, Tom Eagle," Roland pointed out.

Ferris scowled. "Jensen ain't no half-breed who grew up in this valley. He don't know the area at all. Way I figure, his reaction to what happened today will go one of two ways: Either he'll hightail it back to your old man to try and find out why there was an ambush waitin' for him . . . or, bein' a tough hombre and maybe seein' it as more of a personal matter with the ones who actually put the heat on him, could be he'll stick around and try to get his answers direct. No matter, we'll be happy to accommodate him. He tries runnin', Dog will track him and we'll stop him short. He sticks around, we'll stop him just as short at anything else he has in mind to try."

"You'd better," Roland told him.

Ferris shifted his weight from one foot to the other and glowered down at the glass in his hand, appearing suddenly uneasy about something.

"What is it? What's the matter?" Roland wanted to know.

"Well, uh . . . I was just thinkin' about the men I've got to do what needs doin'. We cut back on my crew not so long ago, remember? After we got the last of the sodbusters chased out of the valley. I sent quite a few pretty good guns packin'." Ferris's broad forehead filled with deep creases. "And now, with five men just took out of commission, and all of a sudden faced with runnin' down both Tom Eagle *and* this Jensen varmint . . ."

Roland glared at him. "So what do you expect me to do about it? Wave a magic wand and magically conjure you some more gun hands? It would take days to send out for more men and for them to get here."

Ferris's head bobbed. "I know, I know. Unless maybe you'd let me borrow a few men from the minin' crew. Some of those boys are pretty rough cobs. They'd do to fill in the gaps and ride with my other boys until we could get some other reinforcements."

"Oh, that's a great idea. Mace Vernon is going to love letting go of some of his miners," Roland said sarcastically. "He's always whining for more help as it is."

"Never mind. It was just a thought, Boss." Ferris squared his broad shoulders. "I'll make do with what I got. We'll focus on Jensen first—he's got to be stopped. Then we'll get back around to that pain-in-the-neck half-breed. His days are numbered, too!"

"I sure hope so," Roland said. "I'll hold off contacting my father about any of this, in the hope you can make short work of catching up with Jensen. The old man will be anxious for a report, though, so I won't be able to delay giving him one for very long. Is the telegraph still operating?"

"It was the last I knew . . . unless that blasted half-breed cut it again," Ferris answered.

A corner of Roland's mouth lifted wryly. "If nothing else, that might make a convenient excuse in case I *do* want to delay contacting the old man."

Ferris shifted his weight somewhat nervously, not knowing what to say to that.

Roland took another drink and then said, "Best be on your way then, Hack. Be sure to get that head of yours looked at. Check on the other injured men, too, and prepare the rest for what needs to be done tomorrow." He paused and then heaved a heavy sigh before adding, "Before you ride out in the morning, check with me at my office. In the meantime, I'll see what I can do to convince Vernon to free up some of his men."

"I'd be mighty obliged, Boss. That would help a heap."

"It had better," Roland said through clenched teeth. "One way or other, I expect you to run down Luke Jensen and bring him here to stand before me in chains."

Ferris's eyes blazed. "I mean to make that happen, Boss. He may not be standin' real steady, but I'll have him here."

Once Ferris was gone, Roland stood looking at the closed door for several seconds. His expression appeared stern, deep in thought.

Abruptly, he tossed back the remains of his brandy

then turned his gaze to Ying-Su. Setting aside the glass, he smiled thinly, saying, "Now that I've given that odious creature his assignment, my dear, I have one for you. We shall retire to the other room where you will apply your considerable charm and skills toward helping me to forget, at least for a time, that I am forced to deal with such unpleasant men and related matters."

Ying-Su held Roland's gaze for a long moment, her expression impassive. Then, without a word, she rose to her feet and moved obediently toward him.

Chapter 15

Setting a tireless, steady pace, Tom Eagle led the ascent up into the Spearpoint Mountains. The rain diminished again as they climbed, but not completely, and as they went higher, more and more wind gusts began whistling through gaps in the tall rock outcroppings. The unbroken cloud cover hurried the onset of evening and the thickening gloom of approaching night.

At last, topping a ragged incline that flattened out onto a broad, gravelly ledge running below higher peaks, Eagle reined up twenty yards short of a narrow canyon that appeared choked by jagged pieces of landslide rubble. When Luke pulled up alongside him, the former sheriff gestured and asked, "What do you see?"

"Looks like a dead end. Is that a recent slide?"

Eagle grinned. "Nope. It's not a recent slide and it's not a dead end. But a lot of work went into makin' it look that way."

"Work by you?"

"Not by me. By a stubborn old prospector who spent most of his life diggin' in these mountains. He always believed he was on the brink of a big strike and he always suspicioned others were watchin' him, waitin' to make their move on him. So when he struck some mighty promisin' color back in that canyon, he took steps to keep it hid away from anybody else who might come sniffin' around."

"He dynamited the canyon mouth," Luke guessed.

"That's right. Then he spent weeks and weeks clearin' a narrow, twisty trail through it—a maze-like path complete with a few dead ends that most folks would never spot to begin with and then likely could never follow even if they did stumble into it."

"Sounds like a powerful lot of precaution." Luke lifted his eyebrows. "You called the old prospector stubborn and suspicious. Maybe a little crazy to boot?"

"Reckon he got that way at some point durin' all the years he spent chasin' his lonely dream."

"Did it finally pay off? Did he find anything worthwhile back there in the canyon?"

"Nothing worth even a fraction of all the work he put into it. A palmful of gold dust, a nugget or two no bigger than a teardrop. A sad deal," Eagle summed up, with a genuine trace of the sentiment showing on his face.

"So how do you know all of this?"

"I happened on him one day where he lay dyin', right over yonder"—Eagle pointed—"just outside the edge of the boulders. He'd been out huntin' for fresh meat, as I was. He had what I guess must have been a heart attack. He was tryin' to crawl back to his dig, back to a mule and an old dog he'd left tied up while he was away. He was worried what would happen to 'em if he didn't make it back—that nobody'd ever find 'em and they might not be able to make it out on their own.

"Because of that," Eagle went on, "because of those critters—the only living things he'd had any regular contact with for years—he wouldn't let me load him on my horse and try to get him back to the doctor in Hard Rock. Not right away. He insisted that first I let him lead me through the maze so we could see to his animals."

The grim expression on Eagle's face made it plain enough to Luke what had happened next. "The old prospector never made it back out of that canyon, did he?"

"I buried him in there. Just like he would have wanted," Eagle replied. "He never even got the chance to tell me his name, but I put up a decent marker for him anyway. Afterwards, I took the mule back to town and turned it over to the livery proprietor, then took the dog home to my daughter."

"You have a daughter?" Luke asked, surprised.

Eagle gave him a look. "Yeah, I have a daughter. And a son and a wife. Even a half-breed can have a family, you know. Ain't like I've always been a fugitive on the run from false charges against me. Not so very long ago, remember, I was a respected member of society. Until the Devil—in the form of Parker Dixon—set his horns to rip it all away from me. In case you still don't get it, my family is the biggest part of why I'm continuin' to fight Dixon as hard as I am."

"Okay. If I didn't before, I get it now," Luke said.

Both men were quiet for a minute, ducking their heads and pulling their hat brims down over their faces as a sudden gust of wind whipped across the ledge, lashing them with cold rain.

When the wind gust had passed, Eagle lifted his face and said, "Reckon that was a sign for me to quit spoutin' ancient history and get us on in where there's some shelter. In case you ain't figured out the rest of it, helpin' that old prospector all those years back came in mighty handy—the way things have a funny way of turnin' out sometimes—when Dixon's bunch started drivin' decent folks away. It gave me a place to bring the handful who was willin' to try and stick it out, even if it meant goin' into hidin' for a spell."

"Including your family?"

"Right at the heart of it," Eagle assured him. "It ain't exactly paradise back in there but it's got all the basics—helped along by what I'm able to add with my huntin' and foragin'—to see us through. Follow me. You'll soon find out for yourself."

Once again, Eagle led the way. He rode straight up to what looked like an impenetrable wall of tumbled, broken boulders. At the last minute, he abruptly nosed his mount into a slight gap between two of the jagged pieces—a gap that even the keen eyes of Luke would have had trouble spotting on his own. From there, proceeding in single file, men and horses wound their way through what was indeed a maze-like series of cramped twists and turns. With so many switchbacks, it was hard for Luke to determine how far they were actually moving forward into the canyon. Before long, though, they received a greeting that seemed to signal they might be nearing their destination.

The greeting came in the form of a large dog, a dripping wet yellow mongrel, who suddenly appeared on the crown of a tilted rock slab just a few yards ahead of Eagle. The half-breed checked his horse and Luke heard him call out, "Beulah, old girl. There you are! Been waitin' for me, have you?"

The dog yipped a response, her tail wagging happily.

"Don't tell me," muttered Luke. "That must be the dog you inherited from the old prospector?"

"Not quite," Eagle said over his shoulder. "That was Buford. He left us a while back. This is one of his offspring, though. And that's her brother, Beau, right behind you."

Luke twisted in his saddle and saw a second dog— a close twin to Beulah except for being a bit thicker through the chest and shoulders—poised only a few feet behind the dun packhorse.

"They stand guard over the entrance," said Eagle, confirming what Luke had begun to figure out. "Anybody but the handful they're trained to recognize tries to pass through, they give us warning. And if nobody calls 'em off, they do more than that."

"In other words," Luke said, "if I wasn't riding along with you, old Beau back here would be fixing to take me out of this saddle about now."

Eagle grinned. "No. He'd have done that before you ever got this close."

What they were "this close" to came in sight just a few minutes later when, announced now by the freely barking dogs, Eagle led them the rest of the way out of the boulder maze and they found themselves in a widened section of the canyon. Here its sandy floor was free from any blockage except for a few heaps of broken rock that had crumbled off naturally and fallen from one of the high, steep walls that rose on either side. Also here, less than fifty yards ahead of where they emerged, lay the encampment that Eagle and other refugees from Hard Rock and the surrounding valley—people driven from their homes but not willing to run all the way—had put together as a temporary community until they could win back their rightful one.

The heart of the camp appeared to be a timber-framed opening—the old prospector's original dig, Luke surmised—carved into the canyon's north wall. Extending out from this was a large canopy, approximately twelve feet square and nearly as high off the ground, made up of several stitched-together canvas tarps and suspended on rough-hewn wooden poles.

In the center of the shelter thus provided burned a good-sized campfire with some large pots suspended over the flames on iron rods. A few smaller pots were balanced on stones that ringed the fire. Huddled under the canopy, mostly grouped close to the fire, were about twenty people, men, women, and children. Alerted by the barking dogs, the majority of their faces displayed anxious smiles at the sight of Eagle—smiles that faltered somewhat upon also noting Luke. Nevertheless, the bounty hunter suspected that, had it not been for the rain, several of the folks would have come forward to greet them.

Advancing to the canopy, Eagle wasted no time swinging down from his saddle then stepping under the protective canvas and into the embrace of an attractive, dark-haired woman. It was clear this must be his wife and the young girl and boy—about sixteen and thirteen, respectively, Luke judged them to be—who edged closer to the pair, were their children.

Easing out of the embrace, Eagle placed his hands on his wife's shoulders and gently pressed her back to arm's length. "I never want to cut short a hug from you, Janie darlin'," he said, "but look what you're gettin' out of it—soaked near as bad as me."

"I don't care," Jane Eagle insisted. "I'm so glad to have you back safe that I just want to wrap you in my arms and not let you go again. That's how much I worry when you go out on one of your escapades."

"Aw now," Eagle told her, "how many times have I told you that the only frettin' you need to do when I'm away is for any of Dixon's thugs I happen to run across."

"Like I give a hoot about any of that bunch!" Jane sniffed.

Eagle laughed. "That's my girl. But here, let me introduce you—the rest of you listen up, too!—to somebody you *ought* to give a hoot about." He motioned for Luke to come in under the canopy, and when he did, the former sheriff clapped one hand on his shoulder and said, "Folks, I want you all to meet Luke Jensen. Luke showed up in Hard Rock a little earlier today and Dixon's gun wolves didn't waste no time takin' a run at him. Only trouble was, Luke didn't hardly hold still for it. He went to work tyin' knots in several of their tails and even chopped off a couple of 'em, permanent-like."

There was a general rumbling of favorable responses.

"For that reason," Eagle went on, "I brung him back

with me. He has his own reasons for stickin' around and buckin' Dixon's hardcases. But just how deep he wants to dig in his heels as far as our overall situation, remains to be seen. He might stick for a day, a week, or a month. He might be gone in the morning. He has no obligation, so that's his call to make. But for however long he *does* stick, I want everybody to show him respect and make him feel welcome, you hear?"

This drew another wave of assenting voices.

Eagle nodded. "Okay. I'll get to full introductions all the way around in short order. But ahead of that, it looks like our arrivin' here came as an interruption to your supper. That means y'all are wantin' to get on with it and, I assure you, me and Luke are wantin' just as bad to join you. So let's go ahead and chow down, and I can finish up introductions as we eat.

"I see a couple of young fellas, though," Eagle added, "who I'm nominatin' to take care of a little chore before they join in the feed. That chore is puttin' away the horses me and Luke just rode in on." He turned to the boy Luke had earlier taken to be the former sheriff's son. "Davy, how about you and your buddy LeRoy see to that?"

"Yessir," the boy replied.

Eagle looked over at Luke. "You mind the boys handlin' your gear?"

"Not at all."

Turning back to Davy, Eagle said, "You heard the man. It's your job to live up to the trust bein' put in you. Strip the horses down, haul the gear into the old mine shaft where it'll be safe and dry. Those two big gunny sacks on the dun pack animal are mine—they go with the rest of our supplies. The remainder of the gear on the dun and on the paint are Mr. Jensen's, put them together in a separate pile. After that, take the horses over to the corral. It should be okay to let 'em drink a little, but not too much. Then turn 'em loose so they can get at the hay with the others."

Davy trotted off to carry out his orders, a red-haired boy about the same size and age following on his heels.

Looking after them, Luke said, "You appear to have a good boy there. The redheaded one, too. Willing workers."

"Everybody in this camp has to pull their share," Eagle said sternly. "It's a hard life for all. For a couple young lads like Davy and LeRoy, it'll mold 'em one way or the other—either make 'em strong and able to endure, or handicap 'em into thinkin' too deep on the hardship and feelin' sorry for themselves for the rest of their days."

Luke regarded him. It felt like the half-breed was talking about something beyond the potential future of the two boys—or, possibly, not something beyond at all, but rather behind, like perhaps Eagle's own boyhood. Luke felt the urge to ask him more, but held it in check.

Abruptly, the stern look left Eagle's face and he was grinning when his gaze returned to Luke. "Come on," he said. "Those boys can handle the chore of puttin' away the horses okay, let's you and me go tackle the chore of puttin' away some of the supper that's waitin' for us."

Chapter 16

The supper consisted of venison stew, slabs of cornbread with fresh-churned butter, and wild greens boiled in bacon grease. Coffee and hot or cold tea were available to drink. This was all spread out on a long table made from split tree trunks with the up-turned flat sides planed smooth and varnished to a glossy finish.

While the bowls of food and pots of drink were passed back and forth, following a brief prayer spoken by an elderly gent with a totally bald crown and a mane of white hair flowing down the back of his neck, Eagle began making the promised additional introductions around the table.

As names were given for the new faces surrounding him, Luke nodded politely in response and made a mental note of each as they were presented. As a consequence of his trade, Luke had developed a strong knack for remembering names and faces and there was enough distinction in this group of refugees so that he felt fairly confident he'd be able to recall all of their identities pretty well by the time the meal was over.

In total, there were eight women, four youngsters, and ten men, not counting Eagle. Considering the situation they were in—the struggle to turn back Parker Dixon's forces from maintaining the takeover of their town and valley—Luke automatically appraised the men and based on their appearance judged which ones might amount to anything in a direct confrontation against the likes of Hacksaw Ferris's gun wolves.

Sadly, his conclusion wasn't promising. Less than half, from what he saw in his quick once-over, looked as though they might be able to stack up, and even a couple of them were marginal.

Whit Barlow, a rawboned widower in his late forties, seemed like one of the better prospects. He, along with his tomboyish seventeen-year-old daughter Betty, had been struggling to make a go of a small horse ranch before Ferris's gunnies ruined them—stampeding the herd, shooting several head, then burning their cabin and corrals. Barlow exhibited the kind of tough spirit and thirst for revenge that under the right circumstances could deliver some serious payback to the interlopers. And if Betty had been a boy, her kind of pluck, though decidedly green, would have had the potential for fighting at his father's side.

Howard MacGregor, a solid physical specimen of thirty or so who'd had a small but promising farm that he worked with his wife Colleen before Ferris's gang ran them off, was another who looked capable of putting up a good fight.

The remainder of Luke's four consisted of a couple of old prospectors—Isaac Turley and Red Baker—who'd been driven from their mountain claim. Both men were up in years, but the hardscrabble life they'd

led for decades in their pursuit of gold, scraping out
barely enough to keep going and keep their dream
alive, had toughened and hardened them to a pair of
walking, talking slabs of rawhide. And their rage at
getting chased from finally being on the brink of "the
big one" had them equally primed to strike back.

That left Ben Pettigrew, formerly the town's blacksmith, a man competent at his trade and powerfully
built from the waist up—but limited by having only
one leg, courtesy of a Civil War cannon ball. Pettigrew's eighteen-year-old son Heath might have been
a prospect if he'd had his father to fight beside, but
lacking that and exhibiting a bit of chip-on-his-shoulder
attitude, marked him as having limitations.

Next came Neal Vickers, the town barber, an ami-
able and willing gent who suffered from being so
overweight that his mobility was restricted to frequently needing to sit and catch his breath. Then
there was Dewey Akron, also a victim of the late war—
in his case mentally affected by the carnage he'd seen,
to the point of becoming a quietly babbling shell
who'd previously existed by swamping out saloons for
sleeping privileges and a daily plate of beans to go with
whatever he could mooch in the way of alcohol to
dull the scenes of horror that played inside his head.

And finally, two gentlemen whose advanced years
made them too slow and frail to contemplate participating in any kind of physical conflict: Jonathan Wray,
who had said the pre-meal grace, skilled at boot repair
and leather work, and Clarence Copley, a widower
who dabbled in cabinet making.

All told, with such a meager assemblage of what
Luke would term "fighting men" at his disposal, Tom

Eagle's hope of somehow reclaiming his town and valley seemed like an impossible task. Luke couldn't help recalling the question he'd earlier put to the former sheriff about what was keeping him in the fray? The response Eagle had given then seemed even more admirable in the face of this—yet also more impractical, if not downright hopeless.

But at the same time, Luke also couldn't help remind himself, neither had *he* opted to ride away from the trouble he'd found here. What was more, as he took in the welcoming faces of the people around him, people he was now breaking bread with, he realized he was feeling even more drawn into it . . .

Halfway through supper, the rain suddenly stopped. By the time everyone was done eating, the cloud cover that had remained so stubbornly in place all through the day finally began opening up and sections of clear sky with the faint glimmer of a few early stars were able to peek through.

This break in the weather provided the chance for Eagle to draw Luke back out from under the canopy and show him the rest of the encampment's layout. This basically amounted to a row of various-sized tents and rough-hewn lean-tos spread along the north canyon wall, these being the individual living quarters for the folks Luke had just met. Supper, the main meal of the day, was always taken collectively under the big canopy, which served as a sort of "village square" for the camp; meetings and Sunday prayer services were also held there. Other meals, personal and family matters, and sleeping arrangements took place in the separate dwellings.

Against the opposite wall of the canyon, a corral and a larger lean-to that constituted a "barn" had been erected for the animals—a collection made up of eight horses (not counting Luke's two), three pigs, three goats, and a smattering of chickens. Farther down the valley, Eagle pointed out, there was a plentiful water source and some good-sized patches of graze for the horses and goats, to go with the sacks of grain that had been brought in by those owning animals.

Eagle also told Luke how the nameless old prospector's original dig, the mine shaft extending into the north wall where supplies and miscellaneous gear were stored, was being gradually expanded by the men of the group in anticipation of winter.

"If things haven't been settled by then and there are some of us still hangin' on," he explained, "that will give us the shelter we'll need to keep warm and dry in order to survive even the harshest weather. The shaft goes back pretty far now, and if we keep scourin' away to deepen and widen it even more, we'll have room to fit all who are willin' to stick it out." Then, his somber expression shifting to a sudden grin, he added, "Maybe we'll strike gold in the process and end up bein' able to *buy* our valley back from Dixon . . . not that I'd be willin' to make it so easy on that snake, even if I could."

The two men had been stretching their legs as they talked and by now had reached a corner of the corral quite a ways from the others. Luke stopped and leaned against one of the posts, eyeing his host.

"You really prepared to carry on this fight for that long?" he asked.

Eagle met his eyes. "I'm prepared to keep goin' until hell freezes over or until I'm six feet in the ground. One or the other."

"And your wife and kids—is it worth the risk to them? What would become of them if you do end up in the ground?"

"It's for Jane and the kids that I'm doin' this," Eagle insisted. "If I *don't* make a stand against Dixon, what have I got? I was nothing but another half-breed caught between two worlds before I took the sheriff job that nobody else wanted and from there made myself and the badge into something that mattered and was respected. Dixon's done his best to not only take all that away from me but to also ruin my name and my chances for startin' over anywhere else. It ain't in me not to fight against lettin' him get away with that. And when Jane gave me her heart, she understood how I was and we both understood we would stand together to face whatever trouble came our way."

"You're a lucky man to have a woman like that at your side."

"I know."

"What about the others? Are they as committed as you to this fight?"

"They share in Dixon havin' took everything from 'em and leavin' 'em with no good options, if that's what you mean. Do they have my same thirst for revenge or as strong a will to fight? I can't say for sure. I believe most of them do. But then, once you get past will, you come down to things like ability and endurance, right?"

The question hung in the air for a long moment. Luke knew it was rhetorical.

"I saw you all durin' supper, takin' stock of the other men in my group," Eagle went on. "What did you conclude?"

Now it was Luke's turn to pose a rhetorical question. "As a fighting force to throw against the likes of Hacksaw Ferris and his bunch?" He paused just a beat, then continued. "Maybe half of them look able to put up a fair scrap. I'm talking out away from here, that is—taking the fight *to* Dixon's men. So that excludes the one-legged blacksmith and the heavy, ponderous fella who can hardly get around. If it came to defending this encampment, you could probably add them as well. Along with everybody else, came to that. But I'm guessing that letting this place be discovered and making a stand here is what you want only as a last resort."

Eagle nodded. "You're thinkin' about the same as me. As far as what I got in the way of men as well as how best to use 'em. One or two halfway decent riflemen could hold off an army from making it through that boulder maze. But sooner or later, a siege would wear down and starve the encampment . . . No, the only way to beat Dixon is to do it out there in the valley. Throw the fight against him, like you said."

"But if his gunnies did discover your camp and tried to get at you here, is there a back door for folks to get out?" Luke asked.

"I wouldn't bottle everybody up if there wasn't," Eagle told him. Then he pointed, adding, "The canyon runs for another half mile or so off to the west, with high, steep cliffs on either side that can't be scaled up or down. At the far end, where it pinches shut, there's a waterfall that pours down from some higher source. The water continues on in a fast-moving stream that steps the rest of the way down the mountain over three or four shorter falls until it goes windin' off into the valley at the bottom. Runnin' beside that stream and down along the sides of those smaller falls is a rocky path that can be followed. Not by any horse, but people on foot, movin' in single file and pickin' their way careful, can manage it. That's our back door."

Luke glanced over toward the big canopy where most of the others were still gathered. "Brings us back to what you've got in the way of a force that can ride out to confront Dixon's thugs. I know you've done some supply gathering and harassing, but have any of the others gone with you?"

"No, not so far," Eagle admitted. "Up until only a short time ago, we were gettin' things put together here so's everybody had acceptable livin' accommodations and there was a reasonable order to things. But I got a couple men—Whit Barlow, mainly, and Turley and Baker, that pair of old prospectors—who are itchin' to get out and do some strikin' back. Pretty soon, whether I got any kind of plan ready or not, I may not be able to hold 'em back."

Luke considered for a minute and then, his mouth curving into a lopsided grin, he said, "Well, then I reckon we'd better get to work and come up with a plan."

Eagle eyed him under an arched brow. "You mean that? You dealin' yourself in deep enough to ride out with us?"

"I told you. I mean to find out what Dixon's game is where I'm concerned, and then turn it back on him and shove it down his throat." Luke's grin turned cold, his teeth becoming bared like a feral animal's. "I might as well have some company while I'm doing that and at the same time help you find a way to take his plans and come up with a place to shove them, too!"

"Oh, I've got some ideas for that. Believe me I do," Eagle assured him. "In fact—"

He was interrupted by the hurried approach of his wife, coming from the direction of the big canopy. "Tom?" she said anxiously. "Have you seen Dewey Akron? Is he out here with you?"

Eagle scowled. "No. No, I haven't seen him since we were eating. What's happened?"

"I don't now for sure." Jane's pretty face looked worried. "Nobody can find him. I fear he's wandered off again!"

Chapter 17

"Aw, blast it. This happens every once in a while, whenever the ugliness in his head starts stirrin' up," Eagle told Luke as they hurried back toward the canopy with Jane. "Dewey goes to wanderin', thinkin' he's lost on a battlefield full of dead men, steppin' over the bodies tryin' to find his way back to his command."

Luke felt a pang of sympathy for the tormented old soldier, but didn't know what to say. They reached the others, who were milling around, talking among themselves, and looking as anxious as Jane Eagle.

As Eagle reached them, Isaac Turley, one of the prospectors who'd been driven off his claim, said, "I checked his hut, Tom, but he's not in there."

Pettigrew, the former blacksmith, balancing himself on a sheepskin-padded crutch, reported, "I looked all through the mine shaft, no sign of him there, either."

"All right," said Eagle, "who can remember the last anybody saw of him? I know he was here at the start of the meal because I introduced Jensen to him. What about after that?"

There was a moment of silence while everybody traded looks, then a trim, attractive woman who'd been introduced earlier to Luke as Dinah Mercer, at one time the proprietress of a café in Hard Rock, said, "I fixed his plate for him when we were ready to eat. He took it and went over and sat on that stool beside the mine opening, like he often does when he's in one of his moods. When I looked around a little later, to see if he wanted anything more to eat, he was gone. But I don't know when he got up and moved."

"So he was in one of his moods, then?" Eagle asked.

Again the quiet exchange of looks before Turley spoke again. "Yeah, I noticed he was startin' to get a little fidgety late in the afternoon. From bein' cooped up on account of the weather, I guess. He mumbled something about the constant drummin' of the rain soundin' like the tromp of Rebel infantry. I gave him a snort of my home brew, thinkin' it might calm him down some. He went to his hut for a while after that and I didn't see no more of him until it was grub time. I didn't get a chance to notice how he was actin' then."

Eagle sighed. "Well, the only thing for it is to break up into some search parties and go find him. Turley, you and Baker go look through the other dwellings to see if he got confused and ducked into one of them instead of his own by mistake. Anybody who doesn't want their place searched by someone else, go do it yourself. Barlow, how about you and Heath try the landslide? See if he wandered into the boulder maze again. Me and Jensen will go on down the canyon to the west, although I don't know how he could have gone far in that direction without somebody noticing.

Grab some lanterns and at least be thankful we don't have to contend with the rain for this."

"Perhaps, if she would be so kind, Mrs. Wray could get her violin and play something," suggested Dinah Mercer. "We all know how much Dewey enjoys that. If he hasn't wandered too far, maybe he'll hear it and be attracted back on his own."

"Good idea," agreed Eagle. "I'm sure Mrs. Wray wouldn't mind."

"Of course not," replied Edna Wray, a tiny, white-haired lady standing nearby. "Anything to help soothe that poor suffering man and keep him from harm."

"I'll go fetch your instrument, my dear," announced her husband Jonathan as he turned and marched in the direction of their tent.

Eagle picked up an oil lantern and turned to Luke. "Hope you don't mind that I volunteered you to accompany me. It shouldn't take long to find the poor devil—most likely he's in the boulder maze. Once we get him accounted for then you and me can settle down a bit, too. Get out of these wet clothes and set you up with a place to bunk down for the night."

"Sounds good," Luke said. "I've spread my bedroll everywhere from deserts to mountains and I've slept in the beds of the finest hotels. When it's time to catch some shut-eye, I can manage just about anywhere."

As they moved farther away from the camp, the sky overhead continued to clear. Wind high up in the clouds was breaking them up into small clumps and shoving them rapidly apart from one another, making room for larger slices of star-sprinkled sky. As the vision of the two men adjusted to the silver-blue wash of starlight, the glow of the lantern Eagle carried became less necessary. Behind them, the lilting strains of a violin began floating on the night air.

"The woman who suggested the violin music, the one you said used to run a café in town," Luke said. "She seemed like a pretty level-headed sort."

"She is," Eagle agreed. "Dinah Mercer was a real fine addition to the town, and equally so to our group here. And in case you didn't notice, mighty easy on the eyes."

"I noticed."

Eagle grinned. "Uh-huh. I noticed you noticin'. Hard to believe any fool of a man would run out on a gal like that, ain't it?"

"That what happened to her?"

"That's the story that eventually made its way around town after she showed up." Eagle shrugged. "But since I try to steer clear of gossip, I guess all I can say for sure is that she's unattached and don't seem interested in lookin' to change it."

They continued on, spread several yards apart so they could scan each side of the canyon as they moved along. Although Luke didn't have a lantern, the starlight provided enough illumination by now that he couldn't have missed anything as big as a man.

All at once Eagle stopped moving.

"What's the matter? You see something?" Luke asked.

"No. I don't see anything . . . but neither do I hear anything. Nothing but Mrs. Wray's violin," said Eagle.

Luke understood then. As soon as the rain had stopped, the night sounds of nature had started to fill the canyon. Birds chirping, the thrum of insects.

They'd been absent during the rain but then had returned and became a quiet constant in the background . . . until now. Now they were absent again.

Luke glanced over his shoulder, back at the camp. He and Eagle had come nearly a quarter mile, farther than he'd realized.

"There's something out here with us. Some critter . . . and I don't mean just Dewey," Eagle said, his voice more hushed than before.

"You got bear or cougar up in these mountains?" Luke wanted to know.

"Not much in the way of bear. But we've got cougar for sure. And one in particular who's earned hisself the name Ol' Rip. He's been visitin' the valley every summer for the past three or four years. Big son, seems to get bigger each season. I know he's back again this year on account of I ran across his tracks one day last week. And judgin' by the spread of the paw and how deep it was sunk in the ground, he ain't shrunk any. Maybe two hundred pounds by now."

"You figure he's stalking the camp?"

"No, not that I saw any sign of. Too much activity around there, too many fires burnin' too much of the time. Anyway, Ol' Rip's got easier pickin's down in the valley with all the livestock that got run off and left behind, left roamin' free. If that's him ahead of us, I'd guess he was caved up somewhere higher durin' the rain and is on the prowl now to get down and find himself some of that stock to feed on. Only thing to divert him would be if he caught wind of something closer before then. Something like Dewey, if he wandered this far."

"I didn't bring my rifle with me," Luke said.

"Neither did I," replied Eagle. "I didn't even think to strap my gunbelt back on after I shucked it when I sat down to supper."

"I've got my Remingtons," Luke told him. *Always*, he added mentally.

Eagle edged over, narrowing the distance between them. "Ain't nobody hailed from back at the camp that they found Dewey yet, meanin' the blame fool might actually have come this direction after all. So I need to keep lookin'. How about you loan me one of your pistols and you go back and get a rifle?"

"I'll loan you one of my pistols," Luke said, lifting his left-hand Remington from its holster and holding it out. "But we'll both stay here and keep looking."

Eagle took the gun, saying, "You're as blamed stubborn as me."

"No need to be insulting."

They continued forward again, closer together now. All of a sudden, Luke found himself wishing that the starlight he'd thought so plentiful a little while ago was a whole lot brighter.

Eagle raised his voice and called ahead, "Dewey! Dewey Akron! This is Sheriff Tom Eagle. Are you out here somewhere?"

From a pool of thick shadows off high to the right came the deep, half-growl, half-hiss of a big hunting cat.

Eagle swore. "That's Ol' Rip! He's warnin' us off. He wouldn't do that unless he's got his prey all staked out and ready to pounce."

From the edge of the same shadow pool came a weak, slightly quavering voice. "Sheriff Eagle! There's a Reb patrol just over that rise. Keep it down or you'll have 'em right on top of—"

The agonized shriek that cut off the rest of Dewey's words was simultaneously mixed with the snarl and rumbling roar of the cougar, followed by the sounds of bodies tumbling to the ground and then thrashing wildly about.

"Dewey!" Eagle shouted as he broke into a run.

Luke was racing right beside him.

Both men veered toward the pool of deep shadows out of which the sounds of the struggle were issuing. As they drew closer, murky forms became discernible— the huge cougar, eyes blazing like white-hot coals, on top of the flailing man, mauling him, trying to drag him away.

"Throw the lantern!" Luke shouted. "Aim it as close as you can to give us some light!"

Eagle didn't hesitate to do as instructed. The lantern arced end over end through the air and hit the ground mere inches behind the digging hind paws of the big cat. Glass shattered and a blossom of instantly ignited coal oil flared out, spreading onto the stubbled grass that grew across this end of the canyon floor. Ol' Rip roared and mauled more frantically than ever, refusing to let go of that which he had claimed for his own. Whether from the fire licking around his legs or from the attacking cougar—or both—Dewey was shrieking in concert.

With his arm extended, the borrowed Remington gripped steady in his fist, Eagle said, "I still can't get a clear shot—not without the risk of hittin' Dewey!"

Luke was locked in a similar pose and frozen by the

same dilemma. But he didn't stay frozen for very long. Shifting the Remington from his right hand to his left, he hurled himself forward. At the same time, he reached back with his temporarily emptied hand and filled it anew, wrapping it around the bone handle of the ten-inch Bowie knife that rode in a sheath just behind the holster on that side. He jerked the Bowie free and swung it ahead of himself as he ran.

Reaching the struggling forms on the edge of the burning grass, Luke launched himself over the flames in a flying tackle, twisting his upper body so that his left shoulder slammed into the ribs of the attacking cougar. The impact drove Ol' Rip off the screaming, flailing Dewey and sent him rolling and twisting away. Luke's momentum carried him with the cat, his face pressed hard against its fetid fur, his knife slashing wildly, blindly, as he himself kicked and twisted to try and keep clear of the slashing talons of the hind legs.

This new entanglement of man and beast tumbled to the ground, unavoidably wrapped together. The cougar was shrieking in continuous rage, fangs bared and claws blurred in constant motion, seeking desperately to sink into flesh and muscle, to maim and rip in keeping with the name bestowed upon it. Luke, trying to kick free from these savage threats, kept stabbing and slicing with the Bowie. He also continued to grip the Remington in his left fist but writhing and struggling at such close quarters wasn't allowing him any chance to get the muzzle turned in order to squeeze off a shot.

But then, suddenly, he didn't need to. His Remington spoke. Once, twice, in rapid succession. Only it wasn't the Remington in his hand, he realized—it was the one he'd loaned to Eagle. And with each wonderful-sounding roar, the body of the cougar slamming and grinding against him spasmed and jerked away, diverted from the intensity of the struggle they were locked in. When a third shot split the night, Luke could feel a great shudder pass the full length of Ol' Rip. Then the big cat's body went completely limp and all Luke could think about was kicking and shoving frantically to get out from under its smothering weight and to get clear of the hot blood running down over him . . .

Chapter 18

"He finally lifted his head in a way that gave me the opening to take a shot," Tom Eagle was explaining for the third or fourth time, still flushed with excitement. "But it was Luke who did the hard work—him and his knife. He had Ol' Rip wore down and sluggish to the point of providin' me that opening."

Luke rolled his eyes. "If that critter was worn down and sluggish, it sure as blazes wasn't noticeable to me," he said. "But if you insist on giving me part of the credit, I'm too tired to argue."

They were once again under the encampment's big canopy. Sounds of the commotion that ensued from the unexpected encounter with Ol' Rip had brought several of the others racing down the canyon, brandishing rifles and lanterns. The big cat had been dispatched by the time they got there, but their assistance with the injuries to Luke and Dewey was most welcome.

Luke, though battered and scraped from head to toe, was able to stand and walk on his own. Dewey, however, had been torn up considerably worse. For him, Betty Barlow had gone running back to fetch a blanket that they loaded the mauled man on and used like a stretcher to get him returned to the camp.

Dewey was now sprawled on the split log table with Jonathan and Edna Wray giving care to his numerous gashes and bites. The Wrays made an efficient team. Once the worst of the bleeding wounds were sufficiently stanched and cleaned, Jonathan's leather-stitching skills got put to use closing the lacerations and then Edna applied healing salve and dressings. Copious amounts of whiskey poured down the patient's gullet dulled his pain as much as possible, but it also increased his state of delusion. He kept rambling about Rebs boiling over the rise, and to him, the shrieks made by Ol' Rip during his attack had been the infamous Rebel yell that chilled and left haunting memories ingrained in many a Yankee veteran of the late war.

While Mr. and Mrs. Wray were taking care of Dewey, Luke was being tended to by Dinah Mercer. He was seated a ways down the table from where the other treatment was taking place, stripped to the waist, while the attractive former café owner cleaned his wounds, having already announced that none appeared in need of stitches.

A handful of others were clustered around, holding lanterns high to provide illumination for the work being done, looking on anxiously and listening to hear more about what had happened. Tom Eagle was prominent in their midst, proving more than willing to fill in the details.

"Wading into Ol' Rip with nothing but a knife— that ranks right up there with one of the nerviest displays I ever heard tell of," stated Whit Barlow, one of those gathered close. He paused, then cocked one eyebrow slyly before adding, "Comes to a display of good sense, though, Jensen . . . on that front, I can't say as I'd rate it quite so high."

Everybody had a good chuckle over that, including Luke. "Friend, I couldn't agree with you more," he told Barlow.

Their laughter was cut short by an elongated groan of pain—partly physical, partly mental—issued by Dewey Akron. Glancing in his direction, Tom Eagle said, "Well, I'll tell you one person who for certain don't care what anybody calls what Luke did. Nervy or lacking good sense, either way, you can bet that Dewey is plenty grateful for it."

"Maybe so," Luke allowed. "But don't shortchange yourself in the process, Sheriff. After all, it was your pistol shots that had the final say on Ol' Rip and saved Dewey and me both from getting torn apart worse than we did."

"Expressing your gratitude is a commendable thing," remarked Dinah Mercer as she leaned close to tighten one of Luke's bandages into place. "So long as you remember that the sheriff didn't keep you entirely from damage. You need to keep a close eye on these wounds to make sure no infection starts to set in."

"Aw, Luke's too tough to worry about a piddly little thing like that," Eagle scoffed. "More like if Ol' Rip had managed to slip away and run off back up into the hills, then maybe *he* would've been the one needin' to worry about infection from chompin' into Luke."

This got another smattering of laughter, but Dinah's

expression remained quite serious as her eyes gazed directly into Luke's, their faces only a few inches apart.

"The possibility of infection is no joking matter," she said. "That applies not only to what the cougar did to you but also to those other cuts on your face from some kind of earlier encounter."

Luke involuntarily touched the area she was referring to, the pitting to his cheek that was the result of tombstone and bullet shrapnel striking him when he'd made his escape dash through the church cemetery. "These?" he said, frowning. "I got the bleeding stopped on these several hours ago."

"I can see that. I can also see that the bleeding may have stopped but some of the fragments that caused it are still embedded in the flesh. It appears some are bits of stone. But others, unless I'm mistaken, are bits of lead from a bullet slug. Did you realize that?"

"I'm aware of how it happened," Luke answered. "And yeah, a fragmented bullet could be part of it."

Dinah's gaze remained steady. "Then I expect you're also aware of the dangers of lead poisoning?"

"Hey, come on, Dinah," said Eagle, taking a more serious interest in the exchange. "You're gettin' a little carried away, ain't you? This fella just survived a tussle with a mountain lion, for cryin' out loud. You think a few scratches on his cheek pose some kind of serious worry for him?"

Jane Eagle, moving up beside her husband, said, "Dinah knows what she's doing, and what she's saying only makes sense. If there's even the slightest risk of infection from those cuts, why not treat it?"

"I've got some tweezers in my tent that I could

fetch for digging out that lead," said Dinah. "Getting it out of there and then treating the wound with some salve would be the safest way."

Luke winced. "Digging chunks of lead out of my face might be a safe idea to you, but you'll excuse me if I say it doesn't sound particularly pleasant to me."

Dinah arched the smooth line of one eyebrow. "A valiant cougar wrestler like you concerned about me doing a little probing with a pair of tweezers? Come now, Mr. Jensen, think of your reputation."

"I tried speakin' up for you, pal. But," said Eagle, casting a wary glance over at his wife, "but I think we're both losin' ground here. Probably be best for you to go ahead and get that took care of. You've still got to skin out of those wet duds, too, and I need to arrange some kind of sleepin' quarters for you. I can see to that while Dinah finishes fixin' you up."

Luke let out a resigned sigh. He said to Dinah, "All right. Looks like you win. Go fetch your digging tools and let's get it over with. It's not like I've got to worry about you spoiling my good looks."

Dinah smiled. "I'll do my best not to scar you up too hideously. But for the best results, how about you come with me to my tent? The lighting will be better there and I've got everything I'll need in addition to the tweezers." She glanced up at Eagle. "Maybe the sheriff could have someone bring you a clean, dry shirt after he lays out the rest of your gear?"

"Sure. I'll do that," Eagle agreed.

To Luke, Dinah said, "You can also bring along this other shirt we took off you. I'll have a look at it for possible mending, but from what I saw, I'm afraid it may be too badly ripped to save."

"I appreciate all of this attention, ma'am, but you really don't have to go to so much trouble," Luke told her.

"And you didn't have to go to the trouble you did to help save Dewey, which was far more extreme than anything I'm offering. Yet you did," Dinah replied. "People helping each other in times of need is what gives us hope to continue on. It's really that simple, and ought not be considered anything particularly special."

Luke regarded her. She was indeed an attractive woman. Middle thirties, average height, trimly built with high, firm breasts pushing against the front of the crisp white blouse she wore. A face more bold and handsome rather than delicately beautiful; full lips and deep, rich brown eyes all surrounded by a swirl of wheat blond hair.

"That's a real nice sentiment," he said to her. "You'll have to pardon me for not having had much exposure to that sort of outlook. The kind of owlhoots I spend too much time around see other folks, especially in times of need, as being that much weaker and more vulnerable for the plucking."

"So is that why you do what you do? Hunt down owlhoots, as you call them, in order to stop them from preying on others?"

Luke didn't respond right away. Then: "I'd be less than truthful if I denied that the money I collect for bringing in fugitives is mostly why I do what I do. But

I'd like to believe that in the process, I'm also doing some good in a broader sense."

"Of course you are," Dinah insisted. "The removal of dangerous men and the threat they pose to good, honest people—no matter your motives—can only be viewed as something worthwhile."

A corner of Luke's mouth lifted in a wry smile. "You wouldn't have to travel very far to get an argument on that, ma'am. A lot of folks see bounty hunters like me as little more than hired guns operating on a thin edge of the law and being not too far removed from those they track down."

Dinah gave a dismissive sniff. "I've heard such talk. Not about you, but bounty hunters in general. I have a stubborn habit, however, of not letting the viewpoints of others make up my mind for me. You see, I *have* traveled far enough to know that people—even decent, well-meaning ones—can sometimes be petty and narrow-minded."

Another loud groan from Dewey caused everyone's attention to once more swing in that direction. After the tormented man settled back down again, it suddenly dawned on both Luke and Dinah that their conversation had become focused largely to the exclusion of the others around them. This brought a faint flush to Dinah's cheeks as she squared her shoulders and said, "If we're going to attend to getting that lead dug out, we'd best get to it then. I should try to be back here when Mr. and Mrs. Wray are done stitching and patching Dewey. Sometimes, when he's having one of his episodes, I'm able to help soothe him."

"Yeah," said Luke. "I can see how you'd have a soothing effect on a man."

She averted her eyes in response and her flush deepened.

"You two go ahead," Eagle urged them, unable to hold back a faintly amused expression. "I'll get that dry shirt sent along directly."

Chapter 19

"All I wanna know is what am I supposed to be running around here—a mining operation, or a recruitment center for hired guns?"

Mace Vernon was unhappy and wasn't holding back on expressing his feelings. A tall, ruggedly built man of forty, he stood with his feet planted wide and his square slab of a chin jutted out defiantly below a scowling ledge of furry brows and intense blue eyes. In his meaty hands he held a short-billed cloth cap that he'd jerked off his headful of sandy hair when he entered Roland Dixon's office. As he spoke, he was twisting and wringing the cap like he wished it was somebody's neck.

Behind his desk, Roland regarded his mining foreman with a flat, tolerant gaze. When he'd sent for the man first thing this morning he had fully expected this kind of reaction and part of him even felt a touch of empathy. But he couldn't help it, he had to do what he felt rated the highest priority.

"I guess I need to remind you, Mace," he said calmly, "that your main purpose here—like everyone else present, including me—is as an employee of

Dixon Enterprises. Yes, your primary duty has been overseeing the mining operation of the Gold Button and you've done a commendable job, even under the pressure of maintaining a decent yield out of a strike that hasn't proven as rich as originally hoped for."

"I know my job, sir," Vernon said stiffly. "And I've never complained about the pressure of keeping up an acceptable yield, even under tough circumstances. But because I know my job is why I'm protesting that yanking a half dozen men off my crew is gonna make it nearly impossible to keep up quota. I'm already working most of 'em twelve, sometimes fourteen hours a day. I don't see how I can make up the difference for the loss of even a couple, let alone six."

"Whip some of those lazy Chinee a little harder, that's all you gotta do," spoke up Hack Ferris from where he sat slouched in a chair over against the wall.

Vernon shot him a scathing look. "I don't need no lip out of you, telling me how to run my crew. You want to worry about something, worry about that pack of so-called hardcases you're supposed to be in charge of. Seems to me if they spent less time in the whore cribs and practiced with their six-shooters as hard as they do tipping up liquor bottles, maybe they could do a better job of hitting what they aim at and not get shot up so bad themselves!"

Ferris started to shove up out of his chair and Vernon turned quickly, bracing to meet him.

"Stop it!" Roland shouted, freezing both men. He stood up behind his desk, hands balled into fists that he slammed down hard on the polished surface. "Don't I have enough aggravation without my two top men butting heads with each other? Don't we all have too much invested in this valley?" Roland paused, but his expression stayed dark. "It was my father's idea to bring in this Jensen character. Send him here and then have him apprehended, but make sure he was kept alive—those were his instructions. The same ones I passed on to Hack."

Roland looked at Vernon and went on, "I didn't bother to tell you about any of that. There was no need for you to know or concern yourself. You still had your hands full with your mining responsibilities and there was every reason to expect that the apprehension of one lone stranger wouldn't pose much of a problem."

Vernon frowned. "You say your father *sent* Jensen here—and then gave orders to capture him as soon as he showed up?"

"Don't try to make sense of it," Roland said peevishly. "Some kind of ancient score the old man is looking to settle in some overly elaborate way. I'm not privy to all the details myself. I wish I didn't know any of it, that none of us here had been brought into it at all. Unfortunately, that's not the case."

"So what happened?" Vernon asked. "What went wrong?"

"The stranger was a gun-twirlin' bearcat we had no warnin' to expect, that's what happened," Ferris said bitterly. "Add to that our orders to take him alive—havin' to pull our punches, in other words, when it came to shootin' back—and the slippery varmint got away from us. But before he did, he put the hurt on five of my men, two of 'em permanent-like." The gun boss jabbed a thumb toward the lumpy bandage covering the back of his head, adding, "And he nearly cooked my goose, too."

Vernon's mouth pulled into a tight line. He hesitated a moment, then said, "You got my regrets on the injuries and for losing some of your men. What I said before . . ."

"That's better," Roland was quick to interject. "You two don't have to like each other, but I need you to get along or at least not fight against one another. You understand? If we make it through this current rough patch, we have every right to find ourselves on the brink of a very sweet opportunity. Once all the modern equipment starts rolling in and those new shafts hit that sweet mother lode we're assured is there waiting, then everything in this formerly remote corner of nowhere is going to change and change big. If my father's plan for making over the valley and the town the way he envisions it starts to pan out— and I wouldn't bet against the old pirate—we'll be right there on the ground floor of it all. Shoot, I'm counting on being mayor of the new town. I'll put you two fellas on my city council and set you up in prime businesses, whatever line you want."

Ferris's eyebrows lifted. "I want a saloon! With dancin' girls . . . Man, wouldn't that be the life?"

Vernon remained silent, not being so quick to get caught up in the fantasies Roland was painting.

Returning to the realities of the present, a somber-faced Roland said, "But first we've got to finish clearing away these problems standing in our way. That annoying flea Tom Eagle still has to be swatted, but first and foremost is catching that Jensen scoundrel before he causes more trouble. In order to do that as quickly as possible, we need to throw a wide enough net. That's why we need more men. Some of your miners, Vernon."

Showing signs of relenting somewhat, Vernon nevertheless saw fit to remind everybody, "That's the thing, though. My men are miners, not hard-riding manhunters."

"You've got plenty of hombres on your crew who know how to ride," Ferris said. "What's more, I'm willin' to bet some of 'em have wrapped their mitts around a six-gun somewhere along the way before they ever took up a pick handle."

"Surely you can select some adequate men," Roland appealed to Vernon. "It's only for a limited time. Hopefully just a day or so. Maybe it can be wrapped up as quickly as today. Our best chance for that is to act fast and make a wide sweep."

"We figure Jensen was kept holed up somewhere last night by the rain," Ferris explained. "Since he don't know the area and has no reason to stick around after the way we slammed the door on him, we're guessin' he'll head back for Helena the same way he came in. That means goin' through Balfour Gap off to the south. At first light, I sent most of my boys to ride out hard, aimin' to get ahead of him and be ready to cut him off if he makes it that far. As soon as you can supply me some more men, I mean for them to join me and Dog DeMarist, my tracker. We'll get on Jensen's trail and either run him down or run him up against those boys I got waitin' for him. Either way, we'll clamp down on him and I don't intend for him to squirt away from me again!"

Vernon's hands quit twisting his cap and he heaved

a ragged sigh. "All right, I guess that's how it has to be," he said without enthusiasm. "Give me a few minutes to go round up some men."

"Just don't send me none of them lazy Chinee," Ferris told him.

Vernon shot him another menacing look and Roland was quick to say, "You can trust Mace to pick men best suited for the job."

Vernon continued to glare at Ferris for a long count. Before going out the door, he said, "You see to it the men I give you come back in one piece. They don't, I'm holding you personally responsible."

Chapter 20

"That ungrateful pup! I never figured he had enough sand to pull a stunt like this." As he made this declaration, Ben Pettigrew raked his eyes over all those gathered about him, almost like he was challenging anyone to take issue with his words.

When a response came, it was from his wife Lucille, standing right beside him. The two made quite a visual contrast, him so broad and hulking, even balanced on the crutch that helped support him, her just a tiny slip of a woman but with a spark in her eye and a boldness to her posture and a lift in her chin when she spoke.

"What did you expect?" she demanded of her husband in a biting tone. "Maybe if you hadn't treated Heath so harshly and told him practically every day that he *didn't* measure up to your idea of having enough sand, you wouldn't have driven him away."

Pettigrew's mouth dropped. "You're blaming this on me?"

"I'm blaming it on all of us. All of us," Lucille said, cutting her gaze to Tom and Jane Eagle, "who played a part in treating Heath and Belinda like children and not even showing them enough respect to hear them out and allow them to make their case for wanting to be together."

"We understood well enough their feelings for one another, Lucille," Jane Eagle replied earnestly. "My goodness, none of us are so cold or ancient we don't remember feeling that way ourselves."

"Why then? Why were we so determined to discourage them, to keep them apart?" Lucille wanted to know.

Jane said, "I don't agree that we brushed them off like children. But the fact is, my Belinda, even now, is only sixteen."

"And how old were you, Jane, when you and Tom married?"

Jane faltered at giving a reply.

"I already know the answer. Seventeen. Same as me. And I'll bet most of the other married or formerly married women here weren't a whole lot older." Lucille looked around. "Am I wrong?"

The encampment had woken that morning to the realization that two of its members—Heath Pettigrew and Belinda Eagle—had run off together during the night. Heath had left nothing in the way of an explanation.

Belinda, on the other hand, had left a rather lengthy note pinned to her pillow and addressed to her mother. The crumpled slip of paper was even now clutched in Jane's hand.

Dearest Mother—Please do not worry or be vexed with me. Heath and I have gone off to be together. He will take good care of me. We are deeply in love and have reached the conclusion that this is the only

*way for us to have a life with each other. In town,
before the trouble, it was bad enough but there still
seemed hope. The way things are now, there may be
none. This is not our fight and getting caught in it
may ruin any chance for us if we don't take this
action. Please try to understand.*

> *All my love to Father, Davy, and you*
> —*Belinda*

It hadn't taken long for the news of this surprising
development to spread, and as each member of the
refugee party heard, they came to the main canopy,
gathering to discuss and offer whatever they could
in the way of help. Not everyone present had been
aware of the burgeoning romance between the two
young people back in Hard Rock—"before the trouble," as Belinda put it in her note—nor the way their
parents had quashed it (or believed they had) back
then. That bit of history was being revealed to all,
along with the rest of what had now transpired.

A grim-faced, obviously shaken Tom Eagle joined
in the exchange between his wife and Lucille Pettigrew. This meant, out of necessity though he would
have preferred to have kept it more private, also addressing everyone else who was gathered around.

"Sometimes age—or maturity might be a better
word—ain't measured in just years. The fact of the
matter is that Belinda, now at sixteen or even in another year or two at seventeen or eighteen, may still
not be as mature as Jane was at that age. Probably the
same for you, too, Lucille. I guess you could say we
maybe sheltered her too much. Whatever the reason,
that's the way we saw it, her mother and me, when this

whole thing started between her and Heath and why we discouraged it. It was never anything against your boy Heath. You and Ben had your own reasons for holdin' him back."

"He wasn't ready, neither," Pettigrew stated. "If he'd have come to me like a man, face to face, and told me he wanted to strike out on his own, I would have had a chance to work with him a little bit, try to prepare him. But he never gave me a clue. The first I knew he had any notions along those lines—before this latest shenanigan—he was already wanting to haul off and get hitched. He was no more ready for that than I was for . . . for . . ."

Eagle's eyes narrowed. "For what, Ben? What weren't you ready for?"

Pettigrew stammered some more before finally managing a response. "For seeing my son make a fool of himself. For seeing him break his ma's heart and . . . and everything else that a foolhardy thing like this could lead to."

"Like you someday havin' grandchildren with Indian blood in 'em? Tell the truth. Ain't that been your biggest objection to Heath and Belinda all along?" Eagle demanded.

"You got no call to say that, Tom," Pettigrew protested. "I was always square with you, always showed you the respect you earned and deserved as sheriff."

"Yeah, you put on a real good act whenever I was around," Eagle said. "But what about some of the things you said behind my back about me and Indians in general? I didn't even have to hear about 'em to know. I've been around people like you all my life and I already knew. I could *smell* it on you right from the first, the way you really felt about me bein' a half-breed. You think you were the only one who thought about potential grandkids? You think I wanted any grandchild of *mine* growin' up around your kind of hate?"

"Stop it, the both of you!" Lucille said sharply. "This isn't the time to let yourselves be distracted by that kind of bitterness."

"Lucille's right," Jane was quick to add. "If you two had all that resentment bottled up in you, you should have found a way to work it out long before this. Now is not the time."

Luke chose that moment to speak up from where he'd been standing quietly on the periphery of the gathering. "I know I'm a newcomer to all this, an out-sider," he said in a level tone as he stepped forward. "And I don't know anything about the history between the two youngsters or the hard feelings that obviously have been brewing between their fathers. But what the mothers are saying is exactly right—none of that matters right now. The thing that does is the fact that Heath and Belinda may have placed themselves in danger and we should be concentrating on what to do about it."

The faces of Jane and Lucille immediately pinched with anxiety.

"Now wait a minute, Jensen," said Whit Barlow. "I know they're not my kids so it's easier for me to be a little calmer. But aren't you laying it on a little strong with this danger talk? The parents are upset enough, no need to make it worse. What's the big danger? It's summer, the weather is agreeable, they took a decent amount of provisions with 'em. And they *are* nearly full grown. I suggest the best thing is to let 'em get this running-off notion out of their heads and they'll come to their senses quick enough. The rest of today, probably tonight, maybe a stretch of the next day . . . by tomorrow evening I'm betting they'll be showing up right back here on their own."

Before anyone else could say anything, it was Barlow's tomboyish daughter Betty who responded, saying in a strong, clear voice, "You're wrong, Pa."

Chapter 21

Having caused all eyes to swing in her direction, Betty Barlow stood her ground and spoke the rest of what she had to say, directing her own gaze to the two sets of affected parents.

"And so are the rest of you—wrong in the way you're thinking. You're still seeing Belinda and Heath as just a couple of kids. Children caught up in a romantic fantasy. You haven't learned anything because you haven't taken time to really listen to them, to what they want, to believe how truly in love they are. Belinda kept telling me how trapped they felt, how they didn't see any—"

Jane interrupted the girl. "Belinda talked to you about this? She told you they were going to run away together?"

"She told me they were thinking about it, how they didn't see no other way. But I never had no idea they'd made up their minds for sure, or that it was going to be last night."

"Did she say where they planned to go?"

Betty shook her head. "No. She never talked about that."

Tom Eagle turned to his son. "How about you, Davy? Did your sister say anything to you about any of this?"

The boy shook his head earnestly. "Uh-uh. I knew she was still moonin' over Heath, but that's all. I never had no idea they were planning to run off. Honest, Pa."

Lucille Pettigrew stepped closer to Luke and gazed up at him with a deeply concerned expression. "What did you mean before when you said we should worry about them being in danger?"

Luke looked down at her for a second before lifting his eyes and once more sweeping his gaze across the others. "I'd think it should be obvious to all of you. Who's prowling that whole valley out there and doing so now with an extra dose of anger because of the toll I took on them yesterday?"

"Hack Ferris and his boys—Dixon's thugs," Eagle said.

Luke nodded. "They'll be mainly on the lookout for me, but that certainly won't stop them from pouncing if they should happen to catch sight of those youngsters. Wouldn't you say?"

Eagle grimaced. "Yeah. They'd pounce for sure."

Several of the women onlookers gave sharp intakes of breaths.

"You must go after our children then, immediately," implored Jane. "We can't risk Heath and our daughter falling into the hands of those devils!"

"I spoke wrong before. What you're saying is on the mark, Jensen, and I'm a fool for not thinking of it sooner," declared a scowling Whit Barlow. Turning to Eagle, he added, "I'd be proud to ride with you, Tom. Say the word and I can be saddled up in two shakes."

"Same for me," said Howard MacGregor, the stocky, dour-faced farmer who'd had his crops burned and was run off his land. "I'll have to borrow a horse but I'd sure welcome the chance to ride out against those burnin', thievin' scoundrels!"

Suddenly, everybody seemed to be yammering excitedly all at once. Urging, offering advice, volunteering, asking questions . . . until Tom Eagle was forced to raise his arms and issue a shrill whistle to quiet things down.

"Everybody take it easy! Give me a chance to think. I know you all mean well and you all want to help in your own way. But we need to calm down and take a minute to put together some kind of plan before we go chargin' out like nothing more than an unruly mob!"

"You want my advice," said Luke, standing beside him, "I'd keep it to a small, fast-moving force. Not more than three or four men."

Eagle arched a brow. "You think that's enough?"

"The more men we ride out with, the more apt we'd be to get spotted ourselves," Luke pointed out. "And the last thing we want on this particular outing is to end up trading lead with Ferris or any of his coyotes. Even if we took every available man, we couldn't match them gun for gun. What's more, if we got caught up in a shoot-out, that would keep us from looking for the kids, meaning they'd still be at risk for falling into bad hands."

"I see what you mean," Eagle grated. "A small handful of us riding fast and alert would have the best chance of catching up with the kids and then keeping all of us away from Ferris's bunch until we can make it back here."

"Jensen keeps on making good sense," said Barlow. He added, "That is, as long as I'm still included in riding out with you."

"And me. I mean to go along, too."

Thrusting the tip of his crutch hard into the ground, Ben Pettigrew pushed his single leg into a long step forward. Then, replanting the crutch, he squared his broad shoulders and stood steadfast against the uncertain looks brought about by his declaration.

"I know," he said, addressing Eagle directly. "I'm a one-legged gimp who can't mount a horse without the help of a tree stump or fence rail or some such. But once in the saddle, I can stay there. And if it comes to it, I'm as good or better a shot than anybody here except you or Jensen. No getting around the fact you and I have our differences, Tom, and neither did me and Heath see eye to eye on a lot of things . . . but he's my son. You can't ask me not to go along to help bring him back."

Eagle stood unblinking under Pettigrew's gaze for a long moment. Then, the rigidness in his posture visibly easing, he said in a quiet voice, "No, I guess I can't."

Pettigrew's wife placed a hand on one of her husband's thick forearms. "Are you sure, Ben?"

His brows pinching together, the blacksmith replied,

"Don't you think it's about time I started doing better by the boy? Yeah, Lucille, I'm sure I need to do this."

Eagle cut his eyes to MacGregor. "Don't ever think I ain't grateful for your offer to ride with us, Howard. But as I guess you heard, it seems like a smart idea for us to keep our number trimmed down this time out. I hope you understand."

MacGregor pressed his lips together and gave a faint nod. "Whatever you think is best, Tom."

"For what it's worth, it eases my mind considerable to know you'll be keepin' an eye on things here. And once we get things settled with these doggone kids, I promise we'll soon be headin' back out on another sweep, this time directly against Dixon's gun wolves. Comes to that, I'll make sure you're a part of it."

MacGregor's tightly pressed lips curved up ever so slightly at the corners. "You can bet I'll be holding you to that."

"And you can double-down on bettin' me and Red will be wantin' in on some of that action, too!" barked Isaac Turley, one of the leathery old prospectors who happened to be standing nearby.

"We sure will be," Red Baker, his partner, added for emphasis.

Isaac was tall and pinch-faced, with a shock of snow white hair that was always spilling down over his forehead and an equally white walrus mustache that he kept surprisingly well trimmed in contrast to his slouch hat, run-down boots, and worn out, overly patched shirt and trousers. Red was half a head shorter and, though of equal age, still had a headful of the rust-colored hair that had earned him his nickname despite the never cleanly shaven whiskers bristling on his jawline being spiked with silver. His attire was just as worn and patched as his partner's, except he displayed a fondness for bright-colored patches that never came close to matching the garment they were sewn over.

"This is a real nice camp we've put together here," Isaac said. "Far more comfortable livin' than me and Red are used to, as a matter of fact. And that there is a problem, you see."

"It is?" said Eagle, immediately regretting he'd given Isaac a reason to talk some more.

"You bet. Comfortable livin' is the worst thing for old-timers like me and Red," Isaac said firmly. "Layin' around all comfortable-like is how a body's joints start stiffenin' up and their muscles turn flabby. And that's when old age moves in and grabs hold and refuses to let go. Then pretty quick you got nothing but a codger who ain't worth spit except for barely hobblin' around."

"That's a fact, that's how it happens," Red echoed agreeably.

Isaac picked up again, saying, "And that's exactly what *ain't* gonna happen to Red and me. We're men of action, used to hard livin' and hard work. If we ain't careful, the high livin' and good eats pourin' over us in this camp is gonna plumb rob us of our youth! We can't let that happen."

"No, we can't," said Red.

Pinning Eagle with an intense stare, Isaac said, "That's why we need the same promise out of you that you just gave MacGregor, Sheriff. You gotta say you'll be sure to take us along the next time you ride out on some kind of escapade."

"We'll stay behind this time and help MacGregor keep an eye on things around here," said Red. "But if'n you make us wait too much longer, we might all of a sudden stiffen up and be too blamed hobbled to do you any good if'n you *did* need us."

Barely managing to keep a straight face, Eagle made the two old-timers a promise. "You got it, fellas. The next time anybody rides out on any kind of 'escapade,' I'll be sure to see to it that you two are included. I don't want to have no part of robbin' you of your youth."

Red wagged a cautionary finger. "That's smart thinkin' on your part. You want us in tip-top form. You get that, you'll be mighty glad to have us to call on."

Chapter 22

"Off to the left of us—that's east, right?"

"Uh-huh."

"I don't think I've ever been out this way. All the land in that direction is so bare and, well, kinda ugly. Nothing but jagged, rocky hills and dry, twisted gullies. Barely any grass and only a few prickly-looking bushes. I wouldn't want to live there. It looks downright depressing."

"That's why they call it the badlands. And why nobody does live there."

"We're not going through it, are we?"

"Not if I can help it."

"But we're kinda in it now, the way we're going. Moving along the edge of it, I mean."

"That's the idea. Our way is south but I'm skirting the edge of the badlands because of all the rocky ground. It don't hardly pick up any tracks, see, in case anybody tries following us."

"You're so clever. You think of everything, don't you?"

Heath Pettigrew's chest swelled under the words of praise. Praise wasn't something he'd heard very much of in his eighteen years of life. He liked it. It sounded good, felt good . . . almost as good as Belinda Eagle's arms wrapped around him. And having the words come from her, the girl he loved, made it all the better.

"I hope I've thought of everything," he said in response. "I'm sure trying. I want to think of everything from here on out that will help us avoid problems and make our life together as good as it can be."

"Just *being* together will make our life good. Finally and forever!" Belinda exclaimed. At sixteen, she was an exceptionally pretty girl on the brink of womanhood. She was somewhat on the short side, not quite four inches over five feet, trim and well proportioned, though a bit bustier than most girls her age, or even her own mother for that matter. Her most distinguishing features were her large, liquid dark eyes and her long, silky black hair that reached all the way to the small of her back.

"I like hearing you say that, that just us being together would be enough to make you happy," Heath responded. "But I want to give you a lot more than that. I want you to be happy, but I also want you to have nice clothes and nice things about you. I know it will take a while, but one day I mean to shower you in fineries like nobody in Hard Rock ever imagined."

Two years older than Belinda, Heath stood just a whisker under six feet, taller than his father, but leaner in build. Still, he was square-shouldered and packed with sinewy muscle gained from helping out in the blacksmith shop. He had his father's curly brown hair and heavy brow, which added to the brooding expression he often wore, but the latter was reasonably offset by the pale, intelligent eyes he'd gotten from his mother.

They rode on for a ways without further conversation, doubled-up on a tall, heavy-chested bay that Heath held to a steady but moderate pace. With a strong horse under him and Belinda pressed against his back, Heath felt like he could ride forever just like this. The climbing sun in a cloudless sky beating against the side of his face from the east, a faint breeze brushing past his shoulder from the northwest, and nothing but open, rolling country ahead angling away from the badlands for as far as he could see.

"Do you think they will?" Belinda asked abruptly, her breath warm on the back of his neck.

Belinda had a sometimes maddening habit of suddenly blurting out a comment or question that was perfectly in tune with a thought passing through her mind but on a subject that might be minutes or hours or even days removed from any prior discussion of the matter. Over time, Heath had found himself being able to once in a while recognize the genesis for such remarks and respond without missing a beat. But this morning wasn't one of those occasions.

So he had to ask, "Do I think who will do what?"

"Do you think someone from the camp will come after us, try to track the way we're going?"

Heath twisted his mouth sourly. "I've been wondering about that myself. If it was only up to just my old man, I don't expect he'd bother. He's been telling me for most as long as I can remember how worthless I am, what a big disappointment. I figure he'd be glad to get rid of me. One less mouth to worry about feeding."

"I know your father is a hard man, it's his nature," Belinda said. "But I find it difficult to believe he truly dislikes you, his own son. Besides, there's also your mother. She doesn't treat you so bad, does she?"

"No. Ma's okay as far as how she treats me. But that don't mean she ever spoke up against the old man for the way he carried on. Leastways not that I ever heard."

"I'm sorry for you, sorry you grew up in a home where you doubted your parents loved you. That's so sad. But if it helps, when we're off on our own and have a home of our own, you'll never have to doubt that it will be filled with *my* love for you."

Heath's ears burned and he knew he was blushing. It made him feel funny to hear Belinda talk like that, but at the same time it thrilled him. He never wanted her to stop thinking about him that way or to stop telling him. And he never wanted to do anything that might cause her to stop.

"Unfortunately, the same can't be said about your parents, especially your father," he said. Regretting his choice of words as soon as they were out of his mouth, he quickly added, "I don't mean it's unfortunate your folks love you. I meant that, because they do, I figure there's a good chance your dad will come after us. After you. If he does, everybody knows what a good tracker he is—my puny attempts to hide our trail probably won't slow him down much at all."

"If he does find us," Belinda said through gritted teeth, "it won't make no difference. Not in the long run. He can tie me up and haul me back if he's a mind to, but unless he's prepared to keep me in chains I'll just run away all over again. And again and again, however many times it takes. Sooner or later they'll all have to get it through their heads that we're in love and we're determined to be together and there's nothing they can do to stop us."

"Unless your dad decides to shoot me or run me plumb out of the territory or some such," Heath said glumly. "He'd never hurt you, but I can see him being a lot less charitable toward me."

"He wouldn't dare!" Belinda declared. "If he did, I'd never forgive him. I'd . . . I'd hate him forever!"

Heath put one of his hands gently over hers, where they were clasped together just above his belt buckle. "I wouldn't want that," he said. "As big a grudge as I got against my old man, I don't reckon I really even hate him. I wouldn't want us being together to be the cause of so much bitterness."

Belinda was quiet for a long moment, until she asked, "What hope do we have then? If you're convinced my father is going to come after us and catch us, yet you're not prepared to fight back, then what are we even doing this for?"

"We're doing this, like you put it a minute ago, to show everybody how determined we are to be together," Heath told her. "And I never said I wasn't willing to fight, I just said I didn't want it to end up in hate."

"What if they're as determined as we are? If both sides keep refusing to give, how can hard feelings *not* start to build?"

"Maybe," Heath said, "because other hard feelings will get in the way. Maybe that's gonna turn out to give us a chance. Maybe what the two of us are doing won't rate the full attention of even your father."

"That didn't make any sense." Although Heath couldn't see it, Belinda's pretty face scrunched into an annoyed scowl. "Don't tease me with riddles at a time like this!"

"It wasn't a riddle," Heath said defensively. "Look, you asked me a minute ago what hope I think we have, right? Well, I put a lot of thought into that before I ever gave you the sign that last night was the night we were going to light out. Did you ever wonder why I suddenly decided then was the right time, after we'd talked about it but put it off so many times before? Well, the reason why was on account of that Jensen fella showing up."

"Him? What difference does he make to our situation?"

"Because I got a hunch that he might cause your dad to have a whole different set of things demanding his attention. Didn't you see the two of them together? The kind of excitement they generated, like sparks flying off two chunks of steel striking against one another? It was there when they first got back to camp and talked about how Jensen had tangled with Hack Ferris's curly wolves and how your dad pitched in to help him. And then it was there again, maybe even more so, after they got done killing Ol' Rip."

"I still don't see . . ."

"Look, what's the biggest thing that's been driving your dad ever since he gathered everybody together in that mountain camp?" Heath said. Not waiting for an answer, he went on. "He wants folks to stick with him and rise up to reclaim our town and valley, right?

That's the dream of everybody who's holed up with him, ain't it?"

"Of course. Most of them have no place else to go."

"But other than the stuff your dad has been doing on his own—the harassing, stealing supplies, cutting the telegraph wire, and whatnot—what has anybody else done in the way of anything you could actually call striking back against Dixon's thugs? Let's face it, if you add up all the other men in our camp, you've got pretty sorry makings for any kind of effective army."

"But we've got several good men," Belinda countered. "Mr. Barlow and Mr. MacGregor are strong and stout. And your dad is plenty rugged."

"Yeah, my old man's still got plenty of bark on him and could tear it up in a close-in fight—but not riding out against Ferris and the rest of Dixon's hired guns." Heath snorted derisively. "It'd take my old man a half hour to even climb on a horse. Face it, the only two men in our camp who are proven fighting men, actual war veterans, are a couple cripples as a result. My dad and goofy ol' Dewey Akron. One crippled physically, the other crippled in the head."

"That's mean. And I don't see what any of it's got to do with Mr. Jensen or why it might make a difference as far as whether my father may or may not come after me."

"Because," Heath said, "Jensen gives your dad exactly what he's been lacking. At least *the start* of a fighting force against Ferris and the others."

"But how much difference can one man make?"

"Plenty, from what he's shown so far. Your dad claimed he left four or five of Ferris's thugs laying in the dirt back in Hard Rock. And then he went after

Ol' Rip last night with nothing more than a knife. Besides, it ain't just what he can do himself, it's what he can help stir inside the other men. Including your father."

"My father doesn't need anybody to stir anything in him. He's been carrying this fight against Dixon practically all on his own since the very beginning," Belinda pointed out.

"And that's exactly the point I'm trying to make," said Heath. "Now that he's got an equally strong man to stand beside him and help prod along the others, I'm thinking he's bound to be mighty anxious to finally hit back against Dixon's gun toughs. Especially now when they're smarting from tangling with Jensen the first time. Strike while the iron is hot, as the old saying goes.

"Which brings me to the point of thinking that your dad might not be as quick to come chasing after us as he would be if he didn't have to balance it against leaving that iron to cool down. After all, by taking off like we did, we're not only showing how much we want to be together but we're also abandoning the dream and the cause of all the others. The cause, like you said a minute ago, nobody has put more into than your dad and everything he's had to do practically alone up until now."

Belinda was quiet for several moments before she said, "You really think he might see it that way? That my father would put the fight against Dixon ahead of coming after us?"

"I can't say for sure. I'm just telling you what went into my thinking." Now it was Heath who went quiet for a spell before speaking again. "You almost sound like you'd be disappointed if your father *didn't* track us down. That's not how you feel, is it?"

Belinda's arms tightened around him and she was quick with reassurance. "No, of course not." She paused a moment and then added in a quieter voice, almost as if to herself, "That's not it at all."

Chapter 23

"I'd like it a whole lot better," Pinkeye Scarns was lamenting, "if we could just shoot him. I mean, looky here, we got practically the perfect setup. We split ourselves into the rocks off on either side, wait for him to ride out there in the middle of the gap, then hit him with a crossfire. It'd be all over, slick as pie."

"Maybe killin' a man ain't *supposed* to go as slick as pie. You ever consider that?" drawled Clarence Horn from where he stood leaning leisurely against a smooth slab of rock off to one side of Pinkeye.

Pinkeye scowled. "Whatcha mean by that? You sayin' I ain't got the right to think about a piece of business the way I want, that I can only look at it the way I'm *supposed* to? Who has the say over what men in our line of work should feel or think about what we do? You all of a sudden get bit by the religion bug or something, Horn? You—a hired gun who's planted more men than you got whiskers on your chin?"

The abnormality that perpetually tinted the irises of both of Pinkeye's eyes the color that earned him his nickname was prone to deepening nearly to full red when he got annoyed or angry. A trace of this change was in evidence now as he fired off the retort to Horn.

A runt all his life, suffering a diminutive size in addition to pushed-in facial features dominated by flat, flaring, pig-like nostrils and bulging eyes that displayed their odd color to the point of practically begging to be commented on, Pinkeye had grown up the brunt of endless ridicule. Only after he picked up a gun for the first time and discovered he was pretty handy with one, did he find the means to retaliate against all the teasing and unkind remarks he'd had to endure up to that point.

And retaliate he did, often at the most minuscule thing he took to be disrespectful or disparaging. Such as the off-hand bit of musing from Horn, as if it were some kind of personal challenge to Pinkeye's way of looking at things.

Horn was a grizzled old veteran who'd seen Pinkeye huff and puff over little or nothing too many times to respond seriously to his latest display of raised hackles. At fifty, with his easy Texas drawl and mild, seen-it-all-before eyes, Horn still had a trace of lightning left in his draw even though the rest of him moved slow and somewhat wearily, never wasting a single motion. He'd killed a score or more men in his time, and though more likely loomed in his future, he seemed in no particular hurry for it.

On that subject now, in response to Pinkeye's chuffing, Horn said, "Yeah, I've planted my share of men. More than my share. So maybe that don't give me the right to say how anybody else oughta feel about it. But I can speak for my own feelings and it ain't got nothing to do with religion, neither. What it does have to do with is . . . well, balance. Weighin' one thing against another. And by that I mean that snuffin' out the life of a man, a human being, shouldn't be taken as lightly as swattin' a mosquito or plinkin' the head off a rattler. That's all I was sayin'. Do you see what I mean?"

Pinkeye continued to scowl at him, only gradually it turned into more a look of confusion than annoyance. "No, I don't," he said dully. "But never mind. You not makin' sense fits right in with the rest of what we're in the middle of here. It's no wonder none of us are thinkin' or talkin' straight. How can we, on account of this 'take him alive' bull? What kind of crazy business is that, anyway? You know good and well those Dixons ain't goin' to all this trouble to catch Jensen just so's they can chew the fat with him over brandy and see-gars. He must have done something to really piss 'em off royal, so they got some kind of special payback in mind. Which means he's gonna end up dead anyway, so why not just get it over with? That's what I'd like to know."

"Well then," said Paul Grimsby, the third man hunkered in the nest of boulders with Pinkeye and Horn, "maybe when we get back to Hard Rock with this Jensen varmint, you can march right up to Roland Dixon and demand some answers to all those things you're fretting about. Better yet, maybe his old man will be coming 'round for a visit and you can corner both of 'em together and find out everything you want to know. How would that be?"

Pinkeye's mouth sagged open. "What are you sayin'? Yeah, like I'm apt to pull a fool stunt like that. That would take the crazy cake for sure."

Grimsby regarded him. He was a solid six-footer, about forty, with a weathered face bracketed by thick sideburns gone prematurely white. Penetrating blue eyes under a ledge of brows still stark black gave him a stern, no-nonsense air.

"Why not?" he demanded now in a tone that fit his appearance. "You could be the spokesman for the whole lot of us. I know quite a few of the boys have got some of those same questions."

"To hell with that notion." Pinkeye shook his head vigorously. "I ain't gonna brace no Dixons with no bunch of questions on why they want something done a certain way."

"Why not?" Grimsby said again. "You got all these questions and you just got done spouting 'em out, along with saying how crazy the Dixons are. I think they might appreciate hearing all the things wrong with their ideas and what good ones you got to improve them."

Pinkeye shrank back a half step from Grimsby, like he'd suddenly learned the man was carrying a disease. "This is some kind of joke, right? I ain't got no ideas about improvin' nothing. That ain't for me to say."

"Why not, Pinkeye?"

"Whatcha mean, 'why not'? 'Cause it ain't my job, that's why! All I am is a hired gun."

Grimsby set his teeth on edge and glared at the little man cowering away from him. "That's right. All you are is a hired gun," he grated. "That means you do what you're told in order to earn your pay. You do what you're told and you keep your yap shut while you're doing it. Leastways that's how it goes when you're working for me. And since Hack put me in charge of this little shindig until he shows up, that's what it amounts to—you working for me." The heat in Grimsby's eyes intensified. "Understood?"

Pinkeye licked his lips. "Jeez, Paul. Sure, I understand that. No need to land on a fella so hard. I didn't mean no harm. You know I always do my job when it counts. I was just makin' conversation to help pass the time, that's all."

"You've done nothing but flap your gums since we rode out this morning," Grimsby growled. "You made enough conversation to help pass about six months. So enough is enough. My ears need a rest, and so does Horn's and everybody else's."

"All you had to do was say something," Pinkeye muttered.

"Then consider it said," Grimsby told him. "Any more yammering, I'll send you up to relieve either Touhy or Karpis on one of the lookout posts and you can listen to yourself."

The three men were positioned in a jumble of boulders and weather-scoured rock slabs accumulated around the base of a high, stony peak that rose behind and above them. The peak was the culmination of a long ridge reaching in from the west, most of it covered by brush and trees with a few outcrops of rock until it ended abruptly at a cliff that dropped almost straight down. To the east, on the other side of a flat, grassy expanse about a hundred yards wide, another cliff face rose to a similar peak and then another ridge, this one meandering away farther east until it was lost in the barren, baked humps and jagged arroyos of the badlands sprawl that lay beyond.

The flat, north-south stretch between these peaks—

or shoulders, as some called them—was known as Balfour Pass. Depending which way one was headed, this could be considered either the gateway to or the exit from the Hard Rock Valley. For the purpose that brought Grimsby and the others here this morning, they were viewing it as the exit on the road to Helena—the road they anticipated Luke Jensen to be taking in his flight from the harsh reception he'd received upon his arrival yesterday. If and when he showed up, it was their assignment—as issued by Hacksaw Ferris—to stop him.

"Comes to climbin' up and relievin' one of those other fellas," Horn said, shifting his weight from one foot to the other and cranking his head from side to side to work out the kinks, "I wouldn't mind takin' a turn. Be a chance to stretch my legs a mite and keep from crampin' up."

"Appreciate the offer," Grimsby said. "But I'd just as soon you stayed down here on the ground, close to the horses. In case Jensen shows up and tries to make a run for it, you're one of our best riders if we have to give chase."

The horses for the three men—as well as for Alvin Touhy and Rimrock Karpis, the lookouts Grimsby had stationed up high on each of the shoulders bordering the pass—were hobbled nearby but out of sight, deep in some underbrush that grew back around a corner of cliff.

Shrugging in response to Grimsby's rationale, Horn said, "Okay. If that's how you want it."

"With any luck, if Jensen does make an appearance," Grimsby explained further, "Hack and Dog and those other boys they're bringing will be tight on his tail and we'll be able to squeeze him between us. If he's smart, he'll see that he's caught in the jaws of a trap and it ought to take the fight out of him."

Pinkeye couldn't hold back. "Yeah, but think how much easier and surer it could be if not for that 'take him alive' baloney. Then we could use my idea of—" He caught himself in time, before he said too much, and clapped his mouth shut tight to hold back any more words. Except for meekly adding, "Never mind. That other idea should work swell."

A minute later, Grimsby said, "Looks like we're about to find out. Judging by the way Touhy is all of a sudden motioning from over across the way"—he pointed— "I take it he's spotted somebody approaching."

Horn and Pinkeye both perked up, becoming more alert.

"There's what I been hopin' to hear," declared Horn.

"Me too," agreed Pinkeye. Then, to Grimsby, he added, "But, say, do you think one of us maybe oughta go over there with Touhy? Sorta balance things on either side of the gap?"

Grimsby nodded. "Good idea. You go ahead and scoot on over. Stay low, and remind Touhy I said for neither of you to do anything until I give the signal."

"Got it," said Pinkeye, snatching up his Henry rifle from where it had been leaning against a boulder at his elbow.

"We've covered a good distance. Better even than I thought," said Heath Pettigrew. He jutted his chin, indicating something up ahead. "Looky there. See those shoulders of high ground up yonder and that opening between 'em? That's what folks call Balfour Gap. We get through that, we're well away from home and on the main road to Helena and anywhere else we decide to go."

Belinda rested her chin on his shoulder and gazed ahead at where he'd indicated. "I've heard folks talk about Balfour Gap before," she said. "I sure had it pictured different, though. I thought it would be . . . I don't know. Bigger, more impressive somehow."

"Well, it's impressive to me," Heath responded. "It marks the first big step for us getting clear of everything we're leaving behind. On the other side, like I said, is everywhere else. The rest of the world— whatever is waiting for the two of us, as long as we're together."

Chapter 24

Ben Pettigrew's broad forehead puckered above his frown. "You sure we're following the right trail?" he asked. "That boy of mine can be wrongheaded, I know, but even he wouldn't be foolish enough to strike out across the badlands."

"We're on the right trail," Eagle assured him. "But don't worry, I don't think Heath and Belinda are aimin' to take on the badlands."

Pettigrew squinted as he looked out across the sprawl of stark, ragged land stretching to the east. "This is where the tracks brought us, ain't it? To the edge of what sure looks like the badlands to me."

The two men, along with Whit Barlow, indeed sat their horses at a point on the narrow end of the valley where the richer, grassier land that spread wide to the west and north, below the northern curve of the Spearpoints, pinched down and gave way to the rocky, sun-blasted wasteland Pettigrew was squinting at. Upon exiting the hidden entrance to their mountain encampment, they'd had little trouble picking up the trail of the fleeing young lovers.

The ground, still soft from the recent rain, showed

their marks clearly. Not surprisingly, these marks at first led south, the logical way out of the valley and away from Hard Rock. Also not surprisingly, after only a short ways, the trail began curving to the east, making a loop around the abandoned town. To the west and north lay the Gold Button mine and it would be logical for the couple to reason that going that way would mean greater risk of running into Hack Ferris's thugs or some other of Dixon's men traveling back and forth between the mine and the town they now claimed. For that reason, the loop to the east made good sense. But when the trail veered off more sharply and ended up disappearing into the rocky, broken ground of the badlands, that gave the trackers some pause to wonder.

"You're right, as far as you're sayin'," Eagle allowed. Then, peering past Pettigrew, he added, "But bein' on the edge of rough country is hardly the same as headin' out across it."

"What's the point, then?" Barlow wanted to know. "Why cut all the way over here?"

"How about to cause exactly this confusion?" Eagle countered. "All of a sudden their tracks ain't so clear and we're caught wonderin' for sure which way they went. Slows us down, maybe even throws us off their trail for a while if we make a wrong decision."

Pettigrew considered this for a minute and then his expression shifted, seemed to brighten a bit. "I'll be durned. If my boy thought all that out . . . well, from his end, for what he's trying to accomplish, that's kind of smart figuring, wouldn't you say?"

Hearing the gruff blacksmith say something that

was even a borderline compliment to his son caught
Eagle off guard for a minute. A part of him almost
wanted to acknowledge it as a good thing. But then
he remembered Belinda's part in this and he was
damned if he was going to share in any charitable
thoughts toward the boy who was attempting to take
her away.

"Might be smart figurin'," he grumbled, "if he was
tryin' to pull it on somebody who couldn't track a
plow horse through a tomato patch. But I'd like to
think I'm a little sharper than that. And so's Jensen,
by the look of it."

His gaze swung in the direction of Luke, who had
dismounted from his paint some minutes earlier and
was now walking the tall horse about thirty yards
within the perimeter of the broken land and sixty
or seventy yards farther down, off to the south. He
stepped slowly, his head tipped forward, eyes closely
scanning the ground.

Barlow followed Eagle's gaze. "What's he up to
away over there?"

"Tryin' to pick up sign of the kids," Eagle explained.

"He can do that? He can spot sign in amongst all
those rock slabs and hardpan?"

"Uh-huh. If it's there, he'll be able to find it."

Pettigrew cocked a shaggy eyebrow. "And I suppose
you could, too?"

"Expect I could, yeah." A wry grin briefly touched
Eagle's mouth. "I'm half Injun, remember? Us bucks
practically crawl out of the womb knowin' how to
track and hunt and take scalps."

Pettigrew scowled. "Hey, that wasn't called for. I

never meant nothing by what I said. It was just a question."

Eagle's mouth started to tighten, but then he relented. "Yeah, I guess it was at that. Look, Pettigrew, it's important for me and you to pull together on this. It took grit for you to saddle up and go after those youngsters. I give you credit for that, and I don't aim to say or do anything to make it harder on you."

Pettigrew responded with a nod. "Whatever was said or done or thought in the past . . . well, however this current business works out, I'd like to think we maybe can get past that other altogether."

"Be good to hope for that. Up to us to make it work," said Eagle.

Further discussion on the matter was interrupted by a shout from Luke. "Over here," he called.

Eagle, Pettigrew, and Barlow gigged their horses into motion.

When they reached him, Luke said, "Looks to me like they're continuing to move south, but just doing it over this broken ground so as to try and hide their tracks." He pointed down where he stood. "Some recently disturbed gravel here and back that way a few yards there's a fresh horseshoe scrape on the side of a rock. Appears they're doing it smart—setting their horse to a long, steady stride but not attempting to run it as a precaution against having it step wrong in some of this rubble and maybe pulling up lame."

Pettigrew shook his head. "That boy of mine . . . I never would have thought he had the savvy for thinking of stuff like that." He glanced over at Eagle. "Not to shortchange your daughter. Maybe she's helping with his thinking."

"I doubt that," Eagle replied. "Belinda's a sharp gal when it comes to many things, but she's never taken any interest in the outdoors. I'd say these steps they're takin' are all owed to Heath."

Pettigrew twisted his mouth sourly. "Hell of a thing, ain't it? The first time I'm feeling kinda proud of my son and it has to come in the middle of a shenanigan like this."

The other three men exchanged glances, not knowing quite what to say to that.

"The thing is," Luke said, "we know they're still moving south and—judging by the freshness of this disturbed gravel—I'd say they're no more than three hours ahead of us."

"If that's the case, if we know the direction they're going and we figure they're slowed down some by choosing to travel over this rough ground," said Barlow, "can't we just move back out onto the grass and ride parallel to 'em? That way, on better ground, we could push our horses harder and catch up that much quicker."

"That might work," Luke agreed, "as long as they didn't decide to shift direction at some point. If we don't stick to actually following their trail, we might miss that."

"But what other direction are they going to go?" Pettigrew asked. "We've already ruled out them trying to *cross* the badlands. And if they all of a sudden swing west, they're going to run smack into the Flathead Mountains. The only thing that leaves, short of turning around and going back home, is to continue on south . . . don't it?"

"Be nice to think they'd do that—turn around and go home," Eagle said somewhat wistfully. "But I can't see that happenin'. Leastways not yet. They've got their minds made up and they're plowin' ahead real determined-like. Take a lot more time or miles, I think, for them to get discouraged enough to turn back."

"So that goes right back to them sticking with south and us being able to count on it. Certainly as far as Balfour Gap," said Barlow. "Getting off the main trail to Helena might be open to them after that, but I can't think of anything that'd make sense before then. And if we ride hard and they keep picking their way over rough ground, trying to fool us, we surely ought to be able to beat them to the gap."

"What's this Balfour Gap?" Luke wanted to know.

"Basically, it marks the southern edge of our valley," Eagle explained. "It's where the badlands reach in the farthest on one side, before they start to taper off altogether, and where some long fingers of heavily forested ridges and hills stretch out from the Flatheads off to the west. The gap, as the name says, is an opening in between that has become heavily used as part of the main route for freighting ore and travel in general. You must have come through it on your way here."

Luke nodded, vaguely remembering an area that fit the description. "Like Barlow says, then, it seems pretty likely that's where Belinda and Heath are headed."

"I guess so," Eagle said somewhat reluctantly. "The only possible wrinkle might be—since Heath is so bent on throwing us off—if they didn't actually *use* the gap. Those wooded ridges to the west are passable, it's just that they're obviously harder to go over than usin' the flat, open gap. Was I in the position of those kids, though, thinkin' somebody was on my tail, that's exactly the way I'd do it. Once over those ridges, then they'd have a fair amount of other options that could keep them totally off the main trail."

Luke studied him, one eyebrow lifting. "You almost sound like you're starting to pull for those kids."

Some deepened color crept up Eagle's neck. "That's ridiculous. Why would I be pullin' for my daughter to make good on runnin' away? She's lucky she's past the age for a good old-fashioned spankin' when I do catch up with her. In the meantime . . . Okay, doggone it, I'll admit that the spunk and determination those two are showin' is . . . well, I kinda admire it. But that don't mean I intend to hold off runnin' 'em down. For their own safety, we have to keep in mind, as much as anything."

"Uh-huh," said Luke. "And something else you might want to keep in mind is that when we do catch up with them and you get them back home, in addition to being too old to spank, maybe it's time to start realizing that your daughter is grown up in other ways as well."

"Maybe so. But comin' to grips with that is gonna be a lot harder than trackin' her down, I can tell you that," Eagle muttered.

"Yeah, and I reckon I got some new feelin's to come to grips with, too, where my boy is concerned," admitted Pettigrew. "But before we're faced with dealing with any of that—"

His words were cut off by a sudden onslaught of sounds that were far too familiar to Luke. The wind-rip of bullets slicing close through the air was unmistakable once you'd heard it, and it was something Luke had heard too many times. It was unsettling enough on its own, but what was even worse was the accompanying thud of slugs striking meat and bone. Suddenly, both of those sounds were taking place all about them as a volley of lead came pouring down on the four men. The boom of distant rifles followed belatedly but by then the horses were already shrieking and rearing up in panic and trying to twist away as bullets pounded into them.

Eagle's mount crumpled under him and the half-breed barely managed to kick out of his stirrups and roll free to keep from getting pinned. Barlow, the best horseman of the group, sprang nimbly clear of his bay as soon as he felt the animal jerk and start to go down from the rounds striking it. Pettigrew went toppling off the back of his horse as the animal reared wildly and tried to bolt as slugs slammed into its shoulder and neck. It was able to lunge for one or two long strides before its legs buckled completely and it crashed heavily to the ground.

As the only one not in his saddle, Luke immediately let go of the paint's reins and, seeing what was happening, swatted it away with his hat. "Run! Git!" he shouted. The paint wheeled and sprang off. As far as Luke could tell, it escaped being hit. He had only a fraction of a second to make that assessment, however, before he was turning in a spin of his own and then diving to the ground, scrambling to get in behind some of the larger rocks strewn along this outer edge of the badlands. As he did so, he caught movement out of the corner of his eye from the other three, causing him to shout again, "Stay low! Find cover!"

Chapter 25

From behind a fringe of thick grass topping a low hill some two hundred yards west of the four trackers, Hacksaw Ferris called for a halt to the shooting. "Hold it! Hold your fire. We did what we needed to, we've got 'em set afoot. They got nowhere to go and no way to get there. We can take our time finishin' 'em."

Along the crest of the hill to either side of Ferris, the seven men accompanying him did as he'd ordered and quit triggering their rifles. Immediately to Ferris's right, Dog DeMarist cackled gleefully.

"Ain't you glad you listened to my idea about making a sweep across the valley north of town, looking for sign of that Jensen varmint in case he wasn't so quick to take off south like you figured? Paid off pretty good, wouldn't you say?"

"I got to hand it to you, it sure did," Ferris allowed. "We not only ran across Jensen but we caught him in the company of that blasted Tom Eagle. There's a double stroke of luck I never would have counted on in a month of Sundays! How they hooked up together, I don't know."

"What about the other two with 'em? You recognize them?"

"One of 'em I think I recognized as the gimp who used to be the town blacksmith. The other was one of the ranchers or farmers I thought we ran off. But it don't matter. Whoever they are, it's too bad for 'em they threw in with Eagle and Jensen."

"Bad for them but plenty good for us," DeMarist crowed. "Only why ain't the curs even botherin' to shoot back?"

"Because now that we've ceased fire, they got nothing to shoot at and they're too smart to burn up ammunition with no glimpse of a target," Ferris answered. "Make sure everybody keeps their head down, though, 'cause I'm sure they're itchin' to take a shot if they *do* get a target."

Stretched out on his belly beside Ferris, DeMarist was a long, lean individual dressed in a buckskin shirt and striped pants tucked into high boots. The planes of his narrow face all angled forward in a kind of wedge that ended on an oversized hook nose with a small slash of a mouth below it and beady eyes set too close on either side. Underneath his weak, backward-sloping chin, in the center of his scrawny neck, was a lump of Adam's apple almost as big as his nose.

To the other side of Ferris, one of the commandeered miners, a man in a black and red plaid cap, said, "I think I also caught a piece of one of the men—the husky one who fell backward off his horse when the animal was taking its own bullets."

"Just as long as nobody hit the hombre in black. I told you all how we got to take him alive," Ferris was quick to caution. And then, after a moment's consideration, he added, "Come to think of it, it would suit me right down to the ground if we could take that 'breed alive, too. After all the aggravation he's caused and the ways he's made us look foolish over these past couple months, I got some personal reasons for wantin' to have a little fun with that buck before he dies. Just snuffin' his wick out with a bullet would be too quick and easy on him."

DeMarist cackled again. "Puttin' an Injun through some torment before you do him in, I like the sound of that. Everybody knows how plenty of good white men was put through hell by red devils like him before they was finally allowed to die."

"That's ancient history. I'd be doin' this strictly for myself," Ferris said through gritted teeth. "But before we get to countin' our chickens, let's remember we still got some moppin' up to do. Both Jensen and Eagle have proved themselves pretty slick in the past, and I don't aim to let either of 'em slip through my fingers again."

"Whatcha got in mind?" DeMarist wanted to know.

Without answering him, Ferris turned to the man in the plaid cap. "Nils, who would you say is the best rider in this bunch of fellas Mace Vernon lent to me?"

"That's easy. Ol' Tucker right here next to me. He used to be a bronc stomper all down through Wyoming and Nebraska."

Ferris craned his neck and called to Tucker, a grizzled, gray-whiskered old gent in a slouch hat. "Tucker, you know how to find Balfour Gap?"

"Reckon I do, yeah," came the answer.

"Good. I want you to slide back to where we left our horses, grab a good one, and hightail it as hard as you can ride to the gap. You'll find some more of my men waitin' there. One of 'em's named Paul Grimsby, good-sized fella with bushy white sideburns."

"I know Grimsby."

"Tell him we got both Tom Eagle and Luke Jensen pinned down and I want all the guns I can get to help flush 'em out and make sure nobody squirts away from us. You got that?"

"Easy enough."

"Hop to it, then. Pound out there as hard as you can, bring 'em back here on the double."

Tucker snapped a quick nod and slipped away wordlessly.

When he was gone, DeMarist said, "Is that it? We gonna just wait here until Grimsby and the others show up?"

"Not quite," answered Ferris. He turned again to the plaid-capped man on the other side of him. "Nils, how good a shot are you?"

"Above average, I'd say," came the reply. "I grew up in the Wisconsin jack pines shooting squirrels with my grandpa's old muzzleloader. These newer re-peating rifles"—his eyes flicked momentarily to the Winchester in his hands—"are more accurate and give you more rounds to throw. Fella'd have to be pretty poor not to bring down what he set a bead on with one of these."

"Who's another good shot from the other men with us?"

Nils looked thoughtful for a moment. "Don't

exactly know about everybody. Shooting isn't something we usually have need or time for back at the Gold Button. But young Smiley Buchner, down there on the end, I do know that he goes out for fresh meat every now and then and never comes back with an empty game sack."

Ferris called down the line and summoned Buchner. He came slipping along the rear of the other men, showing himself to be a twenty-year-old of average build with lank, straw-colored hair, pock-marked cheeks from childhood measles, and a very earnest expression. When he dropped into place so that he, Ferris, DeMarist, and Nils were grouped close together, making sure to keep back from the crest of the hill, Ferris explained what he had in mind.

"We got those troublemakin' rascals pinned down good," he said. "With no horses to try and ride clear on and us holdin' the front door shut with lead, the only chance they got to get away is to snake backwards into the badlands. I don't think they're gonna be in a hurry to try that, but before too long I figure they might see it as their only way. Short of surrenderin' to us, that is—which I can pretty much guarantee they ain't gonna be willin' to do."

"We keep 'em pinned down long enough for 'em to start gettin' hungry and thirsty," DeMarist said, "their willpower might weaken considerable."

Ferris shook his head. "No, I don't see 'em waitin' that long before they try the back door. I don't want to drag it out that long myself." He swept his eyes over Nils and Buchner. "That's why I want you two to hold here and keep poppin' to make it hard for 'em to move. Don't pour it on too steady, but enough so's they know you're here. And keep shiftin' back and forth along this crest to try and make 'em think there's more than just two of you."

As the two miners nodded, DeMarist said, "What are the rest of us gonna be doin'?"

"Like I said, I don't aim to drag this out any longer than necessary," Ferris told him. "That's why the rest of us are gonna drift back a ways. Then, you take two men with you to the south and I'll take the remainin' man with me to the north, and we'll swing out wide until we reach spots where we make our own way into those badlands. That way, whether they stay where they are or try to snake out the back, we'll be able to tighten in on 'em!"

"I like it!" exclaimed DeMarist.

Ferris grunted. "Whether you do or don't, that's the way it's gonna be. Spread the word for the others to get ready to move out. Tell 'em we'll be leavin' our horses behind. The clop of a horse's hooves in all those rocks would announce us about like a marchin' band. Gather up any extra cartridges you can, so we can be sure to leave these two boys with plenty. But before you do that, hold on a minute. I'm gonna call out to them jaspers, give them a chance to surrender. I know they won't, but I want to let 'em know who and what they're up against. Let it work on their minds as the mornin' ticks on, make 'em think we're fixin' to just wait 'em out."

While the others eyed him, Ferris hitched up a little closer to the crest and hollered out, "Hey down there! Jensen! Eagle! I don't know how you two managed to hook up, but if you thought it was gonna bring either of you any luck, it sorta backfired, didn't it? I want to thank you, though, for bein' so obligin' to me. Instead of havin' to chase down the two of you separate, I got you both bottled up tidy as can be!"

There was a slight pause before Tom Eagle's voice called back. "Is that you, Hacksaw?"

"You know good and well it is, 'breed! It was just a matter of time before your sneaky hit-and-run games backfired on you, just like all the other stupid Injuns."

"Nothing's over 'til it's over, you blowhard bag of guts!" Eagle sneered. "You say you got us bottled up? Whyn't you come on down and have a sip out of our bottle, see how the taste suits you?"

Ferris gave a nasty snort. "I'll be down in due time, don't you worry. I'm gonna let you and the others simmer for a while as all those bare rocks you're nestled in start to heat up. With your horses dead or gone and a dozen guns trained on your little hidey holes, just hopin' for an obligin' head to pop up, you sure ain't goin' nowhere. Unless, that is, you're willin' to show some smarts for a change and do this the easy way. Toss out your guns, step forward with your hands raised, and it can all be over painless-like."

"Yeah. Painless except for the bullets waitin' for us."

"Aw, 'breed, you got no imagination," Ferris clucked. "I wouldn't ask these fine fellas to gun you down in cold blood and have that on their consciences for the rest of their days. For you, especially, I look forward to a little time just the two of us. And as for your new pal Jensen, he ought to have it figured out by now that Mr. Dixon wants him alive—at least until Mr. Dixon has a chance to spend his own brand of time with the man in black."

A new voice, Jensen's, called back. "That sounds real inviting. Bring your Mr. Dixon on down here. I would very much enjoy a conversation with *him*!"

"Enough of this!" Ferris spat. "Be stubborn, the both of you. I expected nothing less, but I gave you your chance. So stay there, enjoy a few hours bakin' in the sun. We'll see if you sing a different tune after all the sweat is boiled out of you and your dried-out tongues are swollen in your mouths!"

Edging back once more from the crest of the hill, Ferris motioned to DeMarist. "Go ahead, get the other men ready and scare up some spare cartridges for these two, like I said before."

As DeMarist peeled off to do as bidden, Ferris again focused on Nils and Buchner. "Okay, I'm countin' on you two fellas. Mainly remember to keep your heads down and not to shoot that hombre in black. Also, in case something starts to get out of hand somehow, I want you to fire off five rapid-fire shots. Then reload as quick as you can and fire off five more the same way. That'll be a signal to me and the others that you're in trouble and we'll quick-like double back this way. Got it?"

Young Buchner's head bobbed again. "We got it, sir. We'll hold here and give you all the time you need to do what you have to out there."

Ferris scowled. "If Tucker makes it back with Grimsby and the other men, do the same thing but in a series of only three shots. That'll let me know they're here and, depending how things stand out there in the rough, how I'll want to respond. When Grimsby gets here, tell him to just hold on until he gets some kind of signal from me."

Chapter 26

Luke Jensen swore under his breath. He was blasted sick of being ambushed and, as a result, forced to eat dust and crawl on the ground behind rocks like some kind of lizard!

On the other hand, the calmer portion of his brain reminded him, such activity, unpleasant though it might be, was definitely preferable to being *successfully* ambushed and dropped into a puddle of his own blood.

"Okay, what's our situation—anybody hit?"

The question came from Tom Eagle after things quieted down following the exchange with Hacksaw Ferris. Instead of scrambling to the rocks, Tom had rolled in tight behind the carcass of his fallen horse.

"I'm okay, just scraped up a bit," answered Luke.

"Same for me," spoke up Barlow.

After a slight pause, Pettigrew responded, "I'm okay, too, but a slug from those dirty bushwhackers did manage to find me."

"Find you how bad? What do you mean exactly?" Eagle wanted to know.

"I took one through my stump." Pettigrew chuckled

dryly. Like both Luke and Barlow, he had wormed his way in behind some broken rubble big enough to hide his bulk. "I'd call that lucky, wouldn't you? The dumb buzzards planted one in the part of me that was already half wrecked instead of taking out something that mattered. Went through the meaty part on the back side of my thigh, not even bleeding very much."

"Find something to tie around it if you can," said Eagle. "It's important to get it plugged. Even losin' a slow dribble of blood will start to take a toll on you before long."

Pettigrew chuckled again. "Thanks for the concern. I already survived losing half of this doggone thing, I think I know it's kinda important to take care of what's left. But speaking of something to be concerned about . . . how did Ferris and those other polecats know where to find us anyway?"

"Just pure dumb luck, is all I can figure," said Eagle. "They must have been out searching, most likely looking for some sign of Jensen or me, who they're always on the lookout for."

"That makes sense," agreed Barlow. "It's sorta like Jensen warned us when the kids went missing—how they were at risk for running into some of that bunch making a general search."

"Better us than the kids, I guess," Eagle muttered. "I'm surprised Ferris has his wolves rangin' over this close to the badlands, but blast it, I still shoulda been more alert than to let us get caught in an ambush like we did."

"You don't have the only set of eyes and ears in our group," Luke reminded him, "so don't try to shoulder it all. What's done is done. The thing now is to figure a way out of this fix we've landed in."

"With twelve guns out there staring down our pie holes," said Barlow, "that's going to take some fancy figuring."

"In the first place, I think that's an exaggeration," Luke told him. "Ferris would naturally want to lay it on thicker than is actually the case, aiming to make us squirm as much as possible. More like half that many would fit with the number of hombres left after my skirmish with them yesterday. Although, I've got to admit, I'm a little surprised that Ferris is even among them."

"He's tough, you can't sell him short on that," said Eagle. "But I agree with Luke on the number of men he's got out there with him. You all see that grassy hill where the shootin' came from, right? The powder smoke haze is fadin' now but you can still tell the spread of it. Ain't wide enough for no dozen guns, not by my judgment. I'd agree with half, maybe one or two more."

"So only six or eight guns trained on us . . . That still leaves us a mighty long ways from being in good shape." Barlow was fighting it, but there was a ragged edge of fear stabbing into his voice.

"Take it easy," Eagle told him. "We might be without horses, but it ain't like we're without guns of our own."

"And we've only got those other guns trained on us," Luke added, "if we stay where they figure we are."

"You thinkin' what I'm thinkin'?" Eagle said.

"Reckon so," Luke answered.

Pettigrew was quick to say, "Okay. How about filling in the rest of us? What have you got in mind?"

"Mainly I got in mind to not hold still and let this play out the way Ferris just painted it," said Eagle.

"Him and his boys can't charge us, not without coming down off that hill and exposing themselves in the open," Luke pointed out. "They try that, we'd have the advantage of cover and we could cut 'em to pieces."

Barlow said, "You heard Ferris. He's smarter than to try that. He's gonna wait us out, let us bake and go thirsty and hungry until we're ready to give up. In the meantime, he can send somebody off to get provisions to keep him and the others in fine shape."

"We're only bottled up if we let ourselves be," Luke insisted. "All you have to do is look over your shoulder, Barlow. There's miles of rocks and hills and arroyos back there. All we have to do is fade back, lose ourselves in those badlands, and work our way out again, somewhere we no longer have gun muzzles staring us in the face."

"They'll swarm after us!"

"Not right away they won't," said Eagle. "We leave one man here to keep Ferris's coyotes at bay while the other three slip away. If Ferris sends men out wide to curl in and follow into the badlands—well, once in those jagged rocks and twisty canyons, numbers won't count near as much. One man could be as effective as twenty. With a little luck he could maybe start pickin' off a few of the coyotes, one at a time, and possibly even turn the whole tide."

"That's too risky," protested Barlow. "That might be the kind of cat-and-mouse stuff you've been getting away with, but not everybody's suited the same. A person could get twisted around in those badlands and wander for days. And even if one of us did work his way clear, what then? He'd still have no horse, no way to help anybody else or try to get back to the mountain camp."

"Come on, Whit," Eagle snapped. "The whole valley is full of horses who've been left to roam free after all the ranchers and farmers got chased off their spreads. You ought to know that as well or better than anybody. Some of those horses runnin' out there are yours. If anybody would have a good chance to catch one, it'd be you."

"No matter the odds, doing it like Tom is saying gives us our best chance," said Luke. "If we stay here and play Ferris's waiting game, there's no guarantee he won't still sneak some men out wide for the purpose of trying to flank us. They manage to work their way unseen into the rough and then close in on us from behind and to our sides, we'd be durned near helpless. I don't intend to hold still for that."

"That don't sound like anything I want to hold still for, neither," growled Pettigrew. "What they're sayin' makes sense, Barlow. We've got to do whatever it takes, not just to save our own skins but for the sake of makin' sure at least one of us makes it back to warn the others in the encampment."

A sudden volley of shots from the grassy hill silenced any further discussion for the better part of a minute. Bullets whined off the rocks concealing the four trackers, kicking up a cloud of chalky dust filled with wildly spinning stone fragments. The dull smack of more rounds striking the already dead horses could also be heard.

Then, as suddenly as it had started, the shooting stopped.

A handful of seconds into this silence, Barlow thrust up from behind his cover and fired off four frantic return rounds as fast as he could squeeze the trigger of his handgun. "Yellow polecats! Show yourselves!"

No sooner had he dropped back down than another volley from the hill heavily pounded his specific boulder.

When silence again fell over the scene, Luke said, "Did that make you feel better, Barlow? Even if it did, it was a dumb play. All you accomplished was to pinpoint your exact position and waste some ammunition killing a few blades of grass. Boneheaded moves like that won't do you or any of us a bit of good!"

Nobody said anything more for a minute until Barlow responded, "You're right, Jensen. You're right." His voice was a little ragged, fighting to regain control. "Look, I'm sorry I let myself get rattled. It won't happen no more. And the notion of us fading back away from here and working our way clear out through the badlands, you and Eagle are right about that, too. It's our only chance."

"Okay then. Now that that's agreed on, the only thing left is decidin' which of us stays behind to cover the other three," said Pettigrew.

"That's easy," Eagle was quick to reply. "I'm the one who's snugged in here behind my horse. The rest of you have only got your handguns while I've got access to my rifle and canteen. That puts me in the best shape to stay here and make a stand."

Pettigrew emitted another of his dry chuckles. "I

figured you'd say that, Tom. But you're overlookin' one little detail—me and my gimpiness. I told you I'd be okay as long as I was on a horse. Well that ain't the case no more and a one-legged man ain't exactly built for scrambling around out there in that rough country. Plus, the more I work this leg the more I'll agitate the wound and cause added bleeding. So, for once in my life, being handicapped makes *me* the one in the best shape for doing something—and that's staying here and covering the front door."

Once again nobody spoke for several seconds.

Until Eagle finally said, "You make a strong argument, Pettigrew."

"If my argument is strong, then that ought to be the end of it," Pettigrew told him. "Look, I never talk about it much, but I lost the bottom half of my leg helpin' defend Little Round Top at Gettysburg. So on top of everything else, I've got some experience holding the line under tough conditions. You leave me your rifle and canteen, I reckon I can hold out here."

There was another stretch of silence, this time broken by Luke. "Sounds to me like Pettigrew is the right man for the job. The best thing the rest of us can do is work our way clear and make his stand count for something."

Chapter 27

One by one, with Pettigrew using Eagle's Winchester to provide cover fire, Luke, Eagle, and Barlow edged back away from the spots where they'd initially taken refuge. As each made it deeper into the badlands, the rock outcrops grew larger and more frequent and their exposure to the rifle fire from the hill dropped dramatically.

About two hundred yards in, they converged in a deep, ragged-walled gully. The sun overhead was climbing closer to its noon peak and both the air and the bare rock surfaces all around them were growing steadily hotter. All three men were already dripping sweat and caked with dust. From back near the front edge of the broken terrain, where Pettigrew remained, they could hear the shots he was exchanging with the men on the grassy hill growing more sporadic and farther apart.

"So far so good," Eagle declared. "Now it's time for us to split up and finish makin' this pay off."

"Do you know these badlands at all?" Luke said.

Eagle shook his head. "Nobody does, really. Nothing in here worth spending time to learn about. I only know that it's widest up to the north where it eventually feeds into the Spearpoints. To the south it's narrower and eventually tapers off into some prairie once again. But by narrower, I mean it's still dozens and dozens of trackless miles."

"That's okay, I don't aim to pass through it," said Luke. "I'll go ahead and split off, though—but only for a ways."

"What do you mean? Why only for a ways?"

"Occurs to me," Luke said, "that if Ferris didn't already send some men to flank us before, he surely will now after seeing that some of us decided not to stay pinned down up front. That makes me change my mind how I mean to play my part of this. Instead of making a run for it, I'm going to hang around and do some hunting of my own. It'll give me the chance to pick off some of those flankers and not only trim their overall number but also keep them off Pettigrew's back."

"I like the sound of that part. Pettigrew won't stand a chance if they get into these rocks and work their way around behind him."

"Why don't we all stay and make a fight of it then— from here, deeper in the rocks?" said Barlow.

Luke gave a quick, firm shake of his head. "No. Somebody still has to concentrate on getting all the way clear—if for no other reason than for the sake of the others in the encampment. You and Eagle know the valley to the north, right? If you can make it out of these badlands up that way, where some of the ranches and farms used to be, your familiarity with the area will give you the best chance for at least one of you to find water and shelter and eventually one of those horses running loose. Then you can make it the rest of the way."

"What about you?"

Luke smiled a wolf's smile. "Don't worry about me. Those flankers won't be coming around without guns and canteens. I got a feeling I'll be acquiring all the water and ammunition I'll need to get me through. Then, if I manage to keep me and Pettigrew alive until nightfall, I know a few more tricks."

Barlow eyed him with a mix of awe and uncertainty. "You're not short on confidence, I've got to hand you that," he murmured.

"You never win by planning to fail," Luke told him. "And even more certain is that nobody ever accomplished anything by squatting in an over-baked gully just talking about it." He looked at Eagle. "You got anything to add?"

Eagle held his gaze for a long count and then said, "Only this: Dinah Mercer would be mighty disappointed if you end up wastin' all the attention she put into soothin' those cuts and bruises of yours."

"In that case," Luke told him, "I'll try extra hard not to disappoint the soothing Miss Mercer."

A half hour passed before Luke heard the sound of someone moving through the rocks not far from where he'd positioned himself. After Eagle and Barlow departed, Luke had also moved out of the deep gully. But he didn't go far. Less than twenty yards away he spotted a rock formation that rose up about fifteen feet higher than anything else around it. He calculated its height and shape—that of a giant, lop-sided mushroom—would suit him well as a lookout point from which he could watch for the approach of the men he suspected Ferris would be sending.

Once atop the outcrop, he found the surface there to be worn relatively smooth by the elements. Dropping to his belly and pushing close to the edge of the highest point, he was able to look out and down and see a good distance in all directions. He was almost able to see Pettigrew where he remained hunkered, continuing to trade sporadic shots with the ambushers on the hill beyond. While he couldn't actually catch sight of the blacksmith, he spotted periodic puffs of powder smoke rise up when Pettigrew took his shots.

For a brief time Luke had been able to track the withdrawal of Eagle and Barlow, but they quickly disappeared into the sea of sun-blasted humps and ragged cuts that stretched for miles to the north. In one sense this was a relief, seeing how easily they could lose themselves in the rugged terrain, but at the same time it served to remind him how easy it also would be for Ferris's men to keep themselves concealed if they came slipping around like he expected.

That was why the sound—the soft rattle of pebbles being dislodged by something brushing too hard against a rock face—was so welcome. It gave him at least a rough idea where to focus. Although the unevenness and twists of the rocky surroundings had a way of sometimes distorting the exact source of a noise, it nevertheless provided a general direction. In this case, it was off to Luke's left.

Turning slowly, cautiously, so as not to give anything away with his own movement, Luke shifted around in order to be facing more toward where he'd heard the sound. The bleached, sun-washed surface under him was hot and growing hotter, pressing through his clothes and threatening to blister his bare hands. But he willed himself to ignore the pain, to concentrate on matters more serious, matters upon which hinged life or death.

More minutes ticked by. Silence again now, except for an occasional exchange of distant shots between Pettigrew and the ambushers on the hill. Luke was listening so hard, so intently, that he picked up the faint sigh of a breeze that he otherwise never would have noticed.

"Ouch!" This exclamation from a man encountering some sudden discomfort as he slipped through the rugged terrain was involuntary and little more than the sound of a deep breath. But Luke was focused so sharply that it rang out loud and clear to him. What was more, he felt confident in being able to pinpoint with reasonable accuracy where the words had come from.

His gaze settled on the same narrow, deep gully in which he, Eagle, and Barlow had briefly spent time earlier. The gully snaked crookedly below his present elevated position. And while he and the others had occupied it more to the west, whoever was down there now—the man who'd issued the short curse—was more to the east, deeper into the full badlands. It made sense that he could have entered the cut farther back and then decided to use its deep cover to advance toward where Pettigrew was shooting.

Everything was quiet again now. While he had yet to catch a glimpse of the skulker, Luke felt sure he was just a short ways back behind one of the sharp twists of the gully. He could imagine that, cursing himself for having been unable to hold back the sudden exclamation, the individual who'd made it was frozen very still, listening and hoping intently that his mistake hadn't drawn undue attention. He would allow some time to pass to make sure and then, if he heard nothing as a result, he would advance again . . .

And when he did, Luke would be watching and waiting.

Chapter 28

Poised, ready for the man in the gully to resume his advance, Luke's attention was suddenly split by a new noise from a new location. The clatter of a falling stone, this time even louder and more distinct than the initial rattle of a few pebbles, reached his ear. Turning his head, he caught a glimpse of a man in a yellow shirt and a short-billed black cap ducking in behind a tall, cone-shaped rock. This individual was no more than a dozen yards off, perhaps even closer than the still unseen skulker down in the gully to the south.

Luke bared his teeth in a bitter grin. All at once he had a wealth of would-be flankers to deal with.

Not that he was complaining. He had two Remingtons, each with a full wheel. Luke slowly, silently drew the .44s and held one ready in each hand. His only concern was that, by opening up on the first skulker who clearly showed himself, he would be revealing his position to the remaining one.

Luke swung his gaze back to the gully. He wondered if the hombre down there had heard the falling stone that signaled the nearness of his cohort. If he did, he'd likely stay frozen in place that much longer, waiting to see what came next.

On the other hand, it seemed certain that the man behind the tall rock cone had no reason yet to be aware of anyone else being close by. If he was betting on the situation, Luke mused, odds would seem to favor the man behind the rock cone being the one to first reveal himself further.

No sooner had this thought crossed the black-clad bounty hunter's mind than both men edged into sight, almost simultaneously. Now he was faced with the dilemma he had only pondered before: which man to shoot first and which one to give a chance at firing on him in response? Both were brandishing Winchester repeating rifles and each looked equally grim and willing to pull the trigger.

Luke's solution was to rest his right-hand Remington on the rock surface before him and reach back for the Bowie knife sheathed on his hip behind the now-empty holster on that side.

Generally speaking, Bowie knives were not crafted or balanced for throwing. They were heavy, durable, wickedly bladed weapons made for in-close slashing and stabbing and gut-splitting. But he had taken time during long periods on the trail to refine and re-balance it a bit and put in a good deal of practice toward additionally making it a reliable throwing weapon.

The man down in the gully was to Luke's left; the man making his way around the rock cone was slightly to his right. Although he could shoot just as well with either hand, Luke had discovered that his knife-throwing accuracy was considerably better with his right hand. He got the proper grip on the Bowie, snugged the Remington in his left fist . . . flicked his eyes one final time to each of the approaching men, mentally fixing their positions . . . then he shoved up and went to work.

The Bowie streaked down with a short whistling sound that ended in a meaty *thunk!* as the blade sank to the hilt in the chest of the man in the gully. His knees buckled and he fell to the ground. Twisting smoothly at the waist, Luke extended his left-hand Remington and triggered two rapid-fire rounds, both of which found their target, the man by the rock cone, hitting him six inches below his gaping mouth and punching two red-rimmed holes high in his chest that slammed him hard against the rock face and left him sliding slowly down.

The dull echo of Luke's two shots rolled across the baked, barren landscape and that should have been it, at least for the moment.

But it wasn't.

As he was reaching for the Remington he'd briefly laid aside, Luke heard two near-simultaneous sounds. First, by a fraction of a second, came another unmistakable *thrrrp!* of a bullet slicing the air a mere inch above his head—and then the report of the rifle that had fired it. If Luke hadn't leaned forward to pick up his gun, that bullet would have laid open his brains!

In a continuation of the leaning motion that had saved his life, Luke finished snatching up his second Remington and then threw himself all the way belly-down flat again. Instantly, he went into a series of frantic rolls across the slanted slab of rock that was his perch. Two more shots came in rapid succession, one of the bullets skimming the spot where he had flopped just a moment earlier, kicking up a geyser of dust and stone chips in his wake.

That strike enabled Luke to recognize that the shooter was off to the south, not far from the rock cone where now lay the body of the second man Luke had just killed. Furthermore, the downward angle of the shot, the way it had gouged in, indicated that the rifleman was shooting from his own elevated position, equally as high or higher than Luke's—making it time for the bounty hunter to abandon his platform.

Continuing to roll, Luke reached the north edge of the high rock slab. Checking his momentum only briefly, he twisted and swung his legs over the edge. Braced on his elbows, still gripping his twin .44s, he dangled that way for half a second. Another slug sizzled in, gouging a long, grit-spitting furrow half an inch from Luke's right elbow. He lunged backward with his head and shoulders, at the same time straightening his arms. As he faded back and away from the edge of the slanted slab, he blazed a pair of rounds from each Remington.

The drop to the base of the mushroom-shaped formation was about seven feet from where his feet had dangled. Even though he bent his knees on impact, the landing was still jarring due to his inability to tuck and roll forward into the rise of the outcrop directly in front of him. Instead Luke had to fall back somewhat off balance. He took the second impact mostly on his rump, lucky not to crack his head on any of the other jagged rocks crowded close on all sides. Regardless, the final result left him sprawled awkwardly with part of his wind knocked out of him.

Although he now had the full width and height of the mushroom rock between him and the new shooter, Luke knew he couldn't stay in one spot for very long. The shooter, emboldened by having forced Luke off his high perch, would likely try to press his advantage by advancing quickly in hopes of perhaps having wounded or at least stunned his target. Luke welcomed the thought of the man being in a hurry to work his way closer. All he had to do was shift to the right position and be ready for him.

With that thought running through his mind, Luke pushed himself to his feet. He paused like that, braced against the side of the mushroom rock, and took time to suck some air back into his lungs, getting his breathing leveled off while he replaced the spent cartridges in his Remingtons.

But scarcely had he finished re-filling the cylinders before, half a foot off from his right shoulder, a fist-sized chunk of rock exploded outward in a spray of stone shrapnel and dust. With the crack of the rifle shot that had sent the bullet ringing in his ears, Luke once more threw himself to the ground and squirmed in tight behind a line of ragged, moderate-sized boulders.

Surprisingly, no more shots followed immediately on the heels of the first. Instead, after a tense pause, a voice called out. A voice that had become too blasted familiar to Luke—that of Hacksaw Ferris.

"Jensen, for an hombre who's supposed to be hell on wheels, you sure spend a lot of time crawlin' on your belly like a worm!"

Luke hesitated a moment before replying. Then, deciding he had nothing to lose since his position was already revealed, he called back, "You ought to know about belly-crawling, you ambushing snake!"

"Look who's callin' names. I seem to recollect that there's a name for somebody who tries slidin' out the back door and leavin' all his pards in a tight spot the way you seem to be doin'. A name and a color— yellow."

Good, Luke thought. *Let him think I'm making a run for it on my own and none of the others are involved.* "You think I care about your opinion of me?" he grated insolently.

Ferris snickered. "Something you *should* care about is that the shot I just took could have blown out a chunk of your skull just as easy as it did a piece of the rock you was standin' beside."

"What I recognize," Luke countered, "is that there's a big difference between throwing lead and throwing it accurately. You and your boys have been trying for me for two days now and you haven't hit anything yet. In the meantime, how many of yours have I cut down?"

Now a tremor of rage crept into Ferris's voice. "You know we got orders to take you alive. Wasn't for that, you'd've been ventilated like a piece of Swiss cheese long before this."

Sensing he was getting under the hired thug's skin, Luke kept digging. "That sounds to me like just a lame excuse for not being able to get the job done. By the way, if you want a current count on how things tally up for one side versus the other, chalk up two more for me. On second thought, make that tally mark with permanent ink. Because that's how I took 'em out—permanently."

Ferris said hatefully, "My orders may be to take you alive, but nobody said *how much* alive. I already owe you plenty for the burns and bruises on the back of my neck and shoulders. I ain't forgot those. And the more you keep runnin' your mouth, the bigger the debt you're pilin' up. I'm thinkin' you're earnin' yourself a nice round of Injun-style carvin' before you get handed over to Parker Dixon!"

Still working to gouge the barb deeper, Luke said, "That would mean getting close enough to put your hands on me. I don't think you got the guts for that. If I'm wrong, come right ahead and prove it."

Ferris, perhaps realizing he was being intentionally egged on, went quiet.

Luke took the opportunity to mentally step back and do some quick re-appraising of his own. For starters, he knew that his exchange with Ferris—while it might have had some value as far as goading the man into being careless—also had eaten up time that was very likely being used by the shooter Luke suspected of working his way in closer from the south.

Abruptly, Ferris called out again, confirming Luke's thought. "DeMarist? Dog! You still out there somewhere?"

Chapter 29

After a pause, a voice from behind Luke, still back on the other side of the mushroom rock, responded somewhat cautiously to Ferris's query. "You bet I am. And I'm about to be landin' with both feet on that slippery son of Satan you're bandyin' words with!"

"Is it true what he said?" Ferris wanted to know. "Did he cut down a couple of the men over there with you?"

"Appears that way. I don't hear or see no sign of 'em movin' around no more. But I nearly did for that sidewinder in return," DeMarist growled. "Just a lucky last-second duck of his head is the only thing that saved him from gettin' his punkin blowed clean off!"

Ferris sputtered. "Then it sounds like it was a good thing he *did* duck! How many times do I have to tell you—"

DeMarist cut him off. "I know, I know. Keep the devil alive. I've heard that enough I want to puke! I get Jensen in my sights again, I'm gonna plant a bullet anywhere I can. If he don't survive where it hits, well, then I guess I'll have to take it up with Dixon afterwards."

"Them's some mighty dangerous words, Dog," Ferris warned, a hard edge to his voice.

"I can't help it, Hack. That's the way I see it," De-Marist came back, sounding firm. "I signed on for dangerous work, yeah—but not for suicide."

"Hey," Luke shouted into the middle of this. "If you fellas want to hash things out between you, go right ahead and take all the time you need. But me, I got places to go and things to do. So, if you don't mind, I'll just be on my way and you two can jabber all you want."

"You ain't gonna be on your way to nowhere," snarled Ferris. "Not less'n it's at the end of my gun. If you was half as smart as you pretend to be, you'd see that you're all out of chances."

"If I had a nickel for every time some cheap hired gun like you has told me I was out of chances," Luke said with a taunting laugh, "I'd have enough money to buy and sell your Parker Dixon about ten times over."

"But you don't, do you?" Ferris sneered back. "I'll admit you're pretty good. If it was just me and Dog puttin' the squeeze on you, maybe you *would* have a chance. But you're forgettin' how many of us 'cheap hired guns' there are. Yeah, you got lucky and cut down a couple of Dog's men. But he's got plenty more spread out over there with him, and I got even more backin' me over here. Tell him, Dog. Ain't that right?"

Apparently DeMarist was caught off guard by the sudden question. But he recovered quickly and managed to stammer, "Uh, yeah. That's right, Hack. My boys are primed to swarm this varmint as soon as you give the word. They're itchin' to get some payback for their pards he gunned down!"

Luke had to chuckle at these pitifully obvious histrionics meant to make him think he had a force of men closing in on him from either side. Instead it convinced him of just the opposite. He believed now that DeMarist had *no more* men with him after losing the two who'd gotten killed. On top of that, Luke was willing to bet that Ferris probably had only one or two with him.

Armed with this conviction, placing a bet was exactly what Luke was fixing to do—betting his hide that, under the guns of only DeMarist and Ferris, he could get away with bolting to some new cover and eventually work his way to a new position.

"What do you say, Jensen?" Ferris called out. "You can hear how it is—why not make it easy on yourself? You do that, I'll even give a break to Eagle and those others who are crawlin' around somewhere out there in those rocks with you. I'll settle for ridin' away with you and give the rest of 'em a pass for today. Not to say I won't be comin' after 'em again some other time, especially if Eagle keeps stirrin' up trouble. But, for today, I'll settle for just you."

"Whew! That's such a generous offer it plumb takes my breath away," Luke said sarcastically. "Only trouble is, I wouldn't trust the word of a lying, bushwhacking polecat like you if you told me the sky was blue!"

His voice quavering with rage, Ferris responded, "All right, here's my word on something I guarantee you *can* trust—I'm gonna make you pay for that smart mouth of yours and before I turn you over to Parker

Dixon you're gonna be the sorriest sack of misery anybody could ever imagine!"

"And I'm gonna lend a hand in makin' sure of that!" DeMarist crowed gleefully.

Having the two thugs caught up in trying to outdo each other with menacing threats, Luke decided, gave him as good a chance as he was likely to get. All during the exchanges over the past several minutes, his eyes had been ceaselessly scanning his surroundings, both immediate and at various distances. Scanning and calculating, weighing the odds for success in reaching a position that would make him better off.

Somewhat ironically, his gaze kept returning to the deep, ragged gully that twisted erratically through this whole area—the same slash in the earth where, in a spot off to the west, he and the others had first recon-noitered, and where the flanker with Luke's Bowie knife in him now lay dead to the east. Although it wouldn't do as a permanent position to try and hold, especially if a rifleman gained an elevated spot on either side, the best thing the gully's narrow depth offered was a means for Luke, in a crouched-over run and thus virtually out of sight, to follow its twisting route until he could get clear from being pinched directly between Ferris and DeMarist.

No matter what, Luke couldn't afford to remain where he was; his cover was too limited. If he didn't move, it was just a matter of time before either Ferris or DeMarist—or both—made it to where they could draw an unobstructed bead on him.

With his mind made up and his stalkers busy spouting words aimed at trying to scare him into sur-render rather than triggering lead to force the issue,

Luke shoved to his feet and sprang forward. He leaped over the line of low boulders and hit the ground on the other side, heels digging hard, propelling him on. Rifles immediately cracked from off to the north and then the south, bullets sizzling in low, aiming to cut his legs out from under him. Geysers of dirt and dust erupted as the slugs hammered the ground.

Luke zigged a half yard to his left and then zagged back right, always hurtling forward toward the gully. When he was three feet away, he threw himself into another dive, landing on his chest and forearms and whipping his legs around so that his feet went over the edge first. The rest of him followed and he toppled into the deep cut. Luckily the bottom was strewn with mostly gravel and sand, no chunks of jagged rock, so his landing was not particularly graceful but also not harmful.

Gathering his legs under him again, Luke settled into a low crouch, a Remington still gripped in each fist. Just above his head, more bullets gnawed harmlessly at the rim of the gully on both sides. The bounty hunter smiled with grim satisfaction. He was puffing for breath, dripping sweat, and his clothes were caked with enough dust and grime to nearly obscure their underlying black color—but he was still in one piece and he'd just succeeded in pulling a fast one on his hunters.

The rifle fire abruptly ceased and only moments after it did, Ferris was venting his frustration again. "See? Didn't I tell you? He's a blasted worm and now he's found a new worm hole to burrow into!"

"Relax," DeMarist called back. "He may have bought himself a little more time, but not that much. That gully can't go on forever. If he tries followin' it west, he'll run right back into fire from our boys on the hill. He crawls east, we'll be waitin' for him to pop his head up and it'll be all over."

"If you don't have anybody out there who can shoot any better," Luke called out, going right back to his taunting ways, "I could spend the rest of the day popping up and down like a jack-in-the-box and the only worry I'd have would be from my legs getting tired."

Now it was DeMarist's frustration that erupted. "You see there, Hack? You hear him? He knows we ain't supposed to shoot to kill and he's mockin' us over it! That's the final straw, I tell you. No more! I get him in my sights again, I'll be aimin' to put him down permanent-like and to hell with Parker Dixon. And you, too, if you're too stubborn to see the foolishness that's gonna end up gettin' the lot of us killed."

When Ferris replied, it was like the words were scraped over some of the surrounding jagged rocks. "I'm gonna pretend I didn't hear that, Dog. But I'm warnin' you for the last time to quit talkin' like that."

With the tension between the two men hanging heavy over the scene, things went very quiet. But in that stretch of tense silence, Luke was planning, taking advantage of the temporary lack of focus on him.

Fifteen yards up the gully to the west—the direction DeMarist was convinced Luke would never go—the gnarled gray spine of an ancient saltbush that must have sprung up at some past time when the gully held moisture still clung stubbornly to one side. It gave Luke an idea. It was an old trick, but "old tricks" get to be that way by enduring and still working from time to time. He was willing to gamble that this might be one of those times.

Staying low, Luke holstered his guns and began moving along the bottom of the twisty gully. Upon reaching the dead old saltbrush remains, Luke quickly unbuttoned his shirt and stripped it off. The sun was hot on his bare back but it felt good to peel away the sodden garment. Wrapping the shirt around his hands so his palms were protected from the rough stalk of the bush, he slowly tugged out and down until he snapped away a section of the growth about three feet long with some smaller branches flaring out up and down its length.

His two hunters were still jawing at each other, with DeMarist saying, "It's a helluva thing for you to threaten me that way, Hack, after all we been through together."

"It ain't how I want it," Ferris replied. "But I'm the one who'll be called to account by the Dixons if their orders ain't followed. I got a right to think of my own hide, too, don't I?"

"What about the hides of the good boys who've already been cut down by this skunk, and those who might be next in line if we keep messin' around with a killer?" DeMarist demanded.

Ferris didn't have an answer for that right away and things went quiet again.

Staying low, making short, quick movements, Luke unwrapped the shirt from his hands and draped it over the length of a saltbush stalk. He buttoned two of the shirt's buttons to hold it in place. Next he removed his hat and hung it on the top spike of the stalk. Twisting around so that he was facing south, he was ready.

Based on the exchange of words with Ferris, Luke believed he had DeMarist's position pretty closely fixed. He was the closer of the two, off to the south and at a somewhat elevated spot. These factors, combined with DeMarist's insistence he was ready to shoot to kill the next chance he got, were what made Luke choose him to try this ploy on.

With the shirt- and hat-decorated saltbush stalk gripped in his left hand, held carefully below the rim of the gully, Luke reached out and wrapped his right hand around an apple-sized chunk of rock. Reaching up, he flipped the piece of rock out to where it clattered nicely amongst some other rocks just beyond the edge of the gully. A second later, he shoved the decoy stalk, held at arm's length, up where it could be plainly seen.

"There he is!" DeMarist bellowed. An instant after that, his rifle barked.

As soon as he felt the shiver of a bullet's impact run through the stalk and down to his left hand, Luke thrust his legs straight. Rising, he drew his right-hand Remington in a fast, smooth motion, swinging his arm up and over the rim of the gully. There was DeMarist, fully exposed from the waist up, behind an egg-shaped boulder twenty yards away. His rifle was extended and he was just triggering a second round into the decoy when Luke centered the muzzle of his .44 on him and squeezed his own trigger. DeMarist's face disappeared in a red splash and he toppled backward, the rifle slipping from his dead fingers and dropping down over the face of the boulder.

Chapter 30

Luke dropped back down onto the gully floor as a pair of shots rang out from the north. One of them nicked a shoulder of the decoy as he yanked it down, the other gouged into the gully rim to one side.

"Little late joining the party there, weren't you, Ferris?" Luke jeered. "Or could it be you hesitated just enough, on purpose, to allow me to take care of your insubordinate man for you?"

"That's a dirty lie!" Ferris bellowed. "I rode with Dog DeMarist near ten years. I considered him a friend and practically my right arm, and now you've blowed his face off!"

"If he wouldn't have stuck his nose in my business, he'd still have his face. You might want to think about that," Luke told him as he began unbuttoning his shirt and removing it from the saltbush stalk.

"You're gonna pay, blast you—pay in blood!"

"Ferris, don't you get tired of hearing your own feeble threats?" Luke prodded. "Especially with your army melting around you like snow in July?"

"With Parker Dixon's money footin' the bill, an

army can be built back up soon enough," Ferris argued. "And given what you've done on top of how bad he wanted you in the first place, you can't fight back hard enough or run away far enough to escape what he'll send after you!"

"In case you haven't noticed, I'm not doing any running. All I want is for Dixon himself to show up and reveal his intentions for me in person."

Before Ferris could reply, the shooting to the west—from the hill where the ambush had begun— seemed to take on a kind of urgency. A series of evenly spaced shots were triggered. Five of them. Then, after a slight pause, five more in the same steady cadence.

Luke paused in the act of putting his shirt back on and listened intently. Spaced precisely like they'd been, the shots indicated some kind of signal, he decided. The fact that all other shooting from the hill then ceased and Ferris, too, went completely silent, convinced him all the more.

Luke waited, staying still and silent himself.

A signal meaning what?

There were no more shots coming from Pettigrew, either. Did that mean the rugged blacksmith had been overrun? Was that the message the signal was sending? Or was Pettigrew merely holding his fire, sparing ammo, because he was taking no incoming rounds to shoot back at?

Luke finished buttoning his shirt and secured his hat on his head. Things had taken an unexpected and strange turn. He believed he had whittled the forces against him out here in the rough down to

Ferris and maybe one more man, and he'd begun contemplating how he would make his next counter-move on them.

But now, suddenly, all that had changed. Every-thing was different, or at least *felt* different. Based on nothing he could actually see or hear, Luke never-theless had a strong sense that Ferris was quietly withdrawing, moving away.

Aiming to try and prod him some more, Luke called, "What's the matter, Ferris? Cat got your tongue?"

Nothing. A silence that somehow seemed even deeper than before.

Luke reached down and grabbed another chunk of rock, a melon-sized one this time. This one he heaved a good distance to the north, in the general direction where he figured Ferris to be. The big rock landed and then bounced and clattered loudly before coming to rest. But it got no reaction. None whatsoever.

Minutes ticked by. Everything stayed quiet.

Removing his hat again, Luke poked his head slowly, cautiously up to where he could peer over the lip of the gully. With both .44s drawn and held ready, he swept his gaze thoroughly over the rugged land-scape to the north. Nothing moved or stirred in the slightest. And Luke's sense that there was no longer anyone out there—that Ferris and whoever he might have had with him had slipped away—grew stronger than ever.

More minutes ticked past. Luke continued to rake his gaze over the surroundings, his ears perked as intently as his eyes. Nothing moved, not a whisper of sound reached him.

He dropped back down and returned the hat to his head. For another minute or so he did nothing but glare down at the sandy, gravelly floor of the gully, pondering. Then, abruptly, Luke pushed into motion once more. Keeping in a low crouch, he began following the twisting cut toward the west.

When he came within sight of Pettigrew's broad back, Luke froze in place and just watched, studying before he moved any closer. After about half a minute, the blacksmith reached up and rubbed behind his ear. A smile of relief briefly touched Luke's lips. So Pettigrew hadn't stopped shooting because he was overrun and lying dead, riddled with bullets. He appeared to be okay, still hunkered in roughly the same spot he'd been when Luke and the others left him more than two hours earlier.

Keeping behind a protective slab of rock in case Pettigrew overreacted to a voice coming from behind him, Luke called in a low voice, "Don't shoot, Pettigrew! It's me, Jensen."

Pettigrew twisted around hurriedly. But recognizing the voice, he checked himself from raising his rifle. His brows pinching into a tight scowl, he said, "Jensen! What are you doing back here?"

"I missed your sunny disposition," Luke replied dryly. "Keep me covered, I'm moving up."

Pettigrew turned back around and aimed his scowl out at the grassy hill. "Come ahead," he said over his shoulder. "I'm ready to give you cover, but the way things all of a sudden turned silent a little while ago, I doubt it's gonna be necessary."

Luke advanced in quick, smooth movements, keeping cautiously low in spite of there evidently being little reason to do so. A final short sprint brought him up to where he was able to drop in alongside Pettigrew.

"What the hell's going on? I've been hearing a lot of shooting from back there—didn't Eagle or Barlow make it?"

"On the contrary, I have every reason to believe they got out fine," Luke told him. "They broke north, the quickest way to try and make it back to the encampment. The shooting you heard was all concentrated on me. I stayed behind to run interference and thin the herd some."

"Thin the herd?"

"Head off the men—including Ferris himself—who were attempting a flanking maneuver," Luke explained. "I saw to it that three of them failed."

"Ferris one of 'em?"

"Unfortunately not."

"Too bad."

"Tell me about it," Luke muttered. "I had things narrowed down to Ferris and maybe one other man when that odd pattern of shots sounded from up on the hill. It was clearly a signal of some kind. Whatever it meant, it was enough to make Ferris suddenly withdraw from the skirmish we had going. My guess is that he must have circled around and back up to the other side of that hill."

"Could be," Pettigrew allowed. "I didn't see no sign of anybody coming or going, but there's sure something different than before going on over there. I got a notion, though I can't say why—it's one of those things you *feel* more than you *know*, you understand what I mean? Anyway, what I'm thinking is that more men showed up than there was when this first started. Who they are or where they came from, I can't say. But I think those shots might've been a message saying they'd arrived. And then, right after that, all the other shooting stopped."

"Yeah, that's the way it was back there in the rocks, too," Luke said. As they talked, his gaze, like Pettigrew's, was constantly raking the grassy hill and the rolling countryside all around. "How are you holding up? How's the leg? You didn't take any more hits, did you?"

"Nothing to amount to anything," Pettigrew scoffed. "Got stung with few stone chips when a couple of their shots came a mite close. But that was my fault for ducking too slow. Mostly, they can't shoot for beans. As far as the bullet hole in the leg, it's throbbing to beat the band. Dang sure letting me know it's there, but nothing I can't handle. And the blood's just seeping a little."

Luke glanced down at the wounded stump. Before he and the others had departed earlier, they'd wrapped Barlow's undershirt around the thigh, covering both the entrance and exit holes made by the bullet, then had cinched it tight with laces from Pettigrew's own shoes to keep pressure applied to help stanch the bleeding. By the look of the scarlet stain on the underside of the thigh, it appeared to Luke that there was more than just a little seeping going on but he made no comment.

Instead he asked, "How about ammunition? How much do you have left?"

"Not much for the rifle," Pettigrew admitted, the first hint of despair noticeable in his voice. "But I've still got the handgun and shell belt that Eagle left me. One good charge from those varmints on the hill, though, would pretty much burn up the whole works. But you know what? Right about now I'd almost welcome that. Whatever this is that's going on right now, is giving me the fantods. I can't believe I'm saying this, but I think I'd rather go back to the shooting."

Luke couldn't suppress a lopsided grin. "Yeah. I don't know how smart it is, but there are times when just blazing away feels like the best thing."

It was less than a minute after that when the rifle with the white cloth tied to its barrel—a piece torn from someone's shirt, it appeared—thrust above the crest of the grassy hill and waved slowly back and forth.

And then the too familiar voice of Hacksaw Ferris— obviously having circled back around, the way Luke had guessed—called down.

"You down there in the rocks! Hold your fire. We're coming out under a flag of truce. We want to parley. Trust me, you'll want to hear what we have to say."

"Ferris!" Luke said through gritted teeth. "I wouldn't trust him if . . . But never mind, we can't afford not to find out what this is all about. You do the talking. It's not necessary right now for him to know I'm here."

Pettigrew nodded. Then he called out, "Come ahead. Slow and easy. You'll have guns trained on you at all times, so don't be stupid enough to try any tricks."

There was a slight hesitation and then a man on horseback, holding high the rifle with the white flag tied to it, came into view and rode slowly down the slope of the hill. Behind him came another horse with two slender figures occupying its saddle. A length of lasso could be seen encircling the pair, binding them tight together. A blanket was draped over the heads of the two figures, and to either side of the horse carrying them rode a man holding a rifle aimed at the pair from a distance of mere inches. Last came Ferris on a black-maned gelding.

Halfway down the slope, the rider with the flag shifted to one side and reined up. The horse carrying double moved up and also stopped, the riflemen crowded close on either side following suit. Ferris moved up on the outside of the flag man and checked his gelding.

"I know that yellow dog Jensen took off on you," Ferris called. "But is Tom Eagle still down there?"

"It's for us to know who's here and who ain't," Pettigrew told him. "Just go ahead and say your piece."

Ferris looked displeased with the answer. But then, after a moment, he said, "All right. It makes no difference right now, but I guarantee you're gonna want to pass on to Eagle and Jensen what I've got to say and you'd better do it pronto. It starts with this—" Ferris waved his right hand with a bit of a flourish, causing one of the riflemen to reach out suddenly and yank the blanket off the bound pair, revealing their previously concealed identities.

Pettigrew groaned at what he saw. "That's my boy! That's Heath and Belinda Eagle. Those animals have got our kids!"

Chapter 31

Nothing but somber expressions were in evidence on the faces of all gathered under the main canopy of the mountain encampment. Tears glistened in the eyes of the women, and the mothers of the two captives fought hard to hold back sobs. Long shadows cast by the sun sinking behind the ragged line of the western horizon only added a sense of deepening gloom to the scene.

After Hacksaw Ferris and his men had made their revelation followed by the demands that went with it, they'd withdrawn—still with their prisoners—back over the crest of the hill. A short time later the fading rumble of horses' hooves signaled their complete departure.

Once he'd made a quick reconnoiter to determine their leaving was not some kind of trick, Luke had returned for Pettigrew. The gang had left behind a single horse, not out of any measure of compassion, but strictly for the sake of enabling someone to ride away and carry word of their demands.

Luke quickly helped Pettigrew get mounted, intending for them to ride double back to the mountain camp where, in addition to the unfortunate news they had to deliver, the wounded man's leg could get some medical attention. Hopefully—either when they got there or on the way—they'd get the chance to reunite with Eagle and Barlow.

Before he joined the burly blacksmith on horseback, however, Luke's ears had picked up the thud of approaching hooves. He'd spun around with drawn guns, thinking a betrayal was in the works after all. But instead, to his surprise and delight, his gaze had fallen on the heavy-chested paint he'd inherited, the one he'd managed to swat away at the start of the ambush in order to save it from the fate of the other horses Ferris's gang mowed down. Now, with the shooting finally over, some sense of loyalty or other instinct was bringing the animal back around and its arrival couldn't have been more timely or welcome.

Mounted individually as a result of the paint's return, Luke and Pettigrew had wasted no more time getting their horses aimed north toward the Spearpoints. Luke set a steady pace but moderated it somewhat in deference to the wounded blacksmith's condition. But no complaining had come from the grim-faced Pettigrew. Luke could barely imagine what it took for the man to bear up under the pain from the bullet holes in his leg, not to mention the added torment at the thought of his son being in the hands of ruthless cutthroats.

In one more badly needed stroke of luck, as the two riders were making their sweep northward and veering away from the badlands, they'd been spotted and hailed by none other than Eagle and Barlow.

The pair had only recently emerged from the broken land, having successfully avoided any encounter with Ferris's flanking attempt on their side, and were making their way across the prairie on the lookout for some of the former ranch horses they hoped to find roaming free.

Being able to double up with Luke and Pettigrew solved their lack of mounts, and after they'd been hit with the gut-punch news about the young couple having been captured by Ferris's bunch, that's how the four of them had proceeded to the mountain camp.

Once there, after Pettigrew was laid out on the big table so Mr. and Mrs. Wray could begin treating his leg wound, Eagle had addressed the others who were assembled, looking on expectantly, awaiting his report. Hugging his wife tight against him with one arm, he spoke in halting, agonized words and told them how Belinda and Heath were now captives of Hacksaw Ferris's pack of curly wolves.

Then he laid out the rest of it, the demands made for getting them released unharmed—that being that he and Luke Jensen lay down their arms and hand themselves over to the gang by noon the following day. Once the two men were in custody, Belinda and Heath would be released and they, along with all the rest of the refugees, would be allowed forty-eight hours of safe passage to completely vacate the valley.

Any who remained after that could expect to be hunted down and killed.

The fate in store for Eagle and Luke was left unspoken.

That was how things stood in the thickening twilight

as the somber-faced group under the canopy was left trying to come to grips with what they'd been told and then reach a decision on what to do in response.

Into the somewhat stunned quiet that hung over the scene following Eagle's report, Jonathan Wray, even as he continued to work on Pettigrew's leg, spoke in a flat, calm voice.

"It's been increasingly obvious for some time," he said, "that the men who invaded our town and valley are violent, merciless vermin. That they represent an allegedly respectable businessman like Parker Dixon makes no difference. It's equally clear that, under the surface, he must be from the same loathsome species— as is his son. In other words, any belief that even a morsel of decency or trustworthiness exists anywhere within that entire group of thieves and killers would be nothing short of lunacy."

"For Christ's sake, Jonathan," grumbled Clarence Copley, formerly the town's highly skilled but cantankerous old cabinet maker, "stow that highfalutin talk and speak plain. You're a leather-stitcher, not a dad-blasted lawyer."

"What my Jonathan is saying, quite plainly enough if you ask me," said Edna Wray, working beside her husband, "is that anyone who thinks those villains can be trusted to uphold any deal they claim to make, is a fool."

Copley tossed up his hands in a frustrated gesture. "Anybody with half a brain knows that. Why didn't you just say it that way, Jonathan?"

Mary Hobart, the widowed mother of Davy Eagle's young friend LeRoy, looked stricken. "Wait a minute. Am I hearing right? Are some of you actually suggesting that we *not* negotiate with those men? They have the children. That's a fact, a terrible one, that we can't ignore."

Still wrapped in the embrace of her husband's arm, Jane Eagle said in a somewhat dulled tone, "Trust me, Mary, no one is ignoring that fact. But the other hard, painful fact is that meeting the demands of the men holding them is no guarantee Belinda and Heath will be released. In fact, if there is any guarantee, it is just the opposite."

"What's more," said Neal Vickers, the badly overweight former barber who'd long had deep but unspoken feelings for Mary Hobart, "if Tom and Mr. Jensen willingly gave themselves up and the gang proves untrustworthy, then everyone will be worse off. Without those two, our chances to defend ourselves and survive would be greatly diminished."

"But what about the promise of safe passage if we cooperate?" Mary wailed.

"That's an even bigger lie than the claim they'd release the kids," said Tom Eagle, speaking for the first time since concluding his report on Ferris's demands. His voice containing an uncharacteristically harsh edge, he added, "If Parker Dixon wants to continue havin' his way, he can no longer afford for any of us to live."

"But hold on," said Howard MacGregor, frowning. "Dixon *has* let families leave safely in the past."

"That was in the beginnin'," Eagle replied, "when Dixon had those lawyer types paradin' around, tryin' to make it all look like business propositions. When that didn't root folks out fast enough, what came next? The killin' and burnin', right? That's what drove all of us here, to this last holdout. And now that he took things that far, Dixon can't ease up and let a couple dozen respectable folks wander away to start talkin' about the things his coyote pack has done."

Now it was Ben Pettigrew who joined in. Propping himself up on one elbow, he said, "Eagle paints a grim picture, but he's telling it straight. I got a firsthand taste of those snakes and I can tell you they're as cold and heartless as exactly that—a nest of snakes. Most of you from around town know that the history of things between me and my son ain't been very good. Something I lay here now mighty ashamed of. I hope it ain't too late to try and make amends for the way I treated him and I'd lay down my life if it meant a way to get him away from Ferris's bunch. But giving in to the demands they're making—that ain't the answer."

His wife Lucille, standing close to where he lay, reached out and placed her hand in his, silently signifying her agreement.

"What is the answer then?" Isobel, one of the spinster Byerly sisters, wanted to know.

When no one else responded right away, Dinah Mercer settled her penetrating gaze on Luke and said, "We haven't heard anything from Mr. Jensen yet. Since he figures prominently in this—one way or another—I think we should find out what he has to say."

Chapter 32

"Do you really think you can put together a plan that will work?"

Luke smiled tolerantly at Dinah's question. "I think there's a reasonable chance, yes, or I wouldn't have suggested it. Contrary to how it might seem from time to time, I'm not suicidal. But whether or not our attempt will succeed, no one can say until it plays out. There's always the risk of something unexpected cropping up, something no amount of advance planning manages to take into consideration."

"You sound like you do this sort of thing frequently."

Luke replied, "If you mean a rescue raid, no, that's not a common thing for me. But if you mean finding myself crossways of unpleasant individuals who, for one reason or other, are bent on doing me harm—then, yeah, I guess that does happen with a fair amount of frequency."

"I have a feeling you wouldn't have it any other way," said Dinah Mercer. "After all, that's your trade—seeking out unpleasant individuals."

"I seek them out to put them behind bars," Luke

told her. "It's up to them how troublesome they want to make being taken into custody. It'd suit me just fine if all of them came along peaceably."

"Well, judging by the scars you've accumulated," Dinah observed, "that appears not to happen very often."

The two of them had repaired again to Dinah's tent where she was once more cleaning and re-dressing Luke's cuts and abrasions from his first meeting with the Ferris gang and then his subsequent encounter with Ol' Rip. He sat with his shirt off, she leaning close to administer the necessary care. Lanterns with their wicks turned up brightly were positioned near on either side.

Outside the tent, full darkness had settled and the movements of others in the encampment could be heard as they went about their business following the breakup of the meeting under the main canopy.

That meeting had ended after Luke, upon being prompted by Dinah, stated his belief that the only chance for Belinda and Heath to ever re-join their families would be if they were forcibly *taken* from their captors. Eagle, Pettigrew, and Barlow had instantly agreed. An intense general discussion involving all present had ensued until, with full sanction from the families of the captive youngsters, the majority also came to favor the idea of Eagle and Jensen putting together a plan for a rescue raid.

But first, both men—along with Barlow and Pettigrew, once the Wrays were done treating the latter—required some time to get themselves collected and cleaned up following their ordeal in the badlands.

They arranged to get together again an hour before midnight in order to finalize preparations.

In response to Dinah's comment about the scars decorating his torso and to a somewhat lesser extent his face, Luke said, "In certain European societies, a scar is considered a badge of honor. It marks the character of a man."

Leaning still closer to apply a fresh dab of salve to Luke's shrapnel-pitted cheek, and with the trace of an impish glint showing in her deep brown eyes, Dinah replied, "That being the case, I guess you'd be considered quite the honorable character in those circles."

Luke was increasingly aware of her nearness. The fresh, soapy, all-over woman scent of her filled his nostrils, overriding even the tang of the salve she was applying.

"I'd like to think I conduct myself with a degree of honor wherever I'm at," he said. Then, a huskiness edging into his voice, he added, "Which leads me to warn you that spending too much time alone with you like this is starting to give me inclinations I fear are *not* strictly honorable."

Dinah stopped dabbing on the salve and the palm of her hand came to rest softly on his cheek. Her eyes boldly meeting his, she said, "Whether or not such inclinations are dishonorable would depend on how they are met, wouldn't you say?"

The touch of her hand sent a warmth coursing through Luke. Still, he protested, "You have a standing, a status, with the people surrounding us. No matter how this situation we're caught up in works out, I'll be moving on, one way or another. But you need to consider having to face the consequences of a reckless, impulsive decision you may regret."

"The people who count, already know and respect me," Dinah said firmly. "Anyone else, I don't give a hang about. I'm an adult woman, a widow, who's had to be strong and on my own for several years now. That means I'm quite capable of making decisions and standing by them. What's more, we both know that before it's over, there's the chance none of us may come out of this thing alive. The only regret I can see myself having is to let this moment pass, to *not* give in to the impulse, even if—"

Luke didn't let her finish. He brushed away the tin of salve Dinah held in one hand, letting it drop to the floor, and pulled her into his arms. Their lips met and held for a long, passionate kiss. Soon the lanterns were turned down to a soft glow and then, entwined once more in an embrace, their lips continuing to urgently, hungrily seek each other's, they sank back together into the deepened shadows . . .

Chapter 33

Hacksaw Ferris lowered the bottle of whiskey from his mouth and emitted a satisfied sigh.

"Now there's some decent corn squeezin's," he declared. "I generally favor rye, but I'm in such a good mood this evenin' that I'm willin' to be more accommodatin'." He set his gaze on the man seated across the table from him. "Sorry we ain't got none of that fancy stuff you got a taste for, Boss. But I'd sure be honored if you'd reconsider and have a touch with us all the same. You know, to sort of celebrate the good fortune that's come our way."

Roland Dixon's return gaze was impassive. "Thanks, but I'll pass on having a drink just now," he said. "And as for the celebrating, I—being a bird in the hand type—suggest it might be a bit premature for that, anyway."

Ferris squinted. "I've got where I can most of the time wrangle out the meanin' in those big words you use, Boss. But every once in a while you still manage to stump me when you string a bunch of 'em together. What's havin' a bird in the hand or anywhere else got to do with anything? And what do you mean by a celebration bein' 'pre-mitcher'?"

"Premature," said Paul Grimsby, the third man sitting at the table. "Means too soon—like counting on something to turn out a certain way before it has time to play out on its own."

"And surely," added Roland, "you've heard the old saying about a bird in the hand being better than two in the bush."

Ferris scowled. "So you're sayin' I'm puttin' too much stock in those brats we got stashed in a room upstairs bein' able to fetch Jensen and that pesky half-breed. Is that it? And you figure Jensen amounted to a 'bird in the hand' when I was tradin' lead with him back there in the badlands—that I shoulda stuck with that instead of switchin' tactics the way I did after Grimsby showed up with the kids. That what you're sayin'?"

"By your own account," Roland reminded him, "Jensen was within twenty or thirty yards of your grasp."

"And you think that meant he was gonna hold nice and still while I waltzed up and glommed onto him, eh?" Ferris bared his teeth in a sneer. "Did you forget the part where I also told you he'd just got done killin' three of my men—one of 'em bein' Dog DeMarist, my best man?"

"You know I never held DeMarist in as high a regard as you, though I'm naturally sorry for the loss of him and the others," Roland said. "But their misfortune doesn't equate to Jensen being some kind of phantom too elusive for *anyone* to capture—especially when Grimsby had just shown up with five more men.

I have to question why, in lieu of giving up the pursuit of Jensen for the sake of using the children as hostages, you didn't take those added men and swarm the area where you knew your quarry to be."

His lips curling with disdain, Ferris said, "You ever been out in those badlands, Mister Dixon? You ever even *seen* 'em?"

"Of course I've seen them."

"Then did you happen to notice how they stretch for miles and miles? Nothing but baked, barren rocks and gullies and ragged peaks over which a man can't be tracked—and a thousand cracks and crevices where he can hide, sometimes where another man could pass within three or four feet and never spot him." Ferris's sneer stayed in place. "Did any of that register with you? Because that's how it is out there. And if I'd taken Grimsby and his boys back out there with me, it *would* have been like chasin' a phantom."

"You managed to find him the first time," Roland pointed out.

"Purely by accident," Ferris grunted. "We was aimin' to flank around on the shooters up front. We wasn't expectin' to run into Jensen and neither was he expectin' us. Once we locked horns, and us bein' hamstrung by our orders to take him alive, it turned lopsided in a hurry even though we started out havin' him outnumbered. He was shootin' to kill, we was returnin' fire only to wound or try to flush him into the open. If I'd gone back in with Grimsby and his boys under those same orders—even if we could've managed to find Jensen again—not a lot of reason to expect it wouldn't have turned into more of the same."

"I'm getting awfully tired of hearing that same old excuse about how you're hampered by the require-ment to take Jensen alive," Roland said petulantly.

"And I'm gettin' awful tired of losin' men on ac-count of it!" Ferris barked back.

This increasingly heated exchange was taking place in what had, until a couple months earlier, been the main room of the Elkhorn Saloon in down-town Hard Rock. It was located on the main street, diagonally across from the one-time more ornate High Plains Palace, the saloon Luke Jensen, strictly by happenstance, had chosen for his fiery confronta-tion with Ferris's men after he first arrived in town. Prior to that, once they'd run off all the honest Hard Rock citizens, Ferris and his curly wolves had claimed the Elkhorn as their hangout while they finished mopping up the rest of the valley.

They'd long since stripped the Palace of all or most of its liquor and other trappings that had any appeal and hauled them over to the Elkhorn, resulting in no real remorse when Jensen left the Palace in flames. General consensus among the gang in the wake of that act, however, was that if *their place* had received such treatment, then there'd be no corner of Montana remote enough for Jensen to hide.

"What's done is done," said Paul Grimsby in a calm, level voice aimed at cutting through the rising tension between Ferris and Roland Dixon. "The thing to remember is that having these two kids as hostages—especially when we know the girl is Tom Eagle's daughter—*does* give us an awful strong bargaining chip, Mr. Dixon. It might prove the best chance we've had yet, especially for taking the men alive."

Roland glared at Ferris, still smarting at having a subordinate talk back to him in a raised voice. Glancing around the room, however—a space filled with lounging, heavily armed men who were putting on a show of acting indifferent while clearly straining to hear every word—it registered with him that this force was made up of men used to backing Ferris. Men accustomed to doing what they were told to do and taking what they were told to take and looking to Ferris to see they got paid for it. And while the pay for their current work originated as Dixon money, that was no assurance they would give any consideration to this fact when it came to where their loyalty lay.

"Very well," Roland said stiffly. "What is done is done, indeed. It appears I have little choice but to join you gentlemen in your fervent belief that using these children as bargaining chips will accomplish the desired results." His gaze lifted to the stairway that led up to a row of doors on the second floor. "You say you have them in a room up there?"

"Uh-huh. That's right."

"I trust you have them adequately secured."

Ferris chuckled throatily. "Secure? Them brats are locked down safer than a gold shipment from your mine—one of the regular ones, I mean, not one of the ones we phonied up to look like it got robbed by Tom Eagle." Then he chuckled some more.

Roland pushed back from the table and stood up. "Very well," he said again. "I need to get back to my quarters at the Gold Button. I'll return here in time for the exchange tomorrow. Noon, correct?"

"That's the way we set it up."

"Let's hope all goes according to plan," Roland said. Then, offhandedly, he added, "Especially so the capture of Jensen can be completed by the time my father arrives later in the day."

This drew a startled reaction from both Ferris and Grimsby, both men jerking suddenly upright in their chairs.

"What's that?" Ferris demanded. "You sayin' your old man is gonna be here tomorrow?"

Roland made little attempt to hide the smugness he felt for having so obviously rattled the gang leader who'd been displaying a belligerent streak just moments earlier. Much as he personally loathed his father, Roland nevertheless marveled at—and didn't hesitate to *use*, when it suited his purpose—the power conveyed by the mere mention of his name.

"Oh," the younger Dixon said now, his attempt at an innocent tone fully transparent, "I guess in all the excitement upon hearing about your hostages and all, I was distracted from mentioning that development before. Be that as it may, as soon as the telegraph line was once again repaired earlier today, I received notice that Father was on his way. It seems he left Helena not long after sending Jensen—apparently displaying some premature confidence of his own that the man would be promptly apprehended on his arrival here."

"Didn't you notify him otherwise?" asked Grimsby.

"I just told you, the telegraph line was down," Roland replied.

"How about after it got to workin' again? Did you

send word about all the trouble we ran into with that devil?" Ferris wanted to know.

Roland spread his hands. "How could I? Father was already on the trail. Where would I send any such notification in hopes of it reaching him?" He paused, continuing to adopt the innocent veneer. "But luckily it turns out to be a moot point, right? Providing, that is, this hostage swap you're so certain of works out like you've been assuring me it would."

"Come on now," growled Ferris. "You've seen how it is with Jensen and Eagle both. Ain't nothing a dead certain thing when it comes to them."

Roland's expression suddenly turned cold and flat. "In that case," he said, shifting his tone to match, "you'd better have some kind of backup plan ready. And while you're explaining it to the old man and hoping he'll even take time to listen, maybe you can also convince him how your failures have all been the fault of his orders to take Jensen alive."

Chapter 34

By midnight they had their plan worked out.

Eagle was seated at the head of the long table under the camp's central canopy, Luke immediately to his right. Clustered close in around them were the rest of the men who would be participating in the rescue raid: Barlow, Howard MacGregor, and the two old prospectors, Isaac Turley and Red Baker.

Also present was an ashen-faced Ben Pettigrew, whose input toward the planning was more than welcome, though he was in no shape to be riding out with the others this time. He would stay behind to be in charge of the camp.

Additionally, the other men who would be remaining behind had respectfully been invited to attend the meeting, though they sat slightly apart from the raid participants, listening, saying little. This group was made up of Jonathan Wray, Clarence Copley, Neal Vickers, and a brooding Dewey Akron. The women of the camp were all in their tents, opting to give their men the time and space they needed to plan the mission, though it was a safe bet that each was listening intently and would come flooding out as soon as things were settled and the meeting started to break up.

Tom Eagle leaned forward now, knuckles planted on the tabletop before him, and swept a somber gaze over those gathered in close as he announced, "Well, I guess that's it then. You've all heard and agreed with how we got things figured, and those of you who'll be riding with us each know what your part will be once we get there. Any final questions?"

His gaze continued its slow sweep, lingering briefly on the face of each man.

"I got a question," said MacGregor. He inclined his head toward distant flickers of lightning in the night sky. "That storm away off yonder. What if it moves in and hits us when we're in the middle of things?"

Eagle didn't say anything. Barlow, his mouth curving into a lopsided grin, answered for him, saying, "Well, Howard, then I reckon what'll happen is that we'll all get a little wet."

Chuckles came from the other men. MacGregor looked flustered for a moment, then ended up joining them. "Okay, okay. I didn't mean for it to sound as dumb as it did. I just wanted to make sure it wouldn't make any difference as far as delaying us or calling things off or anything."

"It'd take a helluva lot more than a little rain," Eagle rasped, "to turn me back from goin' after my daughter."

"Besides," Luke added, "a good thunderstorm would make it harder for our enemies to see or hear us. But at the same time, if it comes to that, we'll also have to deal with those conditions. Meaning it'll be all the more important when things start busting loose for each man to follow his moves as assigned—do *what* you're supposed to do, *when* you're supposed to do it."

"I can't stress strongly enough," spoke up Pettigrew, "that the best chance for pulling this off and keeping your hides intact in the process, is for everybody to listen to Eagle and Jensen. They'll get you through it. I'm beggin' you for your own sake, and for the sake of bringing my boy and Belinda Eagle back with you."

MacGregor regarded him. "We'll do everything in our power to get your boy back, Ben."

Isaac Turley cleared his throat. "That's all well and good," he declared. "Ain't a one of us here not in favor of gettin' back those young'uns who've got themselves in a fix with them lowdown owlhoots. Couldn't be no clearer that we're all chompin' to get at it. But I gotta say one more time that jeopardizin' yet *another* youngster to help get the job done, that plumb sticks in my craw something fierce."

As he finished this statement, the old prospector's troubled gaze came to rest on the narrow space between where MacGregor and Barlow sat with their elbows resting on the table. Within that space, almost lost in the shadows slicing across it, the pale oval of Betty Barlow's face pushed slightly forward. The young tomboy's expression was set in the same stubborn, semi-pugnacious look that all who knew her were used to seeing. She appeared like she wanted to respond to Turley but was holding herself in check.

Somewhat hurriedly, as if he wanted to be sure and speak before his daughter lost her restraint, Whit

Barlow said, "Come on, Isaac. We've already gone through this. I appreciate your concern for my daughter, but doggone it, I'd be the first to try and hold her back if I didn't believe she could do us some good and we could keep her safe."

Not holding back any longer, though in a polite, tolerant tone, Betty herself said, "Thanks for worrying about me, Mr. Turley. But everybody knows I can ride as good or better than anyone in the valley. And I can shoot good, too, if need be."

"Now don't start that," her father was again quick to say. "You're coming along to help with the horses, not get involved in any shooting."

"I'm just saying I'd be willing and able, if it came to that," the girl said stubbornly. "You nearly worked your tail off putting our horse herd together, Pa, and I worked and rode beside you as hard as anybody half again my size, man or boy. I understand that riding out to save Belinda and Heath is our main goal tonight and I understand, too, what my role is. But if I get the chance to sink a slug in one of those lowlife skunks who busted up our herd and caused us to lose our ranch, it's gonna be mighty hard for me not to pull the trigger."

Luke smiled faintly in spite of himself, admiring the girl's spunk. "Nobody will begrudge you a potshot if the opportunity presents itself," he told her. "Just make sure your trigger urge don't get in the way of doing your main job of taking care of our horses."

Betty gave a sharp nod. "I say it won't, it won't."

Luke cut his gaze to the reluctant old prospector. "That goes for you too, Turley. The girl's in, it's already been decided. If you're going to keep fretting

about her, then that means your full concentration
won't be where it belongs. Bullets start flying out there
later on, your mind better be where it's supposed to
be, you hear?"

"You don't need to worry about me, mister," Turley
grunted. "Comes lead slingin' time, both my mind
and aim will be straight!"

"All right then. Anybody else got anything?" Eagle
said, showing signs of impatience.

That was enough to cause MacGregor to hesitate
before he went ahead and said, "Yeah, I got a question. You're putting a lot of faith in the Elkhorn
Saloon as the place where they'll be holding those
kids. What if we hit town and they're not there?"

"The Elkhorn is the only place that makes sense.
Them namin' the main street out front as the spot
where they want to make the trade for Jensen and me
makes it all the more certain," Eagle said confidently.

"But what if, leastways for tonight, they take the
kids somewhere else? Like maybe up to the Gold
Button mine?"

Eagle shook his head. "Hack Ferris's thinkin' ain't
that complicated. Be too much trouble to haul the
kids all the way up to the mine and then back down
again tomorrow for the trade. Besides, I can't see
young Dixon allowin' any part of the dirty dealin's
right in his front yard. He's kept the Gold Button
strictly a minin' operation for the most part, not
lettin' the nastiness takin' place throughout the rest
of the valley reach in. Don't see no reason for him to
change now." The former sheriff set his jaw firmly.
"No, I'm convinced the Elkhorn is where we'll find
the kids. Ferris and his boys have taken it over, made

it their hangout for weeks now. It's where they'll feel the most confident . . . and, because of that, where I'm bettin' we got a chance to find 'em relaxed and least expectin' us."

"That's good enough for me," said Luke. "And if we *should* find something different, then we'll just have to adapt."

Eagle's impatience showed again. "If we're gonna do this, we need to get a move on. Time for everybody to get your gear together and saddled up. We'll head out from the corral area in fifteen minutes."

Half an hour later, they'd emerged from the boulder maze that guarded the entrance to the mountain encampment and were starting across the rolling grassland of the valley. Jensen and Eagle rode at the head of the little column. Barlow and his daughter came next, then MacGregor, then Turley and Baker, all following in a fairly tight group.

Wind gusts from the northwest were growing chillier and more frequent. High overhead, a cold silver moon was still managing to peek through on occasion, but thickening, rapidly skidding clouds blotted it out with increasing frequency.

As they moved along at a steady gait, Luke said to Eagle, "The layout of this saloon we're targeting—I take it you're pretty familiar with it from your peacekeeping days?"

"Way more than I ever wanted to be," Eagle replied sourly. "The Elkhorn was one of those places that just seemed to naturally attract rowdy types. You probably know the kind I mean. Brawls, shootin's, stabbin's were all common occurrences that I got called in to tame down. Guess it stands to reason that it's the kind of joint Ferris and his bunch would flock to and settle in after they ran all the decent folks out of town. Anything higher-toned, like the Palace that you put a torch to, would never be to their taste. Too bad it wasn't the Elkhorn you cut a swath through the other day when you first introduced yourself to that sorry pack."

"I was moving kind of fast so I can't say positively," Luke drawled, "but I'm pretty sure I didn't miss any welcome mats laid out to greet me—only gun muzzles aimed my way."

"Been there myself," said Eagle.

A sudden gust of cold, damp wind whipped down over a grassy knob and cut through the riders with a low moan.

"Getting back to the layout of the Elkhorn," Luke said after the gust had passed. "You think there's any chance that Ferris's men might have changed anything in the time they've been there? Anything that might alter the layout from what you're familiar with?"

Eagle grunted. "No, other than pilin' up empty whiskey bottles and other trash, I can't see them makin' any changes to amount to anything. Layout's pretty basic, don't really see how or why they would. Downstairs there's the main barroom with a store-room and small office behind the bar. Then here's an open stairway that goes up and feeds straight back to a short hall on the second floor with six rooms, three on each side. Closed stairwell at the back that opens directly to an alley. Can't get much simpler than that."

"And glass windows in front, you said, right?"

"One on each side of the batwings. Not big, fancy-lettered ones like the Palace, but sizable enough to see through okay." Eagle cast a sidelong glance over at the bounty hunter. "Something botherin' you?"

"Nothing in particular," Luke said. "Just chewing over some things."

"If you got a chunk of gristle that ain't goin' down, might be best to just spit it out," Eagle suggested.

Luke gave it a moment, then said, "Okay. It makes sense for them to have the kids at the Elkhorn, just like you said. But not having a better idea exactly *where* in the building they're being held is gnawing at me some."

"They'll be in one of the rooms upstairs, right? Probably one of the middle ones. Hardest place for anybody to get at, ain't that how we figured it?" Eagle's tone was very earnest, that of someone trying hard to be convincing—maybe in part to himself. "With guards at each end of the hall and men also likely in some or all of the other rooms. Plus whoever we'll find passed out—almost a certainty at three o'clock in the mornin'—downstairs in the barroom. Maybe a guard or two down there as well, though at that hour I wouldn't expect much in the way of them bein' on real sharp lookout."

"They might be sloppy, lowlife scum. But no matter what else they are or aren't, they're a gang of ruthless killers. We need to be sure to keep that in mind and not take anything about them too lightly," Luke advised.

Eagle scowled in his direction. "You think you need to remind me of that? Me, of all people? If I sound like I'm takin' the actions of this pack of vermin too lightly, it's only because I know 'em so well from trackin' and watchin' 'em over the past two months. Yeah, they might be dangerous and even cunning. But I'm tellin' you they're also lazy and not overly bright. That's why I'm bettin'—with my own daughter's life on the line—that their little pea brains ain't in no way expectin' or ready for us to show up tonight and hit 'em right in their own stronghold."

"I hope you're right," Luke told him. "But no matter how big our element of surprise, simply storming the joint and trying to safely pull the kids out of the middle of the building with gunfire on all sides . . . that's going to be mighty tricky."

The anger left Eagle's scowl, replaced by intense concern and curiosity. "So what else is there? You got something in mind?"

Luke's expression turned brooding. "I don't know yet. I'll know better after I've had the chance to give that saloon a good looking over."

Another howling gust passed over them.

"Appears more and more like you're gonna have to do that looking through a hard rain," Eagle observed.

"Fine by me. I'd welcome it," Luke replied grimly.

Chapter 35

"You awake, Belinda gal?" Heath Pettigrew's voice was low and hushed in the near total darkness.

Frequent gusts of wind rattled the room's single window a few feet away. Now and then, the flicker of distant lightning lanced through the filmy curtain and very briefly diminished the deep shadows with short bursts of illumination.

"Of course I'm awake. How could I sleep under these awful conditions?" came Belinda Eagle's tense response.

Heath wished he could see her, wished he could look on her lovely face. Although, at the same time, he knew the anguish he surely would find there—the same anguish he could hear in her voice—would only pain him more. Under almost any other circumstances imaginable, having her so close, pressed tight against him, the warmth and scent of her filling his senses, would have been wonderful and satisfying. But not now, not this way . . . The two of them trussed together, back to back, their hands and feet bound individually and then still more wraps of coarse rope lashing them into a bundle then tossed onto the filthy bed where they could do nothing but wait and wonder.

Heath whispered again, "Up until a few minutes ago, the way you were breathing, I thought you *had* fallen asleep. I wished you had, so you could escape from all of this, at least for a little while."

"I . . . I guess I was, actually," replied Belinda after a moment. "I don't know how I managed it, but you're right. It was a relief for the precious little while it lasted."

"Good. I'm glad for that much," Heath said.

"I'm sorry if I was testy with you when you first asked me."

"It's all right. These *are* awful conditions and you have every right to be testy and more," Heath groaned. "Belinda, I can't tell you how sorry I am that I got you into this fix."

"Don't do that to yourself," Belinda was quick to say. "We're in this fix because of decisions we made together. You're no more to blame than I am."

"But I'm supposed to be the man," Heath protested. "A man takes a woman for his wife, he's supposed to protect her, take care of her no matter what! And look how far I got. Those dirty skunks came out of the rocks back at Balfour Pass and clunked me on the head and I never got even a lick in against 'em. Some fine protector I am. And now here we are, hogtied like a couple sides of beef ready for the barbecue spit."

"We're still alive, aren't we?" Belinda countered. Then, realizing her response had been sharp and perhaps a little too loud, she fell silent, listening intently for any sound out in the hallway that might indicate she'd drawn the attention of one of their captors. Thankfully, the late night quiet surrounding them was broken only by another gust of wind rattling the window.

When she felt it was safe to speak again, Belinda said in a more subdued whisper, "As long as we're alive, there's hope. You've got to remember and believe that. And me, too. I need to keep from feeling sorry for myself and you need to quit blaming yourself."

"Those are good words. Brave and inspiring and all," allowed Heath, trying to sound stirred by them but coming across decidedly flat. "Only trouble is, they don't do a doggone thing to loosen these ropes holding us down. And until that changes, we're at the mercy of Hack Ferris and his thugs and whatever they got in mind for us."

"We already know what that is," Belinda reminded him. "They're hoping to trade us for my father and Mr. Jensen."

"Your father's too smart for that," Heath said. "He's got to know he can't trust the likes of Ferris. Still, his love for you might be enough for him to go ahead and take the risk in order to save you."

Belinda said, "That's hardly a comforting thought— that my father might be trading his life for mine."

"It's like I was saying before about a man doing whatever it takes to protect the women in his life," Heath replied. "That goes for daughters as well as wives."

"And it goes for a man protecting others in his life, too," Belinda said pointedly.

"What do you mean?"

"You know darn well what I mean. That voice down

in the rocks when Ferris was making his demands on the trade for us . . . that was your father, Heath, and you darn well know it."

Heath didn't answer right away. Then: "It sounded like him. But I'm havin' trouble wrappin' my head around it. Him climbing on a horse, coming all that way for . . . well, for us. Even after we did what we did."

"For you," Belinda corrected. "For his son. No matter what you'd done."

Heath was quiet again, until he said, "It's hard to picture him doing that. I don't quite know what to think. But I'm glad he made it through that ambush okay."

"So am I," Belinda said. "I can't lie, I want desperately to be saved somehow. I want both of us to be safe and still have the future together we dreamed about. But, no matter what, I don't want those things to come at the cost of anybody else's life."

Heath ached with wanting to hold her, to comfort her. But all he could do was say, "I hear you, gal. But I'm sorry to say it ain't in our hands how any of that turns out."

Paul Grimsby finished closing and latching the outside door of the Elkhorn Saloon's front entrance, blocking the wind howling increasingly stronger out in the street and halting the irritating way it was causing the batwings to slap back and forth.

"There," he announced, turning back to the main barroom of the establishment. "Crazy weather! Hot enough to fry an egg out on the rocks of those badlands earlier today and now that wind is colder than a mother-in-law's kiss."

Sprawled back in a chair pulled up to a table in the middle of the room, Hacksaw Ferris grunted around a lopsided grin.

"What would you know about a mother-in-law's kiss, cold or otherwise, you backdoor rascal? In order to have a mother-in-law, you'd first have to have a bride— and what gal would ever marry the likes of you?"

"You'd be surprised," Grimsby replied as he sauntered back to hitch up his own chair at the table. "Been many a filly over the years who was ready to fluff up a bed, hang lace curtains, and go to settin' up housekeepin' with yours truly if I'd've popped the question."

"Haw! Long as you keep mixin' loco weed with your liquor, I reckon you're apt to go right on havin' such far-fetched dreams," Ferris said, reaching for a half full whiskey bottle in front of him. From it, he poured generous slugs of amber liquid into a nearby pair of glasses, then placed the bottle upright again. "Stick to who-hit-John all by its lonesome, maybe with some beer now and then, you'll keep a lot clearer head. Once your skull quits poundin' the next morning, that is."

"Sound advice, no doubt," allowed Grimsby. "If I had a nickel for every time I heard it, I'd be a very wealthy man." He took a sip of his whiskey and then lowered it, chuckling. "And if I had another nickel for every time I failed to follow it, I'd be even wealthier."

Both men guffawed dutifully at the admission. The half-drained bottle of whiskey standing between them was obviously not the first they had shared this night.

The clock on the wall behind the bar showed a few minutes past two. All around Ferris and Grimsby, amidst a generous array of empty whiskey bottles, other members of their gang were sprawled in corners, on benches, one fellow atop the pool table—each enjoying some well-oiled slumber in the wake of the celebrating they had decided was warranted. The ragged sound of their snoring rivaled the low rumble of the slowly approaching thunder outside.

"Speakin' of pounding skulls," Ferris said, his gaze sweeping over the scene, "it looks like there's gonna be quite a contest come mornin' as far as who's gonna be sufferin' the worst one. But they'd better be quick about shakin' off the effects and have themselves in shape for the big trade tomorrow, or I'll be doin' me some skull-bustin' that'll make their hangovers seem like cases of the sniffles."

"Aw, they'll come out of it okay. They always do," said Grimsby. "Lookin' forward to that trade. Bein' able to hand over the Jensen hombre *and* that pain-in-the-ass Tom Eagle, puttin' 'em right in the hands of the he-bull Parker Dixon hisself—that's what gave 'em good cause to celebrate. And us, too, Hack, no matter snot-nosed Roland's pukey little remarks about bein' premature."

"I know that," Ferris grumbled. "Roland can go stand in a corner for all I care. I just got a twinge of guilt, I guess, for holdin' a shindig like this with Dog DeMarist havin' so recently bit the dust out there in those badlands. I liked Ol' Dog. I'm gonna miss him."

"All of us are," Grimsby told him. "And Dog would be the first one to tell you not to feel guilty or hold back just because his time came due. You know he would."

Ferris continued to glare down into his glass for another minute before a corner of his mouth abruptly lifted in a wry smile. "Yeah, Ol' Dog was always quick to look for a reason to celebrate, no denyin' that." After tossing down its remains, he brought the emptied glass back down to the tabletop with a loud thump. "Reckon it's time for me and you to grab a few hours of shut-eye ourselves, so we're in shape for the doin's tomorrow."

"I'll drink to that," said Grimsby, draining his own glass.

Ferris's gaze swung across the room to the stairs that led up to the second floor. "But if I take to sawin' logs for a spell, I got a concern about one of these hungover horned toads wakin' up with a notion to sneak in a visit to that little gal up there. I've seen the way they all look at her, even though I put her strictly off limits."

"Kinda hard to blame 'em for looking," said Grimsby. "She's a little young for my tastes, but you got to admit she's showing all the parts of a full-growed woman."

"That's no excuse," Ferris growled. "It's important she stays unsullied for when we trot her out in front of her old man tomorrow."

"I get that."

"Who've you got up there guardin' that upstairs hallway?"

"I got Pinkeye Scarns at the back end. Got to admit, him I wouldn't trust around a woman no farther than I can throw this building," said Grimsby. "But up front, closest to the door of the room where we stowed the girl and her boyfriend, I put Clarence Horn. Horn is as solid as a rock. You tell him how you want something, that's the way you'll get it."

Ferris nodded. "Good. I trust Horn. Now I can rest easy for some shut-eye. Got me a cot in that office behind the bar, I'm gonna sack out there. Suggest you find a spot and do the same. See you again an hour or so past sunup."

Chapter 36

"Well? You've had your up-close look. Bring to mind anything else on how you want to go about this?" Tom Eagle wanted to know.

"Matter of fact, I think so," answered Luke, continuing to study the tall, well-lighted building across the street. A battered slab of wood painted with the word ELKHORN was suspended on short chains above the front door. The steadily gusting wind that whipped down Hard Rock's main drag was buffeting this sign mercilessly, the overworked lengths of chain clinking and squawking above the howl of the gusts.

"Those second floor windows," Luke said, pointing. "There's one for each of the rooms you said we'd find up there, three to a side."

"Uh-huh," agreed Eagle. "But they're about fifteen up from the ground. So what are you gettin' at?"

"Fifteen feet from the ground," Luke echoed, "but only about three feet down from the edge of that flat roof right above."

The bounty hunter and the former sheriff were crouched in a pool of deep shadows that filled the mouth of a narrow alley diagonally across the street from the Elkhorn Saloon. The others were strung out behind them, keeping still and quiet.

Though no rain was falling yet, the sky overhead was roiling with purple-black clouds out of which regularly issued pitchforks of brilliant lightning and ominous rumbles of thunder.

"If a couple of men made it to that roof," Luke continued, "they could drop ropes over the side and have pretty easy access to any of those rooms—in particular, in case I'm not making myself clear, the middle one on each side. Since we're likely to find the youngsters in one of those rooms, that would put one of us right in there with them and another just across the hall."

"Just bust through those windows, you mean?"

"That would be the quickest way."

Eagle frowned. "You think the storm will be loud enough to hide the noise of that?"

"Not counting on the storm," Luke replied. "I've got in mind a bigger distraction, one that would panic those holed-up rats, especially any of the ones caught upstairs. Something they wouldn't immediately recognize as an attempt to get the kids and therefore something that would delay the start of any shooting. Whoever ended up in the room with Belinda and Heath could use that delay to get them to the window and down to the ground using the same rope dropped from the roof earlier. Betty Barlow could be waiting down below with horses to get all three of 'em clear, hopefully ahead of the fireworks that are bound to come next."

"You make it all sound mighty slick." A flutter of lightning showed Eagle's eyes regarding Luke intently. "I think I got a hunch what's comin', but go ahead and tell me. What's gonna provide this big distraction you figure will throw the rats into such an obliging panic?"

Luke grinned as he jerked a thumb over his shoulder to indicate the burned-out Palace Saloon they were crouched next to. "My old friend fire," he said. "It worked pretty good for me against that coyote pack once, I think there's enough luck left in it for another round."

Twenty minutes later, the rescuers had regrouped in a grove of trees two dozen yards behind the Elkhorn Saloon. Stabs of lightning cast everything in stuttering bursts of illumination as wind whipped branches wildly back and forth above the heads of the group. Three horses tied to the trunks of the trees skittered and chuffed nervously.

Turley and Baker and the rest of the horses were not here. Those horses were tied at the back of the alley than ran alongside the Palace. The old prospectors had taken up positions out front of the Elkhorn, in shadows just back from each corner of the saloon. Armed with double-barreled shotguns, they were primed to shred the front windows with twelve gauge loads and then follow them in with intent to sweep clean the whole barroom.

At the rear, while Luke, Eagle, and MacGregor looked on, Whit Barlow and his daughter Betty were

advancing toward the building, twirling the widening
loops of lassos as they walked. Each had their eyes
lifted to a point on the corners of the roof where a
rather ornate cornice design featured molded knobs
over which they meant to drop their loops. Almost
simultaneously, as if at some unseen signal, father and
daughter threw their lassos and each snugly captured
their target. After a couple of final tugs to make sure
the catch would hold, the pair left the ropes hanging
and turned to hurry back to the grove.

"There are your stairways to the top," Barlow said
somewhat breathlessly to Luke and Eagle.

Luke nodded. "The lightning flashes will enable
you to see well enough to track our progress. Once
we get the ropes re-attached somewhere, you'll spot
us dropping them down over the sides at the center
windows. As soon as you see that, make your move on
the real stairway—the one inside."

"I jimmied the lock on that back door so you'll
have no trouble getting through it," Eagle said,
sweeping his gaze over Barlow and MacGregor. "Once
inside, there's a small landing at the bottom of a steep
stairwell. You won't have much room so you'll need
to be careful not to make too much noise with your
equipment. I suspect there'll be a guard in the hall at
the top of the stairs."

The equipment he referred to sat on the grass at
the men's feet, a gallon jug of kerosene and two open
pails filled with bits of kindling wood and straw.

"The next tricky part will be, once you've got
flames lickin' up the walls real good, to squeeze past

'em and make it partway up the stairs so you're ready for when the excitin' part kicks in."

"Relieved to hear that," MacGregor said sarcastically. "I was afraid I was going to get bored waiting on those stairs with nothing to do but keep the pesky flames swatted off my backside."

"The wind and thunder that will help cover any sounds we make on the roof or those back stairs," Luke said, "is going to work against us when it comes to hearing the ruckus that'll break out as soon as somebody realizes there's a fire. So we'll have to listen close in order to use that as the key for our next moves. That's when Eagle and I will go down and in through the windows. You two"—indicating Barlow and MacGregor—"are bound to be sighted when those hall guards come to the stairwell to investigate the fire. You'll have to shoot your way up from there and the sound of your gunfire will signal Turley and Baker to go to work from the street. Watch for Eagle and me to join you in the hallway as soon as the kids are down, then the four of us will make our way out the front."

"You make that trip out the front sound mighty easy," remarked Barlow.

"It's not likely to be any more intense than in that hallway. The two old-timers will be covering us from the street and their shotguns ought to have the way partly cleared by the time we start down to the barroom," Luke reminded him. Then his gaze shifted to Betty. "And as soon as you spot Belinda and Heath being lowered from one of the windows, you bring the horses up in order to get them—and yourself—away from here. No matter what you hear behind you, don't slow down or stop. Ride as hard as you can straight back to camp and wait for us there."

"I know my job," the young girl assured him.

Luke grinned. "I know you do. And if you ride like you throw a lasso, you'll do it just fine."

"That's right," added Eagle. "If not for you and your pa, it might've taken me all winter to make those rope tosses."

Luke cocked an eyebrow at him. "Well, now that they've been made, I hope you're faster than that at climbing up one of them."

"You want to make it a race?" came the challenge.

Luke waved him off. "I'll settle for making it to the roof without either one of us breaking our necks. Come on."

Scaling the corner of the building, Luke discovered, was somewhat less difficult than he expected. Not easy by any means, but his raw physical strength combined with the niches he was able to find in the structure that provided adequate toeholds made the ascent steady and even fairly rapid.

Even so, he was breathing hard by the time he pulled himself up over the edge, and despite the cold wind lashing him, there was sweat dripping down inside his shirt. He rolled out onto the flat roof and lay there for just a moment, knowing he couldn't afford the luxury of completely catching his breath.

Pushing up into a crouch, Luke looked around and saw that Eagle, too, had made it up over the edge. When Eagle glanced in his direction, the pair exchanged silent nods of acknowledgment and then quickly turned to the task of pulling up the dangling ropes.

With the coiled rope over his shoulder and still in a half-crouch, Luke catfooted toward the middle of the roof where a sturdy brick chimney—presumably rising from a large central stove or fireplace below—thrust up obligingly. Eagle chose the same target for re-fastening his rope, and one after the other, they dropped their loops over it.

The two men regarded each other for just a moment as lightning flickered overhead.

"We're not leaving here without your daughter," Luke said.

"My sentiments exactly," replied Eagle.

Then they backed away in opposite directions and seconds later were dropping their ropes over the sides of the building.

Chapter 37

Luke knelt at the edge of the roof, just back from the ornate cornice. His mind raced. He wished he didn't have this lag time, the waiting for Barlow and MacGregor to set their fire. Time in which to think, to question the changes he'd made to the original plan. All the shooting that was bound to ensue with the kids in the heart of the building and therefore right in the middle of it had seemed far too risky. What they had underway now was definitely less so . . . *if* the timing was right and if each individual component clicked the way it was supposed to.

Luke listened intently, hoping hard to hear the first shout of alarm, willing the flames that would produce such a response to spread rapidly.

It seemed to be taking Barlow and MacGregor a long time . . .

Luke realized he was gripping the rope so hard that his right hand was starting to cramp around it. He switched to his left and shook the right, loosening it, flexing the fingers to work out the stiffness.

Then, finally, he heard it. Faintly at first, muted by

the howling wind and the intervening layers of roof and ceiling and walls. A frantic voice, words unintelligible. Then louder, accompanied by the thump of running feet and fists pounding on doors. And then the words that told it all: "Fire! Fire!"

Luke lunged from his kneeling position. He dropped momentarily onto his rump, swinging his legs over the side. Then, twisting his body so that he was facing inward toward the building, he pushed back over the edge and began lowering himself hand over hand down the rope. His feet kicked away from the structure in short hops as he dropped down.

When he was level with the window, he kicked away a little harder and shifted his body pendulum-like so that he was centered on the rectangular opening. He steadied himself there briefly, feet planted on the sill below the pattern of four glass panes separated into equal-sized sections by strips of flimsy wood dividers. Then he straightened his legs in the hardest kick so far, swinging his body five feet out and away. When the arc of the swing ended and he started to go in reverse, back toward the window, he lifted his feet and thrust his boot heels straight ahead.

As expected, the barrier of cheap glass and flimsy wood offered barely any resistance. The wood splintered and broke, the panes of glass shattered and fell clattering, partly into the room, partly down the outside of the building. Luke's forward momentum was barely slowed. He sailed into the darkened room and tumbled, swatting away a tangle of filmy curtains and dropping immediately into a short roll. He felt a few stabs of pain in his left shoulder, the one he lowered to take the weight of the roll, as shards of broken glass sliced in. But he could tell instantly that the cuts were nothing serious.

In a hurry to get his feet under him once more, Luke reached out in the darkness, hoping to grab something to help balance himself. His hand closed on the iron frame of a bed's footboard.

At the same time, the deep, gargling rumble of a snore came from just beyond the footboard, and with it was issued the unmistakable stink of exhaled breath that had been liberally soused in rotgut whiskey.

So, in that moment, Luke knew two things: He hadn't arrived in the room where the youngsters were being held captive, but he *was* in the presence of at least one of their captors, a varmint who was sprawled in an obligingly drunken slumber.

What was more, judging by the boom of shotguns coming from outside the room and down in the direction of the barroom, along with the crackle of additional gunfire that had started up directly out in the hall, other pieces of his plan sounded like they were happening as intended.

Now, if Eagle's entry into the other middle room, the one directly across the hall, had succeeded in finding the kids, then everything would really be clicking into place.

All of this flashed through Luke's mind in a fraction of a second. And even as he thought it, he knew things might be going good for the moment, but there was a long way to go before this was over and all hides—the ones that mattered—were still intact.

Luke's attention swung to the snoring hombre on the bed. All he could make out in the lightning flashes that stabbed through the window was a lumpy shape, a long, large one. Whoever this drunken slob was, this human snake who hired out to cold-bloodedly kill and ravage for the likes of Hack Ferris and Parker Dixon, Luke didn't have to contemplate long before making the icy decision that here was a hide that did *not* matter.

He was in the act of rising to his feet, meaning to move around to the side of the bed, his right hand already drifting toward one of his Remingtons, when the door suddenly burst open.

"Roust up! Roust up, blast it! We got a bad fire spreadin' out here!" squawked the spindly, frog-faced figure who filled the doorway.

The figure hollered this toward the lump on the bed. But even as the last words tumbled from his mouth, he noticed Luke straightening up at the foot of the bed.

"Who in blazes are you?" the gunman demanded, starting to raise the rifle he was holding.

"The last person you're going to see this side of hell," Luke answered. And then the hand that had been only drifting toward the Remington was suddenly filled with the big revolver and its muzzle was spitting flame and death.

The two slugs that it hurled in rapid succession slammed into the man and jerked his body into a crazy spin even as it was flung back hard against the door on the opposite side of the hall. The frail, cheaply made slab of wood popped open with a crackling of splinters and the dead man dropped through the opening like a sack of mail tossed from a freight car.

"Wha-what? Did somebody say fire?"

The room was now filled with illumination from the hallway. Whipping his head around, Luke saw the big man on the bed rearing up, clawing to get untangled from his blankets. His hair was standing on end and his bloodshot eyes were wild, confused. But when those eyes landed on Luke, the confusion suddenly left them, replaced by a split second of suspicion giving way to instant, raw anger.

There was a holstered gun on the nightstand. The big man made a grab for it. Turning only slightly from his stance in the doorway, Luke drew his left-hand Remington and reaching almost casually across his body triggered a single round that snapped the big man's head back and caused his upper body to follow in a heavy flop that left him once more prone and motionless with outflung arms dangling limply over the sides of the mattress.

Outside the room, in addition to the shots Luke had just added, the sound of gunfire was crashing and roaring from all directions, high and low. Acrid black smoke from the stairwell fire rolled forward, curling down from the hallway ceiling. Mingled in it were layers of powder smoke from the numerous blazing weapons.

But through the noise and smoke, courtesy of his room's door standing ajar and the one across the way likewise knocked open and blocked that way by the first gunman's body, Luke saw a heartening sight: Tom Eagle, frantically cutting away ropes that had been binding his daughter and Heath Pettigrew. Not only were the youngsters there in the room, but they looked to be unharmed and in relatively good shape.

Eagle's eyes darted in Luke's direction. Seeing the bounty hunter was okay and there was no immediate threat at hand, he quickly returned his focus to the task of pulling away the now-loosened ropes his knife had sliced through. Both Belinda and Heath were also helping, struggling and yanking to free themselves the rest of the way.

Chapter 38

Bullets continued to sizzle back and forth the length of the hall and the intermittent roar of shotguns exchanging fire with pistols and rifles downstairs assailed Luke's ears as well.

Luke dropped to one knee, placing his head at an unexpected level, and made some quick peeks around the door frame on either side, assessing the situation out in the hall. It wasn't particularly good, but it could have been worse. Barlow and MacGregor were in doorways toward the rear, leaning out at intervals to trade lead with three owlhoots at the front of the hall.

One of the latter was also in a doorway, a second was firing from back around the corner of the small landing at the mouth of the hall, the third was sprawled on the steps of the open stairway that led down to the barroom, popping up periodically to trigger a long-barreled Colt over the body of a fallen comrade that he was using for cover. Farther back toward the rear of the hall, lay another dead man and beyond him the flames from the back stairs were leaping and crackling higher as they licked hungrily up and forward.

Luke straightened up and called out, "Barlow! MacGregor! Are you okay?"

"We won't be for much longer, not with that fire closing in on us so fast—and MacGregor has been hit in the leg!" came the response from Barlow.

"How bad is it?"

"I'll be okay," MacGregor answered for himself.

"But he ain't gonna stay that way—not with all the blood he's losing," amended Barlow.

Luke's gaze returned to the room across the way. The youngsters were completely free of their ropes now and Eagle had them crowded over to the window. Heath was already out over the sill, hanging on the rope with one hand while reaching to assist Belinda with the other.

A pair of bullets skimmed across the frame of Luke's doorway, digging furrows in the wood and throwing a spray of splinters. Luke was far enough back so that it had no effect except to annoy him.

Calling once more to Barlow and MacGregor, the bounty hunter said, "Hang on just a minute longer, but get set. Eagle and I will give you cover to move forward. Can you double-time as far as the next room, MacGregor—the one across from me?"

"I'll do my best."

"I'll drag him if I have to," said Barlow.

"Good. If you make it that far," Luke said, "then you can help him out the window and down the rope too! You two get on across the street, to the horses— then get out of here. Back to the camp where that leg can be taken care of!"

"What about you and Eagle?"

"Don't worry about us," Luke told him. "We've still

got Turley and Baker covering us from the front and we've still got some rats to finish exterminating down in that barroom!"

In the room opposite his, Luke could see that Belinda and Heath were both out the window and had dropped from sight. Eagle leaned out, gazing down on their descent for a moment, then he spun and came rushing up to the doorway.

Luke called over to him. "You hear what I just said?"

Eagle nodded. "Enough."

Luke's eyes bored into him. "You with me?"

Eagle's gaze came back, just as intense. "All the way."

At that exact moment the flaming back stairwell gave way, collapsing in a prolonged rumble that shook the whole building as it belched a spark-infused cloud of boiling, choking black smoke. The cloud billowed upward and forward, rolling the length of the hallway and creating a smoke screen that couldn't have been better timed.

"Now!" Luke hollered to Barlow and MacGregor.

Without taking time to see if his command was obeyed, Luke leaned out of his doorway with both arms extended and a .44 fisted at the end of each. As fast as he could cock and squeeze the triggers, he began pouring lead toward the three hombres at the front of the hall. The swirling, choking smoke made clear vision next to impossible but accuracy, in this case, was secondary to keeping the varmints pinned down and not throwing lead at Barlow and MacGregor as they made their move. In his doorway, Eagle was doing the same, though with a single pistol.

As his Remington hammers began clicking on empty

chambers, from the corner of his eye Luke saw Barlow and MacGregor lurch and stumble through Eagle's doorway. They nearly fell over the prone form of the dead man but managed to maintain their footing. And then, with Barlow half supporting, half dragging his companion, they stumbled toward the window. The smoke hadn't poured as thickly into the room as it was out in the hall, so Luke could follow their progress fairly well.

As he nimbly reloaded the Remingtons, he called over to Eagle. "Help them get started down. I'll pour another round at our friends up front while you're taking care of that, then it will be our turn to take advantage of this smoke screen."

"Just don't kill 'em all until I get the chance to join in," Eagle said before turning to go assist the men at the window.

Just as Luke finished reloading his guns, one of the varmints at the end of the hall—evidently having heard his remark about using the smoke screen—shouted out, "You come right ahead and see what it gets you! Smoke don't stop bullets!"

Keying on the man's voice and simultaneously catching sight of a blurred shape through a sliver of separation in the churning black clouds, Luke fired his right-hand Remington and was rewarded by hearing a sharp yelp of pain and seeing the blurred shape jerk away. "Nope, it sure don't," Luke drawled.

By the time Luke had emptied his wheels again and was once more reloading, Eagle reappeared in the opposite doorway. "You ready?" he wanted to know.

The fire at the rear of the hall was crackling higher and louder and the smoke rolling ahead of it was still plenty thick, but not as much so as a couple minutes earlier. Luke gritted his teeth and said, "Ain't going to be no better time. Let's go!"

Together the two men surged from their respective doorways and started down the hall, bent forward in low crouches, guns blazing, throwing a wall of lead ahead of themselves. Opposing lead was sent to greet them, bullets ripping the air high and low, sometimes missing by mere inches, other times gouging the walls a foot off target. The distance to cover was only a few yards, though in the roiling, blinding smoke it seemed more.

Rushing headlong through the poor visibility, Luke ended up inadvertently running straight into one of the owlhoots—the man who'd been firing from the front doorway on the bounty hunter's side of the hall. Their bodies collided hard, making a meaty thud. Luke's momentum drove the other man back against the door frame, a loud grunt of pain and a mouthful of sour breath exploding out of him.

But that didn't mean the fight was out of him. Gasping a curse, he swung up one arm and tried to club the gun he was holding against the side of Luke's head. Luke jerked back in time to take only a glancing blow from the attempt, and then responded with his left-hand Remington in the true manner a gun was made for—at point-blank range, the muzzle of the big revolver roared and the slug it discharged blew apart the would-be clubber's heart.

The suddenly limp body of the now dead cuss was unable to slide to the floor right away because Luke was, for the moment, still jammed against him, holding him pinned upright against the door frame. Out of the corner of his eye, Luke saw the remaining second floor gang member, the one who'd been shooting from behind the corner of the landing, suddenly fly backward, throwing his arms wide, as he took a bullet from Eagle. The man staggered a half step and then pitched into a lifeless heap practically on top of the body that already lay just above the lip of the open stairway—the body the shooter previously firing from the steps had been using for cover.

This gave Luke an idea. Momentarily holstering his Remingtons, he grabbed the man he'd just killed by a double handful of shirtfront, then jerked him from the doorway and dragged him forward until he was close enough to give his limp form a hard shove to send it flopping down onto the dead sprawls of the other two men.

Drawing his Remys again, Luke gave Eagle a sidelong glance and said somewhat breathily out the corner of his mouth, "Now we've got us a barricade to shoot from behind." Then he moved forward and dropped in behind the low wall of carcasses.

"I'll be damned," Eagle muttered. A moment later, wearing a rake-hell grin, he fell in beside Luke.

Their hard-won vantage point gave them their first look at what the situation was down in the barroom below. The smoke rolling out from the hallway was drifting down, mingling with a haze of powder smoke already present in the air down there, but the larger, higher-ceilinged room was able to absorb much of it and leave details only slightly murky, at least for the moment.

The glass of the front windows bordering the

batwing doors had long since been blasted into nonexistence and Turley and Baker were still at work on the outside, throwing intermittent shotgun blasts through each gaping opening. At least four lifeless, badly shredded recipients of those blasts decorated the floor of the barroom. Five other gang members appeared still alive—two returning fire from behind the bar, one from behind the pool table, and two others from behind overturned round-topped card tables whose splintered, pellet-pocked surfaces indicated they were barely providing adequate cover.

None of these five men seemed as yet to have realized that their upstairs cohorts had just been wiped out. Even worse for them would be when they realized that their current positions, which provided cover against the shotgunners outside the windows, gave them virtually no protection from the two men now poised above them at the top of the stairway.

"This is gonna be like shootin' fish in a barrel," Eagle growled in a low whisper. "And the first bloated carp I mean to bag is Hack Ferris squattin' there behind the bar."

"There's only one problem with that," Luke said.

Eagle scowled. "What do you mean? You're not gettin' cold feet on me, are you? We're sittin' on the brink of exterminatin' this whole nest of rats—the very words I heard you use just a few minutes ago."

"Yeah, and that would be a huge step toward solving your trouble. I understand that and I'll go along if it's the only way," Luke allowed. "But, if there's any chance, I'd sure like to take Ferris alive, at least long enough to try and find out what's behind this whole business about Dixon setting me up the way he did."

Eagle opened his mouth to respond but what he meant to say never got the chance to be spoken. Because it was stopped by an enraged roar and the slap of heavy boots pounding the floor directly behind him and Luke. Both men whirled around to see what was happening.

What met their startled eyes was the sight of a huge, wild-eyed man appearing as if born from the tumbling smoke. He was rushing toward them in lumbering strides, arms outstretched, fingers curled into claws, lips bared in an animal snarl. Blood poured from a gash high on his head, above his right eye. Only Luke, in the fraction of a second he had before the giant left his feet and threw all of his momentum and crushing weight into a pulverizing tackle, recognized who he was—the man from the bed in the room where Luke had first entered. The man Luke had thrown a quick shot at as the hombre was reaching for a gun on the nightstand. The way the skunk's head had snapped back and he'd flopped down so motionless, Luke thought he was dead . . . but he'd failed to make sure.

And now, the bounty hunter told himself with a curse, both he and Eagle were going to pay the price for that oversight.

The giant barreled into them like a locomotive. The impact slammed them through the barricade of dead bodies and the whole grisly entanglement—the dead, the living, and the should-have-been-dead—all went rolling and tumbling down the stairs. A boot heel at the end of a loosely whipping leg crashed across Luke's teeth and the breath was driven out of him by the edge of a step sinking deep into his gut. Even though he felt he deserved the punishment, he fought fiercely to stay conscious and keep hold of his guns. If he could do those two things he still had a chance to make amends, he told himself.

But then another boot heel, even heavier this time, came out of nowhere and clubbed savagely across his temple. He instantly lost his fight to stay conscious and, though he had no awareness of it, so did his numbed fingers lose their grip on the Remingtons . . .

Chapter 39

"When we saw the sheriff and that Jensen fella come a-rumblin' tumblin' down those stairs and they ended up conked out cold," Red Baker was explaining, his weathered old face wearing a long, sad expression, "that's when Turley went a little crazy. Instead of hangin' back and firin' in through his window like he'd been doin', he went a-chargin' straight through those batwings, cussin' a blue streak and blastin' away with his shotgun like he meant to wipe out all the rest of Ferris's varmints in one big charge . . . but he didn't make it. Barely took two or three steps afore he got riddled to pieces. One of the rounds split his stubborn old head like an ax blade goin' through a gourd. He hit the floor and I knew he wasn't never gettin' back up again, so I . . . so I turned and lit out."

The old man's voice broke a little on the final words and his shoulders trembled, trying to hold back a sob.

Dinah Mercer reached out and placed a comforting hand on his arm. "It would have been senseless to do anything else," she said gently. "You only would have gotten yourself killed, too."

The others gathered around them under the big meeting canopy murmured words of agreement and consolation to the old prospector.

The first rays of morning sunlight were reaching into the refugee mountain camp out of a partially cloudy sky. After all the previous night's blustery wind and jarring, lightning-laced thunder, no rain had ever fallen. And with the first hint of dawn, the wind had abruptly died and the thick cloud cover had begun to break apart in time for intermittent slices of blue sky and sunlight to start poking through.

A chill remained in the air, however. A chill deepened by the news Baker had brought with him when he showed up in camp, alone, shortly after first light. In the hours immediately preceding him, others returning from the rescue raid on the town— first the freed Belinda and Heath, accompanied by Betty Barlow, then followed by Whit Barlow and Howard MacGregor, even though the latter was suffering a serious leg wound—had all carried reports suggesting complete success. Anticipation had been high for the next arrivals to be the remainder of the rescuers, including the conquering leaders, with accounts of how the final mop-up had gone.

Instead, the account they got was a bitterly ironic twist on what had been hoped for and expected. It boiled down to the original captives now being free and relatively unharmed—but at the cost of one man's life, another getting badly wounded, and two key members of the group left behind in the custody of the ruthless gang members they had just riled to a new height of vengeful rage.

"It's all my fault, mine and Heath's," wailed a still

disheveled-looking Belinda. "If we hadn't run off the way we did and fell into the hands of those awful men, then none of the rest of—"

"Stop it. None of that," her mother cut her off sharply. "What's done is done. You made your choice and so did the men who went after you. No amount of blaming or whining is going to change the results we now must face. But as long as your father is still alive, then I refuse to give up hope that all is lost."

"That's a brave outlook, Jane. And I go along with it, up to a point," Barlow was quick to say. Then, his gaze locking on Baker, he added, "But a lot hinges on the part about Sheriff Tom and Jensen still being alive. Are you sure that's the case, Red?"

A trapped animal look fell over Baker for a moment. Until, his mouth pulling into a tight, determined line, he replied, "That's the way as best I know it. Like I said, I saw 'em fallin' and rollin' down the stairs. But I never saw 'em get shot. And after Ferris and those other snakes cut down Turley, I never heard no more shootin' as I made it to the horses and rode off."

"Then count me in," spoke up Ben Pettigrew from where he sat at the long table with his wife and son pressed in close behind him, "as another voice sayin' that if Eagle and Jensen are alive, then this thing ain't necessarily over." He paused, his eyes sweeping the other faces turned to him, before adding, "If nobody heard it before, then by now you all know that, for a long time, I had little use for Tom Eagle. Didn't have no reason except on account of the Injun blood in him. What was worse, I didn't even have the guts to bad mouth him to his face. But I sure did it plenty behind his back . . . Only I know now I was wrong. Bad wrong. After we got ambushed out there on the edge of those badlands, him and Jensen could have left me—a useless cripple—and never looked back. But they didn't. They treated me square, treated me like a man. A whole one. And we all made it out of there together. Now we got to do everything we can to give them every chance to make it out of this new trouble they're in."

"But how?" said MacGregor, propping himself up on his elbows where he lay stretched out on the table just a few feet away. His pant leg was cut open and peeled back and his bloody, bandaged leg was still extended straight out to facilitate Jonathan and Edna Wray's removal of the bullet that had been in his thigh. Except for the spots of rosy color on his cheeks from the whiskey he'd tossed down to battle the pain, his face was as chalky white as the un-bloodied roll of bandages Mrs. Wray was holding in her hand.

"How?" he said again, his eyes filmy and his voice thick-sounding. "What can we do to help them? What can we do to help ourselves? We never had a chance to begin with, and now it's only turned worse."

His wife Colleen put her hands on his shoulders and tried to get him to lay back and settle down.

"That's the thing we definitely can't do—just give up," said Pettigrew. "Like Jane said, as long as Eagle and Jensen are alive we can't give up hope. And I'll go one better. The rest of us bein' alive counts for something, too. We're not a bunch of helpless babes, are we? Ain't we got our own measure of fight in us?"

"Do we?" said Clarence Copley. "In spirit maybe, but what chance does mere anger and indignation stand against the hardened gunmen we would be facing? Why do you think the sheriff kept us safely tucked away here all the times he went out alone on his excursions? Except for only a few of us—the six who went with him last night, and now that number has been cut by four—he knew our limitations. Like all old men, I hate admitting my best time is past and I have such limitations. But it's a fact, and there's no getting around it. I suggest we all be realistic and accept the hard realities of our situation."

"I, too, am an old man forced to live with knowing I can no longer do certain things," responded Jonathan Wray with a deep frown. "But one of the things I *never* will accept, not as long as I have a breath in me, is to roll over and give up!"

"The limitations Tom saw," Jane said, "were largely imposed by his heart and his refusal to ask others to take what *he* believed to be risks they were unprepared for. An example, something he'd never allow me to do in a hundred years, is the fact I can ride and shoot a gun quite accurately."

"So can I," said Betty Barlow.

"And I as well," spoke up Dinah Mercer.

"Hell's bells," said Isobel, the older of the spinstered Byerly sisters, "I don't know that our old bones could hang together on a horse these days, but my sister and I grew up shootin' squirrels and rabbits in the Tennessee hills where we grew up, practically from the time we could lift a gun."

"And if we hadn't got good at it," agreed her sister Estelle, "we would have gone hungry. Put a couple of those fancy repeatin' rifles in our hands and stick that fat-bottomed Hack Ferris or some of his cutthroats in front of us and watch us plant a pattern of lead in 'em you could cover with a teaspoon."

"That's right," added Isobel. "We was taught not to chaw up good meat with our bullets—though I expect no such thing as good meat could be found on any of those rascals."

An expression of astonishment and horror had slowly settled over the face of Mary Hobart. "I can't believe I'm listening to this," she gasped, her voice strangled by emotion. "Are you people all mad? We're no kind of *fighting force*! Like Howard MacGregor said, we never were. And now, more than ever . . . Can't you see? The only chance we have is to throw ourselves on the mercy of Parker Dixon. He's a wealthy, respected man. Ruthless in his business dealings perhaps, but not some sort of bloodthirsty monster. He already has everything he wants from us—our land, our businesses, our dignity. Destroying us the rest of the way, killing us as you all think he has in mind . . . What would that gain him?"

"He has to. He can't *afford* to leave us alive. I hate to put it so bluntly, Mary," said Neal Vickers in a tolerant yet firm tone, "but those are the facts. We went through all that before, and for you to cling to any other belief is simply unreasonable."

From where he stood with his father and mother, Heath Pettigrew abruptly spoke. "Mr. Vickers is right. All of you who are saying we need to make a stand and fight—with or without Sheriff Tom and Mr. Jensen—are right. They're not going to give us any other choice."

All eyes swung to the young man. Ben Pettigrew

twisted in his seat and looked up at his son. "What are you saying, boy?"

"You need to remember that we were right there in the midst of them for several hours," Heath replied. "When night came they tied us up and shut us away in a room at that saloon. But before that, we were out among 'em and they talked pretty freely."

"What did they say?" somebody prodded.

"For starters," Heath said, his voice growing stronger and surer, "they were never gonna make a fair trade for Belinda and me. It was all a trick to capture the sheriff and Mr. Jensen, just like they've gone and done anyhow. Either way, their intentions were the same. They've got some kind of special plans for those two." His brows pinched tighter together. "Exactly what, was never made clear. But you can bet it ain't anything pleasant."

The grim expressions on the faces of Jane and Belinda grew even more so.

"After that," Heath went on, "something that *was* made plenty clear was that they intend to come after this camp and wipe it out . . . along with everybody in it."

"They know about us being here?" his father asked.

"They've suspected all along that Sheriff Tom had some others backing him. They don't know how many or where we're holed up. When they caught the sheriff and the rest of you in that ambush and saw there were other men riding with him, that clinched it as far as knowing for sure he wasn't strictly on his own. But they still had no way of knowing how many."

"Tell them the rest, Heath," Belinda urged. "Tell them how they tried to force information out of you."

The words caused Heath to wince involuntarily.

Setting his teeth, he said, "They knocked me around pretty good at one point, aiming to get me to reveal the location of our camp and how many of us there are. When I wouldn't tell them anything, they threatened to start in on Belinda as a different way. So I pretended like I gave in and started to talk. But I lied like crazy. Oh, how I lied." The young man chuckled devilishly. "I told 'em there was right around two hundred of us, and that over half was veterans of the war. I claimed Sheriff Tom had been stealing guns and ammunition from all over the valley and that's all we were waiting for, to make sure we had plenty of firepower. In the meantime, I said, we had a tough old drill sergeant who was working every day to get everybody in top shape for the charge."

"And they believed you?" Pettigrew said.

Heath shook his head. "No, I laid it on too thick. So they beat me some more for that. And then they moved on to wanting to know how to find our camp. I told them the truth about the entrance maze but made like I couldn't accurately describe how to find it. Then I acted like I was begging not to be beat no more, so I told them I could take them and *show* them the spot. Dark was coming on so I knew we wouldn't be going out right away. I was buying time. But they seemed to believe me, at least enough for the beatings to stop. Shortly after that, they tied us up and stuck us in that upstairs room for the night."

"That was some mighty brave and clever thinkin', lad," Pettigrew said, beaming up at his son. "I'm proud of you."

"But that's not all. Tell them the rest," Belinda urged once again.

Heath took a quick breath and then expelled it slowly, cheeks puffing out, before saying, "The rest of it is that the big boss, Parker Dixon himself, is due here soon. Sometime this afternoon. He's the one who has some kind of personal beef to settle with Luke Jensen. On top of that, he's bringing more men with him. This is all according to what his son Roland told Ferris when he came by the Elkhorn. We got the lowdown from the talkative little varmint who brought us some supper after they dumped us up in that room. He was all too happy to crow about it, just to make sure we'd enjoy our lousy meal all the less. 'Steel tough gunnies' was his favorite term for the new men Dixon was bringing—men whose job, after the business with Jensen is taken care of, will be, like I said before, to concentrate on finding and destroying this camp and all of us in it."

The final part of Heath's statement hung in the air like a physical weight replacing the canopy over their heads. Under the pressure of this, nobody said anything for what seemed like a long time.

Until Ben Pettigrew finally spoke, summing it up in a gruff, somber tone. "Well, if that ain't plain enough for everybody, I don't know what more it's gonna take. Much as I wish it was otherwise, I don't see how we can do anything to directly help Sheriff Eagle and Jensen. Except to hope, maybe pray, they can come up with something on their own. But what we *can* do—for our own sake and for the sake of everything Sheriff Eagle has been fighting for—is take care of ourselves here. Get ready to fight and defend this place with everything we got if and when the devils come."

"Oh, they're comin', Pa," Heath said with conviction. And then, looking deeply and directly into his father's eyes for the first time in too long, he added, "And when they do, you need to remember something. What me and Belinda did was foolish and maybe even added to bringing this whole thing to a head . . . but I ain't a kid no more. And when it comes to defending this camp and people in it who I love, including the gal I still intend to marry some day, a rifle is gonna fit my hands just as good as yours or anybody else's."

Chapter 40

"Well, well, well, what have we here? The spectacularly stubborn and irksome Tom Eagle and the elusive and mysterious Luke Jensen. Right before my very eyes." Roland Dixon stood with feet planted wide apart, hands clasped behind his back, and regarded the men he was addressing with smug superiority. "I can't deny harboring a good deal of ill will toward you two gentlemen, in keeping with an equal amount you no doubt feel toward me. But I must admit to a genuine appreciation for you so obligingly taking actions that resulted in your early deliverance to me here rather than necessitating another visit to that repulsive town of Hard Rock to view your apprehension there later at noon."

"How about you let us oblige you even more," Eagle replied through clenched teeth, "by takin' that appreciation and chokin' on it!"

The stocky hombre standing directly behind Eagle wasted no time viciously slamming the butt of a Henry repeating rifle across the former sheriff's kidneys. A loud grunt of pain exploded out of Eagle as his head pulled back and his knees buckled. But he stayed on his feet.

Beside the stricken man, Luke lunged reflexively but his restraints prevented him from doing anything more than making a choppy half-step forward. Like Eagle, his wrists were tied behind his back, legs shackled at the ankles, and a leather thong was looped around each of their necks. The man on the other end of Luke's thong was none other than a grinning, nastily chuckling Hacksaw Ferris.

"Whoa up there, hero," Ferris barked. "Where do you think you're goin'?"

"Easy," Roland was quick to admonish. "You know the orders regarding that one. You've complained about them enough. And by the look of him—and the other one as well—you've already pushed the limit of their treatment quite sufficiently."

Both Luke and Eagle were stripped to the waist and a generous pattern of welts and bruises marked their torsos along with more of the same on their faces.

"That ain't a fraction of what the dirty scum deserve!" snarled Ferris. "Look at the rest of what's standin' before you!" He swung his free arm, indicating the five men gathered around him and the captives. They were indeed a sorry-looking lot, having just ridden hard from town out to the Gold Button mining operation. The morning sun, less than two hours risen and glaring through the last of the dissipating clouds left over from last night's empty bluster, shone down on a battered, bleary-eyed, bedraggled bunch with sagging shoulders yet grim, flinty-eyed faces.

"This is all the men I got left, includin' the extra miners you lent me," Ferris went on. "The condition they're in and the loss of all the others is almost entirely due to these two lead-slingin' varmints . . . and you say they've been treated *sufficiently*?"

Roland's smug supremacy withered under the demanding question and the hard stares of the men backing Ferris. "Here now." He cleared his throat. "I certainly understand the thirst for revenge that you and the other men have for the damage these two have inflicted on your comrades. After all, the men who've been lost were comrades of mine, too, in a manner of speaking."

A towering man with streaks of dried blood running down his face and holding a bloodstained bar rag to his forehead stepped forward and said in a booming voice, "I didn't see you at the Elkhorn when these dogs were smothering it with fire and lead. Look at what that gunhawk Jensen did to my head. A half inch lower my skull would have been popped open like a Mexican piñata!"

"Naturally I sympathize for your injury," Roland was quick to assure him. "We have a fine doctor here at the mine who will care for you."

"That's Big Olaf," Ferris said with obvious pride. "If he hadn't survived that bullet crease to his head when Jensen thought he'd killed him, probably *none* of us would be here now to tell about it. It was Olaf who landed on Eagle and Jensen like an avalanche, just when they'd got behind me and Grimsby and the handful of us left in the barroom, aimin' to bushwhack us and wipe us out the rest of the way."

"I share your gratitude for Olaf. Certainly he deserves to be rewarded," Roland said. "That's what I meant when I said I consider all of you *my* comrades as well. As employees of Dixon Enterprises, you see. That also means I feel your loss and share in wanting just punishment."

"Let us take care of it then!" somebody shouted.

"All we need is a tall tree and a couple of strong ropes!" someone else added.

It was Ferris who quickly quelled this talk, chopping the air with his hand and raising his voice above the others. "Knock it off! We already covered that back in town. I explained to you how it was, how Mr. Roland here takes orders same as everybody else down the line. It's his father who's makin' the demands and callin' the shots on this Jensen hombre. Meanin' Mr. Roland has to go along just like the rest of us." He turned plaintively to Roland. "I need you to tell 'em that's so, Boss. Tell 'em how your old man is due here soon and when he shows up he's bound to have some plans for Jensen that will square this whole thing and help get even for Dog and all the others. After everything we've been through, it's important they hear that from you."

"Of course," Roland said, the gang leader's pleading tone making him feel somewhat back in control. He swept his gaze over the men regarding him half angrily, half anxiously. "Of course my father has some severe punishment in mind for Jensen. I don't know exactly what, but I do know he's harbored a hatred for the man a long time. And that's enough for me to be able to assure you that, whatever he metes out, you will find satisfactory."

"What about Eagle?" a voice demanded.

Roland bared his teeth in a cold smile. "Oh, I'm sure my father will not overlook our former sheriff.

He's fully aware what a nuisance Eagle has made of himself these past months. And whatever he has in store for Jensen . . . well, I'm confident there will be enough for Eagle to share in it as well."

"There you have it," declared Ferris. "These curs are going to pay and pay *hard*. And we'll all have a front row seat for enjoyin' it!"

There was a general grumbling of satisfaction from the men.

And then, right on the heels of that, came another extended sound, the sudden murmur of numerous voices. The display taking place out front of Roland's private cabin, it turned out, had drawn the attention of several miners—a crew just finished with breakfast and ready to begin their shift down in the bowels of the Gold Button dig—who were filing out of the mess hall fifty or so yards away. This crew, one of several that worked a cycle of staggered shifts, appeared to be made up almost entirely of Chinese workers. Their expressions were guarded, impassive, yet their interest was obvious by the murmur of curiosity that rippled through them and the way their faces stayed turned to stare even as the movement of their feet dragged with a reluctance to carry them away.

Roland took quick notice of this attention and his reaction showed he wasn't pleased by it. "Here now. What are you slackers staring at?" he demanded. "You've filled your bellies at the company trough, now off with you to work!"

"You're right about that," Ferris was quick to chime in. Turning to glare at the Chinese workers, he inadvertently jerked on the thong around Luke's neck and caused the leather to dig into already raw flesh.

"I won't have no lazy, slant-eyed heathens gawkin' at me. You heard what the boss man said—off with ya, and be quick about it!"

The door of the mess hall opened and Mace Vernon emerged. Behind him stepped a second man, another Caucasian, a dour-faced individual near fifty, with thinning, gray-streaked hair and a pair of round spectacles perched on the end of a long, narrow nose. Vernon paused, first glancing at the line of workers strung out before him, then turning his gaze to Ferris. The scowl on his face seemed to indicate he had heard the gang leader's harsh words.

"What seems to be the problem here?" he wanted to know.

"You're the one with the problem," Ferris responded. "You got yourself a string of Chinee so-called workers there who seem to be more interested in stoppin' to gawk at something that's none of their business instead of movin' their lazy asses on to what *is* supposed to be their business."

"You got a problem with any of my men," Vernon grated, "you speak to me about it, you don't raise your voice to them. Better yet, keep your opinions to yourself and your yap shut altogether where me or my men are concerned."

Vernon swung his attention back to the workers, focusing on one in particular up near the head of the line. "Chang-Ha," he addressed him. "Move the men along. Report to Henderson down in Shaft Number Six, that's where you'll be working today."

Chang-Ha nodded acknowledgment and then, in Chinese, spoke sharply to the other men and motioned for them to get a move on. They fell in behind him and strode away briskly toward the Gold Button's main vertical shaft and the pulley system for the transport cage that lowered and raised workers as well as brought up the loads of ore from the tunnels below.

As the workers marched away, the second man who had come out of the mess hall with Vernon made no effort to mask his own interest in the group gathered before Roland's cabin. Frowning deeply, he advanced toward the group. Vernon followed, although with notably less eagerness.

"What have we here?" muttered the man in glasses as he drew nearer. And then, a moment later, he exclaimed, "It's Sheriff Eagle!"

Managing to stand a little straighter and turn the grimace he'd been wearing ever since the rifle butt blow to his kidneys into a lopsided grin, Eagle greeted him with, "Hiya, Doc. How's the pill pushin' business?"

Chapter 41

Dr. Henry Carstairs drew to within a couple feet of Eagle, surveying his wounds and the way he was bound, then turned and aimed a fierce scowl at Roland, demanding, "What is the meaning of this inhumane treatment!?"

"Looks to me," Roland replied, "like the meaning is clear. We've captured a pair of dangerous hombres and are keeping them restrained so they can cause no further damage."

"What about the fact they're both in need of immediate medical attention?" Carstairs said.

"What about it?" Roland said sarcastically.

"*They're* in need of medical attention?" Ferris sputtered. "What about these other men? Do you see Big Olaf there? And are you forgettin', Doc, that I got burns and bruises on the back of my neck you ain't checked on for days?"

"How could I, with you galloping all over the countryside and never coming back around?" Carstairs reminded him. "What was I supposed to do, go out and chase you down?"

"Speaking of the other men," Vernon cut in. "Where are the rest of the fellas I loaned you, Ferris?"

Ferris glared at him. "They're dead, that's where, thanks to these two varmints the good doctor is so concerned about medically treatin'."

"Now just a minute!" Vernon exploded. His eyes whipped back and forth between Ferris and Roland. "What are things turning into around here? Some kind of bloodbath? A war? I loaned you a half dozen good men only a day ago and now you're telling me they've all been gunned down?"

"It was the risk they took when—" Roland started to say.

"No, it was the risk *I* took for them," Vernon corrected him. "Those men were used to hard work and danger—the kind of danger to be found in a mine shaft—not from the muzzle of a gun. You said you needed men to cover more ground in order to run down that Jensen character. You never mentioned the chance for shooting on a scale that would wipe out the whole lot of them."

"Things don't always go as planned," Roland said coldly. "You know what a thorn in the side this half-breed has been. We weren't aware he had a connection with Jensen. Plus other leftover troublemakers from the valley who unexpectedly reared their stupid, stubborn heads and decided to pitch in."

Carstairs smiled a thin, rather curious smile. "The sheep didn't all knuckle under as easily as your father calculated, did they? Not like me."

"Watch what you say, medicine man," Roland warned him. "You made your deal. Your family was let out safely and set up nice and comfortable in a place far away from what goes on here. You've still got time left to serve before your end of the bargain is satisfied. Be careful you don't let your mouth or your attitude screw it up before then. My father will be here later today in case you want to tell him how lacking his calculations were."

Carstairs blanched and his curious smile turned into a flat, tight line.

"What's this about your father coming?" Vernon said. "This is the first I'm hearing about it."

Roland sighed in exasperation. "I only found out myself late yesterday, after the telegraph lines were once again repaired. This is the first chance I've had to mention it to you. In case you haven't been paying attention, a few other rather pressing matters have been taking place."

Nobody said anything more for a minute. Then Ferris looked at Vernon and said, in a voice that sounded sincere, "I'm sorry about the loss of your men, Vernon. I truly am. I got to know them a little, they were good boys. If it makes any difference, I lost some good fellas, too. A few of them friends I rode with for a long time."

Vernon met his gaze and acknowledged with a faint nod.

"Ain't no gettin' any of 'em back," Big Olaf added, casting his own baleful gaze on Luke and Eagle. "But there's a way for those who done it to pay . . . and when Big Boss Dixon gets here, that'll get took care of soon enough."

"Indeed it will," said Roland, his tone returning to a more in-command one. "But before then there are steps to be taken. Mr. Vernon, I believe you have a mining operation to see to. Dr. Carstairs, as you so astutely observed, you have some patients in need of medical attention. If you repair to the infirmary, Mr. Ferris will bring his men over shortly."

Carstairs's eyes went to Luke and Eagle. "What about them?"

Roland shook his head. "I see no need to tax your skills unnecessarily. They'll keep well enough until my father gets here. Then he can decide what treatment is warranted."

Carstairs didn't move for a minute. Then, with effort, he turned away. "Whatever you say."

Vernon fell in step beside him and they walked off together.

As they did so, Ferris asked, "What do you want to do with these two skunks, Boss? You got some kind of shed or something we can lock 'em in until your old man gets here?"

Roland's expression hardened. "How did things work out the last time you had a pair of prisoners locked away? In a room where you assured me they were quite secure, remember?"

Ferris squinted and shuffled his feet uneasily. "Well, uh . . . yeah. Yeah, but—"

"No 'buts'!" Roland said sharply. He thrust out one arm and pointed at a telegraph pole that stood ten yards off from one corner of his cabin. It rose up from bare ground and nothing else was anywhere near it. "I want them chained to that pole, completely in plain sight. I want two men with rifles standing watch over them at all times. The watchmen can sit in the shade of that wagon across the way. They can have canteens, they can be relieved for a meal if lunchtime rolls around before my father arrives . . . but the prisoners get *nothing*. No one goes near them unless I say otherwise. Understood?"

Ferris nodded. "You bet. You got it, Boss."

"See to it, then," Roland told him. "And get that neck looked at again by the doctor first chance you have."

With that, Roland turned on his heel and started back toward the front door to his cabin. For the first time he realized that Ying-Su was standing there with the door slightly ajar, peering out through a six-inch opening.

"What are you looking at? Get back inside," Roland ordered her harshly.

The exotic beauty wordlessly melted back and disappeared. Roland followed her in and slammed the door shut behind them.

Some time later, after he and Luke had been chained with their backs to the telegraph pole and everyone else had vacated the area except for the two guards sitting a dozen yards away in the shade of a high-wheeled freight wagon, Eagle said quietly, "Look on the bright side. We're prisoners at a gold mine. That's a step up from some dark, musty old cell. Right?"

"Not necessarily," Luke told him. "Not if Parker Dixon takes his time showing up and we start to turn crispy and well done, plunked out here in the sun waiting for him."

"You almost sound like you're eager for him to get here."

"Only for the reason I just said. That, and to finally find out what it is about me he's got stuck so tight in his craw."

Eagle grunted. "No mystery about that where I'm concerned. I've worked real hard to earn myself a spot in his craw."

"If you could go back and do it over, would you do any different?"

"Not one bit."

Luke chuckled dryly. "About what I figured."

Eagle was quiet for a minute, then he said, "No. On second thought, I would do part of it different. I'd get my family, Jane and Belinda and Davy, away somewhere, out of the valley. Then I'd come back and make my fight. Sorta like Doc Carstairs did."

"He doesn't seem to be making much of a fight of it," Luke observed.

"Inside himself he is. Didn't you see the look on his face when Roland reminded him of the hold they've got over him? I don't know the exact deal he made, but the Dixons wanted and needed a doctor for their miners and gang members. You heard the terms. His family is safe, but he's got to stay behind and serve some specified amount of time. I don't know how long, but it appears every minute of it is eatin' him up more and more."

"You make a deal with the Devil, you're likely to get the horns before it's through," Luke said.

They went quiet again for a spell. Until Eagle said, "That ol' sun up there *is* gettin' a mite warm, ain't it?"

"Going to get warmer right along, the higher it climbs. There's hardly a wisp of last night's clouds left in the sky, either, nothing to slide across and provide even a whisker of shade."

"Yeah," Eagle grated. "But Ferris's pet skunks over there under that wagon have got shade, and plenty of it. And canteens of water, too. Watch 'em look our way whenever they tip one up and take a long, gurglin' drink. Just tormentin' us, the lowdown snakes."

"Don't look, then. Don't give them the satisfaction," Luke said.

There followed another stretch of quiet. It was Eagle who broke it again, this time saying, "I reckon somewhere in here, while I still got the chance, I oughta say I'm sorry for gettin' you into this, Jensen."

"Way I recall, I rode to Hard Rock with no invitation from you."

"In the beginnin' maybe. But I'm talkin' about here. Now. You likely wouldn't be in this particular fix if you hadn't agreed to stick with me and my people for a while and then ended up on that raid to get back my daughter and young Heath."

"Which we succeeded at," Luke reminded him. "And, in the process, if I'd shot and killed Big Olaf the way I should have instead of just *thinking* I did, then you might also say we likely wouldn't be in this particular fix. So blame at this point doesn't matter. The only thing we can do is deal with it the best we can."

"You got an idea on how to do that?"

"Not a one."

"I don't suppose you got any kind of weapon hid away on you, either?"

"Nope. They plucked me good and thorough while I was unconscious."

"Well . . . hell."

"Yeah. Or something close to it."

The sun climbed to its zenith and the air hung motionless except for distorting currents of heat.

Big Olaf and another man came out of the mess hall and relieved the original set of guards who had otherwise never ventured away from their wagon. Big Olaf was now sporting a large bandage that covered most of his head and slanted down just above his right eye. As if to prove that the medical attention hadn't improved his disposition any, before taking up his watchman's post he walked over to Luke and Eagle and shoved his face close to call them some filthy names. Then he kicked dirt on each of them and leaned over a little closer to give Luke an extra clout alongside the head.

As he sauntered slowly away to join the other new guard in the shade of the wagon, Luke said, through the fresh trickle of blood running out the corner of his mouth, "In case you're wondering, I'm real annoyed with myself for not blowing that big slob's head off when I had the chance."

Spitting out some dirt that had gotten in his mouth, Eagle said, "Rankles me a fair amount, too."

Another half hour passed before the door to Roland's cabin opened and the Oriental beauty Ying-Su emerged. She was dressed, as always, in black silk that hugged her curves and shimmered in the sunlight like her long, flowing hair. In her hands she held a large ceramic pitcher, maroon in color, with beads of moisture visible on its sides. In long, bold strides that revealed flashes of her ivory legs through slits in the silk skirt, she moved straight toward Luke and Eagle. When she reached them, without saying a word, she began giving them drinks of water from the pitcher, starting with Eagle.

Big Olaf stood up. "Here now! What are you doing there?"

Ying-Su paid him no heed. She moved around the post and put the spout of the pitcher to Luke's mouth.

Big Olaf lumbered forward. "Are you supposed to be doing that? Mr. Roland said nobody but . . . I think you'd better stop. Stop that, you hear me?"

He moved up beside Ying-Su, looming over her. But he was obviously flustered, feeling confident this was not something condoned by Roland yet at the same time fearing to actually lay a hand on the girl in order to try and *make* her stop.

Olaf's indecision was solved by Roland's voice suddenly shouting from the doorway of his cabin. "Ying-Su! What is the meaning—Stop that! Get away from that filthy vermin immediately!"

Roland covered the distance from his cabin in a rush. Olaf backed away. Reaching Ying-Su, Roland roughly grabbed a fistful of hair and silk in one hand and swatted away the water pitcher with the other. The pitcher hit the ground and shattered into a score of pieces.

Still gripping a combination of hair and garment, Roland shook the girl viciously. She finally spoke, rattling off a string of words in Chinese. They were words Roland apparently understood and very clearly did not like. His free hand flashed in an open-palmed slap that cracked sharp and loud.

Ying-Su quit struggling and went silent again. Roland stood glaring at her for a long moment and then released his grip and gave her a shove that sent her staggering back toward the cabin. "Get back inside, you slut," he snarled in English. "Wait for me there, and get ready for a lesson on never flaunting yourself or humiliating me like this in public ever again!"

The girl hung her head and slunk away.

Roland wheeled back to face Olaf. "What part of no one is to go near these men did you not understand?"

"I . . . I was tryin'," Olaf stammered. "But bein' how it was your . . . I mean, I didn't . . . I wasn't sure . . ."

"Well, then let me make it perfectly clear," Roland said through gritted teeth, "so you can be sure to understand it for the future. *No one* gets close to these two unless you hear it authorized *by me* and no one *but* me! Stop them by whatever means necessary. Is that understood?"

"Yes, sir. Absolutely!" Olaf assured him.

Roland stood still for a long moment, nostrils flared, body trembling with barely contained rage. His glare shifted from Olaf to Luke and Eagle, as if he intended to say something to them. But then he didn't, instead simply stomping off and going back inside his cabin.

During the tense seconds when Roland had been berating Ying-Su and all eyes were on them, Luke had—with a quick, smooth, unseen motion—reached out with one foot and pulled back a broken piece of pitcher that he then covered by extending his right leg over it.

Some time later, after things had settled back down, Luke whispered to Eagle, "Remember, a while back, when you asked if I happened to have any kind of weapon hidden away and I said no, I didn't?"

"Yeah. All too well. Why?"

"Well, don't get your hopes up too much, but that might have changed some . . ."

Chapter 42

Parker Dixon arrived at the Gold Button a quarter past two that afternoon. Roland must have had someone on lookout to watch for his approach because, fifteen minutes in advance, a rider came tearing in and went directly to Roland's cabin. A flurry of activity followed in which the same man left the cabin and hurried to the headquarter buildings of the actual mining operation.

A short time later, Mace Vernon, Hack Ferris, Dr. Carstairs, and two men in dress trousers and gartered shirtsleeves who Luke guessed to be engineers, came marching dutifully to gather in front of the cabin. Roland, decked out in a fresh suit jacket and cravat, stepped out and stood with them. Minutes later, the elder Dixon came riding in at the head of a rather impressive caravan. Mounted next to him was Asa Patton.

Eyes sweeping in a quick assessment, Luke counted two dozen heavily armed outriders, half in front of and half at the rear of three canopied freight wagons with a driver and shotgun guard in the seat of each. In between the second and third freight wagons was a fourth vehicle, more like a beefed up buckboard, with an open bed. It, too, had a driver and shotgun guard and seated on a specially constructed bench behind them rode three tall, bareheaded black men clad in loose-fitting burlap shirts with several rows of beads and ornaments dangling around their necks. And behind them, secured to the wagon bed with heavy ropes as thick as a man's wrist, were two steel cages draped in thick sheets of canvas that obscured whatever was inside.

Dixon reined his horse to a halt in front of his son and the men standing with him. Patton silently raised a hand and the line of riders and wagons behind them creaked to a stop as well.

"Good afternoon, Father," greeted Roland. "You made better time than expected."

"Other than a very blustery night after we camped last evening," Dixon replied, "we've enjoyed fair weather the whole way and encountered nothing to delay us."

"Yes," Roland said dryly, "with this formidable entourage, it's hard to imagine anyone attempting to interfere with you."

Dixon's gaze fell on Vernon and the two engineer types who stood expectantly by. "Gentlemen," he addressed them, "I trust you are prepared to discuss operational issues such as we usually do on my visits, and I assure you we will be getting to such matters in due time. But first"—and here his eyes cut sharply to Luke and Eagle—"I have some long overdue business of another nature that will require my full attention for at least the balance of the day. You may remain and observe if you wish. Otherwise, with the exception of Ferris, you are dismissed until further notice."

Roland frowned. "But surely, Father, you must first wish to step inside out of the heat for a few minutes and perhaps freshen up? I have your room prepared as you like it and your favorite beverage ready to—"

Dixon cut him off with a wave of the hand. "In good time, son. All in good time." He swung smoothly down from his mount and Patton followed suit. Dixon motioned Hack Ferris over to him. Holding out his reins, he said, "See to our men and horses. Take the freight wagons and arrange for unloading at the appropriate supply buildings. Then arrange stabling for the horses and show the men to temporary quarters."

"Yessir," said Ferris.

"Leave the wagon with the cages and those who go with it here," Dixon added. "After you've set all that in motion, return here with half the men. Give them time for a drink of cold water, nothing stronger. Have them back here in fifteen minutes."

"Yessir," Ferris said again.

Patton took a step back toward the men and wagons. Jerking his thumb, he told them, "This is Hack Ferris. You heard what Mr. Dixon said. Go with him, all except those of you attached to the cage wagon, and follow his instructions. Half of you will be coming back in short order."

Then he also handed his reins to Ferris and stepped back to rejoin Dixon. Ferris waved his free arm and barked orders and those assigned to him followed him off toward the collection of buildings that marked the heart of the mining operation.

As the wagons rumbled and creaked away, Dixon

abruptly turned from his son and Patton and strode over to where Luke and Eagle sat in their restraints, silently watching and listening.

Looming over Luke, he gazed down with mock concern and said, "My gracious, Mr. Jensen. Look at the way you've let yourself go in just the few days since last we conducted business. Surely the generous advance money I paid you should have afforded you better attire and accommodations than this. What in the world happened?"

"It's a long story," Luke grated. "But as you can see, I got your man Eagle. Here he is, a present from me, all wrapped up. So pay me the rest of what you owe me and I'll be on my way. And this time I'll promise to try and spend the money more wisely."

Dixon showed his teeth in a cold smile. "Very amusing. Did you hear that, Eagle? Your apparent new partner just sold you out. What have you got to say about that? You think it might be that pesky half-breed blood working against you again? The way you just can't seem to get anybody to side with you, no matter what?"

"At least that gives me an excuse," Eagle responded. "You, if you didn't have money to buy people, your loyal followers—even your own son—would sooner side with a diseased rat than the likes of you!"

Olaf, who had moved up from the wagon with the other guard posted there, took a menacing step toward Eagle.

Dixon held up a hand, stopping him. "Let him talk. He has such a short time left to pretend he is any longer of consequence, allow him to waste his breath while he still can."

"It was indeed a stroke of luck to have captured these devils together, Father. But it wasn't *all* luck, by any means," said Roland. "It came at considerable cost to Hack Ferris and his men, and even some of Vernon's miners that he loaned for the sake of being able to cover a greater expanse of ground. I sincerely hope, the first chance you get, that you take time to acknowledge—"

"Yes, yes," Dixon cut him off impatiently. "I'm sure that much brave and devoted effort went into achieving success. Although, I must say that it seems about blasted time where this renegade half-breed is concerned. And as for Jensen, I sent him right into your laps. How difficult could that have been?"

"All I can say, sir," Roland replied in a strained voice, "is that it turned out to be considerably more so than expected."

"Never mind that." Dixon made a dismissive sweep of his hand. "The fact they *are* captured—and together—is what counts. The timing couldn't be better. And that fact, above all else, gives me great pleasure and satisfaction. You can fill me in on incidental details during and after the hunt."

"We're going to proceed with the hunt right away, sir?" asked Patton.

"What hunt?" said Roland.

Ignoring his son, Dixon addressed Patton, saying, "Why not? On the way in, I pointed out to you the perfect terrain just west of here. We have several hours of daylight left and the dogs have been caged up for days. They should certainly be ready for a good workout, wouldn't you say?"

"Well, when you put it that way, I guess there's no reason not to," Patton said, knowing that there'd really been only one correct answer to the question put to him.

"What hunt?" Roland said again.

Still ignoring him, Dixon called and motioned to someone on the remaining wagon. "Ngamba! Come here a moment."

One of the black men clad in burlap and beads rose up, leaped nimbly from the wagon, and trotted obediently over on bare feet. "Yes, Bwana?"

"The dogs, Ngamba—how soon can they be ready for a hunt?" Dixon asked him.

"Be ready whenever Bwana say," came the reply, shaded by a faint accent. "After days in cage, dogs welcome a good run."

Dixon smiled. "Exactly! Start getting the cages uncovered, you and your men. Then stand by, we will soon be giving the hounds a good run indeed."

As Ngamba headed back to the wagon, promptly issuing orders in a foreign tongue to the other two black men, Dixon turned once more to those gathered about him. "Gentlemen, you will have to indulge me in this. I can understand that what I'm about to engage in may not be everyone's cup of tea and, in fact, could be quite distasteful to some of you. For me, you must understand, it is the culmination of being able to pay a long overdue debt, to administer a personal vengeance that I for many years thought was impossible. Once I learned this was no longer the case, little else has consumed me as much as finding a way to make it happen and make it happen in a way that would not only even the score but do so in a manner meaningful enough to equal the loathsomeness of the initial act!"

Roland looked on, his expression appearing concerned to the point of being somewhat frightened. "Father, I never saw you act like this way. I don't understand what this is all about?"

At last Dixon paid some heed to his son. His gaze fell on him with a kind of abrupt gentleness. "No, of course you don't. I never meant for you to. I never wanted you to know the rage and the aching, unanswered thirst for revenge that I endured for so long. Especially when I felt so impotent to do anything about it. But now that's all changed. It is time for you to know. You must, it is right here before you. And you will be part of the culmination, the realization of my revenge and you will understand the depth of family honor that must be upheld and, when necessary, done so with blood."

With Roland now appearing perplexed and perhaps even a little stunned, Dixon stepped over and once more loomed directly over Luke. "And you, you traitorous yellow piece of scum, it is your blood that will be spilled and spilled savagely in order to settle this matter once and for all!"

Chapter 43

Luke peered up at the man standing so menacingly over him and knew he was gazing into the eyes of madness. "Mister," he grated, "if talk was going to get the job done then I might be feeling worried, because you sure know how to sling words. But so far none of them have wounded me in the slightest, and for all that you've babbled on about, I don't have any idea what you're talking about."

"Oh, you will. I'm going to make sure of that," Dixon told him. "This whole exercise would lack impact if no one knew or understood what was behind it."

Over at the remaining wagon, the three black men were busily loosening and starting to remove the tarps from the cages secured to the bed. From within the cages came the sounds of heavy bodies moving restlessly, accompanied by a few low growls and snarls.

"Colonel Russell Lancaster." Dixon stated the name with a kind of reverence. "Do you admit knowing someone by that name? Don't repeat it, I don't want to hear it spoken on your cur's tongue. We both know the answer to my question, and given that, you should begin to realize what this is all about."

Luke knew the name Russell Lancaster. Knew it all too well. His acquaintance with the man went back many years. But the incidents connected to their brief association were as fresh and indelible in Luke's mind as any he'd ever experienced. They were, in fact, life-altering incidents that had set Luke on the path to the man he was and the life he led today.

"Russell," Dixon went on, raising his voice for the purpose of informing the others listening and looking on, "was my older brother. Technically, my half brother—but no siblings ever had a closer bond. His father, whose surname Russell kept, died shortly after he was born. When our mother remarried, I was the next issue only two years later. Russell was special in the eyes of everyone, but none more so than me, his little brother. And in turn, he welcomed me tagging after him from the moment I could take my first steps.

"He was marked for great things in his future, everyone could see it. Politics, law, business, industry . . . whatever he set his mind to, it was a certainty he would excel and succeed at the highest level. And I would have been perfectly proud and content to stand always in his shadow."

Dixon paused for a moment, his voice tightening with emotion, his eyes taking on an intensity that seemed to burn right through Luke and see something far beyond.

"But then," he continued, "that blasted war came. And Russell, naturally, felt compelled to go and serve the cause. Arrangements could have been made to keep him out of combat, but he wouldn't have it. In no time at all he was a colonel. Everyone was proud, even in our fear for him. And then, as we learned from details painstakingly pieced together long after the conflict was done, he was placed in command of a very special mission near the very end, just ahead of the fall of Richmond. A last-ditch effort to save the Confederacy by smuggling all the gold out of the city and delivering it to still-fighting forces for the sake of purchasing food and supplies in hopes to sustain."

"Father," said Roland, "you never spoke of any of this."

"It was too painful . . . and pointless," Dixon murmured distantly. "Most painful of all, as we learned from the information we were eventually able to gather, was the fact that Russell did not fail in his mission at the hands of the enemy. No, it was his own command, his own hand-picked squad of men that caused his demise—traitorous wretches who not only turned on him and killed him but then stole the gold that sealed the fall of the Confederacy!"

Dixon's eyes came back into focus, a focus of pure hate boring once more straight into Luke. "And leading that murderous pack of filth was none other than this thing—I refuse to call him a man—here before me. Luke Jensen, brave and renowned bounty hunter. All lies! In truth, after for years going by an alias to hide his name and guilt, I now reveal him to you as nothing but a cowardly, conniving, backstabbing murderer and thief of the lowest order!"

Luke could feel the eyes of the other men shift from Dixon to him, most of them instantly filled with a measure of loathing. He knew that mere words weren't likely to change any minds—especially not

Dixon's—but with his own life as well as Eagle's clearly on the line, he had to at least try.

"There's some truth in what you just spewed," he said, meeting Dixon's hateful gaze with flinty determination in both his voice and his own glare. "But it's all distorted by wrong conclusions and your overriding blind hate."

"You deny you rode under the command of my brother?"

"No. You got that part right. I rode with him under the circumstances you described and was proud to do so, proud to have been selected for that critical mission."

"Yes," Dixon sneered. "So proud you betrayed the trust placed in you to help carry it out."

"That's not the way it was," Luke protested hotly. "Only half our eight-man squad betrayed the mission and gave up on our cause. And that was only *after* Colonel Lancaster had been killed by enemy fire." Luke watched Dixon's face closely. "There's one of your first big mistakes. No one in our squad murdered your brother. He died fighting bravely when a Union patrol surprised us on some nameless back road near the Georgia border. Had he lived, I've always had a hunch our mission would've held together. But as it turned out, it wouldn't have made any difference as far as the war. The truth of the matter was that we'd already lost by the time our mission began."

"What a convenient rationalization," Dixon snorted. "Just like your pathetically transparent pretense of applauding my brother's bravery and leadership skills."

"I never applauded Lancaster's leadership style, not as part of a pretense or any other way." Luke scowled. "Truth to tell, I found him a pompous little weasel. But when he was alive, he did maintain control, I'll give him that."

"He maintained control exactly because he was *not* pompous. He knew how to lead men, that's all—something a rebellious ruffian like you would never understand or appreciate. Russell had self-assurance and the courage of his convictions!"

Luke sighed wearily, sensing the hopelessness of this exercise. But a Jensen never gave up.

"I already conceded he had courage . . . just not enough to stop a round from a Yankee musket. And after the colonel went down, the rest of the mission started to go to hell pretty quick."

"You say that as if the mission disintegrated of its own accord. As if no treachery was involved in causing it to happen."

"No, there was definitely treachery by part of the men. I already said that, too," Luke responded. "Half of us wanted to continue on and deliver the gold as intended. The other half was ready to give up on what they saw as a lost cause and were primed to desert as rich men with their share of the gold. When four of us stood our ground against that, the other four who wanted to quit convinced us they'd settle for just deserting. We knew we couldn't trust them but figured we could stay on guard and dodge anything they had in mind long enough to make it to Copperhead Mountain, our destination. Well, we were wrong. They ambushed us, killed everybody but me, and got away with the gold. For a while things worked out pretty good for them. They lived in mighty high style. Until, that is, they got crossways of the wrong hombre and met their own bloody end . . . But then, I expect you already know all that, don't you?"

"I know enough," Dixon said tightly. "For a long time I believed all of the murderous vermin responsible for my brother's death were dead themselves and my only regret was that I had no hand in bringing any of it about. But then, lo and behold, the name of Luke Jensen—one of the men under my brother's command who for years had been hiding under the alias of Luke Smith—came to my attention. And that's when I knew there was still one more piece of vermin to exterminate and it was my place, my *calling*, to see it got done and got done right."

"Why the elaborate setup? Why didn't you just have me killed back in Helena and have it over with?" Luke wanted to know. "Or have Patton do it when we were together out on the trail? He'd won my trust, I let my guard down around him"—here Luke's gaze shifted to the hired gun standing nearby, looking back with no expression on his face—"it would have been easy."

"Didn't you hear what I said in the beginning?" Dixon demanded, annoyance ringing in his tone. "To properly avenge Russell's betrayal and death, you must be dispatched in a meaningful and special manner, not merely gunned down like a common villain."

Wheeling suddenly and flinging his arm in a wide flourish, Dixon announced, "And here is the means for doing exactly that!"

What he was gesturing toward was a pair of massive, powerfully muscled dogs being led on chain leashes from their cages by the two black handlers assisting Ngamba. The beasts, each looking to weigh close to a hundred pounds and standing nearly three feet at the shoulders, were sleek and tan in color, with ugly, skull-like heads and a strange pattern to the hair on their backs that made it appear like perpetually raised hackles but angled sharply forward toward the shoulders. Even though they seemed fully under the control of their handlers at the moment, it was easy to imagine them as terrifying if encountered on the loose.

Addressing Luke again, Dixon said, "It must be obvious by now that I sent you to this remote locale under false pretenses, for the purpose of exacting my revenge on you here. When you left Helena, I had not yet precisely decided how, other than it must be something extraordinary. And then, the very afternoon you left, these vicious beauties arrived. I had them shipped directly from South Africa, you see, after a visit from a friend who had gone on safari there and returned with tales and photographs of what he'd encountered. Among the exotic rarities he described and showed evidence of were these magnificent hunters. The Khoikhoi tribe there raises them for lion hunting. Lion hounds they are commonly called—or, more officially, Rhodesian Ridgebacks. I was moved to immediately arrange delivery of some for the purpose of breeding and raising and making them available as hunters and guard dogs here in America.

"And when they arrived so closely in conjunction

with you being sent off to Hard Rock Valley to unknowingly await what I had yet to formulate as a proper revenge . . . well, it was like a wondrously fitting omen."

A spike of raw fear, something he rarely ever experienced, lanced through Luke. And from the men looking on—the same men who'd been so quick to view Luke with loathing and to hang on Dixon's every word as he spun his tale of betrayal and evil and his yearning for what sounded like justifiable payback—came a sudden gasp of alarm.

Chapter 44

"Father," Roland said, his voice ragged with uneasiness, "you're not saying your plan is to sic those savage beasts on these men, are you?"

Dixon frowned, finding not the question but his son's disapproving tone to be offensive. "That's exactly what I'm saying. And why not? A savage act to atone for a savage act. What could be more appropriate than that? First, Jensen and his cohorts turned savagely on my brother. And then, in subsequent years, he's claimed how many more lives as a bounty killer? Is that anything but a savage existence? And Eagle, he's never been anything but a half-civilized savage from the beginning. His recent acts of harassment and thievery and wreckage all through the valley, the acts of a heathen renegade—do you need any more proof than that?"

"But what you're proposing—it's madness!" said Mace Vernon.

"It's that and more," said Carstairs. "It's inhuman to even *think* such a thing. You'll never get away with actually doing it."

"Won't I? Who'll stop me?" hissed Dixon. "This is

my valley now, can't you fools get that through your heads? Once I've opened up the new vein of gold and I've run the last of the riffraff out—meaning that pitiful nest of refugees that Eagle has hidden up in the mountains somewhere, who'll be the next targets for my new pets—then I'll re-build it the way I want with the laws I want and only the people I want in it. If no one can stop me now, who'll dare try to stand in my way then?"

Roland looked like he was going to be sick. Vernon and Carstairs appeared numb, stunned by what they'd just heard, and the two engineers had long since fled away. Only Asa Patton's expression remained stony, unaffected.

"Turn me loose from this post!" howled Eagle, struggling wildly against his restraints. "Let me at those hellhounds of yours. I'll rip their livers and guts out with my bare teeth and then I'll come after you like I should have done at the very first!"

Dixon's only response was to smile a cold, tolerant smile, like he might upon watching a spoiled child throw a temper tantrum.

And that was when Hack Ferris reappeared, leading a dozen of the heavily armed hardcases who had initially arrived as part of Dixon's caravan.

Directing his question to Ferris, who was one of the men now standing close around him, Dixon said, "How much sunlight you figure is left?"

Ferris glanced skyward. "This time of year with a

clear sky? Three, four hours. Then some pretty good half light for a spell past that."

Dixon looked over at Ngamba. "Is that enough time for the dogs? If we allow their quarry a half-hour head start?"

Like Patton, the gruesome business under discussion elicited no outward reaction out of the black man. He said, "Plenty time, Bwana. Dogs not need long."

Dixon smiled. "Excellent. Tell your men to keep the dogs easy for just a while longer." Then he turned to Patton standing at his left elbow. "Go ahead and prepare the quarry as we discussed."

While Dixon's orders were being carried out, Ferris edged away a few steps and went to stand next to Roland who had remained apart from the others. The younger Dixon's face was still set in the sour, uncertain way of someone teetering on the verge of vomiting, and its color had a vaguely greenish tint. Ferris, for all his normal gruffness and tough outer demeanor, looked a bit queasy himself.

They were now all assembled on the edge of the badlands, several miles from the Gold Button. Shortly after Ferris had returned, as assigned, with half of the newly arrived gun toughs, they had ridden hard from the mining operation to this spot. Neither Mace Vernon nor Dr. Carstairs nor any of Ferris's own remaining gang members came with them. Having missed Dixon's lengthy but no less startling revelation on what he planned for Luke and Eagle, Ferris had only heard it during the ride here and it wasn't sitting entirely well with him, either.

"I got to tell you, Boss," he said now, speaking in

a low voice to Roland, "this thing we're about to do . . . it's got a kinda raw edge to it that bites deeper than anything I ever been part of before. Deeper than anything I ever *dreamed* of gettin' mixed up in."

"I know," Roland whispered hoarsely. "I've long been aware that my father could be extremely ruthless. But this . . . I never imagined there was a part of him that was capable of something like this."

Ferris gazed out across the endless expanse of bare, ragged rocks and jagged cliffs falling away into twisting arroyos baking in the mid-afternoon rays of a white hot sun. Gradually, his gaze drifted back and came to rest, briefly, on the leashed lion hounds where they rested calmly on their haunches beside their handlers, loose-fitting black hoods covering their heads. An involuntary shudder passed through Ferris. Then his eyes shifted to where Luke and Eagle were being jerked around and talked to by Patton.

"Those two," he said. "I had me a big hate built up for them and I was lookin' forward to 'em gettin' some real hard treatment before your old man let us finally set their suns. None of that's necessarily changed. But, jeez, what's about to happen to 'em instead of anything I ever pictured . . ."

"Don't say anything. Just hold your tongue," Roland warned him. "There's nothing we can do for them. Trying, even saying the slightest wrong thing, could only make grief for yourself."

"It's real simple," Patton was explaining. "You'll be stripped of everything but your britches. No shirts, no boots, no weapons. Your wrists will stay bound but the shackles will be removed from your ankles. That's the good news—you'll be able to stretch your legs and have a fair shot at outrunning the pretty puppies with the half-hour head start you're going to be given."

"Oh, hell, I was afraid you were gonna make it hard on us," remarked Eagle.

"If you want to take the time," Patton continued, ignoring him, "you can stop and possibly find a jagged edge on some rock that you could use to saw through the ropes on your wrists. I'm not recommending that, mind you, I'm just sayin'. I wouldn't want to be accused of leading you astray because I personally don't see where it would gain you that much, especially considering the time you'd lose."

"Your sense of fair play is inspiring," Luke told him, all the while glaring at the hired gun with hate-filled eyes. Both he and Eagle were on their feet now and Patton had come up to stand carelessly close as he talked. Three of Dixon's gun toughs were standing in a triangle formation only a few feet away, the muzzles of their rifles at all times aimed loosely at the two captives.

Even with his wrists bound, Luke could have reached out and snapped Patton's neck before anybody could stop him. Plus, he couldn't help thinking, maybe the bullets that would then find him would be preferable to the dogs. But the never-give-up survivor ingrained in his core held him in check, reminding him that maybe the dogs weren't necessarily the sure thing everybody was counting on.

"One final thing," Patton said, holding up a set of handcuffs with a four-foot chain between them, "is this little item, the ends of which will be clasped to one wrist on each of you. It's to keep you rascals from trying to split up and force the dogs to do likewise, thinking you might have a better chance with one dog at a time rather than both at once. Frankly, I don't think it would make hardly a lick of difference, but nobody wants to waste time prolonging the inevitable."

As he'd spoken, Patton had studiously avoided meeting Luke's eyes. Now he suddenly lifted his gaze and smiled crookedly.

"I know exactly what's going through your mind, Jensen. You're thinking you could grab me and rip out my throat before any of these fine fellows with rifles had the chance to cut you down. Am I right?"

"Those ain't his thoughts alone," injected Eagle.

Patton didn't break eye contact with Luke. "So why don't you? Ever since you figured out Dixon—and me, by association—had played you for a sucker, you've been beating yourself up for not spotting it sooner and killing me when you had the chance. So why not try it now, why not go for that one small piece of satisfaction?"

"Because you're not worth it," Luke said through gritted teeth.

"Oh? Really?"

"If it was Dixon standing there, it might be different. He'd be dead in a heartbeat. His last."

"And yours."

"Like I said, if it was him it might be different. The certainty of getting rid of Dixon might be worth it. You, you're just a cog in the wheel."

"But an important enough one to have successfully played you and helped get you here. It's too bad,"

Patton said, his crooked smile widening, "because I kinda liked you. And I sensed the feeling was somewhat mutual. At a different time and place, we might even have been friends. Or, if we'd still faced off as enemies, at least it would have been under more straight-up circumstances."

"Like you care."

Patton blinked. "Actually, I kinda do. Can't say I favor going about things the way we are . . . but it's part of the job I'm getting paid to do."

"Keep that in mind," Luke said, his voice now a barely audible rasp. "You might still get your chance to try and earn it straight up."

Chapter 45

The hunt was on!

Luke and Eagle were off and running, beginning their half-hour head start across the barren, blistering sea of jagged, punishing terrain—chained together and barefoot—in advance of the relentless hounds soon to be sent in pursuit.

They set a steady, controlled pace, one they could maintain for a long time as far as their wind and physical stamina went. The real decider on how fast the dogs would catch up would be how much the two men's exposed feet could endure from the slashing, burning landscape.

Barely had they gotten out of sight from Dixon and the rest who were counting down the time before loosing the ridgebacks and joining in the chase, before Luke signaled a halt.

"Already?" Eagle protested. "This is prime time for us to be makin' distance."

"I know, but this is going to help," Luke assured him. "Reach in the hip pocket of my pants, pull out what you find there. Careful, it's sharp."

Looking somewhat doubtful, Eagle did as instructed.

When he withdrew the shard of pottery from Ying-Su's broken pitcher, his expression failed to brighten very much.

"This? This is the weapon you were braggin' about back before Dixon showed up?"

"It took me more than an hour to work that up under the back of my leg and into my pocket without being spotted. Test the edges and tell me if it doesn't beat a jagged rock for cutting these ropes on our wrists."

Eagle lightly touched the ball of his thumb to an edge of the shard, which was basically a curved wedge about two inches long, a little over half that at its widest, and a half inch thick. "Yeah, almost as good as a razor."

Luke held out his bound wrists. "Okay, get to shaving with it then."

In little more than a minute, both men were free of their bonds. Briskly rubbing his chafed wrists, Eagle said, "Man, that feels good. I don't know how much it'll help us in the long run, but it definitely feels better." He held up his left wrist with the handcuff and chain dangling from it. "Now if we could do the same with this blasted thing!"

"Can't have everything," Luke told him. "But there's one more improvement we can make, an even bigger one, if you follow my lead."

As he spoke, Luke had been unbuckling his belt and pulling it out of the waist loops in his pants. When it was free, he held it up before Eagle. "Do the same with yours. Next we're each going to cut two-foot-long strips out of our belts and then use the ropes we just took off our wrists and tie the strips of belt leather to the bottoms of our feet. It will give us a good, tough layer of protection. It might slow our speed some, but it will more than make up for it by how much farther it takes us without our feet getting shredded. It's an old Indian trick I learned."

Eagle's eyebrows lifted. "An old Injun trick? But *I'm* the half-breed here!"

A corner of Luke's mouth quirked up as he began cutting the first strip from his belt. "Must be from the wrong tribe."

They were on the move again.

With their wrists unbound, they could pump their arms as they ran and it made the whole physical act smoother, more natural, less exerting. The chain linking them between handcuffs continued to be mostly a minor annoyance. The slap of their makeshift leather soles was gratifying and although—as Luke had predicted—the feel of them had been rather awkward at first, the protection they provided from the punishing floor of the badlands far outweighed that period of adjustment.

Luke had lost any sense of how much time had passed since they'd started out. He tried not to dwell on it. All they could do was keep going, keep increasing the distance, keep hoping for . . . something. Some break. They'd each kept the buckles from their belts and held them now clenched in their fists, prongs jutted out between fingers, for the sake of adding a little something to any punches they might get close enough to throw, against man or dog.

This time it was Eagle who abruptly signaled a halt.

He paused and immediately poised in a half crouch, his eyes locked on a low rock formation just a few yards ahead. Over his shoulder, he whispered to Luke, "Stay with me but stay back. Move slow, keep the slack out of the chain so it don't clink."

So saying, Eagle crept slowly, cautiously forward. The rock formation he was advancing on consisted of some rounded, pumpkin-sized stones partly embedded into the ground with a flattish slab of rock balanced across the tops of part of them.

Because he was ambidextrous, Luke had accepted his end of the chain being handcuffed to his right wrist, leaving his left hand free, so that Eagle could have his dominant right hand free. It was this hand that the former sheriff held extended out ahead of himself now, thumb and fingers curled loosely, clawlike. The belt buckle he'd been clenching there earlier, he'd temporarily transferred to his left hand.

Luke hung back, watching closely, curiously, keeping the handcuff chain taut. He couldn't figure out what Eagle was up to, but he trusted the man well enough to count on it being something meaningful, something worth taking this amount of time for.

Suddenly, Eagle's clawed hand shot forward. With a deft twist of his wrist at the last possible instant, he flipped the flat rock off balance and forward and drove it down hard between the rounded stones. Something in that formerly shaded pocket thrashed and struggled wildly, kicking up plumes of dust and at the same time issuing one of the most dreaded sounds known to man—the tail buzz of a diamondback rattler!

Eagle kept slamming the edge of the flat rock down and then leaning on it, grinding the snake into the hard stone pocket. He didn't stop grinding until the snake was still and its rattler silent.

Tossing the rock slab aside, Eagle turned and dropped back into a sitting position on the smoother rocks. He was breathing hard and dripping sweat. "I saw that rock formation and I . . . just knew . . . this time of day . . . there was bound to be a fat old rattler in there . . . catchin' hisself some shade."

Luke looked at him, his forehead puckering. "Okay. You obviously were right. But what was the point? You got something against rattlesnakes getting themselves some shade?"

"The point?" Eagle stood up, leaned over and reached into the stone pocket with his free hand. A moment later he lifted out the dead snake and held it up. It was long and indeed fat. Slamming it back down to the ground and nudging with his foot until it was spread out between him and Luke, he squatted down next to it and picked up a chunk of broken rock about eight inches in diameter.

"The point," he said as he started pounding on the fat part of the snake with the rock, rupturing the outer skin and exposing the reptile's insides, "is to get at the innards of this devil's spawn and rub 'em all over our feet and legs. Unless those African trail sniffers are different than any other four-legged critter I ever heard tell of, the scent of this stinky old rattler is gonna make 'em want to steer as wide as they can and have nothing to do with tryin' to follow it."

Luke dropped to his knees beside the snake carcass and reached for a rock of his own. "You really think it will work?"

"If it don't, we can always say it should have," replied

Eagle as he began pulling out handfuls of snake guts
and smearing them on his feet and ankles. "It's an old
Injun trick I heard tell of once—from the Rattlesnake
Tribe, I think it was."

Parker Dixon snapped shut his jewel-encrusted
pocket watch and then shoved it, at the end of its gold
chain, back into his vest.

"It's nearly time. Tell your boys to get ready,
Ngamba," he said to the tall African standing next to
him. Ngamba snapped a quick nod and trotted off
toward the dog handlers.

To Asa Patton, standing next to him on the other
side, Dixon said, "Tell the other men to get ready to
mount up. Also, bring my horse forward."

"Of course," said Patton. He started to turn away,
then paused. "You realize, sir, that riders on horseback aren't going to be able to travel through that
rough country nearly as fast as those dogs."

"Of course I realize that," Dixon replied, mopping
sweat from his face with a brilliant white handkerchief. "But Ngamba and the handlers, who'll be
on foot, can keep up with the dogs remarkably well.
They run like gazelles. And they, in turn, will keep us
signaled on how the hunt is progressing. We won't be
that far behind."

"And when they catch up with Eagle and Jensen
ahead of us?"

Dixon smiled. "Don't worry, they know what to do.
The dogs will keep their quarry 'treed,' I guess you
could say, for want of a better word, until I get there.
Trust me, I've made it very clear that I don't want the

final punishment delivered before I am on hand to see it."

Patton's mouth suppressed what might have been a grimace. "Right. I'll tell the men to get ready to mount up."

Across the way, the dog handlers had removed the hoods from the ridgebacks and unsnapped their leashes. The dogs remained sitting on their haunches but began to whimper expectantly, sensing what was soon to come. The handlers threw to the ground in front of them the boots that had been taken from Luke and Eagle. The dogs sniffed and nudged these with minimal interest at first. But then each of the handlers took from the waistbands of the loincloths they wore under their burlap shirts a pair of hollowed-out cane tubes about a foot and a half long. These they began slowly striking together in a rhythmic pattern.

Clack! Clack-clack! Clack-clack-clack!

As they continued this, the dogs began gnawing and then taking the boots in their teeth and shaking them with increasing aggression.

Roland stepped up beside his father. Frowning, he said, "What are they doing?"

"They're stirring up the dogs," Dixon replied, an almost mesmerized gleam in his eyes as they followed the procedure. "They're preparing them for the hunt, working them into a frenzy and locking them onto the quarry they'll be sent after. I watched them do this in a workout session before we left Helena. It was a fascinating thing to see. I can only imagine what it will be like when performed for real."

Roland backed away again, staring at his father like he was someone he had never seen before.

* * *

As they continued to run, Luke began leading them more to the south and gradually angling back toward the front edge of the badlands.

"You're actin' like you got some place particular in mind," chuffed Eagle beside him. "You ain't figurin' to work back out to the prairie, are you?"

"No, nothing like that," Luke replied. "But I do have an idea. Just keep watching the sky up ahead."

"Ain't what's ahead I'm worried about, it's what's behind."

Not long after Eagle said that, they heard for the first time the distant baying of the dogs being sent after them.

"Just keep watching the sky," Luke said again.

"What are we lookin' for?" Eagle wanted to know.

"Buzzards," came the answer between slaps of running feet.

"Buzzards? Ain't that about the *last* thing we want to see? We don't catch a break, we're gonna soon enough be seein' 'em circlin' straight over our heads."

Chapter 46

"What the hell's going on here? Why the slowdown?" Dixon demanded, reining up his horse and scowling fiercely at the scene before him. He and the other horsemen had unexpectedly caught up with the dogs and their handlers. The latter were scrambling frantically back and forth, banging their cane sticks together loudly and shouting at the dogs as the animals circled and shied away, making guttural, moaning sounds.

Ngamba came over to Dixon, frowning, appearing perplexed and somewhat worried. "Strange juju, Bwana," he said. "The dogs no like, no more want to make chase."

"Well, they'd better *learn* to like it," Dixon roared. "What kind of juju nonsense has gotten into them? I didn't spend all the money and make all the shipping arrangements I did to bring those mongrels over here—not to mention you and those worthless stick beaters—just to watch them mince around in circles! Somebody had better figure out a way to get them back on the hunt again or I'll turn the worthless curs into the most expensive barbecue ever served at the nearest Indian reservation!"

"Here's the problem," announced Patton, who had dismounted and was walking the ground the dogs kept skittering away from. With the barrel of his rifle, he poked down at the ground and then lifted up part of the mutilated rattlesnake skin. The ridgebacks stopped circling, locked their eyes on the gory remains, and growled menacingly. "Looks like Eagle and Jensen killed a rattler and then smeared themselves with its guts to throw the dogs off their scent. The rattler smell is new to the ridgebacks, but instinctively, they're wary of it and don't want anything to do with it."

"You hear that, Ngamba? Tell your boys to figure out a way to make those stupid dogs *un*-wary and be blasted quick about it!" said Dixon.

Ngamba hurried toward the dog handlers, jabbering excitedly. Abruptly, one of the men darted over and took the snake remains off the snout of Patton's rifle. With overly dramatic gestures he hurled the remains to the ground and began jumping up and down on it. Then he leaned over and talked to it, cursing roundly in his native tongue. Next he picked it back up and flung it directly in front of the dogs. The other handler promptly joined in the elaborate selling job and he, too, cursed the snake skin and kicked at it. Then he began chanting, "Akatari! Akatari! Akatari!" as he took up banging his sticks together again.

The ridgebacks were no longer acting skittish and had started to growl with increasing volume, an ominous rumble from deep in their chests. Suddenly one of them pounced on the snake remains and the other did the same an instant later. They took it in their teeth and began shaking it furiously, growling even louder, until they ripped it into two pieces.

Both handlers were chanting and beating their sticks faster and faster.

"Akatari! Aka-akatari!"

Clack-clack! Clack-clack-clack!

Ngamba ran several feet ahead, in the direction his trained eyes had seen some ground spoor indicating where their quarry had continued on. Stopping, he swung his long arm in a sweeping gesture and then called in a high-pitched, ululating wail, "Akatariiii!"

The ridgebacks, worked once again into a fever pitch even greater than before, broke away and raced past Ngamba, convinced to no longer fear the rattler scent but rather be angry at it and want to chase it down.

Returning to his horse and swinging back up into the saddle, Patton said dryly, "Looks like no ridgeback steak for any Injuns tonight. Let's go, we'd better get a move on if we aim to catch up with them again."

Luke slowed his pace and between labored breaths raised an arm and pointed. "There. Those dots ahead low in the sky . . . see them?"

"Okay. Yeah, now I do," panted Eagle.

Both men were nearly spent. Their chests were rising and falling rapidly, they were slick with sweat, their exposed backs and shoulders were bright pink from the sun.

"We've got to keep going. We've got to make it that far," Luke rasped.

It was in that moment that full realization hit Eagle,

an understanding of where Luke was heading, why he was pushing so hard to make it there. "That's got to be close to the spot where those varmints ambushed us the other day . . . Ferris and his bunch . . . the ones you and Pettigrew stayed behind to deal with while Barlow and me made it clear. You thinkin' the bodies of the ones you killed are still there?"

"That's what I'm counting on, yeah," said Luke. "Their bodies and their weapons."

Eagle ran the back of one hand across his dry, cracked lips. "You don't figure anybody's gone back to retrieve 'em?"

"Don't see where they've had much chance. They took the kids hostage, remember, and holed up in Hard Rock for the trade. Then we hit them there last night."

"That seems like a year ago," Eagle groaned.

"Today, the only ones left have been with us at the Gold Button, getting ready for Dixon to show up," added Luke. "I figure the bodies are still out there, and those buzzards up ahead are not only the clincher for that, but they're showing us exactly where."

From behind, for the first time in quite a while, they heard the baying of the ridgebacks. And mingled faintly with that dreaded sound was something new. An odd, snapping noise . . . *Clack-clack. Clack-clack.*

"They're coming fast. Let's move it!" Luke urged.

Time and distance turned into one long, increasingly agonizing blur.

The rocky humps and jagged upthrusts and sudden, twisting arroyos swam before the two half-running, half-staggering men. Sometimes one of them would fall—sometimes both. They would lie there and pant for precious seconds and then drag themselves up and plunge on again. The ropes binding the strips of leather to the bottoms of their feet had begun to fray and break, causing the strips of leather to slip and flap loosely, threatening to trip them and add to the spills. Their hands were blistered from reaching out to grab bare rock surfaces for support and their chests and arms were scraped raw from times when no support was there.

The sun was sinking lower above the horizon but was still a white-hot ball of fury throwing heat and a blinding glare. Twice, Luke looked skyward and saw no sign of the buzzards. Alarm coursed through him until he realized he was looking too far ahead. He had to look *up*, practically straight up, and when he did he saw the usually dreaded sight of the sky scavengers circling almost directly overhead.

They were almost there. So close.

But also close, ever closer, was the baying of the ridgebacks and the strange clacking sounds and voices accompanying them.

Chapter 47

The edge of the gully was there before either man realized it.

Staggering as they were, eyes squinted against stinging sweat as well as the aches and pains that throbbed throughout their bodies, they didn't see it until they were toppling over its rim and dropping in a tangle to the gravelly bottom. For a moment, they just lay there, fighting to regain what little wind they'd had left before the fall knocked out even most of that.

Then, abruptly, Luke sat up straighter. A shadow flicked across them, cast down momentarily from the sky. Luke twisted his head, looking to the right and left. He knew this place! They were in the gully—the twisting slash in the earth that had played an important part in the bounty hunter's survival only the previous day. And now there was the chance for a repeat performance today.

"Eagle! Come on, we can't let up now," Luke urged the former sheriff on the other end of the handcuff chain. He pushed himself to his feet and tugged on the chain, dragging Eagle up as well.

Another shadow flicked over them. A buzzard circling

in the sky above, the center of its pattern seemingly down the gully to their right, off to the west. Luke's breath quickened—not from exhaustion for a change, but from excitement. If he was right, this meant that the body of the first would-be flanker he had killed yesterday, the one he'd used his Bowie knife on, was only a short distance away!

Luke threw himself in that direction, pulling Eagle after him. "Come on," he urged again. "We're almost there!"

The gully twisted maddeningly, running straight for only a few yards at a time before turning abruptly to the right or left, just enough to create a blind corner. Luke kept rounding these corners, his gaze probing anxiously ahead each time, hoping against hope to spot what he so desperately wanted to see. The heavy breathing of both himself and Eagle seemed amplified within the close walls of the gully, puffing like the ragged chugs of a locomotive fighting up a steep grade.

And then at last, there it was! The sprawled, bloated form of what had once been a man, now covered by a buzzing swarm of flies and riddled with gouges and gashes where eyeballs and strips of skin had been plucked and torn away by scavengers. Never had such a grisly sight looked so wonderful to the eyes of a beholder.

Five more yards. Luke took the first step to cover that distance. He could feel renewed strength, pumped from some untapped deep source, starting to course through him.

And then, half a foot ahead of his face, which was

positioned at a level just below the rim of the gully, a set of slavering, fanged jaws thrust out and down over the rim. The rows of razor-sharp teeth slashed the air and at the same time the snarling ridgeback emitted a menacing growl that rolled down and rumbled the length of the gully.

Luke jerked back, nearly unbalancing both himself and Eagle. Both men managed to stay upright, though, and dropped into half crouches, swinging up their fists with the pronged belt buckles clenched in them. Half a yard behind Eagle, the second ridgeback thrust its head over the rim of the gully, baring its own slashing fangs and teeth and issuing another reverberating, nerve-freezing growl. From somewhere unseen, but close by, the jabbering, excited voices of the handlers and the rapid clacking of their cane sticks added to the sudden cacophony.

"No!" said Luke, his voice coming from a guttural place that made it a growl of its own. "We didn't make it this far only to end up dog food. Hang on, we're going for those weapons!"

"Don't wait for me!" Eagle hollered back.

Luke charged forward in a long, lunging step. Timing it just right, he swung his buckle-reinforced fist in a hard, swooping uppercut. At the peak of the swing, his fist crashed into the underside of the first ridgeback's jaw, the metal prong digging in and ripping a long gash as the dog's head was knocked upward and back. The beast twisted and fell away from the edge of the gully, yelping and thrashing in pain and rage.

The rest of the way was clear. Luke bulled forward,

dragging Eagle with him. As he threw himself onto the mutilated corpse and the treasure of weapons it held, the second ridgeback—goaded by the damage it had seen done to its mate and driven by the scent of fresh blood—leaped down into the gully and sprang for Eagle. The half-breed punched and kicked desperately, trying to keep the beast's claws and gnashing teeth at bay.

Reaching blindly through the swarm of a hundred buzzing flies, Luke's hand closed on the dead man's gunbelt, digging and tugging to find its way to the attached holster. His grip closed on the familiar feel of a gun butt and he yanked the six-shooter free even as the wild thrashing and flailing of Eagle fighting against the attacking ridgeback tried to pull him away by virtue of the connecting handcuff chain. But then, with the gun now in hand, Luke went willingly with the pull, twisting around and thrusting his arm across Eagle's shoulder. At point-blank range, he triggered two blasts straight into the dog's savagely contorted face. The animal flew back in a splatter of blood and gore.

But before Luke had a chance to twist around or even pull his arm back from the way it was levered across Eagle's shoulder, the first ridgeback—the one Luke had temporarily knocked away and wounded into an even greater rage—leaped down directly onto his back. The near hundred pounds of clawing, biting beast was a crushing, immobilizing weight. In the tight confines of the gully, Luke not only couldn't turn back around or lift his own torso, but the way he was positioned was also pinning down Eagle.

Worse yet, since he was facing away from the dog,

he couldn't even raise his hands in any defensive
manner. Feeling hot blood gush up over the back of
his neck as the animal's teeth ripped into his shoulder, all he could do was cry out in pain and rage.

This time it was Eagle's reach that saved them.
Even though pinned partially under Luke, the former
sheriff still had a limited view and one arm free. Extending the latter as far as he could, he managed to
seize the handle of the Bowie knife he could see jutting up from where it was sunk in the corpse—Luke's
Bowie, the one he had thrown to kill the stalking
gunman in the first place—and yank it free.

From there, in a desperate, blind lunge, he thrust
his arm upward and slashed viciously when he felt the
blade sink deep into the chest of the ridgeback on top
of Luke. With a gurgling howl of surprise and agony,
the dog rolled away, flailing wildly, taking the knife
with it as it flopped to the floor of the gully. An arc of
blood rose high as it gave its final kicks and then
became totally still.

Once again, Parker Dixon had reined his horse to
a sharp halt. Scowling ahead across the barren, fore-
boding landscape, he said, "What was that? Shots?
Did anybody else hear the sound of shooting?"

Standing in his stirrups, also deeply scowling, Asa
Patton said, "That's sure what it sounded like. Did any
of those handlers have guns?"

"No. They're frightened just being *around* guns,"
Dixon replied.

"How to explain it then? There's not much reason

for anybody else being in this broken country, and it certainly doesn't seem possible for Jensen or the half-breed to have gotten their hands on a gun out here in the middle of nowhere."

Not far to the rear of this discussion, a sudden bolt of sickening fear ran through Hack Ferris. The realization hit him that no, such a thing *wasn't* so impossible. In fact, he knew exactly how and . . . with a sinking feeling of dread . . . *where* the fugitives might have gotten their hands on some weapons.

Looking with alarm in all directions, Ferris inwardly cursed these badlands. An ocean of twisted, grotesque rock formations and shapes, no two exactly alike yet somehow always looking the same. At least that's how it seemed to Hack. Where had this insane chase led them? Were they indeed somewhere close to where that blasted Jensen had cut down Dog DeMarist and those others just yesterday? Ferris had meant to send somebody out to retrieve the bodies first chance he got, but after the raid last night at the Elkhorn Saloon in Hard Rock and then Dixon showing up today and this hunt being set in motion so fast . . .

If he told Dixon and Patton now what he had failed to mention before—no matter that it was partly their fault for taking off on such short notice and not allowing him even a chance to think—it was bound to go hard on him. As increasingly crazy as Dixon was proving himself to be and backed by these new gun toughs on top of that steely-eyed Patton, it might go so hard as them killing him.

Ferris wanted out. Running men down with killer

African dogs had almost been the last straw to begin with. Now possibly facing his own demise due to a simple oversight—a demise maybe even delivered by the same horrible dogs—was definitely too much. He didn't deserve it. Not only was he unwilling to risk facing the ire of Dixon, neither did he want to risk another encounter with Jensen and Eagle. They'd already wiped out nearly his whole crew, maybe it was time to take the hint and steer clear of them while he was still able.

"Ferris! Blast it, what are you daydreaming about?" The sharp words coming from Dixon shook Ferris out of his doomed thoughts. "I asked you, did you hear those shots?"

"Uh, yeah," Ferris answered. "Leastways, I heard something that *might* have been shots. You gotta remember, out here amongst all these rocks sound sometimes does strange things. I don't see how anybody up ahead of us could have got hold of a gun out of thin air."

"No, me neither," Dixon said, his eyebrows pinched tight together.

"It's got to be Ngamba or one of the handlers," said Patton. "One of them must have had a pistol under his shirt and took a pot shot at a coyote or maybe another rattler."

Still brooding, Dixon responded, "It must be something like that. In any event, we've got to continue ahead and find out. Come on, everybody stay sharp and proceed with caution."

As the others started out, Ferris abruptly nosed his horse to one side and swung down from his saddle.

"What's the matter? What are you doing?" Roland Dixon asked him.

"My nag is steppin' funny. Must've picked up a pebble in one of its shoes," Ferris answered without making eye contact. "Shouldn't take but a minute to find it and dig it out. Go on along, I'll catch up . . ."

Chapter 48

Neither Luke nor Eagle had felt moved to harm the dog handlers. They were, after all, basically inno-cents in a strange land caught up in a cruel game they may not have even fully understood. They'd certainly understood the death of their precious dogs, however, and all three had fallen to their knees beside the bodies, mournfully wailing and lamenting the loss.

So that's how Luke and Eagle left them. Ideally, they would have preferred not leaving them behind to give any warning or explanation to the others who would be showing up. But there was no time to deal with them in any effective way short of shooting them, too, and the shooting already done—two rounds to kill one of the dogs and another to break the handcuff chain linking the two fugitives together—had already given sufficient warning to Dixon and the rest.

The best use of the time the pair of battered, exhausted men had before the remainder of their pursuers arrived was to gather up the guns and am-munition from the other two bodies they would find close by. With his bearings now established and feeling somewhat rejuvenated by having the sense of a fighting chance, Luke quickly led the way to the dead men. After stripping them of all useful items, including two mercifully full canteens, they fell into the shade of the tall, mushroom-shaped rock formation Luke had used before, and slaked their thirsts while hastily formulating their next move.

"I got no more run left in me. I vote we pick a spot right here close and make a stand against 'em," Eagle said, quickly summing up his feelings.

"I agree," Luke said without hesitation. "But with one provision."

"What's that?"

"We don't just make a stand—we wipe 'em out. I hate ambushes," the bounty hunter said grimly, "but we've got no choice. If we get into a prolonged shoot-out or running fight, we're right back where we've been. They can hold out indefinitely by sending men to drop back and re-supply, we can't. We've got to end it and end it quick if we want any chance to survive."

Eagle looked at him with eyes that had grown bloodshot from stinging sweat and lancing sunlight. "Like you said back there in the gully—we didn't come this far to end up as dog food. Nor to end up under the boot heel of Parker Dixon, either."

Luke tipped up his canteen and drank some more of its warm, stale contents that under the circumstances tasted better than the finest wine he'd ever sampled. Lowering it, he said, "About Dixon . . . as far as those claims he made saying I betrayed his brother and was part of stealing that Confederate gold shipment near the end of the war—"

Eagle cut him off. "If you're gonna tell me he had it twisted around all wrong, don't bother. You'd be insultin' me by suggestin' that, after knowin' you, I'd have to be *told* you wouldn't be part of anything like that."

Luke gave a short nod. "Thanks."

"What you *can* tell me," Eagle said, after a quick glance skyward, "is what you got in mind for how we're gonna set up to greet Dixon and his bunch in order to leave 'em as buzzard pickin's . . ."

There was nothing elaborate about the plan they came up with. It was simple and cold-blooded. They decided to hit Dixon and his followers as soon as they reached the spot where the dog handlers were still wailing over their slain dogs, before there was too much chance for Ngamba to try and provide an explanation or for the new arrivals to get over their surprise and shift to a more defensive approach.

The terrain immediately on the north side of the gully, where the gun toughs would be riding in, was a rare stretch of flat, open ground covering a semicircular pattern over several yards. This made it well within range for a rifleman up on the flat top of the mushroom-shaped rock formation slightly to the west, the same perch Luke had used earlier—a position Eagle now assumed, armed with a pair of Henry rifles he had taken from the dead men.

A short way to the east of the open area, a low, ragged spine of rocks thrust up and ran along the north rim of the gully. Looping wide around to make sure he was unseen by the dog handlers, Luke squirmed in and crouched among the diminutive peaks, armed with two Colt .45 revolvers and a Winchester rifle.

Between them, Luke and Eagle had over fifty rounds of ready firepower without ever needing to reload.

They didn't have long to wait for the opportunity to use it.

Luke barely had time to get in place before they saw the dust cloud approaching and heard the clatter of horses' hooves on the hard, rocky ground. With Dixon and Patton riding at the head, the group of horsemen slowed when they came within sight of the dog handlers and saw the motionless shapes they were kneeling beside. Then, unable to hold back a half-choked curse, Dixon spurred forward and Patton kept pace. The others lagged only slightly before following, keeping grouped fairly closely together.

Ngamba rose to his feet and began jabbering excitedly with a flurry of hand gestures as Dixon and Patton both hurriedly dismounted and strode toward him. The others crowded up close and halted their horses, spreading out somewhat in accordance with the semi-circular pattern of the flatter ground.

Luke sucked a quick breath, let out half, then held it. There wasn't going to be a better time. By agreement, he was to start it off . . .

And so he did.

Rising up with a Colt in each hand, he said, "Welcome to hell, boys!" and cut loose. A second after his Colts discharged simultaneously, the first report of

Eagle's Henry boomed down from the mushroom rock and lead and blood began filling the air.

The way they'd planned it, due to the angles and proximity of their different firing positions, was that Eagle would sweep from the front into the middle of the pack, Luke would work from the back inward. And that's the way they executed it—execute being a grimly appropriate term. Few, if any, shots from the skilled ambushers missed. Men threw up their arms and toppled from their saddles, screaming horses reared and wheeled this way and that, trying to bolt away, and still more men fell. A few managed to draw their weapons and a handful even got off shots, but all were wild, desperate guesses as there was no real chance in the wild melee for the targets to establish where the incoming rounds were coming from.

It was over quickly. By the time Luke had emptied his revolvers and took up the Winchester, there was no one left to use it on. The only ones still alive were Ngamba and one of the dog handlers. As before, Luke and Eagle had intended no purposeful harm to these men but a stray bullet, ricocheting off something, had taken its toll regardless.

Also, by design, Roland Dixon was left alive. The ambushers had decided ahead of time to allow this, if possible. In the absence of his father, they calculated he would make a useful negotiating tool when they returned to the Gold Button.

As for the power- and revenge-crazed Parker Dixon, he was the first one Eagle had killed. "Not only without regret, but with extreme pleasure," he would say later. The second man to fall under the former sheriff's sights, due to his competence making him a significant threat, had been Asa Patton. When Luke walked among the dead after the shooting was over, he paused for a moment over Patton's corpse and did feel a pang of regret. Not because the scoundrel was dead, but because he hadn't had the chance to face him straight up and do the job himself.

Chapter 49

The celebration at the mountain camp that night was inhibited only by the battered, exhausted condition of the two men whose return was the very cause for the celebration.

Nevertheless, while Luke and Eagle were bathed, salved, bandaged, and then fed and wined to near bursting, the joyous mood in the camp was at full pitch. The mere fact they'd shown up still alive would have been plenty of reason for this, but the promise they brought that some sense of normalcy might actually be in store for the valley—by virtue of Parker Dixon being dead and his son Roland in custody—added all the more.

Not even the temporary presence of Roland in their midst was enough to dampen things, especially after he let it be known he was willing to sign back all property deeds throughout the valley and meet any other demands that would allow his safe return to Helena in order to take over the helm of Dixon business interests there, and strictly there. It was still deemed prudent to keep him bound and under watch, but for his agreeableness, he was given food and drink and not abused in any of the manners that several present had threatened to do at their sight of him.

As for Ngamba and the other dog handler, whose name was M'Botu, they also were given food and drink and generally welcomed and treated with respect. They accepted this and expressed their gratitude yet remained, understandably, reserved and uncertain about all they had seen and been part of. Luke and Eagle had tried to explain to Ngamba why they'd had to do the things they'd done, killing the dogs and then staging the ambush and all, but it nevertheless seemed overwhelming and a bit too frightening for him to fully comprehend. Among his promises, Roland had sworn he would take the pair back to Helena with him and arrange return passage to their homeland.

Later, when things had begun to wind down some, Luke and Dinah Mercer found a few minutes to be alone together. As before, it had been she who'd administered mostly to his battered condition when he first arrived. He was so sore and sunburned and worn down then that even her light touch had caused him to wince sharply a few times. But not so now, when she reached to gently caress his face.

"This must be getting awfully tiresome for you," he said, "patching me up only to have me come back the worse for wear and requiring it all over again."

"You don't hear me complaining, do you?"

"You're not the complaining type."

"I'm just glad that you're able to come back. Especially this time," Dinah replied. "I hate to admit it now, but we weren't holding out much hope of ever seeing you or Tom again. Not after Red Baker's report on how things had gone at the last there in the Elkhorn Saloon."

"Yeah, things were looking pretty bleak for a while," admitted Luke. "But giving up was never in the cards, not for me or Eagle either one."

"No, you're not the type. Just like you said I'm not the complaining type. Especially when I get compensated so well for my time."

At these last words, her eyes flicked meaningfully to her sewing basket. It was there, stuffed deep into the rest of the paraphernalia it contained, that Luke had, before leaving the previous night, stuffed his wallet and all the money it held.

Luke's eyebrows lifted now. "So you found it."

"I could hardly have missed it. I happen to use that basket for purposes besides just stitching you back together."

"I meant for you to discover it without too much trouble . . . in case I didn't make it back." Luke shrugged. "After all, it wouldn't have done you much good if you'd never come across it."

Dinah arched a brow. "You know, there's a name for women who take money from men who have visited their quarters . . . and for men who leave such payments."

Luke felt the heat of a flush pour over his face. "Hey, now wait a minute! You can't think I meant for that to be—"

Dinah put a finger to his lips and shushed him. "Calm down. I was just teasing. I wouldn't have thought it possible, given how sunburned your face already is, for it to turn any redder."

Luke leaned back and groaned. "Don't remind me. That blasted sun and all those hot rocks—I got blisters in places I never knew I had places before. But that salve you put on sure helped. At least I can lean back against something now. As a matter of fact, I feel like I could lean back here right now and sleep for about a month."

"And you've certainly earned the right to." Dinah regarded him as he allowed his eyes to drift shut. "But you can't, can you? It's not over yet. Not until you take Roland back to the Gold Button and finish up there. Isn't that right?"

Without opening his eyes, Luke said, "Yeah. That's where all the deeds and other paperwork are, the stuff Roland needs to sign back over."

"And those remaining gun toughs Dixon brought with him will also be there."

"Roland is our shield against them. That, and the fact that Parker Dixon isn't around to pay them anymore. They're the kind of men who only fight for money. When that dries up, so will they."

Dinah laid her head against his chest. "I hope you're right. I hope something about this valley and all its problems finally starts to work out easier for you."

"Either way," said Luke, "it'll keep until tomorrow, and I'm not going to worry about it until then."

Moments later, Dinah could feel his chest rising and falling with deep, even breaths and pretty soon he was issuing soft, exhausted snores.

They approached the Gold Button two hours past sunrise, Luke and Eagle riding close on either side of

Roland. The latter had his hands tied behind his back and two leather thongs were looped around his neck, one leading off and tied to Luke's saddle horn, the other to Eagle's. In addition, each of the outside men held a twelve gauge shotgun braced on his hip, barrel angled so that the twin bores were aimed at Roland's head from less than a foot's distance.

This was how they rode in, past Roland's private cabin, and up to the front of the mess hall. Curiously, there was no activity in evidence anywhere on the grounds.

Reining in their horses, Luke called out, "Hello, Gold Button! Somebody? We've got some business to conduct here!"

The first sign of a response came from Roland's cabin. The front door opened and Ying-Su emerged. She stepped out with a boldness and with her head and exotically beautiful face held higher than the way it was usually lowered in subservience. Her garb was also different than the usual form-fitting silk; instead she wore loose pants and a flowing blouse.

Then the door of the mess hall opened and Dr. Carstairs and the mine foreman, Mace Vernon, stepped out. For a moment, their expressions were sober, somewhat suspicious. After a good look at what stood before them, however, Carstairs's face broke into an elated grin. "Tom, are you a sight for sore eyes! We thought we'd seen the last of you when you rode out yesterday."

"I had sort of the same feeling," Eagle admitted. "But as you can see, it didn't quite work out that way."

Looking around, frowning, Luke said, "What's

going on around here, Doc? Apart from our surprise appearance, things don't feel the same."

"That's because they're not. Not by a long shot," said Vernon. "You fellas making it back is just icing on the cake. But after you got taken away yesterday, some of us finally decided to grow some guts and reached the breaking point on how far a man can go along with something so sick and wrong."

"I think I like what I'm hearin'," said Eagle. "But maybe you need to put a little finer point on it."

"It's simple enough," Carstairs told him. "As soon as Dixon rode off, those gun toughs he left behind along with the rest of Ferris's boys decided to relax their guard and aim their pistols toward having some fun with the whores the Gold Button keeps on hand for entertaining the crew. While the cat's away sort of thing. At the same time, Vernon and me figured we were overdue to start acting like men and there was never going to be a better chance. So with the help of some of Mace's miners, including all the Chinese workers thanks to Ying-Su urging them on, we got the jump on those rascals and put them under our guns."

"Not to overdo it with the clichés, but we caught 'em with their pants down," Vernon said.

Eagle gave a low whistle. "I don't know from clichés, but that was some mighty slick work!"

"We've got them stuck down in a dead-end mine shaft for the time being, until we could decide what to do with them," said Carstairs. "Now that you're here, *Sheriff*, I guess you can make the call on that."

Roland seemed to be only peripherally listening to any of this. His eyes were on Ying-Su, who had walked over from the cabin. "And you aided in this?" he said to her in a forlorn tone. "I was *good* to you!"

"You made me your personal whore, and I was disgusted by every second of it," she replied in perfect English, her own tone filled with disdain. "What is more, we both know that when you tired of me, you would have brought in a new girl and cast me to the cribs with the others!"

Roland hung his head and looked somehow more deeply hurt and dejected than at any time up until now. After a moment, in a voice barely above a whisper, he said, "You can take the shotguns away now. Untie me and lead me to the safe in the mine office where the deeds and other papers are. I'll sign over everything you want. You have your town and your valley back now."

Chapter 50

Luke hung around Hard Rock Valley for nearly three weeks, recuperating from his injuries, helping out, watching the town and the outlying places like Barlow's horse ranch and MacGregor's farm start to come back to life. With the telegraph lines up and likely to stay up for a while, Dr. Carstairs wasted no time sending for his wife and daughter. Others who'd been driven out but had known present whereabouts were also contacted to see if they had any interest in coming back. Some indicated they would, others were quick to pass.

Ben Pettigrew and his son had plans to expand the blacksmith shop and run it together after Heath and Belinda Eagle got married in the fall. Red Baker headed for the mountains and back to prospecting, alone, as soon as he was able to scrape together enough gear. Before leaving the mountain encampment, Neal Vickers finally got up enough courage to ask the widow Mary Hobart to marry him, but she turned him down, gently, saying she had too many harsh memories of Hard Rock Valley and, against the protests of her son, needed to find somewhere else to live. Ying-Su indicated an interest in rebuilding the Palace Saloon. And Chang-Ha, one of Vernon's lead men at the mine, with whom Ying-Su had been having a secret affair while being kept by Roland, was ready to side her in the venture.

As for Vernon, once Roland had signed the Gold Button over to him, he proceeded to turn it into a joint operation with those miners—white and Chinese alike—who were willing to stay on with him and share in the earnings from whatever they were able to get out. Maybe the mother lode Parker Dixon believed so strongly in was really somewhere to be hit, maybe it wasn't.

For Roland's part, true to his word, he disbanded what was left of his father's gun toughs and, after they got back to Helena, made arrangements for Ngamba and M'Botu to return to their homeland. Outside of that, he delved into Dixon business interests in and around Helena and, as far as anyone knew, never gave another look north toward Hard Rock Valley.

With all the moving and refurbishing and building going on, Dewey Akron was kept busy with enough odd jobs until the saloons opened up again and he could go back to swamping for beer money and a sleeping pallet in a storeroom. But wherever he was and whatever he was doing, inside his head Dewey was always on the lookout for that Rebel patrol just over the rise.

Like Dewey, Luke also carried something inside himself. The urge to move on, to never stay in one place too long. As the days and weeks passed, he felt it building.

And although he didn't know how, others sensed

it also. Which he took for one more sign that he was getting too close, that it was time to drift.

One day he sat on a boardwalk bench cleaning his beloved Remingtons, having retrieved them from the pile of guns taken off the hardcases at the Gold Button before Carstairs and Vernon herded them into a mine shaft. It turned out that Paul Grimsby, one of Hack Ferris's boys (left behind by Ferris, who was still on the run somewhere), had taken a shine to them and was figuring to wear them himself once he heard about Luke getting thrown to the dogs. Since getting them back, Luke had been wiping them down and oiling them incessantly.

Eagle came along and took a seat next to him. He said, "You know, if any of Grimsby *did* rub off on those Remys, I'm pretty sure you've long since got it cleaned away."

"Nothing wrong with a man taking good care of the tools of his trade," Luke responded.

"Uh-huh. About that . . . a fella and his trade, that is . . . You know this place is ready to grow, to bust wide open one of these days. You can see it, can feel the energy building, can't you?"

"Point being?"

"Well, before too long I can see where I might be needin' me a deputy. Of course, I'd have to try you out . . . be sure you got the right makin's and can hold up in a tight spot, you understand . . . But the thing is, there'd be a steady job for the right fella if one was lookin' to settle down hereabouts."

"Uh-huh. That's something to keep in mind. Trouble is, I'm not."

"Not what?"

"Not looking to settle down."

Eagle made a face. "Doggone it, Luke, why not? You don't want to roam all over Creation huntin' down nasty hombres for the rest of your days, do you? And you know blamed well there are more reasons than that, here especially, to think about settlin' down."

Luke grinned. "As a matchmaker, you make a good half-breed . . . from the Rattlesnake Tribe."

"Aw, come on, you know how smitten Dinah is with you."

"Smitten?"

Eagle frowned. "That's one of Jane's words. Women talk, I guess. But that don't make it any less true."

"But it still doesn't change anything, either. And the longer I put it off, the harder it's going to be."

"You know," Eagle said, his mouth tight, "there are also people besides Dinah who wouldn't mind seein' you stick around."

"And to those people, my fondness and gratitude is returned," was Luke's only reply.

Dinah helped make it somewhat easier that night. "I know there's no holding you. I'll accept what has to be, and not beg," she told him. "I just ask two things: When it's time for you to leave, look me in the eye and say good-bye—don't sneak off in the middle of the night. And when you go, don't you leave behind any money for me."

"But you want to start up your café again. You'll need—"

"I'll make out. I always have, I always will. Not another word."

So, in the morning, while she was still sleeping,

Luke had leaned over her and kissed her gently on the cheek. When she opened her eyes and looked up at him, he said, "I'm saying good-bye now."

Then he rode away.

In the first town he came to with a post office, he mailed her some money with a note:

I kept my agreement, I didn't leave money behind. I'm sending this to help get your café going again. That way, if I ever pass back through Hard Rock, I'll always know where I can get a good meal from the prettiest gal in Montana.

–Luke–

**Keep reading for a special excerpt
of a new Western epic
from WILLIAM W. and J. A. JOHNSTONE . . .**

THE FIRST MOUNTAIN MAN
PREACHER'S FRENZY

*Johnstone country. Where the good die young.
And the bad die sooner.*

There are two kinds of traps in the Old West.
One is the kind that Preacher and his buddy, Charlie,
use to catch a mountain-load of fur pelts.
The other is the kind that Charlie steps into—a trap set
by a low-life gambler and his seductive partner in crime
to swindle Charlie out of his fur money. Preacher hates
to see a good friend get robbed. So he sets off after the
grifters—on a riverboat bound for New Orleans.
First he infiltrates the criminal underworld of the
French Quarter. Then he's enslaved on a pirate ship
heading straight to hell. Now there's only one way out
for Preacher. And that's to make a deal with the devil
herself: a female of the species deadlier than the male . . .

*Look for **PREACHER'S FRENZY**,
on sale now wherever books are sold.*

Chapter 1

The alligator lunged at Preacher, massive jaws wide open and sharp teeth ready to clamp down on him with flesh-rending ferocity and bone-crushing power. The mountain man dived out of the way and then flung himself back across the muddy ground, slipping and sliding a little on the bayou bank. The gator writhed after him, its tail thrashing wildly as it pursued him. Preacher had to leap straight up to avoid the next savage attack.

He turned in midair so he faced the same direction when he came down on top of the gator.

Preacher clamped his knees around the deadly reptile's barrel-shaped torso and yanked his hunting knife from the sheath at his waist. As the alligator curled its head around toward him, trying to reach him with those deadly teeth, Preacher leaned forward and rammed the blade into the creature's right eye as hard as he could.

The gator spasmed, thrashing so hard that it almost threw Preacher off. Even in the beast's death throes, those massive jaws continued snapping, so Preacher figured the safest place for him was still on top. He hung on, hugging that wet, scaly hide as he ripped the blade free and struck again and again.

The gator rolled over onto him. Preacher's ribs groaned from the weight. Then abruptly the burden lifted and Preacher found himself on top again—but only long enough for him to grab a breath and replace the air that had been forced out of his lungs.

The gator rolled onto him again and both of them tumbled off the mossy bank into the bayou. Water splashed high around them and flooded into Preacher's mouth, nose, and eyes. He gagged and spat out the stinky, slimy stuff.

A few yards away, the gator continued to flail and send water flying into the air with its futile struggles. Death had claimed the creature already, Preacher's knife having pierced its prehistoric reptilian brain, but that message hadn't caught up with the alligator's body.

Where one of the blasted critters lurked, there could be another—or more—Preacher reminded himself. Not to mention cottonmouth moccasins and who knew what other dangerous things. Best to get out of the bayou as quickly as he could.

As he pulled himself out of the water, a foot in a high-topped black boot stomped down right in front of him, squishing water out of the muddy ground. Preacher stopped and raised his head so his eyes could follow the whipcord-clad leg up to the burly torso of a man pointing a flintlock pistol at his face. From Preacher's angle, the barrel of that pistol looked about as big around as the mouth of a cannon, with the hammer already pulled back and cocked, ready to fire.

"You never should've come into the swamp, mountain man," the fellow said.

Preacher thought about the gator and everything else he had run into in this blasted muck and knew the man spoke the truth.

Preacher made his home in the mountains, and he never should have left.

St. Louis, three weeks earlier

"There she be," Preacher said as he reined Horse to a halt atop a brush-dotted hill with a view down toward the settlement sprawled beside the Mississippi River.

"I know," Charlie Todd said as he brought his horse to a stop, as well. "I've been here before, remember? Aaron and I outfitted here before we headed west."

Even after all this time, Charlie's voice still had a little catch in it when he said his friend's name. They had been close, and Charlie hadn't forgotten—would never forget—the terrible way Aaron Buckley had died.

"I know how you feel, but you're doin' all you can for him," Preacher said. "Takin' his share of the money from those pelts back to his family is more 'n a lot of fellas would do." He jerked a thumb over his shoulder to indicate the four packhorses on lead ropes trailing behind them. Those animals carried bundles of beaver pelts that Preacher and Charlie planned to sell in St. Louis.

Charlie and Aaron came from the same town back

in Virginia, and the two young men had headed west together, looking to make their fortune in the fur trapping business—and have some adventures along the way, to be honest about it.

They had found adventure, all right—more than they had bargained for since teaming up with the rugged mountain man known as Preacher.

"You're sure about not comin' back out here?" Preacher went on as he and Charlie sat on horseback, looking down at St. Louis in the distance. A faint haze of smoke from all the chimneys hung over the settlement, a sure sign of so-called civilization.

Charlie sighed and nodded. "I'm sure, Preacher. I've had enough of the frontier. You're cut out for it, but I'm not."

Preacher regarded his young companion for a moment. Charlie's time in the mountains had toughened him, honing away the soft pudginess, turning his fair skin bronze, giving his features a harder, more seasoned cast than they'd had when Preacher first met him.

But at the same time, Preacher knew the truth of what Charlie said. The young man had survived the wilderness and all its dangers, and he could be justly proud of that fact, but the time had come for him to go home.

"All right," Preacher said. "Let's go sell these furs."

He nudged the rangy gray stallion called Horse into motion and started down the trail made by thousands of saddle mounts and pack animals as fur trappers set out for and returned from the distant mountains. Ahead of them, the big, wolflike cur known only as Dog bounded on down the gentle slope, on the lookout for a rabbit or some other prey in the clumps of brush.

Suddenly, he stopped and stood stiff-legged, the hair on the back of his neck and along his backbone standing up a little.

Preacher heard the low growl that came from the cur's throat and reacted instantly. "Dog, hunt!" he yelled. "Split up, Charlie!"

He jerked Horse to the left even as he shouted the commands. From the corner of his eye, he saw Charlie veer swiftly to the right. Charlie had spent enough time with Preacher to know that he needed to follow the mountain man's orders immediately, without hesitating or even thinking about them.

At the same time, Dog leaped forward, low to the ground. As a rifle boomed from the brush, the ball kicked up dirt well behind the big cur. He disappeared into the growth, his thick fur making him heedless of any branches that might catch and claw at him.

Preacher guided Horse with his knees as he yanked two loaded and primed flintlock pistols from behind the broad belt at his waist. He saw a muzzle flash from the brush close at hand, followed instantly by the roar of a shot and a spurt of powder smoke. A low hum sounded in his ear as the ball passed close.

Thumbing back the hammer of his left-hand pistol, he pointed it and pulled the trigger. The weapon, double-shotted with an extra-heavy charge of powder, bucked hard in Preacher's hand, but his great strength controlled the recoil. The balls ripped through the brush, rewarding the mountain man with a cry of pain.

Somebody else screamed over where the brush thrashed around, and Preacher figured Dog had introduced himself to that ambusher. He threw a glance toward Charlie, still mounted and with his rifle at his shoulder. Preacher fired into the brush in the other direction.

Movement caught Preacher's eye as another man to his left stood up and fired an old-fashioned blunderbuss at him. Preacher had plenty of time to duck, and as he did, he turned in the saddle to bring his right-hand pistol to bear. Smoke and flame billowed from its muzzle and the ambusher flew backward as if slapped by a giant hand. Preacher knew both balls had slammed into the man's chest.

The first man he'd shot wasn't out of the fight after all, he discovered a second later. The would-be killer burst out of the brush, shrieking in rage. Crimson coated the left side of his face from a wound that had laid his cheek open to the bone. One of the balls from Preacher's pistol had ripped along there, and it should have been enough to leave the man whimpering in pain on the ground.

Instead, he used the agony to fuel his anger. He had a tomahawk in each hand and whipped them around as he rushed toward Preacher and Horse.

The stallion trumpeted shrilly. Horse would have reared up to fight back with slashing hooves, but Preacher didn't want his trail partner to get hurt. He kicked his feet free of the stirrups, swung his right leg over Horse's back, and dropped to the ground to meet the assault. He barely had time to let the empty pistols fall to the ground and yank out his knife and his own tomahawk.

The wounded ambusher's arms moved in a whirlwind of motion as he slashed at Preacher, but the mountain man's reflexes were up to the task of avoiding the strokes. He darted and weaved, blocked some of the blows and ducked others, and then he closed in to launch an attack of his own.

The knife in his hand flicked out and sliced through the inside of the man's upper left arm. The blade cut deep, severing muscles and nerves, and the tomahawk in the ambusher's hand dropped from suddenly useless fingers.

The man swung the right-hand tomahawk, coming close enough to knock the broad-brimmed brown hat off the mountain man's head. That was the high-water mark of his attack, though. It had left him open to a sweeping stroke of the tomahawk in Preacher's left hand. The weapon smashed into the side of the man's head with the crunch of bone. His knees buckled, and Preacher stepped back to let him topple forward onto his ruined face.

Seeing no sign of anyone else about to attack him, Preacher turned to see about Charlie. The young man had drawn his pistol, and as Preacher watched, Charlie lifted the weapon and fired it.

Then he exclaimed, "Blast it!"

"He get away?" Preacher called with a dry tone in his voice.

Charlie turned in the saddle to look at him. "Yes,

he made it to a horse and rode off. Shouldn't we go after him?"

"Not sure it'd be worth the bother. You did for one of the varmints, didn't you?"

"I think so—"

"Better be sure," Preacher warned him. "Nothin' more dangerous than a man you think is dead—but ain't."

With a wide-eyed look of alarm on his face, Charlie hurriedly dismounted and drew his other pistol as he stalked into the brush. By the time he came back a minute later, Preacher had already started reloading his pistols.

"The other one on this side is dead, all right," Charlie reported. He swallowed hard. "I, uh, shot him in the head. I aimed for his chest, but I guess the shot went a little high."

"Got the job done, though, I expect." Preacher tucked the ready pistols behind his belt again as Dog emerged from the brush with blood on his muzzle. Preacher nodded toward the cur and added, "So did Dog."

"Why did they ambush us?"

"Those pelts," Preacher said as he leaned his head toward the packhorses, which stood stolidly nearby, still attached by their lead ropes to Horse. "Some fellas think it's a good idea to lurk out here on the trail and wait for somebody to come along with a load of furs they're plannin' to sell in town. This ain't the first time I've been jumped by varmints like that."

"Highwaymen," Charlie said.

"Well . . . this trail ain't exactly a highway, but I reckon it's the same idea."

"What about . . . those men?"

"The carcasses?" Preacher swung up onto Horse's back. "I don't feel like buryin' 'em. Do you?"

"Not really," Charlie replied. "I can't say as I do."

The two men rode on toward St. Louis as overhead, buzzards began to wheel slowly through the sky.

Chapter 2

They delivered their pelts to one of the still-operating fur companies and got a good price for them, although not as lucrative as Preacher had gotten in previous years. The man who ran this branch of the company had known Preacher for a long time, and he gave the mountain man the best price he could.

As they left the business, Preacher commented, "I hate to think about it, but I can see a time comin'—and it ain't too long from now—when fellas won't be able to make a livin' as free trappers anymore, Charlie. The demand for furs ain't what it used to be even a few years ago, and all the companies want to hire a man to work for wages when he goes out trappin'." Preacher shook his head regretfully at the very idea. "When that happens, I reckon I'll have to look for a new line of work. I've hired on to do a particular job now and then, like goin' west with a bunch of pilgrims who needed somebody to guide and look after 'em, but I don't intend to collect wages regularlike."

"Nearly everyone in the world works for wages of one sort or another, Preacher," Charlie pointed out.

"Yeah, but I ain't nearly everyone in the world,"

the mountain man said. He weighed the pouch of gold coins in his hand, then opened the drawstring and took out a few of them. He held out the rest to Charlie and said, "Here. I've got as much as I need."

Charlie stared at him and didn't take the money. "We agreed to equal shares," he said. "You were already generous enough to set aside that much for Aaron's family."

"I've got plenty to pay for a couple of days here in St. Louis and then to outfit me for a trip back to the mountains. I plan on goin' back to that Crow camp and winterin' there with Hawk and Butterfly and our friends." Preacher smiled. "Any more gold would just weigh me down, son."

Charlie still hesitated, but after a moment he reached out and took the pouch from Preacher. "Thank you. I'm going to pass along Aaron's share of the extra money to his family."

"I expected you would. You're an honorable young fella, Charlie."

"You don't know how much it means to me that you think so," Charlie said, his voice thick with emotion.

With their newly acquired funds, they went to a restaurant to have a couple of thick steaks with all the trimmings. Charlie had already put aside the share of the profits he intended to deliver to Aaron Buckley's parents back in Virginia. He and Preacher had agreed that it would be a full third, even though Aaron had been killed before some of the pelts were taken, and now Charlie had the extra coins from Preacher's share to divide, as well.

Money was scant recompense for the loss of a son,

as Charlie put it, but he couldn't do anything else. The past couldn't be changed.

They ate at Trammell's, a decent restaurant that didn't go in for the sort of frills and finery that rich folks liked but served good, solid food at a decent price. The pretty, buxom waitress remembered Preacher from past visits, flirted shamelessly with him, and brought them cups of strong black coffee while they waited for their steaks, potatoes, and biscuits.

"That girl likes you," Charlie said when the waitress had gone.

"Molly?" Preacher grinned and shook his head. "Naw, she just likes to josh around with me. It don't mean nothin'. If I ever tried to take her up on any of the stuff she hints around about, she'd prob'ly run screamin' into the night."

"I wouldn't be so sure about that." Charlie sipped his coffee, leaned forward in his chair, and lowered his voice as he went on. "Now, look at that girl over there. The one sitting by herself in the corner."

Without being too obvious, Preacher looked. An attractive young brunette sat at the other table, well dressed but seeming to lack something of the decorum that a respectable lady ought to have. Of course, a respectable lady wouldn't be sitting by herself in a public accommodation, either. She would be with her father or her husband or, at the very least, her brother.

"Do you think she might like to join us, since she's alone?" Charlie went on.

"She's nice-lookin', all right," Preacher said, "but

maybe not the sort of gal you should be takin' an interest in, Charlie."

"Why in the world not?"

"You said it yourself. She's alone."

Charlie stared at him for a second, then said, "Surely you don't think that means anything. I never took you for the sort to be judgmental about another person."

"I ain't judgin' nobody," Preacher said. "Just tryin' to look out for you, that's all."

"And you know how much I appreciate that. We're not in the wilderness now, though. I think I can take care of myself in a situation such as this." With that, Charlie pushed his chair back and stood up to walk toward the girl's table.

Preacher watched as Charlie spoke to her. He couldn't make out any of the words, but he saw the look of surprise on the young woman's face as if she hadn't expected anyone to talk to her.

Then she smiled, and her already pretty face became even lovelier.

"Well, if she's fishin', she just set the hook," Preacher muttered to himself.

Lucy Tarleton introduced herself after Charlie took her arm and escorted her back to the table he shared with Preacher. The mountain man saw now that she had a small beauty mark on her right cheek, not far from the corner of her mouth. It just made her more attractive.

"I'm pleased to meet you, Miss Tarleton," Preacher said with his natural chivalry.

"Oh, please, call me Lucy," she said brightly. "I don't believe in standing on a lot of formality."

Preacher had long since rejected any sort of formality for himself, but it bothered him to hear a young woman say such a thing. Ladies ought to consider proper behavior important, more so than hairy-legged ol' mountain men did. He knew that his friend Audie, who had been a college professor before giving up that life to become a fur trapper, would call him a *hypocritter*, or some word like that, but he couldn't help feeling that way.

Lucy had plenty of charm to go with her looks, though. Preacher had to give her credit for that. And to hear her tell it, her being out and about alone didn't mean anything scandalous.

"I'm traveling with my aunt," she explained, "and we have lodging at the hotel in the next block. She gets tired so easily, you know, and she decided she preferred to just go on to bed instead of getting something to eat. The hotel doesn't have a dining room, but the clerk told me this was the closest restaurant and a respectable place, so . . . here I am."

"Here you are," Charlie said. "And I'm glad you decided to come."

"Well, a girl has to eat. I'm just so thankful that you approached me, Mr. Todd, so I would have some company."

"Good fortune has smiled on both of us, I'd say."

"Indeed it has! And Mr. Preacher, too, of course."

"Just Preacher," the mountain man said. "No *mister* needed or wanted."

"How did you come by such an unusual name? It's not *actually* your name, is it?"

Preacher shook his head. "No, but folks have been calling me that for so long I sort of disremember what my real moniker is."

That comment stretched the truth considerably. His ma had named him Arthur, as he knew quite well. But he didn't feel like explaining that or how he had come to be called Preacher.

When he resisted telling the story, Charlie said, "Let me. I've heard it plenty of times."

Preacher sighed and waved for him to go ahead.

"When Preacher first began trapping in the mountains as a young man, he clashed with the Blackfoot Indians so often and so successfully that they came to regard him as one of their greatest enemies," Charlie began.

Lucy shivered a little. "Just the very idea of dealing with those bloodthirsty savages terrifies me."

"You can find plenty of good folks out there among the tribes," Preacher said. That included his own son, the young Absaroka warrior Hawk That Soars, who now lived with a band of Crow hundreds of miles from here. Preacher missed the boy, who had fought at his side in numerous adventures after their first meeting when Hawk was nearly grown.

"But not the Blackfeet," Charlie said. He had his own compelling reasons to hate them. "And one time when they captured Preacher, they decided to burn him at the stake."

Lucy shuddered again. "Obviously, they didn't. But what a horrible fate to be faced with."

"I wasn't lookin' forward to it," Preacher said dryly.

"Earlier, when he'd been right here in St. Louis, he had seen a man preaching the gospel on the street. So he began imitating that man. The Blackfeet hadn't gagged him, so even though they tied him to a tree, he started preaching and kept it up the rest of that day and all through the night, never stopping even though he was exhausted and his mouth and throat were as dry as the desert."

Lucy frowned across the table at Preacher and asked, "What did you believe you would accomplish by that? Did you hope for divine intervention?"

"I was hopin' them Blackfeet would think I was touched in the head," Preacher said.

Charlie nodded. "You see, the Indians won't harm a man they believe to be insane. They think it will bring down all sorts of bad luck on them. So even though they had Preacher in their power—a mortal enemy who has gone on to be a thorn in their sides for many years—they felt they had no choice but to let him go." The young man sat back. "So they did. And when other mountain men heard what had happened, they started calling him Preacher. The name stuck and that's what he's been known as ever since."

"What a thrilling tale," Lucy said with a breathless note in her voice.

"Didn't seem too thrillin' at the time," Preacher said. "More like scared and desperate."

"Well, I'm glad you survived."

"So am I," Charlie said. "Preacher has saved my life on numerous occasions."

"The two of you are partners in the fur trapping business?"

"That's right. We just got back to St. Louis today with a season's worth of pelts."

"What do you do with them?" Lucy asked with a curious frown.

"Sell them, of course. That's where beaver hats and beaver robes come from."

The girl laughed. "That *does* make perfect sense. I just never really thought about where such things come from. Have you already sold those . . . pelts, did you call them?"

"That's right. Yes, we sold them to one of the fur companies that has an office and warehouse here. We received a pretty penny for them, too."

Preacher wouldn't have gone so far as to say that, but he supposed Charlie exaggerated in an attempt to impress the girl. Young fellas had been doing that since the beginning of time.

"Well, I've learned a lot today, and enjoyed your company, as well." Lucy drank the last of the coffee in her cup. "But I really should be getting back to the hotel so I can check on my aunt."

"I thought you said she'd gone to bed."

"She has, but the old dear might wake up and need something. She knew I was coming over here for dinner, but she might worry if she knew I wasn't back yet."

"I hoped we could continue our conversation—" Charlie began.

She gave him a dazzling smile and said, "Perhaps we shall. Are you going to be in town for a few days?"

Charlie glanced at Preacher and said, "We hadn't really made any plans yet." He didn't mention that he'd been figuring on heading back to Virginia as soon as possible.

He might have changed those plans some, though, after meeting Lucy Tarleton, Preacher mused.

"Good. I'm sure we'll run into each other again." Her brown eyes twinkled. "Say . . . for dinner here tomorrow?"

"We'll be here," Charlie responded without hesitation. "Won't we, Preacher?"

"Sure," the mountain man said. Let Charlie enjoy himself and end his Western adventures with a pleasant experience, he thought—although he didn't believe for a second that Lucy Tarleton wanted any sort of serious friendship with the young man.

But maybe he'd been wrong about the sort of girl she was, after all.